About Cheryl Adnams

Cheryl Adnams lives in Adelaide, South Australia. She has published four Australian historical romance novels, *The Girl from Eureka*, *The Bushranger's Wife*, *We'll Meet Again* and now *Heart of the River.* Cheryl has a Diploma in Freelance Travel Writing and Photography, has lived and worked in the United States and Canada, and spent two years with a tour company in Switzerland and Austria. Her favourite writing retreats include Positano on the Amalfi Coast and Port Willunga Beach just south of Adelaide. When she's not writing, Cheryl is still creating in her busy full-time job as a learning designer.

If you'd like to know more about Cheryl's books, visit her webpage cheryladnams.com.

Also by Cheryl Adnams

The Bushranger's Wife
We'll Meet Again

Available in ebook

The Girl from Eureka

Heart of the River

Cheryl Adnams

FICTION
HQ

First Published 2024
First Australian Paperback Edition 2024
ISBN 9781867242000

Published by
HQ Fiction
An imprint of Harlequin Enterprises (Australia) Pty Limited (ABN 47 001 180 918), a subsidiary of HarperCollins Publishers Australia Pty Limited (ABN 36 009 913 517)
Level 19, 201 Elizabeth St
SYDNEY NSW 2000
AUSTRALIA

A catalogue record for this book is available from the National Library of Australia
www.librariesaustralia.nla.gov.au

Printed and bound in Australia by McPherson's Printing Group

FSC www.fsc.org MIX Paper | Supporting responsible forestry FSC® C001695

To Mum, For everything. xxx

One

June 1956

'Well, folks, it's official.'

The crowd fell into an expectant hush as the mayor stepped up to the podium.

'The floodwaters coming down the Murray River are looking to be the biggest we've seen in the region since nineteen thirty-one.'

The news was greeted with a symphony of groans, and conversation laced with aggravation broke out among the crowd filling the Mildura Town Hall to capacity.

Isabel Hayward exchanged glances with her mother Audrey as they sat together on uncomfortable wooden folding chairs near the rear of the hall. The noise level soared, with raised voices bouncing off the high ceilings and hard, wooden floors, until she thought her ears might begin to bleed.

The call to attend the town hall meeting had gone out to anyone who lived along the Murray River in the north-west corner of Victoria. While the Riverside Hotel, where Isabel lived and worked with her mum, was situated in the little hamlet of Gol

Gol in New South Wales, it was an easy jaunt for them, and others who lived just on the other side of the river from Mildura, to cross the border and hear what the mayor had to say. Since Mildura was the largest of the Sunraysia towns that included Wentworth, Dareton, Red Cliffs, Buronga, Merbein and as far upriver as Euston and Robinvale, it made sense to hold the important regional meeting there.

Looking around the hall as complaints and concerns were discussed at a rising decibel level, Isabel realised people had travelled a long way to learn what they could about the threat that was slowly creeping downriver towards them. Farmers, still in their work gear, mixed with men in suits and women in dresses, hats and gloves. Isabel looked down at her new denim jeans and scratched at the casserole gravy that she'd spilled on the thigh while making dinner that afternoon. She hadn't had time to change before leaving the pub that evening. Looking around, she was thankful she wasn't the only woman her age wearing trousers.

The bang of the mayor's gavel on the podium jolted Isabel. The banging only added to the hubbub as the mayor tried to regain the attention of the room. She jumped again, even though she'd been prepared for it, as the mayor banged his gavel one more time and shouted for order.

'Come on now, we've known this was coming for a while. The higher-than-average rainfalls in Western Queensland, combined with the last few months of heavy rains in the Murrumbidgee and Lachlan River areas, means the original estimates were about as useful as a chocolate teapot. The bureau reckons the rains here aren't looking like settling down anytime soon either. Upstream the banks of the Murray have already burst in some places like Corryton and we've just got word that the river at Swan Hill is already at fourteen feet. That's only two inches shy of last year's flood peak and we're nowhere near the predicted peak date.'

'Which is when?' someone called out.

'It's looking like mid-August for us at this stage.'

This brought on more shocked and worried murmurs from the assembly.

'That's less than three months away.'

'Look, everyone, Barry can count.'

Laughter mingled with the conversation.

'What's the council gonna do about protecting us?'

'Let's not panic, folks.' The mayor raised his voice, waving his hands in a 'calm down' gesture before the noise could get out of control again. 'We've already started building levees where they were successful according to the old blokes who were here in the big flood of thirty-one.'

'Levees are a bad idea,' someone else called out. 'Let the river take its course. Building levees only makes the flooding that much worse when they break. And they will break. Just like they did in thirty-one.'

Isabel could see his point and wondered which was the lesser of two evils—a slow-creeping inundation? Or a flash flood that could wipe out everything in its path? The statement brought on a mixture of agreement and angry accusations.

'Spoken like a true townie!'

'What about my crops? We can't just let the river take our profits. We have to protect them.'

Impassioned discussions sounded all around Isabel. Some for building the levees, some against it. She could see both sides of the argument so she wasn't about to get involved.

'Yeah, and I'll wager we're not gonna get much help from them bastards in Canberra neither!'

Folks in the rural regions didn't have a lot of time for city politicians, and certainly didn't trust them to help out unless there was something in it for them.

'That's 'cos they're more interested in them bloody stupid sports thing what's comin'.'

The jab had come from the back of the hall and, turning in her chair, Isabel peered through the haze of cigarette smoke to find the owner of the voice. Mr Watkins. She should have known. Eighty years old if he was a day and still working his patch of sultana grapes in Merbein. He'd meant the Olympic Games, of course, which were due to start in Melbourne in November. The huge international event had the whole country buzzing with excitement. Everyone but old Mr Watkins, that was, who had no time for sports or politics. What farmer did?

Before she could turn back in her seat, her eyes fell on a younger man standing behind Mr Watkins. Leaning against the wall, arms folded inside a well-worn, dark brown leather jacket, he looked to Isabel like something out of a movie. James Dean came to mind. There was something about this man's stance that made her think of that same barely suppressed tension Dean had always seemed to exude in the photographs she'd seen in magazines and newspapers—before his tragic death last year, that was.

Trying not to make it look obvious that she was watching him, Isabel fiddled with her coat that was slung over the back of her seat. Peeking up through her eyelashes, she studied him. His dark hair hung long and thick, drifting over his forehead above piercing pale blue eyes that looked deep in concentration as he tilted his head, struggling to hear what the older man beside him was saying. Their olive skin told her they might be new Australians—Italians maybe. Having lived in the area all her life, Isabel thought she knew almost everyone in town. There was no way she'd forget having met the tall, dark and handsome Mediterranean James Dean. She wondered if these men had fled their ravaged home in Europe after the war, in search of a better life for their family. Maybe they'd just moved out from one of the cities to try their hand at farming. Or perhaps they'd always been in the region. She had to admit, they didn't get many new Australians coming to eat or drink at the Riverside. More and more these days Isabel wondered why that was.

Greeks, Italians, and a few of the recently arrived ten-pound poms, had seen Mildura in the midst of a population boom over the last ten years as people fled the war-torn cities and bomb-pocked farmlands of Europe and England. Looking for work, and not afraid of the hard variety, many of them had ended up in rural Australia, leasing parcels of land and quickly building farms and a new life for themselves and their families.

Isabel knew that not everyone in the region was happy about the arrival of so many foreigners to their little piece of rural Australia, but she was fascinated by all the different languages and cultures. As a cook in the hotel her family owned, she was especially fascinated by the varied and exotic foods and recipes they'd brought with them. But right now, it was the exotic good looks of the stranger at the back of the hall that held her interest.

As though feeling her eyes on him, the man turned his head and met her look straight on. Those piercing blue eyes held her green ones a little longer, until she finally had to force herself to look away, the warm flush rising up her neck. God, she'd been caught staring at him. How embarrassing! It wasn't like her to go gooey over a man like that. Shaking her head, she forced herself to tune back into the impending flood being discussed at the front of the room.

'We *are* getting some support from the government,' the mayor assured the room. 'The SEC in Melbourne have sent these two gentlemen to check up on the power stations at Red Cliffs and Mildura. Levees are already being put in place there, but now that we know just how high the water will be, we're gonna have to build them up further.'

'Or we'll all be in the dark!'

'Forget the dark,' Councilman MacKenzie added from his seat on the stage. 'If the floodwaters get into the pumping station we'll be in bigger trouble. The town's taps will dry up and toilet systems won't work. We'd have to truck in water.'

'Electricity and sewage are our number-one priority,' the mayor agreed. 'We'll discuss next steps after these blokes fill us in on what needs to happen around the power stations.'

The mayor stepped aside to allow the two gentlemen from the city to take over the podium. They spoke in a monotone about the power stations and, losing interest in their technical talk, Isabel tuned them out and took the opportunity to glance around the hall again. So many faces she recognised, from her old schoolmates to regulars at the Riverside pub, but plenty of faces she didn't recognise too. Those were from further afield, she figured. Everyone was keen to know just how bad the next few months were going to get.

Spotting her best friend Leanne sitting with her family across the centre aisle, Isabel waved enthusiastically and smothered a laugh as Leanne rolled her eyes and pretended to sleep with boredom at the drone of the officials from Melbourne. From his seat behind her, Ross Burrows tugged on one of Leanne's plaits. Scowling, Leanne turned and gave his hand a slap away. Ross snickered and winked across at Isabel before copping an elbow in the ribs from his best mate Kevin Grey beside him. That began a battle of surreptitious elbowing between the two men. Isabel shook her head. It was hard to believe they'd all turned twenty-one years old this last year.

She continued to watch Ross as he and Kevin fought like naughty schoolboys until Mrs Carsten, their old high school science teacher, whacked them both over the head with her newspaper. Scolded, the two men slunk down in their chairs but continued to jab at one another on the sly as the teacher kept an eagle eye on them, her newspaper still rolled in her hand and at the ready should they step out of line.

Isabel sent Ross a faux look of censure when he grinned back at her. They'd known each other since they'd been knee-high to a wallaby, having attended Gol Gol Primary School then Mildura High School as their parents had done before them.

Lately, though, Ross's attentions towards her had changed from family friend to something more. At first, Isabel had found herself flattered by his interest. Ross was a good-looking man from a wealthy family and could probably have any woman he chose in the region. Why he was suddenly courting her, she still couldn't quite figure out. He'd started asking her out to the movies, or to the dances they held at the supper rooms, right here in the town hall. They'd been out a few times, usually with other friends or couples. He picked her up in his fancy new Holden and dropped her home at the end of the evening, and there'd been one quick kiss behind the footy club rooms after a barbecue just the week before. The kiss hadn't moved the earth for her. She hadn't had many boyfriends growing up but she was sure she was supposed to feel more … well, just … *more*. She feared they were approaching the point where she would need to decide whether it was time to 'fish or cut bait' as her dad used to say. Perhaps they'd just known each other for too long. Where was the mystery? Where was the romance and excitement? More than once she wondered if her ambivalence towards him was because, having known each other since they were in nappies, he was more like a brother to her. The thought had begun to take hold—and that just felt … icky.

Ross sent her a cheeky wink. He may still act like a teenager, but she couldn't deny that Ross had most definitely grown into manhood. He'd lost the boyish roundness in his face. His cheekbones were more defined, his strong jawline showing a five o'clock shadow she knew his mother would not approve of. At sixteen, he'd shot up to a gangly six feet, two inches. Then over the years he'd moved from gangly to brawny so that now his body was one long length of muscle. Not muscle built as a result of a hard day's work in the fields or orchards though. His build, she knew, came from many hours at the local boxing gym and from training and playing Aussie Rules football for the Mildura Demons.

Ross had gone straight from school to work for the family car-sales business—in the office, of course. His dad, Trevor, was the general manager of Burrows Automobiles; although everyone knew it was Trevor's father, Roy, who still held the reins of the business. To his father's disappointment and his wife's dismay, Trevor Burrows tended to spend more time in Isabel's family's pub at Gol Gol than at the car yard on Madden Avenue.

And that association and friendship was just another reason Shirley Burrows didn't approve of her son Ross courting Isabel Hayward, the Riverside publican's daughter.

The meeting wrapped up and the noise in the hall rose to a deafening rumble again as the crowds began to talk and boots hit the hardwood floors, the clatter of chairs adding to the din as they were stacked against the wall. Isabel and her mother joined the river of humanity as it flowed and filtered out of the exits.

'Isabel!'

Just outside the door, as the brisk night air hit her cheeks, she turned and smiled as Leanne, Ross and Kevin shuffled out the door behind her.

'Hi!' Isabel greeted them on the steps, pulling on her favourite old coat to ward off the June chill. 'Big news, hey?'

'Yep, we're gonna get trapped over there in Gol Gol and Buronga when the water comes down,' Ross said, tossing an arm around her and pulling her close. 'We might have to huddle up together against the elements.'

Isabel shrugged him off. 'I doubt it will come to that. Guess we'll just have to wait and see and make sure we get our share of the sandbags.'

'You don't think the pub will go under though, do you, Isabel?' Leanne asked, real concern marring her pretty, pale complexion as she fixed a sky blue, knitted woollen hat over her raven hair.

'Nah. There's no way it could ever get that high,' Ross insisted, wrapping his arm around Isabel's waist to hold her steady as they were shuffled about by the dispersing crowds. 'Of course, you can always come and stay with me, Isabel, if the floodwaters look like taking over the pub.'

'Your house in Buronga is on lower ground than the pub. If we go under, your house will already be well gone.'

She figured the idea of that hadn't struck him before since he frowned at her now.

'I wouldn't worry,' she said quickly. 'I'm sure it won't come to that.'

Isabel caught Ross's mother's thinly veiled look of distaste as she stepped out of the hall and spotted Ross with his arm around her. She looked … expensive. It was the word Isabel always thought of when she saw Shirley Burrows. The outfit she wore now was probably worth more than Isabel earned in a month. The tan skirt was wool, and the sweater set—the colour of the eggs Isabel's chickens laid—was most likely cashmere. Isabel's eyes dropped to Shirley's feet and she admired the low-heeled pumps that matched her fashionable pea green winter coat. Most women had one pair of good black shoes that went with everything. Coloured shoes were a luxury, but she guessed if anyone could afford luxuries it was Shirley Burrows. Her white gloves were still as white as the day she bought them, no doubt. Whereas the old pair Isabel owned, worn first by her mother and then by her, had yellowed over the years of wear regardless of her regular use of the Reckitt's Bag Blue.

Isabel squirmed a little as the woman's gaze skimmed over her own ancient tan coat, her denim trousers and low-heeled, scarred and dirty winter boots.

'Ross, take me to the car, please,' Shirley commanded, fastening the large buttons on her coat. 'I'd like to go home and your father is nowhere to be found as usual.'

Isabel felt Ross slump a little before he removed his arm from her waist. 'Better go. How about a movie at the Ozone on Friday night?'

'Fine,' Isabel agreed, then wondered why she had. Was it to spite Shirley Burrows? Hadn't she just been thinking it was time to cut all ties with Ross?

'Pick you up at six?' he asked as he backed away to follow his mother, who was already halfway down the footpath towards the Burrows' sedan. She nodded and waved goodbye, watching him turn and quickly dash away down the path.

He opened the passenger-side door for his mother before climbing into the driver's seat and starting the car with a roar of the engine. Isabel had never seen Shirley Burrows drive her own car. Either Ross or Trevor would always be at the wheel. Of course, Ross had his own brand-new Holden to get about town in. Owning a car yard meant the Burrows always had the latest model of automobile. Isabel admired Mrs Burrows' new Ford as it sailed past, with its clean burgundy coat and shiny chrome bumper. It certainly made the Haywards' ageing, second-hand, baby blue Holden utility look like a piece of old junk rescued from the scrap heap. But that piece of junk was functional for transporting food and drink supplies from the train station or shops to the pub and it still ran like a dream. Until the old ute gave up the ghost for good, they'd make do.

'Another date with Ross,' Leanne said, bringing her attention back. 'Didn't you say you were thinking of breaking it off with him?'

'We're not officially an item. How do you break something off with someone when you're not actually together? I think we're just friends now. A boy and a girl friend who go out occasionally.'

'I'll bet you a pack of cheese Twisties that Ross thinks you're officially together.'

Chewing on her lip, she worried Leanne was right and just might win that packet of cheese Twisties. 'I just don't think—Hey!'

A bump from behind had her losing her footing on the steps of the hall. As she stumbled and the ground rushed up to meet her, she was suddenly caught around the waist by strong hands that spun her so that instead of facing the ground, she was now looking up at the sky, dipped backwards as though she'd simply been waltzing.

It felt like forever as she lay, bent back, with the warmth of her captor's leather-clad arms blocking the cool breeze. Frozen, in fear of falling as much as in shock, she stared into eyes she'd seen only a short while before inside the hall. Eyes so blue it was like looking up at a summer sky.

He grinned down at her. No longer the dark and brooding James Dean look-alike, instead his handsome face held a cheeky, thrilled sort of a smile, and a dimple winked out at her from his left cheek.

'*Ciao, bella.*'

Her parents were the only ones who had ever called her by that nickname.

'What? H—how ...?'

Being encased in his warm arms, crushed against his warm body, she somehow couldn't seem to find a coherent thought.

His smile wavered and his dark eyebrows furrowed a little over those pools of blue. 'I wish I could say I was sorry for bumping into you, but that would be a lie as we would not have met.'

She opened her mouth to speak, to say something pithy, but nothing came out. Good Lord, he'd made her speechless. She was horrified with herself. What would she do next? Swoon?

Fearing that was exactly what she was doing, she gave his arm a strong tap. 'Up!'

He righted them both and stepped back.

'*Buona notte.*' And with a grin and a dip of his head, he sauntered past her down the footpath whistling 'Till I Waltz Again with You' to where a group of young men, obviously his mates, stood smoking and talking among themselves.

'What was *that*?' Leanne demanded, looking shocked. '*Who* was that? It was like it all happened in slow motion. Did you see how he caught you? It was just like in the movies. Like Fred Astaire taking Ginger Rogers in a spin around the dance floor or something.'

Isabel pulled herself together as Leanne rambled, readjusting her coat that had become skewed as she'd twisted in his arms. 'So he damn well should have caught me since he was the one who sent me flying in the first place.' It came out a little harsher than she'd meant, but she was still spinning from the encounter.

'How did he know your name?' Leanne wondered aloud. 'He called you Bella. Do you know him?'

She shook her head, still a little lost for words. How *did* he know her name? Had he asked? A shiver of a thrill ran through her. Could he really have asked someone about her? She still didn't think she'd ever seen him around before. He definitely didn't frequent her pub. She'd never forget a face like that. She hadn't recognised his friends either. Where had they come from?

The entire region had been notified of the town meeting so maybe he'd come from Irymple or even further afield from Robinvale. She gave herself a mental slap. Why did she care? He was probably just a travelling worker passing through, picking up casual work out at one of the farms or orchards. She'd most likely never see him again.

He'd looked younger close up and even more handsome. There was something about those eyes, that clear, blemish-free, olive-tinted skin set off by those full pink lips, that having been so close to her were now etched into her memory.

'Ready to go, Bella?' Her mother's voice broke into her reverie as she joined them on the steps. 'We have to get back. I told Flo and Albert we'd only be gone an hour and we've been gone well over that.'

Her mum's cousin Flo and her husband Albert lived in one of the bungalows at the bottom of the property by the river and often helped out at the pub.

'Yeah, now that the meeting is finished folks will be heading over the bridge for a pint. Things will get busy. I'm ready to go, Mum.' She hugged her friend. 'See ya, Leanne.'

'Yep. Will I see you at the Soda Fountain on Langtree on Saturday after lunch?' Leanne called out as Isabel followed her mum down the street.

'Why don't you come to the movies Friday night?' Isabel called back.

Leanne screwed up her nose. 'With you and Ross?'

'Please?' Isabel begged, opening the passenger door of the truck parked at the curb. 'You'll help me keep any romantic overtures Ross might try at bay. Just meet me at the Ozone at six. Bring Robby.'

Leanne's eyes widened. 'You want me to bring my brother as my date to the pictures?'

'It's not a date! We're just a group of friends getting together for a night out. Unless you find a date in the meantime.' Isabel's eyebrows bounced up and down suggestively.

'Not likely.' Leanne screwed up her nose.

'Isabel, we really must—'

'Okay, Mum.' She jumped into the cab of the ute as her mum started the engine. 'Bye, Leanne! See you Friday!'

Two

'That smells bloody incredible,' Bruce said as he leaned over the pot of leftover stewed beef, taking a huge inhale before swiping a finger into the gravy.

It was an hour before the dinner seating on Friday and Isabel was putting the finishing touches on the beef and potato pies. Looking at the clock, she increased her pace as Ross was due to pick her up to go to the movies any minute.

'Get your grubby mitts out of that.' Isabel pointed her spoon at Bruce with a warning glare. She pushed her light brown hair from her eyes with her forearm and continued spreading mashed potato across the top of the next pastry cup, already filled with meaty goodness. 'You can offer the leftover meat mix with veggies on the side when the pies sell out.'

'And they will,' he said, tying an apron around his ample girth. He wasn't a fat man, just well built—like a brick outhouse, as her mum would say—and more than capable of ejecting a rowdy drunk or two when the occasion called for it. 'Big crowd out there already. Think everyone's getting a little cabin fever with all this rain.'

'I saw that truckload of blokes arrive an hour ago,' Isabel said, pushing the door to the front bar open slightly to peek out. 'Thirsty men straight in from working on the levees. They've probably had a few pints already.'

'I reckon once they get a sniff of these pies they'll all be staying for tea. I've taught you well.'

'Mm-hmm,' Isabel agreed, albeit reluctantly. She couldn't deny he'd taught her the fundamentals of cooking, but she'd moved on from his basic skills a year ago. Of course, she would never tell him that. Not only did she respect Bruce, but he was her friend too. 'You're a great cook, Bruce, and you know your ground beef patties are famous in three states. Although, I saw this idea in the *Women's Weekly* about adding smashed-up Corn Flakes instead of crumbs to the beef.'

'Corn Flakes? As in Kellogg's Corn Flakes?'

She stopped grating cheese over the top of the pies. 'Yes, it gives the patties a better crunch.'

'Corn Flakes?' he repeated, his frown deepening.

'You just add some salt and pepper, a bit of parsley and there's your crumb mix.'

'I don't think our regulars would go for breakfast cereal on their patties.'

Isabel swallowed back her frustration. 'They'll never know the difference if you don't tell them, and they might surprise you and like it.'

'I think we'll stick with the classic recipe,' he said, and he started laying out the chopped carrots and pumpkin to go in the oven. 'It's a classic for a reason.'

'I suppose,' she murmured, deflated.

Bruce had been the cook at the Riverside pub for almost a decade. Back in the early days of the pub Grandma Louisa, her mum's mum, would always cook more food than was needed by the family in case anyone staying at the hotel wanted to join them for a meal. As a little girl Isabel had liked to help her in the kitchen, rolling dough or stirring pots, while her mum and dad ran the bar out front.

When Gran died, Bruce came to work for them. He'd been a cook during the war and had been based in Tobruk for two years cooking for British and Australian officers. Despite being trained as part of the Catering Corps, his culinary skills were limited to steamed or boiled vegetables, and meals that could be served, as the troops required, to large populations of men in a mess hall.

Not that Isabel could claim to be Le Cordon Bleu trained, but she had excelled at domestic studies in high school. During summer holidays, much of her free time away from her chores at the pub was spent lounging down by the river, devouring the *Australian Women's Weekly*. Not for dress patterns or Hollywood gossip like her friends. No, she'd flick past the latest fashions, and stories about Sir Laurence Olivier and Vivien Leigh's visit to Australia, until she found the recipe section.

The *Women's Weekly* was her bible. She particularly liked it when the magazine did their special international features like 'Danish Delights' or 'How about a Greek Party'. Sadly, her bid to bring a bit of culture into the pub hadn't quite had the result she'd hoped for. Her attempt at making the Greek delicacy, dolmades, had caused patrons to baulk and ask why they were eating soggy blobs of stuffed vine leaves. The customers had also complained when she'd served her stewed veal with rice instead of the usual vegetables.

'Rice is for pudding,' Mr Hanrahan had complained at the bar as plate after plate was returned to the kitchen, the veal gone but the rice still in place. Of course, his comments had been kinder than those of the ex-army men who'd refused to touch that 'Jap food' as they'd called it. She could hardly blame them for that, considering soldiers—some of whom had been kept in prisoner of war camps for years during the war—had been served nothing but one bowl of rice a day by their captors.

Shoving a handful of cheese in her mouth, Isabel chewed away her frustration. She was twenty-one years old, and her life was going nowhere. She dreamed of becoming a proper chef, not just an assistant to a stuck-in-his-ways army cook. The only place she knew of in Australia where she could train to be a chef was the Emily McPherson College.

She hadn't even known the school existed until she'd headed down to Melbourne with a group of friends to see the VFL grand final the year before. While Ross and Kevin had stayed at the luxurious Windsor Hotel, Isabel and Leanne had stayed with Isabel's Auntie Silvia in Fitzroy. Wandering into the city the day before the game, they'd come across the big white building on Russell Street.

'Emily McPherson Building,' Isabel had read across the top of the impressive-looking facade.

'Like the cookbooks?' Leanne had questioned.

'Could be.'

Isabel had watched ladies going in and out of the building and stopped a woman as she passed by on her way up the path. 'Excuse me, but what is this place?'

'The Emily McPherson College,' the woman had responded quickly.

'College? For what?'

'Domestic studies,' the woman said, looking at her watch. 'Dressmaking, design, cooking, all sorts of things.'

Obviously running late, the woman had rushed away and disappeared into the building before Isabel could thank her.

'A cooking school,' Isabel had marvelled. A spark of hope and excitement had been lit within her, and when she returned to

Mildura the day after the Demons got trounced by Footscray in the grand final, she had the application forms to Emily McPherson College tucked safely in her suitcase.

For months she'd worked to put her plan into action, saving the small wage she earned from the pub. When she had enough pounds squirrelled away, she would have the talk with her mum. It was only a six-month course at the college. She figured with Bruce in the kitchen, and cousin Flo helping out, her mum would be able to survive without her for half a year.

She'd sent in her application forms and was jumping with joy when they accepted her for the September intake. It would be perfect because she'd be in Melbourne while the Olympic Games were on. Sports were fine. She didn't mind sports. But she'd read in *The Argus* newspaper that renowned chefs from all over the world were being flown to Australia to cook for the athletes and to provide for the influx of humanity that followed wherever the games were held. Think of what she could learn just by eating meals cooked by award-winning, world-class chefs as, rumour had it, some of those chefs would also be working at restaurants in town. Her plans were about to fall into place and she began to rehearse what she would tell her mother.

But then, early in the year, it had started to rain. And the rain had never stopped.

With trepidation, Isabel had watched as the Murray River began to steadily rise with the influx of water from even more rain up north, and suddenly they were facing the biggest flood crisis in decades.

Knowing what was coming, the threat the rising river could be to the pub, Isabel knew going to Melbourne for six months to study cooking was a dream she could no longer seriously entertain. How could she possibly leave her mum behind to cope when they were faced with the very real possibility of losing their livelihood, their home, to the river. Isabel loved every minute of her work. She loved cooking at the pub, but it wasn't enough. She wished for an outlet for the creativity that was bottled up inside her just dying to spring out.

So she had decided if she was going to be stuck serving the same old fare day in, day out, she at least wanted to be able to create some new dishes to slip into the menu. Having pleaded her case, her mum had finally allowed her to make some small changes to the menu, but only as long as Bruce gave it the final okay.

Just the year before it had become legal for pubs to stay open until ten at night in New South Wales. Victoria hadn't followed suit—pubs were still forced to close at six o'clock—and the change in law had given the Riverside Hotel a huge boost when the number of evening patrons doubled as drinkers from Victoria headed across the river border. Since then, the pub always pulled a steady crowd from the southern state. At the beginning of the new year, Isabel had suggested they put on an evening meal service in the hopes of increasing their profits, with the added motive of stopping patrons from getting too boozed up without any food in their stomachs.

They'd already been providing breakfast, lunch and dinner to hotel guests if they wanted to pay the extra for full board and lodgings, but once they'd added lunch and dinner menu options six days a week the increase in customers meant Bruce gave her the go-ahead to try some new recipes. Of course, he'd laid down the law that she wasn't allowed to serve anything people couldn't recognise or pronounce.

The door that separated the kitchen from the front bar swung open and her mum, with her hair the colour of ripe wheatfields at sunset, tied up in a messy bun, stepped through bringing the din of a noisy dinner crowd with her momentarily before the door swung shut again.

Isabel often lamented that she'd been saddled with a bland mix of hair colour from both her parents. She would have loved the blonde of her mum or the tawny red-brown of her dad, but no, she'd grown up with hair she'd always called 'Murray River brown'.

'Ross is here,' her mum said as she placed a pile of dirty glasses in the sink.

'Oh, righto.' Moving quickly, she opened the door to the oven. The wood had been burning for a few hours so she judged the temperature to be just right. She slid the tray of pies into the oven and set the timer for Bruce. Carefully, she slipped the apron over her head, then fluffed her short sweep of thick hair back into place and straightened her bright yellow dress.

Her mum stepped up and wiped some mashed potato from Isabel's cheek with a chuckle. 'Unless you were saving that for a snack at the pictures,' she said, holding out the potato.

Isabel ate the chunk directly from her mother's finger before giving her a quick kiss on the nose. 'I'll be home before midnight,' she said, gathering her purse and her coat.

Leaving Bruce to deal with the rest of the dinner service, she followed her mum out of the kitchen and stopped near the doorway to the front bar.

There was so much history in this little hotel she called home. It had started life as an inn in the 1800s and used as a way station to change the horses for the Cobb and Co. The original hotel had been a crudely constructed wooden building. Its bones were made of split pine posts, which Isabel could still see in the current building despite the many updates her father had made over the years. He'd wanted to be true to the history of the place, she recalled.

After the war, in the late 1940s, her dad—with the help of his best mate Trevor Burrows and some of their mates—had built a large, semi-enclosed verandah on the river side of the hotel, providing shade from the hot summer sun and a cool, airy seating area. It soon became the main entrance to the pub and the old double doors that had served since the Cobb and Co days were now rarely, if ever, used. A collection of grey box eucalyptus, red river gums and lignum bushes stood between the hotel and the river, but from the verandah you could occasionally catch a glimpse of the sun shining on the water as it flowed idly by. On hot summer nights, Isabel and her mum would drag a mattress out to sleep on the verandah. With the river breezes sweeping through it was much cooler than inside the hotel, and the protective flyscreen helped keep the mosquitos and other bugs away.

The Riverside Hotel was hardly a holiday destination. It was simply a halfway point between Sydney and Adelaide, where travellers or truck drivers could rest their head for a night and enjoy a meal and drink before continuing their journey the next day.

Apart from the bungalow that permanently housed Albert and Flo, in another little hut lived a widower named Perry who received free board and lodging for carrying out some handyman work around the hotel and occasionally helping out in the front bar. Two more bungalows were available for short term accommodation when the hotel was fully occupied.

Gazing around, Isabel had to marvel at the changes the hotel had gone through. Serving meals to locals was usually reserved for restaurants like the Mary Elizabeth over in Mildura, which served three-course luncheons and dinner. But the small dining room at the pub now held five square tables where travellers and locals alike could get a feed, as long as they were happy with whatever was on offer that night. Two choices, no à la carte.

While Isabel lamented the loss of her dream, she was proud of what she and her mum and Bruce had accomplished together over the last year.

She waved at people she knew as she stepped around the old walnut counter her father had extended and restored. They'd celebrated the finished bar the day before her sixteenth birthday by sliding glasses of lemonade up and down the shiny new varnished surface.

That was the last day she'd seen her dad.

Shaking off the heavy memories, Isabel was unsurprised when she didn't see Ross waiting by the front door. He'd probably found someone he knew and popped over for a chat. She scanned the crowd and spotted him talking to his father. Trevor Burrows was hunched at the bar, an Imperial pint half empty in front of him. She winced. The tension in Ross's stance as he spoke quietly in his dad's ear would be obvious to anyone who knew them. The bar had become unusually quiet as several heads turned to watch the exchange. Ross's fists clenched at his side and while Trevor had been sitting sedately at the bar when she'd first spotted them, whatever Ross said had the older man standing so abruptly his stool tumbled back, hitting the hardwood floor with a resounding smack that pulled the attention of all the other patrons in the room.

'You just keep your bloody opinions to yourself, you mama's boy,' Trevor said, his voice loud, his words slurred.

'Or what?'

'Or I'll knock your feckin' block off, that's what.'

'Like to see you try without falling flat on your face,' Ross shot back bitterly.

Trevor made a lunge for Ross, who only had to take one step back and Trevor's swipe went wide, knocking his glass over, the remains of his beer dripping down the front of the bar into a pool on the floor.

Isabel was about to step in when her mum moved in with a cloth and a smile as she wiped away the mess. 'Everything okay here, men?'

Ross's jaw was clenched, his eyes on Trevor's balled fists as the two men faced off.

Isabel rushed across the room as the other patrons in the bar seemed to hold a collective breath. She didn't want a fight in here. She didn't want a fight at all. 'Ross. Let's go, shall we? We'll be late for the movie.'

Ross and Trevor simply continued to glare at each other.

'Mum will take care of Trevor, right, Mum?'

'Yep, we're all good here,' her mum said easily as she poured a fresh beer for Trevor, diluting it with water when he wasn't looking. Wandering around to clean the mess off the floor in front of him, she turned and gave Isabel a warning glance and a tilt of the head towards the door. 'Take off, you two, and enjoy the pictures.'

Isabel took Ross's hand and tugged as she stepped away, hoping he would follow. Eventually he did.

'Smug little bastard,' Trevor said, loud enough for Ross to hear but Isabel continued to grip his hand tightly as she hurried them towards the door and out into the fresh air. The rain that had been a miserable dribble a few hours before had turned torrential.

They stood under the verandah for a moment, watching the rain fall in sheets so thick Isabel seriously wished she could just stay home, but the tension was still rippling off Ross in waves as heavy as the rain and she had to get him away from the pub, and his dad, as quickly as possible.

'Are we going?' she asked, surreptitiously putting herself between him and the door that led back into the pub in case he had ideas of going back in.

He hesitated a moment before nodding. Breathing a sigh of relief, she stood back as he rushed out into the rain, opening the car door for her so she could make the dash and jump in without getting too wet.

Ross ran around the front of the vehicle and leaped in beside her. Isabel dusted water from her coat and shook her hair, relieved when he leaned over the seat to grab a towel. But she stared gobsmacked as he wiped the droplets of water from his own hair, and then the seat and dashboard, before handing the towel to her.

'Thanks.' She screwed her nose up as she took the soggy towel he offered. It was easy to see where his priorities lay—the new model Holden was his pride and joy and the envy of all his mates—but she let the pithy comment on her tongue fade away given his already sullen mood.

When he started the engine, the radio blared to life just as the Crew Cuts were declaring that life could be a dream.

He ran a frustrated hand through his wet hair and put the car in gear. A few moments passed and they were still sitting in the idling car.

'All good?' she questioned, worried that he might be thinking of heading back into the pub.

He gave one quick, curt nod and moved the car out onto the highway.

As they drove across the bridge to Mildura, Ross made no attempt at conversation. Isabel continued to steal sideways glances at his dark and solemn expression, hoping to find a way to pull him out of his sulk.

In the end, she gave up and asked, 'Is it always like that between you and your dad these days?'

He turned his head, looking at her as though he'd almost forgotten she was there.

'He was always a grumpy bugger,' Ross mumbled. He rolled his shoulders. 'But when he's drinking …'

He didn't finish the sentence and Isabel decided it was best not to push. She knew what Trevor was like when he'd been drinking. She'd seen it firsthand. It was why he'd been banned from many of the pubs in Mildura.

He'd always been a regular at the Riverside pub. Audrey didn't put up with any grief from patrons, but she'd never had the heart to turn him away and, perhaps because of his friendship with her dad, Trevor generally behaved himself when he was there.

Driving over the bridge and into Victoria, they turned right into Seventh Street, following the train line that separated the town from the riverfront area, before taking a left into Langtree Avenue. When the clocktower of the T&G Building came into view and Ross began looking for a car park, Isabel asked the question that had been gnawing at her since they'd left the pub.

'What did you say to him to make him so angry?'

'I just suggested he go home and give Mum a hand,' Ross said, slowing the vehicle as he spotted a car park within easy walking distance of the cinema. 'She's getting seriously worried about the floods and trying to prepare the house in case we have to evacuate.'

'That's understandable.'

The Burrows' modern and stately home was situated among orange groves in the riverfront area of Buronga, just five minutes down the road from Gol Gol. They faced a real threat of inundation due to the property's proximity to the river. The levees that were being built to protect the market gardens in the area would also protect the Burrows' home, but Isabel thought it was wise of Mrs Burrows to be prepared.

'She's packing up some of our more valuable belongings to take across to the storage sheds we own out on Etiwanda Avenue. It'd be nice if Dad would give her a hand instead of spending all his time in your pub.'

Isabel winced. The way he'd said 'your pub' had sounded like an accusation. As though it were her fault, and her mother's, that Trevor drank to excess and stayed away from home so much.

Pulling into a car park, Ross cut the engine and sat quietly for a moment. 'Sorry. I'm being a bastard.'

'It's okay,' she returned in a quiet voice.

'Dad wasn't always like this.'

'I know,' Isabel said, trying to conjure a smile. 'I remember him all the way back to when you and I first started primary school together. He was a funny guy. Mum said he and my dad had been best mates since school.'

Ross said nothing so she went on. 'Remember when we used to go camping over near Hattah Lakes? Me and Mum and Dad in our tent or sleeping in the back of the ute in summer, beneath the stars. You and your dad in that caravan. Your mum never came. I always wondered why.'

'Nah, she never was one for camping, even back then,' Ross finally spoke up. 'She and Gran would get the bus down to Adelaide or Melbourne for the weekend and go on shopping trips whenever we went camping.'

'We were barely more than toddlers, but I remember Trevor and my dad taking you and me out on the lakes when they were in flood.'

'Your life jacket was bigger than you.'

She was glad to see a hint of a smile pop out, but it disappeared quickly.

'And then the war started and everything changed,' Ross said. 'He changed.'

She nodded. 'When did Trevor's drinking get out of hand, do you think?'

Ross shrugged. 'During the war, or just after. I don't really remember much about that time. We were what, ten years old when the war ended? I never really understood what he did for the army, probably didn't really care. I mean who really understands what their parents do when they're kids?'

'The war years were a confusing time,' she said. 'Made *more* confusing because we were so young, I suppose. My memories of that time are … limited and jumbled.'

'I asked him once, a few years back, why he didn't go to the war.'

'What did he say?'

'He told me to shut my face. Said I shouldn't talk about the war, that it was none of my goddamn business. I never did get a straight answer out of him. I just assumed he was a coward or something.'

Isabel wasn't surprised. A lot of men didn't like to talk about their experiences during the war. 'Mum said my dad couldn't go to the war. I don't recall why. So he stayed behind. So many kids at school were losing their dads or older brothers, uncles. It was heartbreaking. I remember being so thankful Dad didn't go overseas. But none of that mattered. I still ended up heartbroken.'

'I asked Dad about that too. About your dad, Sam. Asked him how Sam could do what he did.'

Isabel's head snapped around in surprise. 'Did he know?'

'If he did, he wouldn't tell me.' Ross's expression turned dark again. 'And these days he barely talks to me at all.'

'Trevor helped us a lot at first after Dad …' She hesitated. It still hurt to talk about, even after all these years. 'He helped with some maintenance on the pub where he could, stuff Dad would have done, and Mum paid him in drinks. Then he just seemed to give up helping and only came for the drinks.'

'Yeah, now that you mention it, that's when Dad's drinking got really bad. I think he missed your dad. Like you said, they were best mates.'

Isabel nodded. 'They may not have gone overseas, but those years during the war sure did mess both our dads up.'

As they sat in the quiet of the car, a group of young men walked by, laughing and smoking, seemingly undeterred by the misty rain. Their conversation in Italian drifted musically on the breeze as they passed.

Ross sniffed with disdain as he glared out the windscreen at them. 'We won the war but got invaded anyway.'

Isabel winced at his bitter tone. 'Now you sound like your dad.'

He frowned across at her, looked like he was going to argue, but instead opened his door. 'Come on, let's go to the movies.'

Making a quick dash through the rain and into the cinema, they found Leanne and Robby already waiting in the foyer. The Ozone was the original of the three cinemas that now entertained the town of Mildura. Inside the foyer, two grand staircases ascended to the doors that entered the balcony area. In between sat a small refreshment stand and while Robby and Ross went and bought tickets, Isabel and Leanne hovered around, eyeing off the chocolate-coated ice-cream cones and boxes of Jaffas, Minties and Fantales.

'I really shouldn't.' Leanne bit her lip as she gave in and ordered a chocolate-coated ice-cream cone. 'I'm saving for those denim jeans I saw in Shilliday's. I should really go next door to the milk bar and buy snacks there. It's much cheaper.'

'I'll shout you,' Isabel told her, handing the fivepence over to the attendant. 'Mum gave me some extra pay this week. She says we did a roaring trade last Saturday because word got out about my apple pies. I said that was just because the bakery in Mildura had to shut down since its roof collapsed in the heavy rain. The owners were uninsured apparently. They decided to board up the place and head south. I think the bakery over in Gol Gol, next door to the pub, is getting a lot of their bread orders.'

She handed Leanne the ice cream.

'Thanks.' Leanne unwrapped it as Isabel turned away from the counter and bumped straight into someone.

'Oh, I'm sorry,' she said to the chest in her eyeline.

'*Ciao, bella.*'

The familiar voice and words put a hitch in her breath. He was so tall she had to crane her neck back to look up at him. When the impossibly blue eyes met hers and sparkled, she struggled to find her words and when she did, they came out a little harsher than she'd meant. 'Oh. You again? Am I invisible or something? You keep knocking into me?'

His head tilted to the side as he smiled down at her. 'I believe it is you who knocked into me, *bella*.'

'Have we met somewhere before?'

'You mean apart from our dance the other night at the town hall meeting?'

'Yes, apart from that.' She did her best to look annoyed, despite the surprising thrill she felt at seeing him again. 'How do you know my name?'

'I don't know your name.'

'You just said it. And you said it that night, the first time you knocked me over.'

'What did I say?' he asked, bemused now.

'You said "Bella".'

'Yes.'

'Yes.'

He just stared at her, that same broad grin on his far-too-handsome face. Oh dear, was he simple-minded?

She shook her head to clear it and spoke slowly, just in case. 'Let's start again, shall we? My name is Isabel Hayward. You said my name the other night and I want to know how you know who I am.'

An expression of understanding swept across his face, followed by another grin that had her toes curling. 'Ah! Your name is Isabel?'

'Yes,' she said, becoming agitated. 'Why do you keep repeating it?'

'I do not keep repeating it. I was calling you *bella*.'

'How do you …?' She shook her head. They were getting nowhere. 'Only my mother calls me Bella.'

'*Bella*, in Italian, means beautiful.'

'Oh.' Heat crept up into her cheeks. 'Oh!' He was calling her beautiful all this time?

His smile broadened, his pale blue eyes dancing with mischief as the dimple in his left cheek winked out. He extended his hand. 'I am Matteo.'

She took his hand and something fluttered in her stomach at his touch. Rough hands. Worker's hands. 'Hello, Matteo. I'm Bella, I mean Isabel. My name is Isabel. Only Mum calls me Bella. I already told you that, didn't I?' She squeezed her lips together, feeling like a babbling fool.

Stop talking!

But he just continued to smile, his eyes still locked on hers.

'I've got our tickets, Isabel.'

Matteo let go of her hand. Over his shoulder, Isabel couldn't miss the scowl on Ross's face and, moving around Matteo, he tossed a proprietary arm around Isabel's shoulders.

'What do you want?' he all but snarled at Matteo.

Matteo didn't seem at all concerned by Ross's show of machismo. 'Nothing at all. I was just wishing Isabel a good evening.'

'Ross, this is Matteo,' she said, hoping to diffuse anything before it began.

Ross glowered down at Isabel. 'You know this bloke?'

'Um, we met at the town hall meeting on Wednesday.'

Ross grunted, ignoring the hand Matteo had extended. 'She's with me, so why don't you go back to your own kind.'

Matteo's eyebrows shot up and he sent Isabel a pitying look that she interpreted as 'Really? Him?', before he tapped one finger to his temple in salute and stepped around them, walking away to join his friends at the candy bar.

'Well, that was rude,' Isabel murmured to Ross.

'I know. What a clown! Thinking he could make time with my girl.'

'I meant you. You were rude.' Isabel shrugged his arm from around her shoulder. 'There was no need for you to be so abrupt. And I am not *your* girl,' she muttered as she followed him up the curving staircase to the upper level of the cinema.

The tickets for the seats upstairs were more expensive than the lower level but Ross could afford it. Robby and Leanne, on the other hand, could not, and their tickets had them seated downstairs ... along with Matteo and his friends, she noted, looking down on them as she and Ross took their front-row balcony seats.

'You're here with me; that means for tonight, at least, you are my girl. Besides ...' he nodded down to the bottom floor where they could see Matteo and his friends taking their seats, 'he's a reffo.'

'You don't know that,' she said, keeping her voice low. She'd always hated the word many Australians used for refugees. It sounded so derogatory. 'He might not be a refugee; his family might have paid to come to Australia.'

'What's the difference?' Ross snorted. 'They're all reffos from Europe. Who cares how they got here?'

Isabel glared at him, trying her best to keep the lid on her temper. Moviegoers were bustling around as they piled into the cinema and searched for their seat numbers with the aid of the uniformed usher. Despite how disappointed she was with Ross and his lack of tolerance towards new Australians, this was not the place to make a scene.

The first strains of 'God Save the Queen' sounded as the Union Jack waved on screen, and the patrons got to their feet as the national anthem crackled out of the speakers. When they took their seats again, Ross leaned across the aisle to chat with some old schoolmates of his while Isabel sulked, studying the tiny house lights suspended above them like stars. Finally, those lights began to dim and the heavy green curtains parted, bringing the screen to life as the laughing kookaburra on screen led into the newsreels.

News of the upcoming Melbourne Olympic Games flashed across the screen but people around them still talked and laughed, even as the newsreels gave way to the cartoons.

She looked sideways at Ross as he tossed Jaffas back and forth to his mates. She'd always known he'd had little time for new Australians. There the apple didn't fall far from the tree. But while Ross could be thoughtless sometimes, he was rarely deliberately rude or abusive. She couldn't account for his blatant hostility towards Matteo. It must have been the fight with his father that had him out of sorts.

The first film rolled onto the screen and *Long John Silver* didn't exactly excite her. Ross had clearly lost interest as well, since he spent more time talking and laughing and making a pest of himself with his old mates across the aisle. She sunk lower in her chair as people behind them began to send angry shushes down at them. The men quietened for a moment but something in the way they were huddling and whispering had her suspicions rising. What were they up to? Nothing good by the sounds of it.

She realised too late what they'd been planning when she saw Ross lean forward and drop a container of drink over the edge of the balcony. The yells and curses that came from below told her Ross and his mates had hit their mark.

She leaned forward to peer over the balcony. Matteo and his mates, as well as a good portion of the rows around them, stood wiping sticky soft drink from their heads and clothes.

Ross and his mates laughed uproariously.

Isabel did not. Grabbing her purse and coat, she shot him a filthy look and stormed from the cinema.

'Oh, come on,' Ross called after her. 'It was funny!'

She arrived at the bottom of the stairs at the same time as the ushers were heading into the theatre to see who was to blame for the mess they were going to have to clean up. As they went in,

Matteo and his friends pushed their way out of the lower-level doors in a chorus of half Italian, half English, but one hundred percent aggravated. Their hair was wet and messy, their clothes splattered with sticky liquid. The furious look on Matteo's face had her taking a few steps back as he spotted her. He hesitated as his friends headed to the men's room to get cleaned up.

'I'm sorry,' she said quickly.

'Why? Did you throw the cup?'

'No.'

'Then why are you sorry?'

She had no answer for that.

'Did you see who did?'

She hesitated. She didn't like what Ross had done, but she also didn't want to start a fight in the cinema. It seemed now she'd spent most of the evening stopping Ross from getting into a fight. 'I didn't see who it was.'

The look on Matteo's face told her he didn't believe her. He stalked across the foyer, joining his friends in the men's room—thankfully just as Ross came down the stairs. Jordy, one of the ushers and a member of the same football team as Ross, stopped him.

'Ross, did you toss those drinks?'

'Nah, mate, wasn't me.'

Ross chuckled again when Jordy rolled his eyes in disbelief and headed into the cinema with a mop and bucket.

Ross turned to Isabel. 'You coming back in?'

'No,' she shot back. 'That was a stupid, childish thing to do.'

'What?' He snorted out a laugh. 'We didn't hurt anyone. Come on, it's interval in a few moments. Let me buy you a drink.'

'Why? So you can throw that one too? No thanks.'

She folded her arms across her chest in defiance, refusing to move.

'Suit yourself. I'll see you inside for the second film.' He shrugged and joined the crowd that had moved out of the cinema for interval, heading straight to the candy bar.

She wanted to go home. She could find Leanne and Robby. They'd drive her back across the bridge. But she didn't want to ruin their night as well. She glanced around the cinema foyer, at a loss for what to do. She didn't feel like watching another film, but she really had no choice but to wait until Ross was ready to take her home.

The bell rang to sound the end of interval and patrons moved back into the cinema for the second film, leaving the foyer empty and quiet.

Flopping down on one of the velvet-covered bench seats, she dropped her elbows to her knees, her chin in her hands, and studied the pattern in the carpet.

When a pair of large brown and white wing-tip shoes appeared in her eyesight a moment later she sat up abruptly.

'Matteo!' she gasped.

His hair was now slicked back, making him look more dangerous. A wet mark spread across one shoulder of his white shirt where he'd tried to wash out the sticky soft drink. His brown corduroy jacket, held by two fingers and slung over his shoulder, looked as though it had escaped the worst of the liquid bomb.

'Not going back in for the second film?'

She shook her head.

'Matteo, *andiamo, eh*?'

He turned back to his mates who had returned from the men's room and were standing with the door to the theatre open. She could hear the audio from the film, spilling out.

'Go in, I'll be there in a minute,' he answered them.

They sent him shrugs and dismissive waves before disappearing back into the theatre, leaving Isabel and Matteo alone again.

'Where is your boyfriend?' The tone in his question rang with derision.

'He's not my boyfriend.'

'No?' He brightened then, a hint of a smile touching his lips. 'I admit I am pleased to hear it.'

'Again, I'm very sorry.'

'Stop apologising. You didn't do this,' he said, tugging at the wet shirt.

'No, but he did.' She realised too late that she'd given Ross up, and she studied Matteo's expression with concern. Would he go after Ross in the cinema?

He didn't seem angry, just resigned and, as she'd thought, he'd known it all along. 'He is jealous, I think.'

'Of what? Of who?' she asked, genuinely confused.

'Of any man who talks to you, I would imagine,' he said, a look of sympathy crossing his features. 'But especially someone like me. He probably thinks I am a dirty immigrant.'

'Well, he doesn't own me,' she argued. 'I can talk with whomever I want. And you're only dirty because he tossed drink all over you. I'm sorry he did.'

His lips twitched. 'You must stop apologising for something you did not do.' He glanced over her shoulder and out the window. 'It is not raining anymore. Let's take a walk.'

'A walk? It's freezing outside. Your shirt and hair are wet,' she said, stating the obvious. She huffed out a breath, annoyed with herself. She was usually very articulate, but around him she seemed to lose the ability to hold an intelligent conversation. 'What I mean is, you'll catch a cold.'

'No, it will be refreshing.' He held out his hand. 'Come. The moon is shining for once. It would be a shame to waste it.'

'But … I don't know you.'

'What better way to get to know me than a walk and a talk, eh? *Andiamo.*'

She hesitated a moment before taking his hand and letting him help her to her feet. He shrugged into his jacket then pushed open the door, motioning for her to walk out ahead of him. Her shiver was involuntary in the cool June evening and Matteo took her coat from her and held it out for her to slip her arms into. It was such a gentlemanly gesture, and she couldn't help comparing it to Ross and the incident with the wet towel in his car.

Every now and then, a car travelled by as they walked, but mostly it was quiet. She studied him out of the corner of her eye as they passed under streetlamps that relieved the darkness at intermittent intervals. What was she doing? She didn't know this man from Adam. Why on earth was she walking alone with him after dark?

'*Andiamo.*' She tried the word out. 'What does it mean?'

'It means, "we go" or "let's go".'

'*Andiamo,*' she repeated as they walked down Langtree in the direction of the river. 'I like it. *Andiamo.*' She tried with the Italian accent, making him chuckle. 'The Italian language always sounds like a song to me. Your accent, it's not as strong as many of the other Italians I've met.'

'Maybe that's because I'm Australian.'

'Oh, I'm sorry. That was so presumptuous of me. You were born here?'

'Yes. But my parents are from Italy; you are right there. They insisted my brother and I learn Italian as well. So, when I was growing up, we spoke Italian at home and English at school, but always with an accent which caused us many years of trouble.'

'I like the accent, the whole language actually.'

'My parents say it is important to hold onto our heritage.'

'I've never seen you around town before that night at the flood meeting. Are you here to get picking work with the citrus harvest?'

'No, I have lived in the district for about eight years.'

'Eight years?' Isabel couldn't hide the surprise in her voice. 'You've lived in Mildura for eight years?'

'Not Mildura, no.' Taking out a cigarette pack, he offered her one. She shook her head. Her one and only try at cigarettes when she was twelve had ended in a coughing fit and a hiding from her mother with the wooden spoon.

He put one between his lips and lit it. The flame from the lighter gave an orange glow to his cheeks and she thought again how handsome he was. When he exhaled the first puff, the smoke mingled with his warm breath in the cold night air. 'My family leases a block at Buronga. We grow many things. We have a lemon orchard, market gardens with vegetables. We have some vines as well, mostly for wine grapes, and of course glasshouses with the best tomatoes in the district.'

'There's so many of those glasshouses around Buronga. I try to count them when I drive across the bridge. I love how they sparkle in the sunlight,' she gushed. 'It must be nice and warm inside in winter with the sun beating down.'

He laughed and she wondered if he was laughing at her, or with her.

'It is lovely and warm inside,' he agreed. 'It helps the tomatoes to grow big and juicy, ready to be cooked and stored in jars for the winter. And for making the passata.'

'Passata,' she mused. 'That's tomato base sauce, isn't it?'

He looked surprised. 'Yes. How did you know that? It is not very common in Australia.'

'I read a lot of cooking magazines,' she said, stopping in front of Shilliday's store. It had been closed for hours, but someone had left a light on that now cast eerie shadows over the stock inside. 'I'm the cook at our pub, you see. Well, assistant cook. At the Riverside Hotel?'

'The Riverside. I know it.'

'Buronga's less than a five-minute drive from Gol Gol. How come I've never seen you at the pub? It's popular with the young blokes from Mildura.'

'You haven't seen me there *because* it's popular with the young blokes from Mildura,' he said with an easy one-shouldered shrug. 'You see how much they admire us "reffos" or "dagos". Many prefer we did not exist in their district.' He shrugged. '*Va bene.* We prefer to drink at home, to drink wine we make ourselves.'

'You make your own wine?'

He laughed again. 'Don't look so surprised. Many Italians make their own wine and liqueur. It is part of our culture.'

'I'm not surprised, I'm impressed. Turning grapes into something other than sultanas is a rarity in this region.'

'It's only a small vineyard. Just enough grapes for us to press about fifty bottles a year.'

She leaned back against the glass of the Shilliday's window and looked up at him. He was so tall and slim in his brown suit and white shirt. But it was those eyes that captivated her … even in the dark she could see how pale and bright they were.

Finally she had to move her gaze across to the T&G Building just so she could gather her brain cells again.

'You've lived nearby for eight years and we have never met before. I find that astounding.'

He leaned a shoulder against the glass next to her. 'I find it a tragedy.'

He was so close she could smell the spicy aftershave he wore and she was glad it was too dark to see the raging blush that must have been colouring her cheeks.

'Where were you living before?'

He hesitated and she wondered if he hadn't heard her.

'Before you moved here eight years ago,' she added.

'We lived in Adelaide,' he answered finally. 'My family owned a delicatessen before the war but after Papa … went away, my mama, my brother Antonio and I lived with my *zia*, my Aunt Maria.'

'Did your father go back to Europe? To fight in the war?'

Isabel glanced up at him when he didn't answer immediately. The smile was gone and the sparkle in his eyes had dimmed.

'I think it is time to get you back to the cinema,' he said, pushing away from the store window and turning back the way they'd come.

Isabel bit her lip. She knew better than to ask questions about the war. 'Oh, yes, of course.'

Looking back at the T&G Building clock she was shocked it was already half past nine. She'd been enjoying his company so much she hadn't realised they'd been out there walking for over an hour. She wished they could talk some more, but he was right, she needed to be back so that Ross could take her home.

In silent companionship on the return journey, they picked up the pace, arriving at the cinema only to find the doors locked and the lights inside being switched off.

'Oh! I didn't think we were that long.' She looked around and down the road to where Ross had parked the car. It was gone. She groaned. 'Dammit, Ross.'

'He left you?'

'I'm sure when he couldn't find me, he must have thought I'd gone home.' Did she really believe that?

'Come,' Matteo said. 'I will take you home.'

'Are you sure?'

'Of course.' He smiled. 'I'm not going to leave you here alone in the dark and the cold. As you say, the hotel is only five minutes past our property.'

'Alright, thank you.'

Despite her misgivings, Isabel walked with him to his truck and climbed in when he opened the passenger door. It creaked mightily when he closed it. The Ford truck was even older than the ute she and her mother drove but when he started the engine, it purred like a new car. Somebody obviously knew how to keep the vehicle in good condition.

The cabin of the truck seemed too quiet, too intimate as he drove them through the sedate streets towards the bridge. The rain had begun to fall again after the short reprieve that had allowed them their walk, the wipers slicing across the windscreen in rapid flicks to disperse the water.

'I hate this bridge at night,' Isabel murmured as they drove into the gaping metal mouth of the bridge that connected Victoria to New South Wales. She shivered and, wrapping her arms around herself, kept her eyes steadfastly on the road ahead, trying not to think about the fast-flowing river in the dark void below.

'It is a feat of engineering,' Matteo said with obvious admiration. 'The lift in the middle of the bridge that rises to let steamboats through, it's magnificent.'

'It's a death trap,' she argued. Hunching down, she closed her eyes, listening to the familiar rhythmic thump of tyres crossing struts on the bridge beneath her that kept the huge metal structure upright and the car from falling from its precarious perch.

'Only around ten o'clock when the pubs in New South Wales close and the drunks all drive back into Victoria,' Matteo returned.

Her eyes flew open as she sat upright in her seat again, glowering at him. It was the second time a man had thrown the veiled accusation at her that night and it got her back up.

'So, it's our fault that some men don't know when to stop drinking?' she demanded.

'I didn't say that.'

'I'll have you know that when our pub closes Mum and I never let anyone drive who's too drunk. We call their wives or kids and we keep a bungalow free for those who've had too much and have no one to collect them. Old Clarry usually just climbs into the back of his cart and lets his horse take him home.'

Matteo laughed at that. 'The horse makes his way home with the driver asleep in the cart?'

Isabel gave a sharp nod. 'Yep, Sampson knows where he's going. He plods the mile and a half along the Gol Gol North Road to Clarry's block, pulls himself and the cart under the open shed, has a feed and a drink and waits for Clarry to wake up. We run a responsible pub. Why do you think we added the extra meal service?'

'I'm very glad to hear it,' he said, a devious grin touching his lips. 'Ah, look, we have arrived in New South Wales. That wasn't so bad, was it?'

She looked out the window, a little stunned that they were indeed driving back onto solid land.

Eyeing him, she noted his smirk. 'You did that on purpose.'

'What did I do?'

'You kept me occupied, made me defensive so that I wouldn't concentrate on the bridge or the river.'

He smiled across at her. 'Did it work?'

She narrowed her eyes at him, but struggled to keep the little smile from her lips. 'Maybe.'

'You are formidable when you lose your temper,' he joked. 'I must remember that. You are also very protective of your family business.'

'Is that a bad thing?'

'No, it is an admirable thing. Family is everything.' He sobered a little then. 'Only people who have lost family can truly understand that.'

She nodded, thinking of her father, and wondered who it was Matteo had lost.

Three

The rain on the roof of his caravan woke Matteo before dawn. The early hour didn't concern him, he was used to that, and rain should be a blessing to a farmer. But, dammit, it had been pouring rain on and off for over a month now and he was getting tired of constantly being wet from dawn till dusk while he worked the farm with his family.

'Only going to get worse,' he told himself as he rolled his body up so his feet hit the floor.

Hissing, he lifted his feet off the cold linoleum, reaching over to grab a pair of thick woollen socks from the drawer. His last, he noticed. Trying to get washing dry in this weather was about as likely as finding someone to take to the dance at the supper rooms the following Saturday.

Isabel's pretty peaches-and-cream face came to mind as he brushed his teeth over the small sink. He'd enjoyed their walk together last night and she'd seemed relaxed and happy to walk and talk with him. So much so, they'd lost track of time and she'd even allowed him to drive her home. But they'd been very much alone. What were the chances she would go out with him on a real date if he asked? Could he really believe she would agree to be seen publicly with an Italian farmer? New Australians—the polite term for anyone not of English ancestry—were often treated as second-class citizens, and so he and his family, his mates, usually stuck to spending time with folks within their own Italian community. It didn't matter since there were plenty of them across the Sunraysia district. They hardly needed to bother to mingle with anyone outside of their circle. Staring at his reflection in the small mirror above the sink, he stopped brushing his teeth. Did that make them any better than those small-minded folks who saw mixing romantically with new Australians as wrong?

Mirella Carbone had married Alf Whittaker a few years back, he recalled, but they'd been forced to move to Melbourne to escape the vicious gossip they'd faced daily. It wasn't all one-sided either. Matteo knew plenty of people in the Italian community who frowned upon mixing with Australians, or any other cultures for that matter. It made him wonder. If Isabel did say yes to going to the dance with him, would she have enough spine to withstand the talk that would likely follow?

The bang on his door cut into his daydreaming.

'Matteo! Papa's waiting on the tractor to take us out to the far field. Get moving if you want a lift or you'll be walking.'

After spitting out his toothpaste, he wiped his mouth, grabbed his rain jacket and, pulling on his boots, opened the door to greet his brother Antonio's grouchy expression.

'*Buon giorno*, sunshine. What's got your face all puckered up like a cow's arse?'

'The baby is teething.'

'Oh, poor Lucia.' Matteo pouted in sympathy.

'Poor Lucia?' Antonio grumbled. 'Lucia and Loretta are sleeping soundly now. I was kept awake all night by the crying and *I'm* the one who has to work all day on no sleep.'

Matteo figured his brother's wife deserved a medal for putting up with him. 'She's a baby, Antonio. It's hardly her fault.'

'When you are married and have *bambini* to keep you awake all night, you can comment. Speaking of lack of sleep, you got home late last night?'

'You heard me come home?'

'I was awake, remember. Did you go to Dario's for poker after the movies?'

'No, I helped a damsel in distress find her way home.'

'Ah!' Antonio's eyes were suddenly wide open. 'And did you help this damsel into bed as well?'

Matteo just rolled his eyes as they walked together towards the Fergie tractor where their father sat patiently waiting for them.

'I'm a married man,' Antonio grumbled. 'I have to live vicariously through you and your escapades with women. Who was she? Simonetta Pasquale? She's been trying to catch you for years.'

'I know how to run fast,' Matteo said. Simonetta Pasquale was a very attractive, very determined woman a few years older than himself who'd set her sights on Matteo since the first day he and his family had walked into the Italian club at Red Cliffs. He'd be lying if he didn't admit she scared him a little.

'So, if not Simonetta, then who?'

Matteo shrugged. 'You don't know her.'

To stop any further questions, Matteo made a running jump up onto the tractor. '*Buon giorno*, Papa.'

'*Giorno*, boys.'

As the little Fergie tractor lurched and moved down the rows of lemons, Matteo studied his father. Carlo Sorrenti always seemed so calm, so at ease. Nothing ever seemed to bother him. Even when his sons were dragging their feet instead of being in the fields by sun-up, he'd just sit patiently waiting for them to be ready. This outer calmness belied the dark memories Matteo knew were in his papa's head and heart.

At the bottom of the lemon orchard, the tractor halted when they reached their market garden. Between it and the river stretched a long, six-foot wall of dirt that ran the entire length of their property, curving up at right angles at each end. At intermittent intervals, hessian bags and old planks of wood lay over sections of the wall, holding the wall and its delicate foundations together against the biting winds, and hopefully the rising river.

'We need to harvest what we can from this field in case the levee does not hold,' his papa directed when he cut the engine of the tractor. 'This afternoon we need to work with Tony to extend that end of the levee along from that group of trees.' He pointed to where their land met their neighbour Tony's property. 'Past our glasshouses and around to that high point up there.'

'The river won't reach that high.' Antonio shielded his eyes against the rising sun as he looked up the hill.

'Don't be so sure,' his papa said as the three of them jumped down off the tractor. Turning, he pointed. 'See that tree? The one at the edge of the river?'

'The one Matteo used to climb so he could get out of work,' Antonio teased.

Matteo knocked Antonio's hat from his head. It was true he had enjoyed sitting in the V between the heavy branches of the old river gum. It usually sat several feet away from the river, but now its roots and lower trunk were already surrounded by the rising water.

'In the flood of nineteen thirty-one, the river rose right up to where you used to sit, Matteo.'

'Not possible!' Antonio argued.

Matteo had to agree. It was difficult to imagine the river ever getting that high, but an image of their neighbour's living room popped into his head. 'Is that the tree in the photo Tony has on his wall? With the water covering the fields in the background?'

His papa nodded. '*Sì*. That's the one.'

'If he's been through this before, lost crops before, why is he still here?' Antonio asked.

'You would give up your home so easy?'

Matteo saw the usually calm facade of his father crack a little at Antonio's question.

'Tony asked to get a second lease.' His papa pointed up past their boundary line towards the Sturt Highway. 'He wanted that land up closer to the road so that he could plant his crops and build his glasshouses higher up the bank. They denied him.'

'Why?' Matteo asked. 'There's no one working that land. And there are plenty of people who lease more than one parcel of land.'

'Because he's foreign,' Antonio suggested, sneering before he shot off a string of curses in Italian.

'That is what Tony says, but who knows.' His papa shrugged.

Matteo and Antonio stared in awe at the height where the water had reached. The tree sat on the property line between their land and the land Tony still leased. Tony's family had survived the flood of thirty-one and continued to work the land to this day. They owned the largest number of glasshouses in Buronga.

Matteo turned to look back across their market gardens, the orchards, the glasshouses. All of them would have been below the flood line of nineteen thirty-one. Their house and his caravan were thankfully slightly above the line where the water had reached back then, but only just.

They walked into the vegetable garden and Matteo reached down and picked up a pumpkin. 'Papa, these are not quite ripe, and the vine hasn't died yet.'

'They will ripen even after picking,' he answered. 'The vegetables that are inedible, we can sell to the piggery for food. Pigs will eat almost anything.'

'Pigs?' Antonio questioned. 'When did you ever work with livestock, Papa?'

'You live as long as I have, you pick things up.'

Matteo studied his father and recognised the faraway look he so often got. 'Papa, were there pigs where you were—'

'Get moving. We have a lot to do.'

Matteo exchanged glances with Antonio. His brother shook his head at him as their father continued to move down the rows of vegetables, collecting what could be salvaged.

'Another cryptic clue to our papa's life,' Matteo complained quietly.

'Just get to work, Matteo,' Antonio urged, squatting down to check the cauliflower before ripping it from its base. 'I want to be done and back in bed for a siesta at lunchtime.'

'Doesn't it bother you?'

'Yes, it bothers me that I am sleep deprived.'

'No, I mean about Papa. All the unanswered questions.'

'Questions about what?'

Matteo scrubbed his hands across his face as much in frustration as to wipe away the misty rain. 'About what he was doing all that time he was gone. Don't you want to know?'

Antonio straightened, flipping his raincoat hood back. 'Why does it matter now? We got him back. He's home with us.'

'Yes, but he's never been the same,' Matteo argued.

'How would you know what he was really like back then? You were only nine.'

Anger flooded Matteo. 'You think I don't remember? I was there too, you know. I remember every second of that day.'

'That's not what I said.' Antonio shook his head. '*Dio*, why must you go on and on to him. He doesn't want to talk about it. I don't want to talk about it. You have to let it go, Matteo. He has, why can't you?'

Matteo watched Antonio walk away down the garden to join his papa. He wished he was like his brother, content to move forward. Antonio was happy to get on with life and his future with Loretta and his little girl. They'd gotten their papa back, but no matter what Antonio thought, he wasn't the same man. Carlo Sorrenti used to be a vivacious, funny, sparkling light in every room. Matteo may have been only nine years old, but he remembered the carefree, fun-loving man his papa used to be. These days he seemed to move through life sedately, not necessarily damaged by his experience, apparently at ease with the past.

Matteo stared at the wall of dirt a few yards away, separating them from the river, which appeared deceptively serene on the surface, but would be a raging torrent below.

Turning away from the wall, he got back to work.

Isabel was kept busy over the next few days. It seemed the moment she finished serving lunch, she was already preparing for dinner. Folks from the district had started to congregate at the pub as a kind of meeting point to catch up on the latest flood reports, to share road closure information or just to stop in for a chat and the company of friends to try and forget for one night the possible disaster that was bearing down on them.

Carefully lifting the tray of pork roasts from the oven, Isabel placed it on the butcher's block in the centre of the kitchen to rest. She stretched out her back and was wiping the sweat from her brow just as Ross stepped through into the kitchen.

'I can't talk right now, Ross.' It surprised her to hear the snap in her voice. She thought she'd gotten over Ross leaving her at the cinema almost a week ago, but the fact that it had taken him this long to come and see her had her ire rising again.

'What happened to you last Friday night?' he asked, casual as you like.

She stared at him. 'That's it? You're not going to apologise for leaving me alone at the cinema?'

'I thought you'd got a lift home with someone else.' At least he finally had the good grace to look sheepish.

'I did,' she shot back.

'Who?'

Stabbing one of the roasts with a giant fork, she heaved it out of the tray to the carving board with a little more gusto than was necessary.

'I looked for you.'

She shot the sharp knife through the pork, slicing it with expert skill. 'I wasn't gone that long.'

'Where did you go?'

'I went for a walk.'

'With who?'

'A friend.'

'What friend?'

Exhausted, she paused momentarily in her carving. 'What do you want, Ross?'

'I'm sorry I left you. Honestly,' he said, his expression one of genuine remorse. 'Forgive me?'

She rolled her eyes. 'Fine.' And it was fine. If he hadn't left her, she never would have spent a lovely time talking with Matteo. She was glad Ross hadn't pressed her on who exactly she'd gone for a walk with. She'd been so busy with work at the pub that week she hadn't really had much time to think of Matteo. But now she wondered how she might get to see him again.

Ross seemed to brighten then. 'You coming to the footy this weekend? The Demons are playing the Imps at City Oval. I'm starting full forward.'

'Ha! Naturally the football still goes ahead while the region floods.' She wondered if Matteo ever went to the footy, but dismissed that thought just as quickly. She'd have seen him there before now. Soccer, she believed, was the football Italians seemed to worship.

'So? Will you be there? We could go to the Wintersun for a pint or two after the game.'

'Great, a busman's holiday.'

She turned back to the oven and checked the roasting vegetables. 'Ross, I have a pub full of people waiting on a roast dinner. Bruce is over at his brother's property at Buronga. His mother had a turn. The stress of not knowing how high the river will get is upsetting her.'

'Yeah, my mum is going crazy,' Ross said, picking at a piece of crackling and crunching down on it. 'She's been packing for days. She's got the rugs and the family china packed away and half our furniture is being moved out to the storage sheds over on Etiwanda Avenue in Mildura. It's like living in a tomb.'

'There are homes and farms a lot closer to the river than yours, Ross,' she said, thinking of Matteo's family's orchards. 'It'll be more than just rugs and china that will be ruined if the river gets as high as predicted.'

He nodded sombrely before brightening and changing the subject. 'So, Saturday? City Oval? Will you come watch me play?'

'I'll probably be working,' she said, waving her hand across the mess that was the kitchen.

'Well, there's supposed to be a dance at the supper rooms in a few weeks' time. If you aren't interested in the pub or the footy, do you want to go to *that* with me?'

'They're still holding dances? With everything that's going on? Surely folks have more important things on their mind right now.' She hoped to redirect the conversation as she loaded the sliced pork back into the tray, and then into the oven again to stay warm until serving. She really didn't want to go out with Ross again but wasn't sure exactly how to let him down.

Ross shrugged. 'Life goes on, I guess. We're not under water yet. So, are we going? To the dance?'

'Like I said, I'll probably be working.'

'You work too hard,' he said, taking a look around the kitchen with his nose turned up. She could see his mother in him at that moment and her teeth ground together.

'You need to take a break every now and then, Isabel. Bruce doesn't really need you. Get out more, have some fun.'

'I have fun.' Not often while she was with him these days, but she decided she didn't have time to get into that particular conversation right now. 'Besides, it's not about Bruce needing me. I don't just work here because it's our family pub. I actually enjoy cooking. It's what I want to do with my life.'

'Well, you'll do plenty of cooking for your husband when you get married.' Oh, she really wanted to slap that smug look off his face. 'You really want to spend all your time until then cooking meals for random travellers passing through?'

'That's not—You really don't get me, do you?' She closed her eyes and counted to ten; he was pressing her last nerve. 'Look, if I can, I'll come out to the footy on Saturday for a while, okay?'

'Good enough. That pork smells pretty amazing. Gotta admit no one does crackling like you. Mum's is always soggy.' His expression was suddenly one of abject terror. 'Oh, please don't tell her I said that.'

'Not much chance of that,' she murmured. Ross's mother rarely condescended to speak to Isabel. She doubted Shirley would bother to drop in to discuss cooking styles. More and more she was coming to realise that a grown man still afraid of his mummy was not for her.

He stole a piece of bread from the bench with a cheeky wink. 'I think I'll stay for dinner. Talk to you after?'

When he left the kitchen, she let out a sound of frustration and leaned back against the table. Ross was used to getting what he wanted. Despite his father's shortcomings, or maybe because of them, his mother had spoiled Ross, indulged his every desire as a teenager and into manhood. Now, as he was the heir to the Burrows fortune, his mother expected him to marry someone with the right social standing. A debutante. There was no way Isabel would ever have attended one of the region's debutante balls. She didn't come from the right part of society for all that. Not that she cared. Frilly white dresses and gloves were not her idea of a good time.

Whoever Ross married would need to be content to be a homemaker, someone who'd have his dinner on the table on time and provide him with sons to take over the family business. Isabel wanted more from her life. She might reach her dream one day of being a fully qualified chef. Maybe not. One thing was certain though, Ross's mother would never allow him to marry a girl who had ideas and ambitions of her own.

It was another sort of prejudice she supposed. How Mrs Burrows felt about her wasn't so different to how many in the community felt about Matteo and other new Australians in the region.

Over the next few weeks, from Red Cliffs to Merbein, Gol Gol to Wentworth, walls of dirt and sandbags were rising up from the earth at an astounding rate. Families and businesses closest to the banks of the mighty Murray moved into a heightened sense of awareness as the once serene river—the lifeblood of the region—began to widen its path, already inundating the low-lying parts of Buronga and Nichols Point. A giant levee wall was being built up to separate the township of Mildura from the rising river, but many feared it wasn't being built high enough.

Taking advantage of a lull after a less than thriving lunch hour, thanks to the weather keeping folks at home or patrolling the levees, Isabel sat with her mother at the bar writing up a list of food they needed to order from their suppliers. It was getting harder for deliveries to get through with road closures or diversions slowly coming into place across the eastern river regions. Over the border in South Australia, the punt at Kingston had already stopped running, unable to make the crossing safely in the ever-widening and fast-moving river.

Isabel stared listlessly out the window at the incessant drizzle.

'This weather is so miserable,' she moaned. 'When's summer going to get here?'

Her mother snorted out a laugh. 'We've not even reached midwinter, love. It's a ways to go yet till summer.'

'I can't wait. This rain is driving me crazy. I want to swim in the river on a hot Sunday arvo.'

'And then you'll be complaining about the flies and the heat in the kitchen.'

'I'd never do that.'

Shaking her head, and with that patient smile that always frustrated Isabel, her mum moved to the pantry. Nobody had patience like Audrey Hayward. 'Not sure how soon you'll be swimming in the river either, my pet. It's going to take months for the floodwaters to recede once we reach the peak. Back in thirty-one it was almost Christmas before they'd fully left us. And wait till you see the mess it leaves behind.'

Isabel groaned. 'I saw Mr Mackey at the post office yesterday and he reckons that the constant rains are being caused by the recent atomic tests.'

'Surely that can't be right; they were thousands of miles away.' Her mum's voice drifted out of the pantry.

'Says he read it in the *Murray Pioneer* a few days ago.'

'Order twice as much tinned veg than usual. Atomic weather or not, we don't know how easy it will be to get fresh vegetables once the river peaks and cuts the highway. And whatever's left in the ground around here will go off pretty fast if they don't harvest quickly enough.'

'That's if it doesn't get washed away first.' Isabel added tinned goods to the list, her nose wrinkling in distaste. 'I hate cooking with tinned veg.'

'Better than no veg, my sweet.' Her mum pulled containers of herbs to the front of the pantry to count them. 'Better add Keen's mustard to the list too. We're low on that, and white pepper.'

'Mrs Baldwin's garden got washed away this morning,' Isabel said. 'I saw her at the bakery when I went over to get the bread for the day. She was devastated when she got up this morning and looked out to see the water had risen over her entire crop of herbs and her prized hydrangeas.'

'Sadly, they're building the levee behind her place,' her mum said, her brow knitting together as she too glanced out the window at the falling rain. 'Her house is too close to the creek. There was no way they could build the levee between it and her place.'

'She told Arthur at the store that her brother is coming in from Robinvale to help her pack up today,' Isabel said. 'Apparently, he has property safely away from the river and she'll move in there with him. I can't imagine what we'll do if the river rises up and takes the pub. Mum, we don't have anyone, or anywhere to go.'

'It won't come this high.' It was said with the confidence of a woman who'd lived on the river all her life. She stepped down off the ladder and gave Isabel a comforting hug. 'It didn't in the thirty-one floods. Everyone knows if the pub goes, so does the rest of the town. That's why they're building the levee below the bungalows.'

Both women paused their inventory, gazing out the window where they could see Perry, Albert and some of the other local men shifting dirt and clay from a trailer to build the wall that would—should—protect the hotel. It was a battle against time and nature, and damn hard work in the cold and rain.

'We'll be fine, hon, don't fret, okay?'

Isabel nodded and was scribbling items on her list when the front door of the pub swung open bringing the cold wind and a very wet man.

'Constable Masterson.' Isabel greeted the local policeman with a smile. 'What brings you to our humble establishment in the middle of the day?'

'Isabel.' He sent her a nod and one to her mother. 'Audrey.'

He removed his coat, shaking it out in the hallway before he hung it on the peg inside the door, then took off his uniform hat and slipped it under his arm.

Constable Jim Masterson was a tall, lanky man with bright red hair. Isabel always thought the hair teamed with the spattering of freckles made him appear younger than his nearly thirty years. He'd lived in the region all his life, helping his parents on their dairy farm outside Merbein with his three brothers and one sister. He'd been the star full forward of the inaugural Merbein Magpies football team when the Sunraysia Football and Netball League began in the mid-1940s after the war ended. He'd been tipped to go all the way to the VFL and even played a few games for the reserves before he decided to give it up to join the Victoria Police. He stayed in Melbourne to complete basic training, then returned to Mildura. He was married to Isabel's old piano teacher, Melissa, and was a well-respected member of the community and the small police unit that covered Mildura and surrounds.

'Can I get you a drink, Jim?' Audrey asked, stepping behind the bar and lifting an empty pint glass beneath the tap of his favoured lager.

'Just a softy, thanks, Audrey. I'm still on duty.'

She poured him a lemon squash from the bottle and one for herself and Isabel while she was at it.

'Business looks slow,' he said, scanning the room. Only a few of the old locals sat at a corner table, nursing a pint each and smoking. He nodded across at them, and they nodded back.

'Weather's probably keeping them away,' Isabel told him. 'We promised free drinks and a feed to anyone who will help build the levee. The older kids from the local Gol Gol Primary School are coming down soon to help fill sandbags. I stocked up on Heleys soft drinks and made a couple of jam roly poly cakes for our littlest workers.'

Isabel figured the kids would probably think of it as an exciting outing, a way to get out of boring schoolwork—for the first twenty minutes anyway.

'Haven't had too many other takers though.'

Jim nodded, staring out at the swollen river down the hill. 'Yeah, sorry, everyone's over at Red Cliffs to help raise the levee there. Gotta protect the power stations.'

'Oh, of course. No wonder there's no one here. I'm happy to go over and help if needed. Mum can take care of the schoolkids and our levee workers.'

He turned back to them. 'Actually, I was hoping to get your help with something else.'

'Is something wrong, Jim?' Audrey asked.

Isabel had been wondering the same. He looked exhausted—then again who didn't these days—but there was worry and sadness layered in with the exhaustion.

He drank thirstily from the glass of lemon squash before speaking again. 'A boy's gone missing.'

'Missing?' Isabel questioned.

'Went into the river.'

'Oh no! Who?' Her mum laid a hand over her heart.

'Margaret Phillips's boy.'

'Which one?' Isabel asked. The Phillipses had three sons if her memory served.

'Christopher.'

'The youngest? He's, what? Seven?' She turned to her mother, who nodded.

'Poor Margaret. She must be beside herself.'

Jim nodded. 'She is. They all are. The boys feel so bad and not just because of the tanned hides their mother gave them. They were playing with their cousins down by Lock 11 just before lunch. Apparently, Christopher slipped and fell into the river.'

Isabel shuddered involuntarily, as she glanced out the window again. Either she was imagining it, because of her fear for Christopher, or the rain was heavier now, obscuring the view of the river at the bottom of the sloping hill.

'The brothers were able to follow him downstream a way while the cousins ran up to the house to raise the alarm, but they lost sight of him once he got flushed out past Lock Island,' Jim went on. 'We're getting together a search party to patrol both sides of the river in case he was able to climb out somewhere on shore, but with so many folks over at Red Cliffs we're short of people. I'm doing a door to door along this side of the river to see who I can get to help. Melissa's at the station calling anyone and everyone as all officers are out already searching or on other call-outs. We're seriously understaffed just now.'

'I'll go,' Isabel said, hopping off her stool. 'Where are the searchers meeting?'

'We've got some starting at the lock and working downstream on the Victorian side. But there's others on this side of the river starting at River Road as far as Mourquong and working back from there. We're not sure how close you can get to the river from there since the water is already up over the flood plains and some roads are blocked. Anyway, if he went further downstream than that, I doubt he's …' He stopped. Isabel didn't need him to continue. It was near to impossible for a seven-year-old to survive that long in the water. A grown man would struggle to swim that long in the raging torrent the river was now.

'There's police motorboats already on the water,' Jim went on. 'Anyone who's got even a rowboat is helping out, but with so many people out building levees we need all the help we can get.'

'I'll grab my gear.' Isabel rushed out and down the hallway to her room at the rear of the pub. She changed into trousers and thick socks, threw on a woollen jumper and grabbed her emergency bag with its first-aid kit and essential supplies. Living on the river, it was good to be prepared for any eventuality.

After heading back out to the pub, she pulled on her wellington boots and coat. She followed Jim out to the car park, jumped into her truck and tailed his police vehicle as far as Silver City Highway where she turned off towards Mourquong, leaving him to head back across the bridge to Mildura. Turning the truck onto the river road, she spotted the red and white Country Fire Association trucks surrounded by a collection of other vehicles. She parked, then jumped out to join the group of volunteers. Reg, one of the senior CFA men, was just calling them to order. He scanned the crowd with quiet authority. His long face and sallow cheeks had always reminded her of a friendly basset hound, but his usually quick and ready smile was nowhere to be seen.

'Don't take any risks,' he instructed the group of about twenty people. The men clustered close together around Reg's truck and aside from Reg's wife, Patricia, Isabel was the only other woman in the group. 'Those with radios in your cars hold up your hands so folks can see you.'

Isabel lifted her arm. Her dad had kept a radio from when he was in the army. He'd taught her how to use it when she'd been about twelve years old and, on their camping trips, he'd shown her many tips to surviving in the bush and around the river.

'We're searching till sundown and not a moment over,' Reg went on. 'We don't need to be looking for more people out there, so don't get lost and for God's sake don't fall into the river. Good luck and we'll meet back here at five pm.'

Isabel kept her hand up as the volunteers split into pairs. Reg spread a map out over the hood of his Land Rover and handed out quadrants for searching. Knowing it was likely that none of the men would want to be paired with a girl, Isabel stood by, waiting for someone to be left without a choice. She was surprised when Matteo stepped through the throng of men and right up to her.

'Looks like I'm your man.'

'Hi.' She was so delighted to see him she didn't know what else to say. She'd been hoping to run into him again somewhere, but she wished it could have been under nicer circumstances. As other pairs dissipated, Isabel and Matteo hovered over the map, received their assigned search area, and headed back to Isabel's truck.

She climbed into the driver's seat when he opened the door for her. Once he was in, she drove them out along the muddy dirt roads to their starting point. The rain began to fall again and Isabel hoped it would at least stay light until they found the boy.

'It's terrible, isn't it?' Matteo said, making conversation as they stepped out into the rain and walked towards the river. 'He's just a little boy. Do you think he has a chance of surviving that?'

They stood staring at the rushing, muddy water. Trees and debris floated past, bobbing up from the brown swirling torrent before disappearing, only to be tossed back up to the surface again further downstream. A motorboat moved slowly across the other side of the river, searching in the reeds that flanked the Victorian side of the banks.

'Let's start searching,' Isabel replied. Despite knowing the little boy's chances weren't good, she wasn't ready to lose all hope yet.

They walked close to the water's edge, calling Christopher's name intermittently, stopping to examine anything that looked out of place. They'd been told Christopher had been wearing a green jumper and a yellow raincoat, so if he'd kept the coat on, he should be fairly easy to spot. But the river was now more than a mile wide in some places. Each hour, each minute that they didn't find the boy ...

'He must have been so frightened,' she said quietly as they stepped back from the bushes where they'd spotted a piece of fabric. It had turned out to be an old towel.

'You know, when I first moved to the region, I wouldn't go near the river,' Matteo said. 'I can't swim.'

'Not at all?' Isabel had never met anyone who couldn't swim. She'd been a water baby all her life.

'No. But I didn't want to swim in the river anyway. It is brown. Dirty.'

She laughed.

'We sometimes went to the beach at Glenelg in Adelaide, but I always stayed in the shallows.'

'I've never been to the beach,' she said. 'I've never seen the ocean.'

'Really? It is beautiful. Sometimes the water was so clear you could see little fish swimming around your feet. In the river you see nothing. Do you swim?'

She nodded, kicking over a sheet of galvanised iron on the bank. 'I'm a good swimmer. The schools here have swimming lessons at the big pool on Twelfth Street over in Mildura, but my father taught me to swim and about river safety when I was very young. You're right to be respectful of the river. It's different to swimming in a pool. Even when it's not in flood. The current can take you very quickly, and there are snags beneath the surface. Grandma tried swimming across the river from the Victorian side back to Gol Gol one day a few years ago and she got into trouble, so we had to row the boat across to pick her up halfway. I thought we were going to lose her.'

'Your grandmother tried to swim across the river?' Matteo asked, shocked. 'How old was she?'

Isabel burst out laughing. She tried to stop when she saw his confused expression, but just couldn't seem to contain herself. 'I'm sorry.'

'What's so funny?'

'I'm sorry,' Isabel repeated, snorting as she tried to curb her chuckling. 'Grandma is our cat. She's an old ginger cat we adopted when she just showed up one afternoon at the pub. She hung around the front of the pub for days and all the blokes kept feeding her beer on the verandah. We had to take her into our home before she developed a drinking problem.'

'An alcoholic cat that swims across rivers.' Matteo shook his head. 'Now I've heard everything.'

'Really?' Isabel challenged. 'How about an emu that thinks she's a duck.'

'A duck?'

'Maddie, the emu in our little zoo at the pub, she came to us as a little baby chick and used to trail along with the ducks, even swims in the river with her adopted brothers and sisters.'

'I would like to meet Maddie the emu and see your other animals in the zoo.'

'You're welcome any time.'

Silence fell between them. Isabel realised they'd momentarily forgotten the gravity of why they were there. They turned around at the edge of their allotted quadrant and backtracked along the river, hoping to find something, anything, they hadn't seen before. They talked about mundane things, doing their best to keep their minds off the horrible scene they may come across. But there was nothing to be found. Finally, as the sun touched the horizon, Isabel drove them back to the staging area and they reported in with Reg and the CFA. There'd been no sign of little Christopher and now, in the darkness, they had no option but to call off the search.

'Anyone who's available tomorrow, report here first thing in the morning and we'll set some new search areas,' Reg announced, his hound-dog face looking weary now. 'Thanks, everyone. Let's just pray he's still alive out there somewhere.'

Isabel wanted to stay positive, but time and the odds were against little Christopher, and she could see by the solemn expressions of the other searchers that they also believed it was more likely a recovery than a rescue mission now.

Matteo walked Isabel back to her car in the dark with only the headlights of cars swirling around them as people left the area to head home.

'Do you have plans for Saturday night?' Matteo asked.

'I work most Saturday nights.' It was the same thing she'd said to Ross, but this time she actually felt some regret that she couldn't say she had no plans.

'Oh, of course.'

He was quiet for a moment longer and since it didn't look as though he was going to say anything else, Isabel opened her car door.

'Do you ever take a night off?'

She turned back, pausing in the gap between the car and the door. 'Occasionally.'

'There is a dance on Saturday night at the supper rooms.'

'I know.'

'Oh.' His smile faded. 'Someone has already asked you?'

'Uh, no.' She hated lying but she didn't want to tell him that Ross had asked her to go, even though she had declined.

He cheered up considerably. 'Perhaps, if you are able to take the time away, you might like to attend with me.'

'That depends,' she said, a teasing tone in her voice. 'Are you a good dancer?'

He chuckled and the deep throaty sound of his laugh sent a fabulous shiver across her skin. Or maybe it was just the fact that she was soaked to the bone after hours of walking in the misty rain.

'I have been told I am a better than average dancer.'

'Better than average,' she repeated with a laugh. 'Well, that's better than me. I'm a bit of a clumsy Clara on the dance floor.'

'You just need the right partner,' he said with a confidence that showed he obviously meant he was the right partner for her. 'So can I pick you up at the pub on Saturday?'

'Bruce, our head chef, is looking after his ailing mother and so I've been running the kitchen by myself. I won't know if I am able to get away until Saturday morning. If he shows up, I can possibly take the night off. We don't have that many coming in for tea just now with everyone preparing for the possible floodwaters.' She closed her mouth abruptly. Hearing herself babbling like an idiot, she wondered why a man like Matteo would want to take her out dancing. But he only smiled as though she was saying the most fascinating things.

'Then I will make sure I drop by the pub Saturday morning for your answer.'

'Okay.'

She climbed into the driver's seat before she could say anything silly and make him change his mind.

'*Buona notte*, Isabel.'

'Does that mean goodnight?'

'It does.' He winked and closed the door for her.

When Saturday morning rolled around, Isabel made sure she was up and dressed early and preparing the meals for the day's menu. Meatloaf and veggies would do for lunch, and she could get the batter mixed up for the fish for dinner. The potatoes were cut, ready for chips to go in the oven so if Bruce did return, at least she could say that everything was prepared and he could handle the kitchen without her. She hung around the front bar, finding odd jobs to do, wiping down the Formica tables in the dining area, filling salt and pepper shakers. Every time the front door opened her head snapped around and her heart leaped into her throat. But each time, she was disappointed.

When the door opened again, she spun around, flicking the open bottle of tomato sauce she'd been filling.

'What on earth ...?' Her mum lurched back and looked down at the red saucy mess painted across the belly of her apron. 'You shot me! Friendly fire and all! What did I ever do to you?'

Isabel couldn't help the giggle. 'Sorry, Mum.'

She took the cloth Isabel handed her but studied her daughter as she wiped at the mess on her front. 'Why so jumpy, honey? What's going on?'

'I'm waiting for someone,' Isabel said, looking hopefully at the door again as she heard it swing open. On a gust of cold breeze, old Clarry wandered in, taking his usual seat at the end of the bar, lighting up a cigarette as he waited impatiently to be served.

'Be right there, Clarry!' Audrey called before turning back to Isabel. 'Who are you waiting for?'

'Just someone.'

'A young man, perhaps?'

'Mum.' She couldn't help the whine that made her sound like a twelve-year-old.

'Well, if it's a fellow named Matteo, he called on the telephone earlier.'

'Mum!' The whine rose an octave with a touch of accusation added for good measure. 'When did he call?'

'About an hour ago.'

Isabel stared wide-eyed at her mother, following her as she wandered behind the bar and started pouring a pint for Clarry.

'Why didn't you come and get me, or tell me sooner?'

'What? I was busy,' her mum replied and, considering the apron a dead loss, she lifted it carefully over her head, tossing it in the pile with the dirty tea towels. 'I was coming to tell you now.'

'What did he say?'

'He was very polite and has a lovely telephone voice,' her mum said as she opened the drawer and pulled out a clean apron. Isabel eyed the yellow fabric with the horribly out-of-shape sunflower embroidered onto the chest. She'd sewn it in ninth grade and given it to Audrey for her birthday. She cringed, wishing her mum would just toss it away.

A sly grin touched the edge of her mum's mouth as she tied the strings behind her back. 'Matteo has a lovely accent. Very Mario Lanza.'

'Mum!' Isabel closed her eyes, doing her best to keep a firm grip on her patience. Her mother could be such a horrible tease when she wanted to be. 'Concentrate please. What did he say?'

Her mum chuckled, taking obvious delight in tormenting her. 'He said he wanted to take you to the dance at the supper rooms tonight and asked if you were free. I said you were and to pick you up at six.'

'But we don't know if Bruce will be back yet.'

Her mum raised one eyebrow and put a hand on her hip. 'You think I can't handle the kitchen? Who do you think taught you to cook?'

'Bruce, mostly,' Isabel said, thinking her mother deserved the jab after her teasing. 'But you can't run the kitchen and the bar alone on a Saturday night.'

'Honey, I've been running this place since before you were tall enough to reach this bar. You've done most of the preparation for dinner already. If Bruce doesn't return from helping his mum, I can whip up the fried fish and chips. Besides, I can call on Albert and Flo to come serve in the bar if we get busy. Go out with your friends and spend time with a nice man.'

Isabel nodded. She wanted desperately to go out with Matteo, but not if it meant leaving her mother to run the pub alone.

'Anyway, I already called Perry. Told him you were making fish in the beer batter. He said he'd be happy to help in the bar tonight for a free feed. And Florence is willing to clean tables and deliver food. So, tell me about this Matteo,' her mum urged. 'Is he handsome? That lovely voice sounded Italian.'

'Yes. Well, his parents are. Matteo was born in Adelaide.'

'And is it serious?'

'We've only really talked a few times,' Isabel said, squirming. She'd never been one to date much and she rarely spoke with her mother about such things. 'But he's interesting. He's different to most of the boys I grew up with.'

'Different how?'

For starters he's a man and not a boy, she thought, but she didn't want to say that to her mother.

'I'm not sure how to explain it. Anyway, we're just going to the dance at the supper rooms. It's probably nothing special.'

'If you say so.' Her mum's eyebrows bounced up and down.

Isabel shook her head and looked at the clock. 'Almost noon. Better get the meatloaf in the oven for the lunch crowd.' She packed away the condiments and headed for the kitchen.

'Yes, finish your work, Cinderella, or you shall not go to the ball.'

'Mum,' she called when she reached the kitchen door.

'Yes, love?'

'Thank you.'

Her mum winked, blew her a kiss and set about pouring another pint.

Four

Bill Haley's 'Rock Around the Clock' poured out of the supper rooms as Matteo and Isabel arrived at the town hall that evening. The band already had everyone dancing as they hung their coats and hats in the foyer area. Isabel smoothed down her dress. The green short-sleeved number with white buttons running down one side was her best dress. It was usually reserved for weddings and other formal outings, but she'd wanted to make a good impression. It had been totally worth it to see Matteo's face light up when she removed her coat.

Knowing she'd be dancing though, she wasn't about to wear the heeled pumps that usually went with the formal dress, so she'd dug through her wardrobe and found an old pair of black and white saddle shoes which she paired with some bobby socks.

The minute they stepped into the supper rooms Isabel saw three of her old school chums, including Leanne who was happily dancing with the Morrison twins, Barbara and Judy. She waved madly as she spotted Isabel and, leaving the twins, she zig-zagged her way through the dancing couples, stopping short with a shocked expression when she recognised Matteo.

'Oh!' she said, her eyes going wide before shooting a questioning look at Isabel. 'You didn't tell me you were coming, Isabel. I thought you'd be working.'

'It was a last-minute decision. Mum gave me the night off.'

Leanne looked up at Matteo again and back to Isabel, the expectation on her face unmistakable.

Isabel obliged with a chuckle. 'Leanne, this is Matteo.'

'Hi,' Leanne said with a grin of admiration for Matteo.

'*Ciao*, Leanne,' Matteo responded. 'Can I get you ladies a drink?'

'Please,' Leanne said with a nod.

'Thank you, Matteo.'

The moment he was out of earshot Leanne pounced. 'Strike me pink! Isn't that the bloke from the town hall meeting?'

'Yes.'

'Well, golly, how did you end up here with him?' Leanne questioned with excitement. 'Tell me everything. Quickly, before he comes back.'

'You remember how someone threw drinks over the balcony at the movies the other night?'

'Yes, it barely missed me and Robby.'

'Well, that was Ross and his infantile mates.'

'What a ratbag!'

'Hmm, that's one word for it.' Isabel felt her ire rising again just thinking about it. 'Anyway, I was furious and stormed out of the cinema and refused to go back into the movie with Ross after that. I ran into Matteo, cleaning himself up after being drowned in sticky soda. We got talking and long story short, he drove me home. Oh! But that was after Ross up and left me at the cinema.'

'He didn't?'

'He did.'

'What a complete numbat!'

Isabel laughed. It was so nice to have a friend who would be outraged on her behalf and Leanne had such a colourful way about her.

'Wait! Matteo drove you home?'

Isabel nodded.

'But you didn't know him. Weren't you a little afraid?'

'I was a little at first, but he was the perfect gentleman.'

'How exciting. Tell me more.'

Isabel rolled her eyes. 'There's no more to tell. He dropped me home and that was that. But then we were teamed up to search for young Christopher the other evening and he asked me if I'd like to come to the dance with him. And that's all she wrote.'

'No kidding? That's aces!' Leanne said, before concern crossed her pale features. 'Oh, not for poor Christopher though. I heard about him going missing. They haven't found him yet?'

'No, I don't believe so. They haven't given up the search yet though.'

Leanne took Isabel's arm and led her to the corner of the room where they could see Matteo at the drinks counter. 'So, tell me more about Mr Yummy Blue Eyes.'

Isabel chuckled. 'What would you like to know?'

'Does he have any friends that look like him? Or a brother maybe?'

'To be honest I haven't learned much about him yet,' Isabel admitted. 'I know he has a brother, and he was with some friends at the movies, but I didn't meet them. Maybe they'll be here tonight.'

Matteo returned with the drinks and Leanne took hers, gave Isabel a wink and made her exit, joining one of her friends from church. Matteo and Isabel wandered the perimeter of the dance floor. She introduced him to people she knew and tried to ignore the surprised looks people gave her.

Others didn't try to hide their astonishment or even distaste, including Sharon Thompson whose expression resembled that of someone who'd just eaten a lemon. Isabel steered Matteo away from where Sharon stood with several other ex-schoolmates, but when they came across a group of his friends, she recognised the same surprise in their eyes as they studied her.

'You were at the cinema that night,' the one named Aldo said, his face suddenly stony. He looked around the hall as though searching for someone. 'Where is your boyfriend? The one who threw drinks at us over the balcony.'

'He's not my boyfriend,' she denied, glad that Ross had obviously decided not to attend the dance since she'd declined his offer.

'But you were with him.'

Isabel began to feel horribly uncomfortable under the dark-eyed stare of the man. 'Yes, I was there with him, until he threw drinks over the balcony and that's when I left him.'

'She had nothing to do with it, Aldo,' Matteo said, defending her.

Aldo grunted and murmured something in Italian to the other men, who snickered.

She felt Matteo stiffen beside her and fearing an argument was about to break out, she grabbed his arm. 'Oh, I love this song. Matteo, will you dance with me?'

He hesitated a moment, heated eyes still locked on Aldo, until she slid her hand into his. He looked down at their joined hands and back to her face and she was happy to see that his smile had returned.

'Yes, let's dance.'

The band had begun the opening chords of 'Memories are Made of This' and as the lead singer, Keith, the owner of the tyre service store on Deakin Avenue, began to croon in a voice not dissimilar to Dean Martin, Matteo led Isabel to the dance floor.

Mixing in among the other couples, Matteo took her in a waltz hold and began to move her expertly around the floor.

'You're a wonderful dancer,' Isabel said, happy that he seemed to have calmed down since the near altercation with his mates.

'My mama, she insists it is important for men to know how to dance.'

'I think I like your mama,' she said, wondering if Mama Sorrenti would feel the same way about her.

He grinned and she relaxed in his strong arms as he held her close against him. When the band took a break and the jukebox took over, the music changed to an upbeat song.

Matteo grinned wildly. 'This is Elvis Presley,' he said, changing step smoothly into a twisting dance as Mr Presley sang about a girl named Sue, who knew just what to do.

'Who?'

'You don't know who Elvis Presley is? "Jailhouse Rock"?'

'The jukebox at the pub hasn't progressed much past the war years,' she said with a shrug. 'Tommy Dorsey, Bing Crosby, Vera Lynn. If you're lucky you might find something from earlier this decade.'

He took her hand, spinning her out to the fast-paced song before bringing her back into his arms, his feet moving so quickly she could barely keep up. By the time the song ended she was laughing so hard she was terribly out of breath.

'Oh my.' She laughed, dabbing at the perspiration on her brow with her handkerchief as Matteo led her back to the drinks stand. 'Did your mum teach you to dance like that too?'

'No.' He handed her a drink and took a large sip of lemonade. 'The young people at the Italian Club, we love to rock and roll. I just love Elvis Presley. He's got Italian blood, you can see it. I believe he is going to be a big star.'

'I'm sure you're right,' Isabel agreed, still grinning as she sipped at the wonderful cool drink as Leanne joined them again.

'Did you see us?' Isabel asked her, but she quickly noted Leanne's distressed expression. 'What is it? What's happened?'

'They found some of young Christopher's clothes. The coat and the trousers.'

'The missing boy?' Matteo asked.

Leanne nodded.

'How do you know?' Isabel asked, her heart sinking.

'I just saw Melissa Masterson in the ladies' room,' Leanne told them.

'Constable Masterson's wife?' Matteo asked.

'That can't be good.' Isabel looked to Matteo. She found comfort and understanding there in his eyes as he put his arm around her shoulder. They'd searched for the little boy together. 'We always knew it was unlikely they'd find him alive after all this time.'

'Isabel.'

She turned to see who'd called her. 'Kevin. Hi. Have you heard? They found Christopher Phillips's clothes.'

'Yeah, my dad told me this afternoon.' Kevin's dad was Reg, the senior CFA man who had led the search for the boy.

Isabel was going to ask him more questions about the search for Christopher, but Kevin's attentions had turned to Matteo, his expression darkly curious. 'What are you doing here, Isabel? Ross said you had to work tonight.'

'I did. But I got the night off at the last minute. Is Ross here?' Oh Lord, she hoped not. Nervously, she looked past Kevin and around the room.

'No, he's at the footy club,' Kevin said, again turning suspicious eyes on Matteo. 'They put on some drinks and a barbecue after the Demons won the game against the Imps.'

Thank God.

'I think Ross was hoping to see you there today,' Kevin added. 'He played a good game.'

'That's good,' Isabel replied, starting to feel nervous under Kevin's accusatory stare. When he didn't say anything else she took Matteo's arm and began to lead him away. 'Okay, well, it was good to see you, Kevin. We'll see you later.'

'Oh, you can bet on it,' Kevin shot back.

'Who is that?' Matteo asked as she led him out the door of the supper rooms.

'Ross's best mate. You can be sure Ross will hear about me being here with you.' She shivered in the cool night air as they stood under the verandah of the town hall. Outside the rain was pelting down again. 'Suddenly, I'm not feeling in the mood for dancing.'

'Is it the news of the boy's clothes being found? Or because Ross Burrows will soon find out you came to the dance with me instead of him?'

Isabel studied his face carefully, looking for the same jealous ire Ross had displayed. She saw none of it. Only amused interest appeared in his expression. 'If Ross finds out, he finds out. It's none of his business who I do and do not choose to go to dances with.'

'But you lied to him and said you were working tonight and then came out with me.'

'I didn't lie. I was supposed to be working tonight, but when Mum heard you'd asked me to the dance, she gave me the night off.'

'Really?' Matteo stretched out the word. 'So, your mama is happy to give you a night off work for me, but not Ross Burrows?'

'I never asked her for a night off to come here with Ross.'

It was forward of her, she supposed, to let him know that she only wanted to come to the dance with him and no one else. And she could tell by the way he was looking at her that it pleased him.

He took a step closer, touched a hand to her cheek, and her heart did a little kick at the thought that he was going to kiss her. She swallowed hard, watching his pale blue eyes as he moved closer, as his hand touched the small of her back.

Suddenly, the door to the supper rooms flew open and Isabel jumped as a collection of girls tumbled out. They giggled when they spotted Matteo and Isabel standing close together and Matteo dropped his hand and stepped back.

'I should probably take you home,' he said, disappointment lacing his tone.

Not trusting her voice, Isabel nodded mutely.

'I'll get our coats,' he said and left her standing alone on the porch.

She turned to stare out into the heavily falling rain and took deep breaths to try and slow her heart rate.

'The publican's daughter and the reffo farmer's son.'

She heaved out one last heavy breath before turning to face Sharon Thompson. 'Hello, Sharon. How's things at the hairdressing salon?'

'What on earth are you doing with that … Italian?' Sharon asked, that bitter lemon expression back on her face.

So much for trying to redirect the conversation.

Sharon Thompson had been in the same year at Mildura High School with Isabel. A debutante, she'd been one of the most popular girls in school and while they hadn't been enemies, they'd mostly stayed out of each other's way. Isabel hadn't been unpopular, she'd had a close group of friends, but Sharon's group had been a collection of the prettiest, wealthiest—and often the most vapid—girls in Mildura. Isabel being a 'publican's daughter' from Gol Gol—as Sharon had just reminded her—had meant their social circles hadn't crossed all that often.

'What do you usually do at a dance, Sharon? We're dancing.'

'New Australians aren't like us,' Sharon said, tossing her newly acquired, Marilyn Monroe style, platinum blonde hair. A benefit of working at the salon in town was that her hair always reflected the latest styles.

'New Australians eat, they sleep, they work—often harder than most old Australians.' Immediately, Isabel realised her mistake and if she hadn't, the violent expression on Sharon's well-powdered face would have given it away.

'My dad can't work!' she exploded. 'He got injured fighting in Europe during the war. Fighting the Italians, fighting your boy-friend there. Dagos, reffos, wogs, the lot of them can bugger off back to where they came from.'

Sharon's vile words set off Isabel's own fury. She knew better than to be provoked by one of Sharon's attacks, but when something ignited her temper, she had trouble reining it in. She wished she had some of her mother's famous patience, but when she saw injustice, she was incapable of letting it go.

'I feel sorry for you, Sharon. Take a step away from your father's prejudices. There is so much culture you could learn from those dagos, reffos and wogs as you call them.'

'You should stick with your own kind,' Sharon shot back.

'Why do you care who I date?' Isabel asked. 'Call the *Sunraysia Daily*, we've got a scoop! Isabel Hayward goes to the dance with a dago. Woop-de-doo!'

She turned when she heard someone behind her. She hadn't realised Matteo had stepped back out of the rooms onto the porch with their coats. The look of disappointment on his face meant she didn't have to wonder at exactly what point he'd walked out on her sarcastic rant. Stepping forward, he helped her into her coat.

'Good evening, ladies,' Matteo said to the group. He looked out at the teeming rain before turning back to Isabel. 'I will go out and bring the car around.'

'Thank you,' she said weakly, but he was already rushing out into the deluge and the darkness.

Isabel tossed and turned in her bed. She just couldn't settle. Matteo had been very subdued as he'd driven her home. She'd started to explain what had happened with Sharon, but he'd simply turned the radio up and stared out the windscreen. She'd been so furious she could barely remember herself what she'd said. But she did remember using that awful word. Dago. He'd misunderstood her, that's all. Oh, why hadn't she turned down the radio, forced him to listen to her apology?

She stared at the ceiling. The shadow of her little duck night-light hovered over her like a looming spectre. Sharon Thompson had always pushed her buttons. But they weren't in high school anymore. She was older now, she ought to know better. Why did people have to have such ridiculous prejudices against anyone who didn't look like them or talk like them? She'd never been able to get her head around it.

Her mum and dad had always welcomed anyone and everyone into the pub. There had never been any signs banning any specific race or person.

By four in the morning, she'd had enough of herself. She climbed out of bed, pulled on her dressing gown and slippers, and headed for the kitchen. Baking always settled her down. It calmed her. The experimentation with recipes, the feeling of getting her hands into dough, the smell of cake or biscuits. It reminded her of childhood when she would sit with Grandma Louisa in the kitchen, helping her roll out the dough for scones or pie crust.

'What are you doing?'

Isabel broke out of her reverie as her mum came into the kitchen. 'Huh?'

'How long have you been up?'

She looked up at the clock on the wall. 'A while. I wanted to bake. Foundation biscuits.'

She tore off another piece of the sweet dough and popped it in her mouth.

'Looks more like you're eating the dough, just as you used to when you were a kid,' her mum said, pouring herself a cup of tea. She moved in to take a pinch from the block of dough herself. 'Mm, that's good.' She took another lump. 'I think the real question here is, what's eating you?'

'Nothing,' Isabel grumbled.

'Then why are you sitting here at six in the morning, eating raw biscuit dough and looking sorry for yourself?'

Isabel didn't answer, just shoved more dough into her mouth. Even the sweet, sugary goodness couldn't lift her spirits.

'How was the dance last night?'

'Fine.'

'And your new fella?'

Feeling mildly sick, Isabel finally turned the dough out onto the flour-covered bench and began rolling it out. 'I think I messed it up.'

'What happened?'

Isabel slapped the cookie cutters into the dough with more exertion than was required. 'Sharon Thompson was being her usual self, which forced me to be my usual self.'

'What did she say?'

'It's not so much what Sharon said.' Isabel balled up the remaining dough to roll out again. 'It's what I said in response. I let my temper get the better of me and while I was defending

Matteo, he walked out just as I said some things that had to have hurt him.'

'That's not like you,' her mum said, rubbing her back with sympathy. 'Oh, don't get me wrong. You can throw a tantrum with the best of them, but I've never heard you say anything deliberately hurtful.'

'I called him a dago, Mum.'

'Isabel!'

'I mean, I didn't call him that directly,' Isabel explained quickly. 'I was telling Sharon to get over her bigotry but in my usual sarcastic way. It must have sounded like I was agreeing with her. Dammit!' She tossed the wooden rolling pin, so that it rolled on the bench and clattered to the floor.

Her mum bent down and picked it up. 'Well, you know what you have to do.'

'What?'

'Apologise to Matteo.'

'I tried to explain on the way home, but he didn't want to hear it.'

'Make him hear it. If he's worth it, you have to try.'

'I don't know how.' Isabel slumped into a chair, wiping the tears that started to spill. 'I've never been very good with men, Mum, you know that. I was never popular with the boys in school.'

'You were a bit of a tomboy. Daddy's girl through and through.'

The mention of her father had the tears welling again.

'Ross seems to be showing more of an interest these days.'

Isabel took the hanky offered and screwed her nose up. 'I don't feel that way about Ross. I think we've known each other too long. It'd be like dating … my cousin or something.'

'Hmm.' Her mum mimicked Isabel's turned-up nose. 'Well, have you told him you only want to be friends? Men can be very thick-headed when it comes to these things. You'll have to be straight with him if you don't want to see him anymore.'

'I know,' Isabel said. 'Although, I think I've done enough damage to the opposite sex this week.'

'Honesty is always the best policy, pet. Now finish these biscuits and help me get some toast out for the truckies before they leave.'

Isabel didn't have a lot of time to dwell on her romantic problems. Between her shifts cooking at the pub, she volunteered where she could around the region. She wielded a shovel, carted wheelbarrows and filled sandbags for days.

From Nichols Point back towards Cowra Avenue, the river had already claimed farmland and properties. Up to twenty families had been evacuated from the area, making the heartbreaking decision to leave their homes and livelihoods to the fates. Roads to the Nichols Point Cemetery were now officially closed.

It was still over a month until the predicted peak of the floodwaters coming downstream, and still the rain fell. Sometimes it fell so hard, all work had to be suspended on the levees as it was too dangerous with men losing their footing and coming far too close to slipping off the top of the levee into the raging river. Trucks and tractors would get bogged in the mud. It was a miserable time for everyone involved.

When Isabel wasn't working on a levee somewhere, she was busy in the kitchen cooking pies and cakes to take to feed those who worked day and night. At one point, her mother had had to force her into her bedroom for a nap before the dinner service at the pub.

At the height of the activity over at the Mildura levee, they closed the bar for the night and drove across the bridge. When Isabel and her mother arrived at the Cureton Avenue work site it was like a small village. Hundreds of people—men, women and children—drove tractors, continued to shovel sand and clay, and filled sandbags, doing whatever they could to help raise the wall high enough to protect the brickworks and other businesses from the rapidly rising waters. Generators whirred as they pushed power to the electric lights strung from trees, set up so that weak spots in the levee could be easily seen and shored up. Isabel and her mother walked among the workers, handing out food and a welcome slug of rum to warm the wet, freezing men. The Salvation Army had also turned out with sandwiches, pies and tea and coffee. The near constant rain made the work harder. Just as they'd shored up one failing section another part of the levee would begin to leak or crumble.

Isabel shared a cup of tea and listened as some of the returned servicemen, from both world wars, likened the massive effort going on to building the foxholes they'd lived in for years on the cold fields of France or Gallipoli. And when the sirens wailed in the night, more than one veteran broke down, dropping their shovel to run away, or curling into a ball at the foot of the levee. The sirens no doubt reminded them of the horrors of frontline battles. Their bodies had survived, but their minds were clearly much more fragile. It was so hard to watch and it broke Isabel's heart.

By the time the sun was doing its best to push through the clouds on the horizon, with all the pies delivered and devoured, Isabel staggered, exhausted, soaked through and freezing cold, back to the truck to return the trays and containers and to hide the rum since some of the men had become too inebriated to continue being useful. Live and learn, she thought.

She dumped the pie trays in the back of the truck and, opening the front passenger side, leaned in, reaching for the last of the containers of date and walnut roll, vanilla slices and chocolate sultana fudge, made from her Auntie Phyllis's recipe book.

'Let me get those.'

She turned her head and saw Ross standing with his arms open.

'It's okay,' she said. 'I've got it.'

She lifted the containers out and balanced them on the hood of the truck while she arranged them better.

'I didn't see you out there with a shovel or a sandbag,' Isabel said. 'When did you get here?'

'Oh, just now,' he said with a dismissive wave.

Isabel's patience was a thin wire, ready to snap. 'Everyone here is helping. Where've you been?'

'I'll be helping later today at the Rowing Club,' Ross said. 'We're building our own levee down there to protect the clubhouse. All crew members are being called to help and I've been sent to see if we can snag some sandbags.'

'Great.' Isabel wished her comment had sounded less sarcastic, but she was too tired to care, and it seemed Ross hadn't noticed anyway. She turned her back on him to lift the containers of slice, but Ross was determined to talk, it seemed, so she took a moment to rest and leaned against the ute.

'I heard you went to the dance last week after all,' he said.

Uh oh.

'Where'd you hear that?'

She didn't meet his eyes, instead loo~~ked out towards the~~ river where the sun broke through finally, glistening momentarily off the swirling current. She desperately wished for it to warm her frozen bones.

'Kevin said he saw you there, dancing with some bloke.'

She turned around and leaned back on the truck. God, she was too tired for this.

Ross glared down at her. She could all but see the waves of annoyance rolling off him. 'I thought you said you weren't able to go to the dance. You said you were working.'

'Bruce came back. Freed me up to go out at the last minute.' She hated the lie that so quickly jumped out of her mouth and wondered why she even felt compelled to lie.

'So, who's this bloke? Did you go with him? Or did you meet him there?'

As she noted the edge of anger in his voice, her own annoyance leaked through. 'I'm sorry, but why is it any of your business?'

'You lied to me.'

'I didn't lie to you, Ross. I said I was probably working that night and when I said that I thought I would be.'

'You could have called me. When you knew you would be free and that you could go to the dance, you could've called me. I would have taken you.'

'Well, I went with someone else. Ross ...' Isabel hesitated, rubbing her weary eyes. Damn, she was tired, and tired of this whole scene with Ross. 'You and I, we don't fit. We're better as friends. We are friends. Just friends. I'm sorry, but we can never be anything else.'

He looked so taken aback by her statement she wondered how she could have been so mistaken about his affections for her.

'I thought we had something going.'

'Ross, we've only been out together a few times and I can't say any of those times went particularly well.'

'We had fun together. I thought maybe we could even get married one day.'

'Married?' She was completely gobsmacked and couldn't help the little snorting laugh. 'Ross, you don't really mean that.'

'Why not?' he asked. 'We've been friends forever. Our families know each other.'

And your mother can't stand me or mine.

'I'd be good to you, Isabel.'

'I'm sure you would be.' She wasn't so sure anymore. 'But …' She hoped she could get him to see logic. 'Don't you want to marry someone you love, Ross? You don't love me.'

'I could.' He shrugged. It was about as romantic as him saying he could learn to love beetroot. 'Besides, my parents didn't love each other when they got married.'

That was a revelation, Isabel thought. 'How do you know that?'

'I heard Mum telling one of her friends at one of the boozy luncheons she holds at the house,' Ross said. 'She said she was in love with someone else. Some bloke in high school. But whoever he was got together with another girl from school and she figured Dad was a good bet being from one of the richest families in town.'

'Well.' It was all Isabel could think of to say, but it explained a lot about Shirley and Trevor Burrows.

'So, what do you say?'

'Ross, you may not want love, but I do. I'm sorry. You and I can never be together that way.'

He stared at her for a long moment. As though he couldn't understand what she was saying. 'You know, you're not getting any younger and there aren't exactly hundreds of offers coming your way. If you wait for this great love you're so keen on, you might just be waiting forever.'

The stab of that insult was almost too much for her to hold her temper. 'Well, the man I went to the dance with Saturday night seems pretty keen on me.'

'Who?' Ross shot back, his temper spiking now. 'Who is he?'

No way was she telling Ross about Matteo now. In his current mood, she couldn't trust that he wouldn't confront him. She went for evasion instead.

'Ross, you're a good man, most of the time. You just need to find a woman who enjoys being with you. Maybe someone your mother likes, or a woman who is strong enough to stand up to your mother or at least doesn't care that she'll never be good enough to please her.'

Isabel picked up the trays of slices again and headed back across to the staging area where workers were swapping shifts.

'I'm not ready to give up on you, Isabel.'

She didn't bother to respond, just shook her head and kept walking.

He'd meant to just walk to his car, get in and drive home.

After six hours of backbreaking, wet, dirty work to help raise the levee higher at Cureton Avenue, Matteo was swaying on his feet and desperately needed to hit his bed for a few hours before he had to start work all over again working on building up the protective barrier around their own farm. Who could have imagined the river would get so high?

He'd seen Ross approach Isabel and curiosity overcame sleep deprivation, so despite his exhaustion he'd hidden behind a tractor to watch it play out.

He shouldn't care really. She'd made her thoughts about him fairly clear when he'd heard her referring to him as a dago at the dance. He hadn't expected that from her. Was surprised that she would think that way, use *that* word to describe him. He wasn't a man who deluded himself that all women were swept away by his charms, but he could usually tell when a woman was interested in him. He'd been about to kiss her that night, right there on the steps of the town hall supper rooms and she'd been receptive to his advances, until those women had barrelled out of the hall.

Had she been embarrassed to have been caught in a kiss? Or was it that she'd been caught in a kiss with a 'dago' in particular?

Surely she would never have agreed to go to the dance with him in the first place if she'd been embarrassed to be seen with him.

Dio! God. He needed sleep before he drove himself mad with his own thoughts.

He liked her. He liked her quick laugh and self-effacing humour, the smile that lit up her entire face and sent her pretty, green eyes dancing, the thick tumble of hair that changed colour in the sun like the sandplains and dunes out at Mungo. It had been a long time since a woman had kept his interest this long. When he'd shared his thoughts with his brother, Antonio had warned him he was looking for trouble showing interest in an Australian girl.

And what had he said to Antonio?

'I *am* Australian!'

I AM Australian, Matteo thought again now as he watched her interact with Ross Burrows. If she showed any hint of excitement or interest over Burrows' attentions, Matteo would take it on the chin and walk away.

She looked tired. Everyone in the region looked tired. But she also looked sad. He listened to the muted conversation. Had Burrows just proposed marriage to her? Her snort of derision at that amused him, even elicited a weary smile. For a moment anyway, before he remembered how their night at the dance had ended. Perhaps he should have let her explain instead of being so rude and drowning her out with the car radio. He'd enjoyed his time with her ... before that terrible word had come out of her mouth. Watching her fighting back Burrows' advances, he wished he could go over and just lay a kiss on her, right in front of him. Then maybe the bloke would get the message and back off. Content that Isabel was holding her own, he shoved his freezing hands in his pockets and headed back to his car.

Five

Still in her pyjamas, Isabel spent a rare lazy Sunday morning sitting on the couch with a cup of tea, some toast and Vegemite and her copy of the latest *Australian Women's Weekly* magazine in her lap. The big old wooden wireless in the corner was playing a selection of Nat King Cole favourites as she scanned the magazine for the latest recipes while the rain pattered lightly against the window. The pub stayed closed on Sunday and, more often than not, Isabel used the day off to do some cleaning in the kitchen and she and her mum would take inventory, ready to restock for the week ahead.

Isabel flicked through the magazine to find the special Dione Lucas Cookbook supplement. The newspapers had been full of the famous English chef's visit to Australia. The first ever female graduate of Le Cordon Bleu, Mrs Lucas had been the chef in a hotel in Hamburg and, rumour had it, had cooked for Hitler once or twice before the war. She started a school in New York and was one of the first female chefs to cook on American television. They didn't even have television in Australia yet, but there was plenty being said about that in the papers too. According to the magazine, Mrs Lucas was due to deliver cooking demonstrations in David Jones in Sydney. Isabel pouted. She loved living in her small corner of the country, but sometimes the distance from the capital cities meant missing out on things. She so wished she could go and meet the famous chef in Sydney.

Putting her disappointment aside, Isabel thumbed through the sixty-four pages of the insert and marvelled over recipes for Caesar salad, cheese soufflé and lemon meringue pie. She made notes of ingredients and planned to get into the kitchen that afternoon to do some more experimenting.

As Nat King Cole faded away like a stardust memory, the 3MA radio announcer came on the wireless with the latest news. Isabel listened with half an ear as the most recent flood levels were read out, but she sat upright when the man announced that the body of the missing boy had been found by the police motorboat.

Christopher.

Isabel laid her hand across her heart as tears pooled in her eyes. That poor child. And poor Mrs Phillips. The flooding river had claimed its first victim.

At least the rain had given them a reprieve.

That was the only good thing Isabel could take out of the day as she stood in front of the Scout Hall near the corner of Cureton and Karadoc Avenues among the huge gathering of mourners who had come to farewell the little boy lost to the river. He'd been the first—and she wasn't so naive as to think he would be the last—casualty of the floods now well and truly affecting the region.

Isabel found it hard to believe the river could rise any higher as she stood gazing out at the inland sea. The floodwaters had galloped across the racecourse, rendering the levee bank at Cowra Avenue and Park Road useless. Residents in the lowest areas continued to be evacuated and she winced, counting the houses and sheds in the distance, half submerged below the waterline. Rows and rows of vines were now up to, or even past, their fruit in water. Abandoned livelihoods that stood as a reminder to the crowd of mourners just what the mighty Murray, usually a giver of life, could take away at the whim of Mother Nature.

A small blessing—if there was one to be had—was that the cemetery sat on a rise. Forty feet—that was the magic number Isabel had heard the sexton's wife say. If the river reached forty feet, the cemetery and those who rested there would be engulfed. But that meant the cemetery was now an island, its ghostly residents cut off from the living. Young Christopher would be buried without his parents or his older brothers there to send him off.

Isabel tuned back into the service as the priest delivered his benediction. She had to swallow hard against the lump in her throat when they lifted the tiny coffin containing the seven-year-old boy's body into a rowboat. All they could do was stand at the edge of the muddy waters and watch, devastated, as the priest lifted his robes, showing his gumboots beneath, and climbed aboard the small boat with the coffin as Charlie, the cemetery manager, took up the oars and began rowing his way across the waters to the cemetery. A second rowboat carried the flowers that would be laid on Christopher's grave.

Mourners watched for a while until the boat became smaller as it made its way across the newly formed lake towards Nichols Point Cemetery. They gave their condolences to the family and began to move away. With tears streaking her cheeks, Isabel left her mother consoling a friend and turned away from the sad scene, coming face to face with Matteo.

'Oh,' she said, using her fingers to wipe at the tears. 'Hello.'

'Here.' He handed her a handkerchief from the pocket of his formal dark suit.

'Thank you.' She took the hanky and wiped her tears.

'It was a nice service,' Matteo said as people around them made their way back to where cars were parked on the dirt verges of Cureton Avenue.

From beneath her wet lashes, she studied his face for any signs that he was still angry with her. The floods had kept her busy, but every time she'd thought about how the evening at the dance had ended, she'd felt mortified all over again. 'It was a lovely service, and a good turnout. I think half the town must have come to pay their respects.'

'The half that aren't working the levees, yes.'

'I'm surprised to see you here,' she said. 'I heard one of the levees broke over at Buronga early this morning.'

He nodded sadly. 'Yes, some market gardens and some glass-houses were destroyed. We tried very hard to fix the break, but it just crumbled. There aren't enough resources to go around. Five families evacuated. They've moved to the migrant camp across the river for now. Their homes aren't under water yet, but they will be. They are all safe. It is what matters most.'

'Still, it's hard to lose everything like that. So hard.'

She followed his gaze across to the family standing at the water's edge. 'It is harder to lose someone in such terrible circumstances. Harder yet when it is a child.'

'Yes, it's just so tragic.' Isabel sniffed and wiped her eyes again.

'The police found him?'

She nodded and kept her voice low as mourners continued to pass by. 'Yes, a police motorboat. He was found amongst some debris that had washed into a large willow by the side of the river.'

Matteo shook his head sadly. 'It is a blessing to have found his body, I think. To give his family that chance to mourn and say a proper goodbye.'

'Doesn't make it any easier though.'

'It doesn't.'

They both fell silent. The awkwardness between them made her wish the river would just break through the levee and swallow her up.

Taking a deep breath, she mustered the courage to look him in the eye.

'I'm sorry—'

They smiled weakly at one another, as they'd spoken at exactly the same time.

'I'm sorry I have not called or come to visit,' he said.

'I had a wonderful time the other night,' she said, eager to let him know. 'I'm sorry for how it ended, for my part in that.'

His pale eyes locked onto hers. 'You seemed … embarrassed to be with me.'

'No,' she insisted. 'No, I wasn't embarrassed to be there with you.'

'I heard what you said to those women. The word you used.'

Shame enveloped her. 'I know and, Matteo, I am so sorry, but you misheard me.'

'You didn't call me by that name? You didn't call me a dago?'

'Yes, I did but—' She was desperate to explain, desperate for him to understand.

'I wondered if perhaps I misread your feelings. I thought we were enjoying each other's company.'

'We were! I was!' She covered her cheeks with her gloved hands in frustration at herself. 'I wish I had never used that word. I was only repeating what Sharon Thompson said. She made me furious and what you heard was me being sarcastic. She gets under my skin. If you'd come out moments earlier, you would have realised I was defending you.'

'I don't need you to defend me, Isabel, I am a big boy.'

'I know.' She was flustered and tugged off the hat she'd worn for the funeral as she struggled to find the right words. 'Perhaps I was defending me as well. I don't like people judging me, or anyone else, based on stupid things like culture or what someone does for a living. You've suffered with jabs about your culture, I've suffered with jabs about being a barman's daughter.'

'I don't understand this,' he said, looking truly flummoxed. 'My parents would say that a person who owns a *taverna* or a restaurant in Italy is a great businessman.'

'And that's the truth,' Isabel agreed. 'Our family have held the licence on the Riverside Hotel for nearly forty years. We run a respectable establishment. But some people will always find fault in others and if there is no fault, they'll make one up. Girls like Sharon Thompson like to bring people down to make them feel better about themselves. It made me so angry. I lashed out when I shouldn't have. I'm sorry.'

Matteo shrugged. 'The truth of it is that people will talk. It is the way of the world. They'll be confused, even angry, that you and I are friends.'

Isabel's hope dissipated.

Friends? Was that all that was happening between them? Had she done her dash and squashed any ember of what she was sure was a spark between them?

'The war is still fresh in many people's minds. Not everyone can forget that Italy was once the enemy.'

'I understand that, I do,' Isabel said, nodding. 'But what happened in the war has nothing to do with you. You weren't even there. You were a child, and your family were already in Australia by then. Doesn't it make you angry?'

'Obviously it does, or I would not have spent the last week questioning how our lovely night had ended so badly. Then I remembered what my papa says.'

'Which is?'

'He says that we cannot control what people think.'

'Your papa sounds wise.'

'He can be. As much as I would like to sometimes, I cannot fight every man, woman and child who calls me a reffo or dago. I'd be fighting on a daily basis.'

Isabel let out a small knowing laugh. 'No wonder my mother liked you straight away; you have her patience.'

His laugh was sardonic. 'Patience? My father would not agree with that summation of my character.'

They stood quietly again for a moment.

'Your mother likes me?' he asked, breaking the silence. The return of his smile relieved her.

'She thinks you have a lovely telephone voice. Matteo, I truly am sorry for losing my temper and messing things up generally the other night.'

'Well, let's put it down to our first fight, shall we?' he said, lifting a hand to push the hair that had fallen across her forehead. 'Perhaps you will let me take you out again soon.'

Her relief was overwhelming. 'Matteo, I'd really like that.' Biting the corner of her lip, she looked back across to the devastated family by the river. Mrs Phillips was sobbing in the arms of a friend. Isabel's heart broke for the woman. 'But it doesn't quite seem the right time to speak about having fun, does it?'

'I would say the opposite. It is now, during adversity, that we must make the time to have a little fun.'

'Perhaps, but finding the time is the biggest issue right now,' Isabel said, wearily rubbing at her forehead. 'You have to work the farm and you have your own protective measures to take care of. I have the pub to keep afloat—pardon the pun—and work is continuing on our levee too.'

'I will think of something.'

Isabel's mum arrived at the car then and eyed Matteo with interest. 'Ready to go, Bella? We have to get back and open the pub again at noon or there'll be a riot.'

Matteo held out his hand. 'Good day, Mrs Hayward. I am Matteo. We spoke briefly on the telephone the other day.'

Her mum took his hand and shook it with such exuberance Isabel feared she'd break his hand. 'Hello, Matteo. It's nice to meet you. Isabel, you can come along a little later if you'd like to go with Matteo.'

Bless her mother for being so sweet and helpful.

'No, it's okay. I'm coming, Mum. Matteo has to get back to the farm anyway.' She opened the truck door, then turned back and handed him his hanky. 'Bye, Matteo.'

'Keep it,' he said, leaning in to kiss her cheek. 'I will see you soon, Isabel.'

And with that he stepped away to head to his own vehicle.

Isabel climbed into the truck and frowned at her mother's grin. 'What?'

'So, that's Mario Lanza?'

Isabel chuckled at her mother's continued use of the Hollywood star's name to describe Matteo.

'He's a handsome fellow,' she added. 'I assume you made up then, after your little temper tantrum the other night.'

Isabel thought about what Matteo said. 'We're friends. At least, that's what he said. I think that's all he wants to be now. I think I buggered it up.'

Her mum started the engine and gave Isabel a sideways glance of disbelief. 'I have friends. They don't look at me the way he just looked at you.'

'Mum!' she groaned. 'Anyway, some of your male friends *do* look at you like that. You just don't see it.'

'He said he'll see you soon.' It seemed her mother wasn't going to be distracted so easily by Isabel's attempt to deflect attention to her. 'Do you have plans?'

'He asked me to go out with him again.'

'Lovely! Just let me know when and I'll ask Perry or Flo to give us a hand. Although, Bruce is more than capable of cooking without his number two.'

His number two. She'd always be number two if she didn't speak up and tell her mother her plans and dreams.

'About that,' Isabel began, her heart pounding in her chest as they crossed the bridge towards home.

Just say it. Tell her you want to go to cooking school in Melbourne.

'Since we are the owners, I was wondering if perhaps, now that I'm older and have more experience …' She was babbling. 'I …'

Say it.

'I wondered if …'

'If what? Bels, spit it out, will you?'

'I just think that maybe it's time that I took over as number one chef at the Riverside.'

It wasn't exactly what she'd been trying to say, but it wasn't a bad idea either.

'Oh, love, I know you are a great cook,' her mum started as she cut the engine in front of the hotel. 'But you're already spending too much time working at the pub. You're still so young. I want you to have a well-rounded life. You shouldn't be tied to the kitchen six days a week.'

'But I love cooking, Mum. In fact, I love it so much that I want to—'

'Honey, we can't upset Bruce. You know how temperamental he is. And we need him right now.' She grinned again. 'Especially if you want time to go and see your handsome beau.'

Her mum climbed out of the truck and rushed through the rain into the hotel. Frustrated, Isabel banged her head lightly on the dashboard of the truck. She'd almost got it out. Almost managed to tell her mum that she wanted to go to cooking school. Why couldn't she just tell her mother what she wanted?

If only her father were still here. He'd known about her dreams to become a cook since she was thirteen years old. Ever since the day she'd taken the huge Murray cod he and Trevor had caught and made fish cakes with spicy cayenne pepper. Trevor hadn't been overly thrilled with what she'd done with the cod. He'd have preferred his fish grilled or barbecued whole with a bit of lemon. But after a few beers, Trevor had eaten the fish cakes without complaint.

Her dad and Trevor had been out of the army for a few years by then, but it had taken some time for Isabel to get to know her dad again. When she was between the ages of six and eleven, he'd been a ghost, missing for weeks at a time, returning at random intervals for a few days and then disappearing again. Working for the army down in South Australia, she recalled. Although doing what, she had no idea, and had never had the chance to ask.

In the end, it had been her dad who'd talked her mum into letting Isabel start working in the kitchen with Bruce during school holidays. It had also been her dad that had convinced her mum into letting her leave school, and Bruce into letting her work full time as his assistant. He'd always been on her side.

The familiar ache squeezed her heart. The funeral had brought up memories she'd tried to keep buried all these years. Shaking them off, she jumped out of the truck, made the dash through the rain and in the door to their residence where she changed out of the dress she'd worn for the funeral. When she arrived in the kitchen, Bruce had already started frying the kidneys.

'Oh good, you're back,' Bruce said, turning as she pulled an apron from the hook. 'Time to peel the potatoes.'

Isabel screwed up her nose. She grabbed the peeler and sat on the chair, hovering over the pig bin. Peeling potatoes. It was the first thing Bruce had asked her to do when she'd become his assistant at thirteen. If she didn't make a change soon, she'd still be peeling potatoes for him when she was thirty.

Six

As dawn began to lighten the eastern sky, Matteo closed the door of the caravan and began to wander slowly towards the house. It had been a long, arduous and freezing night, but the levee at the Morellis' farm he'd been helping to strengthen was holding steady once again. He'd managed a few hours of sleep after he'd returned at three in the morning and now he wanted a shower, a cup of coffee and a decent feed before he had to start work shoring up their own levee. Stupid thing had started leaking again. The problem was, there weren't enough sandbags to go around, not enough heavy moving equipment to cart dirt and clay in. Thank God they owned a Ferguson tractor. The little Fergie was light and easily manoeuvrable, which made it perfect to navigate the flat top of the narrow levee wall and the slippery clay used to shore up the banks.

Stepping into the kitchen, he went straight for the little coffee pot already heating on the stove. Taking his first sip of the heavenly nectar, he stood at the window and watched the sunrise. The gold was muted by clouds and mist but it persisted and shot rays of hopeful sunshine when the clouds parted. He prayed they'd have a few days of respite after the thirty-one points of rain they'd had yesterday. So much for being the driest continent in the world, as it was often touted. Surely it had to stop sometime.

Despite the short, exhausted burst of sleep he'd managed, he'd dreamed of her again. Isabel. Perhaps when he was finished with his work that afternoon, he would go to the pub to see her. He could even have dinner there at the hotel and try some of her cooking. She would welcome him there. Although the days of him being beaten up for his heritage were long behind him, he did wonder briefly how the other patrons would feel about his presence at the pub … or with Isabel.

He heard the creak of the wooden floorboards in the hallway, followed by his father's raspy smoker's cough as he stepped into the kitchen. Matteo hated the sound of it. His papa had never been a smoker—until the war.

'Good, you're up. Matteo, I need you to go into town this morning and run a few errands for me. Oh, and Mama wants you to pick up the groceries.'

Matteo turned, rubbing wearily at his gritty, sleep-filled eyes. 'But Papa, I was working all night at the Morellis' at Red Cliffs. I'm exhausted.'

'You've slept, have you not?'

'A few hours.'

'We're all making sacrifices to help our friends, Matteo. They will repay us when the time comes.' He poured coffee and stared down the hallway in the direction of the river. 'Your mama has called in an order. Here's a list of items I need from the hardware store. It won't take long.'

It would take the whole blasted morning, Matteo thought as his father handed him the list of errands.

'Why can't you go in?' Matteo asked, even though he knew very well why.

'Because I asked you to go,' his papa said calmly. 'I do not have to explain myself to you, Matteo.'

'No, of course not,' Matteo grumbled. 'You never explain anything.'

There were so many things about his father he didn't understand. His refusal to speak about the years he'd been away from them for one. His papa's reluctance to travel into town was just another quirk of behaviour Matteo had never understood. It annoyed Matteo that he so often had to drop his plans to run errands for his mother, who didn't drive, or his father, who refused to go into town unless it was absolutely necessary.

'Please, I just need you to help me out, Matteo. I'm asking you to do this, *per favore*, without arguing for once.'

'Fine.'

Once he'd finished his breakfast—which he took his time over—Matteo slammed out of the house and stomped across the muddy ground to the truck. With the engine revving, he didn't hear his mama calling him but he wound down the window when he saw her waving madly at him from the verandah.

'Stop at the Capaldis' and collect the cheese on the way home too, please, Matteo,' she called. 'I need the mozzarella for dinner tonight.'

He nodded, grumbled his agreeance.

'And don't forget to check the grocery order before you leave the store!' she called after him as he revved the engine again with a growl that covered his swearing.

He started with his father's list, driving all over town and back to collect the items from the hardware store and the spare parts for the tractor. After checking the order of groceries he'd collected at Shilliday's in Mildura, Matteo placed the boxes of food in the tray of the truck and drove across the bridge back into New South Wales.

As instructed, he stopped off at the Capaldis' block positioned along the river, almost in the shadow of the bridge. Grateful that the rain seemed to be holding off for now, Matteo wandered around the side of the grey weatherboard house when there was no answer to his knock at the door. It took him a while to find the family as they were all at the bottom of the property behind their rows of glasshouses, anxiously watching the river. The council had erected levees in many places around the district, but some farmers only had the choice of evacuating, or spending thousands of pounds to build their own levee if they wanted to stay and save their crops. The river behind the wall of dirt was already higher than where Matteo stood. Had he been standing on the other side of it, he would be chest-deep in water.

'Signor Capaldi,' Matteo called up to where the man stood atop the levee, anxiously studying the water level.

The older man turned to look down at him. 'Oh, Matteo, of course, the cheese.' Davide Capaldi turned and called across to his wife, Nancy, who was sitting near the doorway of the outbuilding where the family made their mozzarella. He could see their teenage son, Marco, stirring the huge pot of cows' milk in hot water, ready to turn into silky mozzarella cheese. A large cart sat outside the shed where they'd been loading packs of the balled, white cheese. The wall of dirt and sandbags was all that stood between the shed and the river.

Matteo climbed his way up the sandbags to join Davide at the top. 'It's rising fast now.'

'*Si*,' Davide said, again with a distracted note in his voice. 'I fear the worst.'

'The levees will hold, won't they?'

'Not if we don't get some help soon.' Davide sounded almost resigned to it. 'We are running low on sandbags. All the work is being done over in Victoria to make sure the power stations and the brickworks don't go under. We have decided to evacuate. My wife's family has a small outbuilding in Irymple. We can continue to make the mozzarella even if our crops go under. If God decides to save our farm, we can return later.'

Matteo felt a little shame creep up over his complaints to his father about his lack of sleep that morning. So many of their friends were losing their businesses and homes.

'What can we do to help? Just call, any time, you know that.'

The Sorrenti orchard and greenhouses were situated a few metres higher up the bank but if the levees failed, they would be in trouble too. His father was right, the Italian community would help without question.

'*Grazie mille*,' Davide returned. 'We will let you know.'

'Well then,' Matteo said, feeling helpless. He extended his hand to Davide. '*Buona fortuna*, my friend. Good luck. *Ciao*.'

As he walked back to the truck with the mozzarella, Matteo glanced back at the ever-widening river. In the distance, perched safely above the waterline, for now, sat the Riverside Hotel. The lunch rush would be over by now, he thought, checking his watch. A grin spread slowly across his lips and decision made, he moved back to the truck. Mama could wait a little longer for her groceries.

Matteo drove the short distance down the highway, then pulled onto the wide patch of dirt that served as the car park for the pub.

He stepped up onto the enclosed verandah, wiped the mud from his boots, then, taking a deep breath, pushed open the door. The interior of the pub was smaller than he'd expected. To the left of him a small square space had been set up with four tables, serving as a dining room. A rather impressive bar made of dark, polished wood extended along the wall in front of him. Matteo thought Isabel was right about the old jukebox in the corner needing an update, as Bing Crosby's bass-baritone crooned out, asking the listener not to fence him in.

Scanning the room, he warily eyed the pair of truckies sitting at the bar nursing pints of lager. A dirty haze of cigarette smoke hung about them as their conversation halted and they studied him just as warily. He stood where he was for a moment, like a soldier surveying a possible field of battle. What the hell was he doing here? He'd never set foot inside the Riverside Hotel before today and the glares of suspicion coming from the men at the bar brought home to him exactly why.

The war had ended over ten years ago, but many former soldiers and their families still carried resentment towards Italians and other nationalities who'd fought for the Axis. They seemed to conveniently forget that the Italians had eventually switched sides when Mussolini had been deposed from power.

He kept his features neutral, refusing to cower. He'd be a hypocrite if he didn't admit that he carried some resentment of his own for what had happened to him, to his family, during the war years.

Matteo had decided he wanted to see a lot more of Isabel Hayward, so he'd have to deal with the stares. He also realised that perhaps it was time to meet her papa. She didn't speak of him much, but Matteo knew that fathers of all nationalities wanted to meet the suitors of their daughters. Now was as good a time as any, he supposed, but he couldn't see anyone serving behind the bar, let alone someone who looked like they might be Isabel's father. Other than the truckies, the average age of patrons looked about seventy years.

A yell from the direction of what he guessed was the kitchen, and the clatter of something hitting the floor, pulled him towards a swinging door at the far end of the bar.

He pushed the door open just enough to poke his head in and grinned when all he could see over the large centre counter was a denim-clad backside.

'Everything okay in here?'

The backside disappeared as Isabel sprung upright.

It took great strength not to laugh out loud at the sight of her. Tomato smeared the front of her denim overalls, and her hair escaped in tufts from the ribbon she had used in an attempt to hold it back while she cooked.

She wiped her forehead, only to smear more tomato across it. 'Oh, hi.'

Pushing completely through the door, he walked around the table and saw the mess on the floor.

'Having a bad day?'

She groaned. 'I was attempting to make a chicken casserole in the French style. Coq au vin. First, I burned it, then I dropped it. Yes, you could say I was having a bad day.'

'Grand cuisine for the pub,' he noted, wiping at the tomato where it had splashed onto the tip of her nose.

'Hmm,' she muttered, seemingly surprised that he'd touched her until he showed her the red smear on his finger. 'Oh, thanks.' She wiped at her nose again before bending down to scoop the mess into the tray of charcoaled chicken. 'What are you doing here?'

'I was passing by.' He squatted to help her and together they lifted the tray to the bench. 'Running errands for my father who refuses to go into town, and I suddenly had this urge to stop in and say hello.' He leaned over slowly and kissed both her cheeks. 'Hello.'

He watched, fascinated, as she suddenly turned shy on him. The colour rising in her cheeks wasn't all from the heat of the kitchen. Interesting; she'd never struck him as particularly shy. She took the tea towel he offered and wiped at her messy overalls, but he noted she wouldn't meet his eyes.

Placing a finger under her chin, he lifted her face up to his, forcing her to look at him. There was that spark again. The same spark he'd felt the night of the dance when they had stood on the steps of the supper rooms, when he'd almost kissed her—before they'd been rudely interrupted. Well, there was no one to interrupt them now. He leaned in again, this time pressing his lips to hers. He held there for a moment, tasting, feeling the warmth of her responding sigh as she sank in. His hands ran up her arms and he felt the goosebumps.

Enough. He shifted back and smiled when she opened her eyes.

'Hi.'

Her breathless greeting made him chuckle. 'Now. What can we do here to save lunch for the customers?'

She shook her head and looked around as though trying to remember where she was.

'Oh, this wasn't for the pub,' she said. Taking the pan, she tipped the ruined contents into the pig bin, the chicken thighs hitting with a hard thud as they bounced against the metal. 'It was just something I was trying. Mum and I would have had it for our dinner tonight. The animals will enjoy it at least.'

'Where are your parents?'

'You didn't see Mum out front?' Isabel asked, frowning as she moved to push open the door to the bar. 'She's there now.'

'No, I didn't see her. I would like to meet your papa at some point too. Is he around?'

Her little frown made him wonder if she wasn't ready for him to meet her father yet. He let it go. 'Perhaps later. For now ...' He dusted his hands together. 'Do you have more of that tomato sauce?'

She eyed him warily before pointing to the stove. 'Yes. Why?'

He went to the pot on the stove and with a wooden spoon, tasted the sauce. The expression on his face was both comical and insulting.

'We can fix this.'

'We?' she asked pointedly.

'*Si*. You have flour? Yeast? Fresh tomatoes?'

'Of course.'

'*Bene*, wait here.'

He disappeared out the rear door of the kitchen and returned moments later with a handful of herbs and a bag that held a strange white ball.

'What is that?'

'This is fresh mozzarella,' he said, opening the bag. He pinched at the ball and stretched it so that a piece came off. Handing it to her, he chuckled as the mix of expressions on her face went from suspicion to interest to enjoyment as she put it in her mouth and chewed. 'It is the best cheese and can be used in so many ways. But for today, I am going to teach you how to make pizza.'

'Pizza?'

'*Si*. It is flat bread with tomato, herbs and cheese mostly, but other foods can be added. Prosciutto, olives, mushrooms, anchovies—'

'I know what pizza is,' she interrupted him.

'Ever made it?'

'No.'

He raised his eyebrows expectantly.

She chuckled. 'Okay. Show me.'

Isabel watched in awe as Matteo mixed the yeast, flour and water like an expert baker. And when he turned it out onto the flour-covered bench … well, who would have thought those farm-roughened hands could be so skilled in the kitchen? When the dough was a nice fluffy ball, he split it in two and set it aside. Isabel took a seat on a stool and poured him a cup of coffee. She poured one for herself as well, to try and douse the flame he'd ignited in her with that kiss. It had been so quick, so light, but her insides had melted, her brain had frozen. And then he'd broken the connection and she understood what it was to ache for someone. She struggled to concentrate on what he was telling her about making pizza as his strong hands had massaged and moulded the dough.

He sipped the coffee, screwed up his nose and put it aside.

'It is better to let the dough sit overnight, but we will have to make do with an hour,' he said, sitting beside her. She could feel the warmth emanating from him and leaned closer.

'True Napoli style pizza has rules as to what you may put on it. Pizza goes back to the eighteenth century and since it was cooked and served by street vendors it was always considered food for the poor.'

'Is this a history lesson?' she asked, finally finding her voice again.

'*Si*. Mama said it is not enough just to be able to cook from a recipe.' His voice was all authority now. 'It is important to know where that recipe came from. Now pay attention,' he told her, with a cheeky wink. 'When Queen Margherita and her husband King Umberto visited Naples, they grew tired of feasting on delicacies, on expensive, fancy food. They demanded to know what was keeping their people so well fed. The best chef in Naples was brought to them.' He halted the history lesson momentarily while he moved to add more wood to the old stove that had been part of the pub's kitchen for decades.

'How did you learn to make pizza?' she asked.

'My papa taught me.'

'Your dad cooks?'

'Only pizza. Don't get me wrong, my mama is the chef of the family.'

'I'd say most women are the chef of the family,' Isabel said, nodding. 'It's unusual for a man to be so handy in the kitchen.

Grilling meat outdoors over the fire pit tends to be the man's domain. I don't recall my dad ever lifting a finger to help my mum with the cooking or housework, even after she'd worked a full shift at the pub.'

'No, I mean my mama is actually a chef,' Matteo clarified. 'She studied with a famous chef in Napoli for two years before she immigrated with her family to Australia.'

'When did your parents emigrate?' Isabel asked.

'They came to this country in 1929. Only two days after they were married.'

'They must have been very young,' Isabel said, with equal amounts of envy and admiration.

'Mama was barely twenty when they left Napoli on the ship,' Matteo said. 'They loved Italy, but they came to this country because there was much conflict, political unrest and poverty and they wanted a better life for their children. My nonno and nonna, my grandparents, owned a *maccelleria*; it's a store that sells meats. Papa worked there when he left school and that's where he met Mama. She came in to buy veal for the restaurant where she worked while she studied. He says he went and ate at that restaurant for two weeks until she agreed to go out with him.'

'That's quite amazing for a woman to become a qualified chef at that time, let alone at twenty years of age.' It fuelled her own hopes that she might be able to achieve her own dreams.

'*Si*, she makes the best pasta and the best *pasticcino*.'

She frowned at the word.

'Desserts.'

She nodded.

'But the Sorrenti men have always been the pizza makers. Papa's grandfather taught his father, he taught Papa, who taught me and my brother, Antonio.'

The hour passed quickly as they chatted and finally Matteo moved one ball of dough back to the flour-covered bench and began kneading it. Then to Isabel's delight, he picked it up in his hands and began to toss it in the air and catch it on his knuckles.

Isabel laughed. 'That's so clever.'

'Do you want to try?' He held out the thin, floppy dough to her on one fist.

'No!' She shook her head. 'No. The way my day has been going, I'll drop it.'

He spread the dough, now almost the size of a dinner plate, on a tin tray, before checking the oven. The wood had burned down so that the coals were glowing red hot.

'Cooking on stone is better, but again, we do with what we have,' he explained.

Deftly, he spread the tomato sauce he had doctored with the herbs he'd brought in from the car.

'It looks amazing,' she said. 'What happened when the queen and king had pizza?'

'The pizza was cooked by the best chef in Napoli and brought to the queen, decorated with the colours of the Italian flag,' he continued, sweeping his hand across the finished product with the bright red tomato, the strange fleshy white cheese called mozzarella and the green leafy basil. 'And so, the first Margherita pizza was created.'

'It's art!'

He nodded proudly. 'Now, it goes into a very hot oven.'

He slid the tray into the oven and checked the heat of the coals.

'Don't you want to set a timer?' she asked.

'No, I will know when it is done.'

'And how long has your family owned this hotel?' he questioned, taking his seat again. 'You said forty years or so?'

'Yep. My grandmother took over the licence on the Riverside Hotel in 1917 with three children in tow and my mum, Audrey, just a bun in the oven,' Isabel said, happy to give him a history lesson of her own. It might not have been about kings and queens but she was proud of her family's story. 'Back then, before the bridge was built, the liquor would be sent up from Melbourne to Mildura and carted across the river punt. That was until the big Spanish influenza epidemic closed the borders. But when they opened again, the punt would also carry anyone who wanted a drink as Mildura was "dry" thanks to it being a temperance colony at the time. Grandma, being a publican from way back, said it was a God-given right for a body to have a drink at the end of a hard day's work. She was quite a character.'

'And you have lived in this hotel all your life?'

'I have.'

'I was thinking as I arrived that I should probably meet your father.'

The happiness she'd felt telling him about the pub dissipated. It was the second time he'd brought up her father since he'd arrived. She should have known the question was coming, but it still felt like a stab in the heart. She'd have to tell him eventually.

'You can't meet my father.' Turning her back, she began to clean up the mess they'd left on the kitchen bench. 'He's not around anymore.'

She felt him move in behind her. He took her shoulders, turning her around. His finger touched beneath her chin and he lifted her head so he could meet her eyes.

'I'm sorry,' he said, his deep voice quiet, his pale blue eyes full of sympathy. 'He died?'

She opened her mouth but couldn't bring herself to speak about what her father did. Even after all these years.

The pity was there on his face, the same pity she always saw when people heard her sad story.

'How old were you?'

'I was sixteen.' She moved away from him again. She did not want to talk about this. Especially not when they'd been having such a good time.

He nodded. 'And so, it is just you and your mama who run the hotel?'

'Yes.' She nodded. 'And we do a damn good job of it too.' She tried not to sound too defensive, but there had been a lot of snide remarks over the years about women not being capable of running a hotel without a man. Grandma Louisa had done it without a husband all those years ago, and all while raising four kids.

She forced herself to smile. 'I've been pulling pints since I was old enough to reach the taps, but I was always happiest in the kitchen. My dream is to be a proper chef one day. Fully trained like your mama. There's a school in Melbourne, a cooking school at the Emily McPherson College. I've been saving up, hoping maybe I would get to go to Melbourne for the course intake in September but …' She stopped. She'd been babbling.

'But?' He urged her to go on.

She shrugged. 'Mum needs me here. Especially now with the floods. Bruce—that's our cook—he makes good food, but he's from the "meat and three veg" school of cooking. He says people don't come here for fancy-schmancy or foreign food. I keep asking him to let me try out new dishes and flavours, but he's happy with the menu as it is and says the customers are as well.'

'But it's your family's pub,' Matteo argued. 'Don't you have the right to try something new if you want to?'

'I do get my way sometimes. Some of my experiments haven't gone down well with the punters though. Small changes are okay.

Mum says we can't afford to upset Bruce. We could never run this place without him.'

'Of course you could.' Matteo waved that off. 'You just need someone to teach you how to cook food so delicious that those "meat and three veg" customers will be willing to try anything you put on the menu. I could ask my mama to teach you.'

Isabel blinked. 'Why would you do that?'

'Why do you think?' he asked, leaning closer to her, making her breath seize in her throat again. 'I like you, Isabel, and I'm hoping that by spending more time with you, you might like me too.'

Her mouth dropped open, but the words got stuck in her throat. She wanted to tell him she liked him too, but she couldn't find the courage. She'd never encountered a man so confident, so open about his intentions without making her feel that she should think herself lucky or honoured that he'd bestowed his attentions upon her.

He smiled. 'But forget about what I want for now. I would like to help you to reach your dream. I will ask my mama if she will teach you.'

'But … why would she? I'm sure she's very busy with the farm and the floods and everything. I couldn't ask her to do that any more than I could ask my mum to let me go to Melbourne.'

'You wouldn't be asking her,' Matteo said easily. 'I will ask her. You can come out to the farm and she will teach you all the *bennissimo* recipes from the home country.'

She didn't want to be a pest, but a real chef teaching her real recipes from Italy was too good to say no to. 'Do you think she would? I mean, I barely know you and she doesn't know me at all.'

'It will all work out, Isabel,' he said, moving in again and sweeping her hair back over her ear.

Her pulse was pounding as he stepped closer, his fingers running along her jaw to her chin. She lost herself in the impossible blue of his eyes, and when he leaned down, her breath stopped altogether. She closed her eyes, waiting, feeling his warmth as he moved closer and closer.

She could almost feel his lips touch hers when suddenly he leaned back. She opened her eyes.

'What? What's wrong?'

'Nothing. The pizza is ready.'

'How can you tell without even looking?'

'Trust me.'

When he bent down to retrieve the pizza from the oven, Isabel took a deep breath to clear her head, but her heart continued to hammer in her chest even as he turned and proudly announced: 'Ah! *Perfetto*!'

With an easy flick of his wrist, he slid the pizza from the tray and onto the wooden chopping board on the bench. He sliced it expertly into triangles, and held a piece out to her. The cheese oozed and the base of the pizza was thin and pliable.

'I'll burn myself,' she said, shaking her head. 'Shouldn't you let it cool a bit?'

'No, it is best served very hot,' he said, and after folding the thin bread in half, he slid the pointed end of the slice into his mouth. He took a bite, then quickly dropped the slice to the table and waved a hand in front of his mouth as he breathed out steam. 'You are right, we need to wait a minute or two.'

She laughed and handed him a glass of water. He drank thirstily and then did a double take at the clock on the wall. 'Oh, *Dio*. I must go. Mama is going to slap my ears. She is waiting for the cheese, for the groceries.'

'You left the groceries in the truck all this time?'

He shrugged. 'It's colder out there today than a Coolgardie safe. But I have taken too long. Mama will be angry. I didn't want to go home straight away.'

'Why not?'

'I was angry that Papa sent me to town to run errands,' he said, his usually happy countenance darkening. 'I'd had very little sleep after working at the Red Cliffs levee until early this morning.'

'You mentioned that your father doesn't like to go to town,' she said. 'Why is that?'

'I'm not really sure. He used to be a very sociable person when I was a boy.' His lips quirked up as he got lost in happy memories. 'We had great adventures when we lived in Adelaide. Day trips to the beach, as I mentioned, and he was always happy and talked to everyone who came into our delicatessen.' The smile faded. 'But he changed after the war.'

'I suppose a lot of people did. It's not surprising.'

'No, not surprising,' Matteo said, a rare lost look marring his beautiful features. 'Just frustrating.'

'Was he a soldier?'

He hesitated. 'No. He was not a soldier.' He didn't offer anything more, his earlier cheery demeanour gone as he seemed to get lost in some dark thought.

'I'm sorry, I didn't mean to pry.' She was curious but she couldn't expect him to talk about his papa when she refused to discuss hers.

His smile returned just as quickly as it had disappeared. 'It's okay. We will talk about that another time. I must go. I have enjoyed being here.'

'Thank you for the pizza. It looks delicious.'

'Share some of that with your mama or it will make you sick,' he instructed with a teasing tone. 'And cook the other one for your dinner. It will be better as the dough will have had more time to rest. Try it with some ham and mushrooms, and artichoke if you have them. Shall I talk with my mama about cooking lessons?'

'Oh, I don't know. I really don't want to be an imposition.'

He began gathering the leftover food he'd brought in with him. 'We are harvesting the lemons next Sunday. Come to the orchard. You can help with the picking and I can introduce you to Mama. She will be cooking on the day. She and some of the other women always cook up a huge feast for lunch and dinner on harvest days. You can try her food and decide if you want her to teach you.'

Isabel's nervousness about the prospect of meeting his family was outweighed by her excitement at the idea of tasting proper Italian food cooked by a real Italian chef. 'I'd love to come and meet your family and help with the picking.'

'Good, that's settled,' Matteo said. He kissed her lightly, his lips lingering on hers a moment before he moved back. His pale blue eyes danced with humour and something else that had Isabel's pulse racing. Then the dimple in his cheek winked as he smiled. 'I look forward to it. *Ciao*.'

In a gust of cold wind as the kitchen door banged behind him, he was gone. But the wonderful scent of him remained, merging with the delectable aroma of the pizza.

'*Ciao*, Matteo.'

'*Nel nome del Padre, del Figlio e dello Spirito Santo. Amen.*'

'Amen.' Matteo crossed himself.

His father said grace at every mealtime. They hadn't attended a Catholic Mass since before the war, but his parents still insisted on giving thanks and being grateful for every meal.

'Pass the *polpette*, Matteo.'

He passed the meatballs to his papa as requested and, taking a breath, launched in. 'Mama, your *polpette* are the best I have ever eaten.'

Gia's proud smile beamed out. '*Grazie*, Matteo.'

The meatballs had always been a favourite of his. 'I always tell Angelo that your *polpette* are much better than his mama's.'

'That's nice, Matteo, but too much pride is sinful.'

'But, Mama, I'm allowed to be proud of you.'

She blew him a kiss across the table, clearly thrilled by his compliments.

Antonio stared at him like he'd grown a second head, but Matteo ignored him and went on. 'In fact, I was just telling another friend what a wonderful and accomplished chef you are.'

'Chef.' Gia made a delicate grunt of derision and despair. 'Not anymore. I left that life behind when I met your papa and he swept me away.' She put her hand over Carlo's, the love shining in her eyes. 'Now I'm merely a housewife, cooking for my men and my beautiful daughter-in-law and the *bambina*.' Gia leaned to her other side to take baby Lucia's tiny hand and cover it with kisses as the little girl gurgled with delight at her nonna.

'He is right, Gia,' Loretta said, smiling at her daughter's laughter and taking a delicate mouthful of pasta. 'You are still a chef.'

Matteo nodded in agreement as his mama stood to get more bread from the oven. 'And I for one think your talents are wasted on just us.'

'Eh?' Antonio was offended and suspicious. 'What do you want, Matteo? What are you buttering her up for?'

Gia slapped the back of Antonio's head lightly as she returned to her seat. 'My son can't treat his mama with respect and admiration?'

'Ow! Mama! I simply meant that Matteo is never so complimentary. He is acting like a *leccaculo*.'

'Don't use that language in front of your mama.' Carlo pointed his fork at Antonio. 'Can we please have a quiet dinner for once?'

'Sorry, Papa,' Antonio said, glaring at Matteo.

Conversation halted, and only the sound of cutlery across china plates filled the kitchen—for about one minute before Matteo dived in again.

'All I'm saying is, I think you could impart your talents to someone who would really appreciate it.'

'I impart,' Gia said. 'I impart to Loretta.'

'And I am appreciative,' Loretta was quick to put in.

'Matteo, why don't you just get to the point?' his papa urged. It wasn't so easy to fool his father.

'I have a friend who wants to be a chef and I thought you might be able to help.'

'Help? Help how?' Gia queried. 'Help who?'

'What friend?' Antonio added.

'Not Teresa Cavuoto's boy?' Gia's eyes were narrowed on him now. 'She's been trying to steal my lasagne recipe for years.'

'No, not Joe,' Matteo snorted. 'He would ruin toast.'

'Then who?'

'Her name is Isabel.'

'Aah.' Antonio dragged out the syllable before he sing-songed, 'Matteo's got a girlfriend. Are you still seeing her?'

'Are you still ten years old?' Matteo shot back, tossing a piece of bread like a frisbee and hitting Antonio in the chest.

'*Ragazzi!*' Gia's voice rose over the argument that ensued. 'Boys!'

'Stop!' The single word from his papa halted all arguments. 'Matteo, who is this woman Antonio speaks of?'

'Her name is Isabel,' Matteo repeated, surprised at how desperately he wanted his family to approve of her. 'She and her mama run the Riverside Hotel. She's a cook there. Assistant cook for now, but she really wants to go to cooking school in Melbourne.'

Gia tutted. 'Australian cooking. Bangers and mash is not a cuisine.'

'She'll take Mama's *polpette* and put them on the menu as rissoles,' Antonio teased. 'It's the only way the customers would eat them.'

'So what?' Matteo shot back, annoyed. 'Who cares what she calls them if it means she gets to serve them fantastic food? She wants to learn, Mama. She wants to go to cooking school but with everything happening with the floods and her mama needing her at the pub, she can't.'

He hesitated, then blurted: 'I told her you might teach her.'

'*Che cosa—?*'

Matteo didn't think he'd ever seen his mother lost for words.

She continued to stare at him, wide-eyed. 'You did what?'

Antonio snorted out a laugh. His papa sat back and sighed, while Loretta dropped her eyes to her pasta, clearly hoping to stay out of the drama.

'Mama, you're the best cook I know.'

'Ah, that explains the sucking up,' Antonio said, earning another slice of bread to the chest.

'Matteo, you can't just offer your mama to teach this woman because you like her.'

He turned to his papa again. 'But I do like her. She is clever and sweet, and she really does want to be a professional cook.'

'She is not Italian?' Gia asked.

'No, she isn't.' He narrowed his eyes. 'What does that matter? Think of it this way, she won't pass on your secrets to any of the other Italian mamas in the region.'

'But she will cook my food in her restaurant,' she said, then aimed a raised eyebrow at Antonio. 'What is "rissoles"?'

Antonio snorted. 'The Riverside is not a restaurant, it's a pub.'

'Shut up, Antonio,' Matteo shot at him angrily. 'You don't know what you're talking about. Why shouldn't she try to better herself and their business, their livelihood?'

This started another insult-slinging match between the brothers.

'*Basta!* Stop! Enough!' Carlo's raised voice rang in their ears.

The arguing ceased once again.

'Antonio, stop teasing,' his papa ordered. 'Matteo, it is admirable she wants to do what she can for the family business, but we have a lot to do here as well. Your mama is a busy woman. Even without the threat of flooding, the need to harvest early, when do you think she would have the time?'

Matteo nodded sadly. His father made a good point. As the river rose higher every day, they had even more work to do just to keep their own family business going.

'She would never expect you to step away from the farm for her. But, Mama, please, just think about it,' Matteo pressed. 'And meet with her.'

'Matteo, you stretch my nerves.' Gia slumped in her chair, taking a large gulp of her wine.

'I invited her to help with the lemon harvest this weekend. And before you argue, we can use all the help we can get.'

'She's a girl who cooks in a pub.' Antonio's nose wrinkled. 'What does she know about the hard work of farming?'

'*Stronzo*!' Gia and Loretta said at the same time. The curse and looks of censure they sent him had Antonio shrinking down in his chair.

'Girls can't work hard?' Gia's glare could have singed the curtains.

Antonio's eyes went wide with fear and apology. 'That's not what I meant.'

'Isabel works harder than any girl I've ever met,' Matteo said, jumping in. 'Day and night she works in that pub. It's just her and her mama and some other cook who never lets her try anything new …' He was babbling. He took a deep breath. 'She'll be helpful. I promise. She'll come and pick lemons and, Mama, when you meet her you can decide if you want to show her some of your recipes.'

His mother's expression didn't alter, so he had no idea if she was open to his idea.

'We can use the help with the picking,' his papa agreed, and Matteo felt the first stirrings of hope. 'Bring your Isabel on the weekend. But it is up to your mama if she wants to help your friend. That is the end of it.'

Knowing his father's word was final, Matteo stood, collecting up the dirty dishes. 'She expects nothing. This was my idea. Meet her. Then you can think about it, Mama.' He disappeared into the kitchen to do the dishes without argument for probably the first time in his life.

With the dishes washed and put away, Matteo headed out to his caravan. His lack of sleep the night before was catching up with him and, since he was due to take a watch of the levee with Antonio at two in the morning, he needed to grab at least a few hours in his bunk before his shift.

He figured he'd done all he could do with his mama on Isabel's behalf. It had surprised him how much he wanted his mother to help Isabel, how much it mattered to him that his family liked her.

He stood for a moment on the step of the caravan and stared out across the orchards silhouetted by the lights down at the levee, the hum of the generator the only thing breaking the usually silent night. On any normal night or day, he could only see the river from here when there was a full moon. Since the Murray had widened its path, crept so far up the banks, he could easily see the murky waters that in the last few days had begun to tease the top of the dirt wall. Would it hold? Or would they lose everything they'd worked so hard for, to build this little patch of red dirt up from nothing into a thriving enterprise? It hadn't been the first time they'd faced the loss of their livelihood.

When they'd lived in Adelaide, their small yard in Campbelltown had held a tiny vegetable patch, a lemon tree, a mandarin tree and an apricot tree. It had been more of a personal orchard than the market garden they'd built here. It was the delicatessen that had been their source of income. Before it had all been taken away. Before the war. Before …

When the war ended, he, his mama and Antonio had made the move up from Adelaide to Mildura to be with his papa, who had already acquired a lease on this land in the small farming community by the river named Buronga.

It had been a long time since he'd thought about their move from Adelaide to the river. The journey had been a long and arduous one, he recalled. He'd been sixteen years old and had experienced a growth spurt over that summer which meant having his long and lanky frame cramped into a bus for nine hours was an experience in discomfort he swore he'd never repeat. Many of the men on board the bus had been new Australians heading out to Riverland towns for work. But there had also been soldiers. Servicemen in their uniforms, returning from the battlefields of Europe to the quiet peace of their home towns. Matteo would never forget their gaunt faces, their hollow and weary eyes. He realised some of those men had probably been the age he was now; only in their early twenties. War—and the horrors they'd witnessed on the battlefields of Europe, in the jungles of Asia—had aged them.

There'd been a few stops at towns along the way—towns so small he wasn't even sure they could be called that—where he'd been able to stretch his legs for ten minutes or so before piling back onto the giant Murray Valley semi-trailer bus. The bus, with its bulbous rear end allowing for two levels of passengers, crossed the wide expanse of river on two different ferries—one at Blanchetown and the other at a place called Kingston. Just getting the bus onto the ferry, beside other cars and trucks on the route, was a marvellous feat. Matteo remembered Mama had been sure they would sink right to the bottom of the river and had become extremely anxious when Matteo and Antonio had jumped off the bus to watch the wire ropes pull the punt across the river.

Even now he could remember the immense relief he'd felt when they'd arrived in Mildura that evening and the bus had pulled into the terminal in Madden Avenue. Not just because he was finally off that damn bus, but because after seven long years, they were finally going to be reunited with their beloved papa.

Passengers had dispersed, collected by family or friends, taking taxis to hotels. The soldiers had been met by tearful family members with long, relieved hugs. Hugs that went on forever. He'd looked forward to doing the same with his father when they finally saw him, but their papa hadn't met them at the bus station. Instead, a man named Frank, who had said he was a friend of Papa's, drove them across the bridge from Victoria into New South Wales.

When they had reached the other side, Frank headed down a dirt road towards the river itself. No houses could be seen, no buildings at all, and his mama had been sure the man was taking them out into the bush to rob and kill them.

Now Matteo looked across the darkness to the little family house with its pretty yellow paint and bright white shutters. Its interior lights glowed out of the windows spotlighting large terracotta pots that sat at each end of the little verandah. Bougainvillea vines, straggly and bare, waited in their slumber for spring to come again so they could bloom in riotous reds and pinks. An old rocking chair his papa had salvaged from a pile of roadside rubbish sat in pride of place waiting until the floods had passed, and his father had time again to relax and enjoy the sweeping views of the orchard and the river below it.

The first time Matteo had seen the house it had been a run-down weatherboard building that might once have been white, but years of neglect had greyed and peeled the paintwork. Red dirt—the same red dirt that seemed to be everywhere in this region—had streaked and stained the cladding where it met the wooden foundations, making it look to Matteo as though the house was bleeding. How did anything grow in all this red dirt, he'd wondered?

Closing his eyes, he could still bring back the overwhelming emotion that had swamped him when the door to the little house had opened and his papa had stepped out. Matteo had just stood where he was, frozen to the spot. He'd been a child when his father had left, barely nine years old, but the memory of him had been vivid in his mind. The man who'd stepped out of the house had not been the man he remembered. He'd expected him to be older, naturally, but not old. No longer broad and muscular, Papa had become thin, not unlike those soldiers he'd seen on the bus. Beneath the dirty brown work shirt with its sleeves rolled up to the elbows, his forearms showed sinewy muscles.

Carlo Sorrenti had always been immaculately dressed in suits and ties. He'd never have been caught dead in the brown pants with badly fraying suspenders to keep them up, boots covered in mud and a fedora hat that had seen better days. His skin sagged, grizzled and lined from too much sun, and when he'd caught Gia when she'd dropped her suitcases and run into his arms, his eyes had closed on tears that left little streams through the dirt on his face.

When his father's eyes opened again they met his, and Matteo had rushed forward, engulfing both his mama and his papa in his long arms. Even now, standing on the steps of his caravan with his eyes closed, he felt the bump as Antonio joined the group and he could see them all, standing together in front of that dilapidated house, wrapped in each other as the last of the evening sun warmed them.

That had been seven years ago.

Looking around at the property again now, Matteo saw just how much work had gone into building this farm, this home. The vegetable gardens, the vineyards, the orchards. It was not just their livelihood, it was their home. He didn't know what they would do if they lost it all to the river. Could they start again? Did his father have it in him to begin again? Matteo wasn't sure he did.

The screen door opened on the little house and his papa stepped out, just as he'd done all those years ago. After seven years apart they'd got their papa back. But not all of him. There were pieces of his papa that were forever lost to those missing years. Pieces he'd buried deep down inside, moments of that time during the war that he refused to share with his family. Matteo wished he didn't care, wished it didn't bother him so much that his papa wouldn't talk about it, wouldn't let him in so he could understand his father better. More often than not it made Matteo frustrated, angry even, that there was a place inside his papa that was always just out of reach.

When Gia stepped out on the porch to join Carlo, Matteo watched as his parents moved into a slow dance to whatever music played in their heads. They'd done that on the first day they'd been reunited at the broken-down old house years ago where his father had envisaged a new life for them. They often danced on the porch. He'd never taken much notice of it before now, Matteo realised.

Feeling like an intruder, Matteo moved back inside. His heart still ached for the time he had lost, time they'd all lost, and for the cruelty that had torn them apart for so many years.

After stripping down to his long underwear, Matteo climbed into bed and pulled up the covers. His parents had always been mushy romantics. It had made him and Antonio gag with discomfort when they were children. He'd taken out a lot of women over the years, but none of them had evoked in him the kind of love he saw between his parents. Many of the mamas in the community were keen to marry their daughters off and he knew several of them had set their sights on him. He'd done a good job of dodging marriage so far, but as he thought of his parents, dancing in the moonlight on the porch, he felt a deep sense of longing, envy even. Was it just that he was getting older? Or was it Isabel that was inciting all these strange romantic feelings? She was very different to any other woman he'd courted. She had her own dreams and ambitions, and it made her interesting to talk to. He wondered; would she dance with him on a rickety old porch when no music played? Could she be the one to make him want to?

The next morning, word got around the Buronga area that a tip truck had dumped loads of sand and dirt by the New South Wales side of the bridge, along with a huge supply of hessian bags that had arrived by train from the Rotary Clubs all across Victoria and New South Wales. Finally, outside help was getting through.

Matteo and his father left Antonio to deal with the farm and drove their truck down to the bridge, immediately joining the working group filling hessian bags. They helped some of the older residents of Gol Gol and Buronga to fill their trucks, utes, and even cars, with whatever sandbags they could carry.

Matteo couldn't help noticing what a good mood his father was in. Papa was chatty with the other residents and workers, many of whom were friends from their Italian community. He was so often reserved and reluctant to be around large groups. They talked of the upcoming citrus harvest, shared stories of the river levels, and discussed when they thought the river would peak and where the danger zones might be along the shores of Buronga and Gol Gol.

Hours later, after all the hessian bags were filled, Matteo and his papa loaded up their own vehicle. Carlo heaved a filled sandbag to Matteo, who stood on the back of the truck, piling the precious cargo into the tray of their Ford.

'We'll pile these up on top of the levee below the lemon orchard,' his papa told him. 'Then I think we deserve some of your mama's *sfogliatella*.'

Matteo snorted out a laugh. 'That's if Antonio hasn't eaten them all.'

But the idea of his mama's sweet and fluffy pastries and a warming cup of coffee had him moving faster.

When he looked back to take the next bag, his papa's smile had disappeared, his shoulders tensing as he quickly handed the sandbag to Matteo.

'Papa, what's wrong?' Matteo asked, confused at the sudden change in his father's demeanour. He turned his head, following his papa's gaze as a truck pulled in beside them.

'Typical,' Matteo grumbled, watching as Ross and his father stepped out of a brand-new Holden ute. 'Burrows shows up when all the hard work is done. He doesn't deserve to take any sandbags.'

'Let's go,' his papa said, lifting the tailgate of the truck and snapping it closed with a bang.

'We can fit more bags, Papa. There's still plenty of room.'

'I said let's go,' he snapped.

'Oi, dago!'

Matteo turned and glared down at the man. 'What did you call my papa?'

Trevor Burrows. The town drunk. Son of the richest man in the district who'd never quite lived up to his father's perfect standing in the town. He didn't know the man well, even less than he knew the son, but he'd heard stories. They owned the posh two-storey house on the edge of Buronga with the best views over the river from the wide, sweeping balcony that circled the top storey. The property's orange groves spread down the flats, but Matteo doubted the Burrows did the work that kept the orchards producing. Matteo guessed, since they'd arrived to collect sandbags, that they'd realised even money couldn't stop the river from taking their home if Mother Nature was so inclined.

'You think you can just show up here and take sandbags after everyone else has slaved to fill them?' Matteo went on.

Ross grinned cockily. 'Yeah, saves us getting grubby like you.'

Furious, Matteo leaped over the side of the truck.

'Matteo, stop.' Carlo put a hand on his son's chest and shook his head, before he turned back to Trevor. 'We were just leaving.'

A few people who still remained in the area had stopped working and were watching the tense exchange with interest.

'You would have left the region years ago if you knew what was good for you,' Trevor shot back.

'I have stayed out of your way. I'd appreciate it if you would do the same.' His papa spoke so quietly Matteo wasn't even sure he'd heard him right.

'Think you can tell me what to do?' Trevor casually leaned an elbow against the hood of his ute but there was a vicious glint in the man's eyes. 'You know who I am?'

Matteo took a step closer to his father in case Trevor decided to get physical. The strong stench of alcohol permeated the man.

'Yes,' his papa said calmly, not moving an inch. 'I know very well who you are. I know everything. You might want to remember that.'

Trevor's face turned a fiery red, his bloodshot eyes wide and wild. Matteo saw some of the other Italian men who'd been watching move a little closer, ready to back them up.

Ross must have seen it too because he started to look nervous. 'Come on, Dad,' Ross urged, reaching out to put a hand on his dad's shoulder. 'Let's just grab some bags and go.'

The flick of Trevor's arm as he pulled away from Ross was so fast, the back of his hand connected with Ross's cheekbone with a crack. Ross staggered back, landing on his backside in the last remaining dregs of soggy sand.

Matteo snorted out a laugh, but his papa just shook his head and stepped past Trevor, holding out a hand to Ross to help him up. 'Are you alright?'

'Stay away from my family, dago.' Trevor shoved Carlo away from Ross.

'I'm fine,' Ross said, pushing himself to standing, his eyes moving from his father to Matteo and his papa and back again as he rubbed his sore cheek.

'What is your problem?' Matteo tried to shove his way past his father to get at Trevor.

'You blokes are everyone's problem,' Trevor grumbled. 'The dago menace. Coming in here and taking our jobs. You should have all been sent home after the war.'

'Our family was in this country before the war even began,' Matteo shot back. 'We've got a right to be here, to work the land we've leased.'

'Land that could have been leased or sold to citizens, not handed out to immigrants.'

'We are citizens,' Matteo shot back. 'Papa is naturalised and I was born here.'

Trevor snorted. 'Naturalisation didn't do you much good during the war, did it?'

'Dad, come on,' Ross tried again. 'People are looking.'

Matteo felt his papa take his wrist. He reluctantly allowed himself to be led back to the truck. Carlo started the engine and pulled the vehicle back out onto the highway as Matteo glared out the window at the Burrows men.

Still fuming, Matteo couldn't let the silence stand. 'Papa, why did you let him talk to you like that?'

'No one wins in arguments like this. A leopard cannot change his spots.'

'A leopard ...?' Matteo growled out of frustration. When had his father become so defeatist? 'It's not about winning. It's about standing up for ourselves, for what's right. Besides, he's just a bully, the town drunk. Everyone knows it.'

'And he should be pitied, not punched,' his papa responded steadily. 'Fighting a man who is clearly unstable is like poking an angry snake. It is not dignified, and it is not smart.'

'Why did you let him push you around? He insulted you, he insulted us.'

'What does that matter? Do you believe what he said?'

'No, but others do.'

'Why do you care what others think of us?'

Matteo shook his head and looked out the window of the truck. 'I don't understand why people have to be like that.'

'War makes villains out of ordinary men.'

'I heard he didn't even go to the war.'

'We all fought the war in our own ways.'

God, he hated it when his papa spoke in those cryptic statements. He never gave a straight answer whenever Matteo asked him about those years during the war. 'What did you mean when you said you know very well who he is?'

Staying silent, his papa just kept his eyes straight ahead on the road.

Matteo tried again. 'He acted like he knew you. I don't remember you ever speaking to him before.'

Nothing.

'Papa, how does he know you?' Nothing. 'Papa!'

'Matteo, stop! It's done. It's over.'

His papa's raised voice shocked Matteo. He hadn't heard his father snap like that in his life. Giving up, Matteo held his tongue. He stewed on the altercation all the way home and cursed Trevor Burrows for ruining his light-hearted morning with his father.

In tense silence, they set about unloading the truck at the bottom of the property. The rain was a misty drizzle, just enough to be annoying, and Matteo's mood was already bad enough without the cold water settling on his hair and eyelashes as he tried to work.

'Papa, I wish you would just tell me why there is so much hatred between you and Trevor Burrows. Help me understand. Where does it come from?'

His father just continued to pile sandbags along the top of the levee, building it higher. He stopped momentarily, staring down into the river. The expression on his face made Matteo wonder what thoughts, what terrible memories, he was seeing in the swirling brown water.

'Papa, please,' Matteo begged. 'You never talk about those years during the war. I can only wonder, can only conjure up the worst in my head.'

'It is in the past, Matteo. Dragging up the past does no one any good. It is where it belongs.'

'Papa—'

'It is not a time I wish to remember or reflect upon. You do not need to know the details of those dark years. It has nothing to do with you. I won't have it affect you or our future. *Per favore*, please, just forget it.'

He watched his father climb back into the truck and drive away up the muddy road through the lemon orchards towards the house.

But it did affect him, Matteo thought bitterly. It had everything to do with him. How could he not understand that? His papa had been absent for years. Years when a young boy had desperately needed his father.

School in Adelaide had been agonising for Matteo. For children of ethnic parents during the war years, it was a constant battle against bigotry and bullying. He'd had more than his fair share of bloody noses by the time he'd become a teenager. But once he'd grown a few inches he'd learned how to fight back. He'd learned how to stand up to the bullies.

In the end it was the necessity to earn extra money that had forced him to leave school and at thirteen years of age, he joined his mama and Antonio working in one of the local market gardens. He'd been excited to be free of maths books and English lessons. Little did he know his mother had expected him to keep up his studies and his evenings were spent, not riding his bike or going to the Italian Club to see Antonetta Mancini, his latest crush, but sitting at their kitchen table as his *zia*—his Aunt Maria—tutored him.

Considering all the help Mr Peterson, the owner of the market garden, got from the women in the Land Army, they'd been lucky that he was happy to take on Italian workers. He didn't seem to care what nationality or gender a person was. If they were willing to work the long hours in the blistering South Australian heat or the bitter cold of winter, he would take them on. Not every businessman in town had been so open-minded or forgiving.

'I need all the help I can get,' Mr Peterson would say good-naturedly. 'Vegetables need to be picked to send to our troops up north. Gotta keep 'em all fed if they're gonna stop the Jap man from coming south. You want to talk about invasion though, them Yanks have taken over our country and not a shot's even been fired.'

Antonio had said it didn't matter that he was joking, that kind of talk could get Mr Peterson labelled a Nazi sympathiser if he wasn't careful. But Matteo remembered Mr Peterson as a funny old man with his big laugh and even bigger round belly nearly popping the suspenders off his trousers. He'd been kind to them, given them jobs, and Matteo had learned more than a thing or two about farming by working at Peterson's.

They'd done what they had to to survive those years their papa had been away. But it was what his father had been doing during those long war years that had helped them establish this farm, in this place beside the river. They'd diversified over the years, learning what fruits and vegetables grew well in the sandy loam along the Murray River. Discovering what could withstand the blistering heat of the Australian summer and what suffered in the frosts of the icy winter mornings.

It was what his papa had learned about surviving and farming in a remote region that had ensured their success. It would break Matteo's heart if they were to lose the farm completely to the ever-widening river.

Matteo looked back across the orchard, towards the house where his father was taking off his boots on the verandah. The altercation with Trevor Burrows nagged at him. His papa and Trevor had spoken as though they'd known each other well. In all the years they'd lived in the region, Matteo couldn't remember one time they'd ever socialised or had any interaction with the Burrows family. None of it made any sense to him. Everyone knew Trevor Burrows was a drunken bully. Before the war, his papa would never have stood for that kind of bullying. It seemed standing up to bullies wasn't something his father had in him anymore.

Turning his back on the river, Matteo started the long walk through the lemon groves towards the house. The misty rain became a heavy deluge, forcing him to quicken his steps as he slipped and slid up the muddy path towards home.

Seven

It had been a rare occasion indeed for Isabel to have a free afternoon to meet Leanne and see a Friday matinee. Bruce had been uncharacteristically kind, saying he would deal with the lunch crowd. Apparently, he had something he wanted to talk to her mum about. Isabel didn't take the time to question him on what that was and all but raced out the door, jumped in the truck and drove across the bridge to see her friend before he could change his mind.

The rain had abated once again as she joined Leanne at the Ozone Cinema and the sun shone bright, momentarily lulling everyone into a false sense of security as they wandered the streets of Mildura, shopping or heading to long lunches at the Grand Hotel.

But by the time she stepped back out of the cinema at three o'clock, the clouds had closed in again and the rain fell in sheets. She bid goodbye to Leanne and then navigated her truck along the wet and puddled roads towards the bridge.

It was then she began to wonder what it was that Bruce had needed to speak to her mum about. Alone. Without her there. She thought back over the last week. She didn't think she'd done anything to upset him lately. They'd been too busy for her to take the time to try and push any of her new creations on Bruce or the pub. Besides, her mind had been occupied with a tall, dark, handsome Italian man and the wonderful kiss they'd shared while the smell of pizza had permeated the air in the kitchen.

Arriving at the other side of the bridge, she was lost in her daydream when she realised the traffic ahead of her had stopped. Squealing, she slammed her foot on the brake, stopping just short of hitting the green Volkswagen Beetle in front. Exhaling the breath that had clogged in her throat, she shook her head and closed her eyes.

'Concentrate on the road, Isabel, not the adorable man with the piercing blue eyes,' she murmured.

Drivers on both sides of the road had stopped and were climbing out of their vehicles. Unable to move forward or get around them, Isabel pulled up the hood of her coat, opened the truck door and stepped into the rain.

'What's going on?' she called over the pattering of the rain on her hood. She wandered across the road to see what it was they were looking at down below.

'Levee down there broke.'

'Oh, not another one.' She rushed forward, and looking down, she couldn't help the swear word that popped out of her mouth. The sight below was heartbreaking. The flat, low-lying area of Buronga was now a muddy, swirling lake. Many of its farmhouses and sheds now stood as little islands in the brown sea. The homes closest to the levee were inundated up to the eaves, and others had been pushed off their foundations, such was the force of the water that had gushed through the gaping hole in the protective wall.

Squinting against the rain, she could see where torrents of water continued to pour in, smothering market gardens. Rows of glasshouses were either smashed or had been lifted with the strength of the inflow and tossed around like discarded toys in a sandpit.

'That's Davide and Nancy Capaldi's place,' someone said. 'All those glasshouses gone. That's thousands of pounds worth of crops.'

'Damn shame that,' another driver added. 'The Eye-talians always grow the best tomatoes.'

'They're not all lost,' Isabel said, pointing across to higher ground. 'Look. There are still at least fifty or sixty glasshouses still standing.'

'For now,' the man uttered, puffing out cold air with a cloud of cigarette smoke.

But there were bound to be more losses. They couldn't see all the properties along this stretch of the river from where they were parked on the Sturt Highway. She wondered how the Sorrentis were faring.

Car horns began to beep behind her as the road became clogged with looky-loos. Drivers took the hint and began to move back to their vehicles. Isabel climbed into her ute and drove slowly along the road back to the pub, trying to catch a glimpse of the Sorrentis' place as she passed. There were too many trees and the rain on the windshield was obstructing her view. She could only hope and pray that their levee was holding.

Soaked to the skin, when Isabel arrived home she headed straight for the residence and her bedroom to change. She decided she'd drive down to the Sorrentis' property to check on them and see what she could do to help. While the pub had the telephone connected, she couldn't call Matteo because they didn't have a phone. Besides that, thanks to the floods and the multiple emergencies, it was averaging four hours to get a call put through by the operator.

She was towel drying her hair when she heard raised voices coming from the pub.

Following the argument to the kitchen, she stared confused and surprised as her usually placid and patient mother faced off with Bruce.

'You can't just up and leave with no notice, Bruce,' her mother was saying.

'Why not?' Bruce argued back. 'I gotta go, Audrey.'

'How will we do without you?'

'Why are you quitting, Bruce?' Isabel asked, worried it had something to do with her. Maybe he'd finally had a gutful of her. Had she pushed him too far?

Bruce turned to face her. 'I gotta get my ma across to Sydney. Her old ticker can't take the worry of another so-called "once in a century" flood. She lived through the big one of thirty-one, and she and my old man evacuated then. But this … this is gonna be much worse. The water is already lapping at the front gate of the property. We've got sandbags piled along the front of the house and around the sides. The levee's broken down there and we haven't even reached the peak yet. If the water keeps rising, they'll lose everything. Mum has lived in that house since she was born. Kept living there even when my brother took over the farm. Her heart is breaking. I'm scared for her health.'

'I just saw the mess down at Buronga. It's really bad, Mum. I was just thinking about heading over to see if I can help.'

'My brother, Colin, said everyone was down there fighting to shore it up, but with the latest rain and the strong winds with it, it was just too much water for the levee to take. The waves on the river were huge. Just one little crack and the whole damn thing crumbled. It all happened so fast. There was nothing anyone could do. Ma is going crazy. She's started packing up the car with whatever they can carry. Colin says he's had enough too. My sister Janet has been wanting to move Mum to Sydney for years. This is the excuse she needed.' Bruce's relationship with his sister Janet had always been strained.

'Maybe you can take your mum to Sydney and get settled and then come back,' Audrey offered.

He shook his head. 'When Mum and Colin go, there's nothing left here for me. I'm sorry, Audrey, I gotta go help my ma. It'll kill her to lose the house, but at least we can save the belongings in it.'

'You have to go now?'

'Mum,' Isabel intervened, taking her apron off the hook behind the kitchen door and lifting it over her still wet hair. 'Go ahead, Bruce. Mum and I will cope just fine. We'll miss you, but we understand, don't we Mum.'

Audrey sighed. 'Of course. Of course we understand. I'm sorry, Bruce, just hold on a moment.'

She disappeared through to the bar and returned a moment later with a handful of pounds. 'Your last pay.'

He took the pounds and shoved them into the pocket of his raincoat before turning to smirk at Isabel. 'You'll do alright, girly. I've taught you the basics. Just try not to poison the customers with any of your crazy recipes.'

His parting shot made Isabel feel a little less sympathetic towards his decision to leave and she turned back to face her mother once he was gone.

'I won't poison anyone, Mum.'

'Oh, I know that.' She dismissed it with an absent wave of her hand.

'I can do this,' Isabel insisted when her mum continued to look worried. 'I can. Trust me. You and me, Mum, we will not only cope, we will thrive.'

Smiling finally, her mum moved across to give her a hug. 'You're my angel.'

They held onto each other for a moment before her mum stepped back and looked at the clock. 'It'll be six before you know it. Pub will be full soon. You'd better get a wriggle on with dinner. Bruce already started the stock. Pea and ham soup will be nice and easy and I defrosted a link of sausages, so bangers and mash ought to go down well in this miserable rain.'

Isabel's plans for heading down to the Sorrentis' place would have to wait.

'I'll take care of it, Mum,' Isabel said, checking on the soup stock. 'I've got this handled.'

Her mum gave her a weak smile and disappeared back out to the bar. Isabel understood her mother's worries. They'd never run the kitchen completely on their own before.

As she glanced around the kitchen, she gave in to her excitement and did a little bum-wiggling dance. She finally had the kitchen to herself. No more trying to convince Bruce to try something new, or begging him to let her change up his recipe slightly to give it more flavour. With Bruce's departure, Isabel felt a weight lifted. She was sorry for his mother and their family home, but in her world, new and exciting possibilities had just opened up.

The dinner service ran smoothly—even without Bruce—and at one in the morning Isabel was still awake, sitting up in bed, flicking through her *Women's Weekly* back issues and all her cookbooks planning new menus for the pub.

She aimed to do a slow release of new meals. Keep at least one of the usual pub grub options for the regular fussy eaters and then perhaps add in something more interesting for those who were keen to take a chance on something new.

As her eyes began to droop, her dad's face popped into her head. While her mum might be nervous about Isabel taking over in the kitchen full time, she knew her father would have been her biggest advocate—had he made a different choice.

The tapping, incessant and annoying, was what woke Isabel. She sat up, removing the magazine page that had stuck to her cheek with her dribble. She'd fallen asleep while reading again. Rubbing the sleep from her eyes, she glanced out the window into the grey morning light. And there was Maddie, her pet emu, tapping on the glass of her window.

She chuckled wearily. If emus could smile, Maddie's said, 'Good morning, where's my breakfast?'

Still wearing her pyjamas, Isabel bundled into her overcoat, pulled on her gumboots and walked out to the shed with Maddie the emu following close at her heels. Loading up her buckets with animal feed was a challenge with Maddie constantly leaning over her, trying to get to the grains.

Isabel and her companion headed back outside and around to the little zoo as the sun spread its rays in a rare show of light after days of incessant rain. As Isabel walked, enjoying the tiny bit of warmth from the sun, Maddie's long neck constantly wound around her as the bird's pointy beak pecked into the bucket.

'Wait your turn, guts,' Isabel told the bird, giving Maddie's feathers a rub. Maddie had been found alone on the Sturt Highway after the father emu had been hit by a truck and killed. The other babies must have scattered, but the truck driver had found Maddie and brought her to the pub. She hadn't been injured, just young and in need of food and water. It was true, what she'd told Matteo about Maddie thinking she was a duck. There'd been a gaggle of ducklings abandoned by their mother, that they'd kept in a box under the warm, wood oven in the pub kitchen. They'd popped Maddie in there for the first few days and by the time all the babies had been strong enough to join the little zoo, Maddie was well and truly part of the little duck family. Maddie had been with them ever since and lived on the grounds of the pub. She could have left any time, but seemed to know she was on a good wicket at the pub so she stayed.

Isabel tipped grain and food scraps into the trough for Maddie before stepping into the pen for the wallaby and kangaroos to pat them and spread their food about. Then she tossed a biscuit of hay to Jerry Lewis, the goat, and filled the bird feeders in the aviary for the galahs and other parrots. Such was their little menagerie of rescued creatures.

Wrapping her coat tighter around her, Isabel wandered down to check the river levels. It was deceptive, the speed of the flow. Only where the river rounded a tree, creating an eddy, could she see the rapid movement of the water. Roger the pelican stood atop the levee, as if on patrol duty, before taking off and gliding majestically to land with a skid on the surface of the river. The current quickly carried him along even as his long beak disappeared into the water, resurfacing with a fair-sized carp that then slid whole down his gullet, before he disappeared from view.

Wandering along the levee, Isabel moved towards the Gol Gol Creek. It was wider—there was no doubting that. Looking for the path of least resistance, the river had entered the little waterway and begun cutting a passage inland. It would widen further up and creep in behind some of the homes and properties on the other side of the Sturt Highway. It could also cut off the highway if the creek rose high enough.

'We're going to have to move the animal pens higher up the bank in the next few days.'

Isabel turned to see her mum had come outside to join her.

'Either that or let them go free.'

'They wouldn't survive out in the wild,' Isabel said. 'They've been babied for too long now.'

'Most of them would adapt.'

'Not Jerry.' Isabel looked back at the old goat in his pen, chewing on his hay. He sent them what sounded like a bay of agreement.

'No, not Jerry,' her mum agreed. 'And Maddie would set herself up on the verandah before she'd go bush. I'll get Perry onto shifting the pens this arvo. So, what's your plan for this lovely Saturday? What's new on the menu now that Bruce is gone?'

'I have some ideas,' Isabel said. 'Don't worry, I know what I'm doing, and I promise I won't go too overboard with the fancy stuff. I'll keep the favourites on the menu, but I want to add a new recipe every few days. We'll see what works and what doesn't.'

'Sounds like a good plan. And what about tomorrow, do you have plans with your lovely fellow?'

Isabel laughed. 'Yes, actually, I'm going to Matteo's family farm to help pick the lemons.' Her smile faded as she remembered. 'That's if they didn't get flooded out when that levee burst yesterday.'

Her mum put her arm around her and squeezed. 'I'm so proud of you, sweetheart. You remind me so much of your dad sometimes. Always willing to give so much of himself to others.'

Isabel gave a weak smile.

Mmm, maybe he gave a little too much of himself to others.

'Better get into the kitchen. I have some fancy, inedible food to create,' Isabel said, her tongue firmly planted in her cheek.

Her mother laughed and they turned away from the speeding river. 'I know you'll do a great job, my sweet.'

Isabel nodded. She was the number one cook at the Riverside Hotel, but in her heart, she felt one more piece of her dream to study in Melbourne die.

Eight

It was still dark when Matteo collected Isabel from the pub at seven in the morning.

She climbed into his ute and huddled down in her thickest winter coat with a jaw-cracking yawn. 'You know, for a publican, this is stupid o'clock.'

Matteo laughed. 'And for a farmer, it is almost midday.' He handed her a thermos. 'Coffee.'

'Oh, I've had my coffee.'

'That swill you gave me the other day is not coffee.'

'What is it then?'

'I don't know, but it is not coffee.'

He twisted the lid off the thermos and poured some coffee into the lid cup. The aroma filled the cabin of the truck, steam rising into the cold air in curling ropes.

Isabel's eyes had still been half closed, but now they widened and her mouth watered at the smell. She took the cup and drank, closing her eyes again with delight.

'Heaven,' she murmured and took another sip.

He chuckled as he revved the engine and moved the truck up away from the rear of the pub. 'Stick with me. If you work hard today I can give you all the coffee you desire.'

'Bribing me with coffee like this, I'll do anything you desire.'

His foot lurched on the brake and she fought to keep the coffee from spilling. When she caught the look of amused shock on his face, her mouth dropped open and her face heated. 'That's not what I meant!'

He chuckled and she slunk down further in her seat with embarrassment.

'*Andiamo*!' she told him, taking another sip of coffee in the hope that she wouldn't say anything else inappropriate.

Still laughing, he put the truck back into gear and pulled out onto the sealed road.

Not long after, they turned off the highway into the low-lying, farming area of Buronga. On the way down, they passed the modern home where Ross lived with his parents. It was a hive of activity. Not one, but two bulldozers were busily shifting dirt, old railway sleepers and sandbags into position along the front of the Burrows' two-storey home.

'Looks like the Burrows will have the strongest levee in town,' Isabel said, spotting Trevor and Ross standing on the balcony watching the work going on. 'I guess it's easy to find help and machinery when you have money. Perhaps they'll offer the bulldozers to help build up the other levees along here.'

'I'm not getting my hopes up,' Matteo murmured. 'But it wouldn't help now anyway.'

After a series of winding turns along the dirt road, he made a right onto a driveway. He twisted and turned the wheel, doing his best to miss the worst of the potholes and mud puddles. As they took the bend under a canopy of box trees, Isabel gasped.

'Oh, Matteo.'

There was so much water. Rows and rows of glasshouses were smashed. Only their metal frames remained with the odd pane of unbroken glass in place, not enough to hold back the surge of muddy water. Further to the right, what had once been market gardens was now a lake, still taking on water through the gap in the useless mound of dirt that had once been the levee.

'You've lost everything.'

'No. Not everything,' Matteo said. 'The beets and zucchinis, yes, but we managed to save some of the pumpkins. We were luckier than many closer to the bridge. But I swear the water rises half a foot every day.'

'I saw the Capaldis' place on Friday. I was going to come and see you, see if you were okay, but then Bruce announced he was leaving and—'

'Bruce left?'

'Yes, but—'

'Congratulations! You are head cook.'

'Well, yes, but—' She paused, watching the honest delight on his handsome features as he drove. 'You amaze me.'

'I amaze you? Why?'

'You've lost so much, your crops, and yet here you are, so happy for me.'

'At least the house didn't go under.' He slowed the truck, cautiously skirting the deceptively serene lake that had once been fields of vegetables, and she saw that the house still stood about fifty feet from where the water had risen.

Isabel reached over and laid her hand over his on the steering wheel. He was trying to be strong, but she could see the pain in his eyes and hear the sadness in his voice.

The house was rustic, like most dwellings on farms and fruit blocks on the New South Wales side of the river, but Isabel could see the little touches that made the small house a home. Green vines wrapped around the verandah poles, blending beautifully with the sunshine yellow paint used to brighten up the dull weatherboard cladding. Two mismatched chairs sat in pride of place on the front porch, one a rocking chair that had obviously been refurbished and re-stained, and Isabel could envisage the family enjoying the cool of a summer evening there after a hard day on the farm. Roses lined the front walk, looking slightly bedraggled and bare in the winter sun. The Sorrentis had added a little touch of Italy to the place in the terracotta pots holding baby lemon trees, the colourfully tiled mosaics on the walls and the creeping bougainvillea winding its way out of pots and along the wide verandah that swept around the house. She imagined that in spring and summer it would burst with colour and provide shade across the walkway to a smaller outbuilding.

'My brother Antonio and his wife Loretta live in there.' Matteo pointed to the outbuilding. 'It gives them a little privacy.'

He pulled the truck to a stop at the side of the house behind a large number of other vehicles.

'You have a lot of cars,' Isabel said as they climbed out of the truck.

'It is harvest,' Matteo said, walking around the front of the truck to join her. 'These cars belong to friends who have come to help pick the fruit. We all help each other out. Since we don't have the gardens to work anymore …' He faltered a little as he gazed across at the ruined crops of vegetables. 'Yesterday I was picking grapes in Merbein, tomorrow we will go to my friend Nico's block in Red Cliffs and help him with his mandarin harvest. Today it is our day. We rotate around the blocks, but with the rising waters we must hurry.'

Instead of going in the front of the house, Matteo led her down the side of the building, passing by an old silver caravan.

'This is where I sleep.'

'In a caravan?'

'Yes. Mama and Papa have the bedroom in the house. There is no room for me. I don't mind. I enjoy having a place to myself. Perhaps I can show you inside later.' He grinned, blue eyes twinkling with mischief.

She was glad to see his smile replace the sadness that had come over him again.

Turning the corner, they found long wooden trestle tables standing bare and expectant. Beyond the yard, the orchard spread out before them, the river water halfway up the trunks of the trees that sat closest to the levee, the valuable fruit suspended and waiting to be saved. Luckily, it looked as if the water was only ankle deep around most of the trees higher up the banks.

'I admit I wasn't sure we'd be picking anything at all today when I saw the levee had broken,' she said. 'I thought it would all be lost and unable to be harvested.'

'It's even more important that we pick the lemons now,' Matteo explained. 'We must remove the fruit before the trees have been standing in the water too long. Eventually they will rot.'

Gazing out at the size of the orchard, Isabel gauged how much the loss of the trees would cost them. Yet men, women and children were scattered among the orchard, working rapidly up and down the rows of lemon trees. What strength it must take to just brush oneself off and get on with the job at hand.

'Are you sure I should be here?' Isabel asked, biting her lip with concern. 'I don't want to be in the way.'

'If you can help pick fruit, you are not in the way,' Matteo said. 'Everyone is welcome.'

She nodded, staring at the magnitude of the disaster before her.

'At lunchtime we will have a feast,' Matteo explained. 'It is what all the Italian farmers do. It's a community. Even in good times, we can't afford to pay money for help with the harvest and so we feed them well. Picking is hard work; we need a lot of food. You'll taste my mama's cooking.'

He stopped by a large wooden box and took out several sets of sturdy working gloves. Then he lifted something over her head.

'An apron?' Isabel asked. 'Am I going to be cooking? I thought I was helping to pick.'

'You are. This is for collecting the fruit in. When it gets full, you would normally transfer it into the big buckets on the ground and someone would come by with the tractor and empty them. But as you can see,' he pointed further out into the orchard where little boats were being rowed down what would have been paths, collecting fruit from the trees on either side, 'the tractor can't make it through the deepest sections of the floods. *Andiamo*. Let's put you to work.'

She followed him to the edge of the orchard where men and women were still able to use ladders in the shallower water and were deftly removing fruit and filling their aprons at an impressive speed. Isabel wondered how the weight of the lemons collecting in their pockets didn't topple them off their perches.

A small Ferguson tractor rumbled behind her with boxes of shiny yellow lemons in the large tray attached to the back.

'Papa!' Matteo called, waving his hat.

'Matteo, where have you been?' the man asked as he cut the engine.

'Papa, I brought you another worker. Isabel Hayward, this is my father, Signor Carlo Sorrenti.'

Matteo's father pushed his hat back on his head and leaned forward with his elbows on the huge steering wheel of the tractor as his eyes narrowed on Isabel. In his late forties, she guessed, Carlo Sorrenti still had a good head of thick, dark hair. Only the slight peppering of grey around his ears, and the wrinkled skin of a man who had spent most of his life working in the sun, showed he was old enough to have two grown sons. She could see where Matteo got his good looks.

'You have come to pick fruit?' he asked.

'I'd like to help if I can,' Isabel said, nerves kicking her heart rate up. 'But I admit I've never done anything like this.'

'You are from town?' His frown deepened.

Isabel chuckled. 'Not exactly.'

'Papa, I told you. Isabel and her mama own the hotel over at Gol Gol. The Haywards have owned the Riverside Hotel since nineteen seventeen.'

Isabel smiled, thrilled that Matteo had remembered. But she didn't miss the miniscule change in Carlo's expression and the stiffening of his spine. It confused her.

'Well, Isabel, ready to go for a boat ride?' Matteo asked, obviously unaware of his father's shift in temperament.

'Anchors aweigh,' she said, her cheery response belying the fact that she was beginning to feel unnerved by Carlo's insistent dark stare.

'Stay here with Papa and I'll see where the nearest boat is.'

'Oh, I can come …' But he was already gone.

Left alone with Carlo, she smiled nervously at him, before turning her attention to the pickers out in the orchards as she waited for Matteo to return. Running a pub, she was used to the range of odd behaviour that humans could display. She tried not to take Carlo's less than welcoming demeanour personally. They'd had a tough few days, had lost so much to the river. It was understandable he would be feeling less than cheery. Or perhaps it was personal. Maybe the Sorrentis wanted their son to be with a nice Italian girl. Maybe this was another family who thought their son could do better than the publican's daughter. She did her best to push her out-of-control thoughts aside.

'Hayward.'

She turned back to Carlo. It hadn't been a question, but there was something in his tone that she couldn't quite place. Accusation? Or just interest?

'That's right,' she confirmed.

'Your mother runs the pub at Gol Gol.'

'Yes. I work there too. We run it together.' Wasn't that what Matteo had just said?

Carlo continued to stare.

'We own it,' she went on when he said nothing. His silent study of her was making her nervous. 'It was passed down through the family when my grandmother died. I work in the kitchen. I'm the assistant cook, well, the only cook now since our head cook just left.'

Realising she was babbling, she stopped talking, but continued to meet his narrowed eyes, refusing to be cowed by the man's deep and unnerving study of her.

Everyone is welcome, Matteo had said. Why did she feel like that didn't include her?

'And your father?'

It was her turn to lose her cheeriness. The usual stab of pain pricked at her heart at the mention of her father. 'Isn't around anymore.'

His expression softened then and he shook his head. 'I am sorry. It is not your fault. *Mi scuse*.'

She stepped back out of the way as he started up the Fergie again and with a loud rattling, the tractor lurched forward down the row.

'That was odd,' she murmured.

'What was odd?'

She spun back quickly, surprised to see Matteo standing behind her again. He'd snuck up on her. 'Hmm? Oh, nothing.' She shook off the strange conversation and forced a smile. 'Put me to work.'

She followed Matteo to where the water lapped at the base of fruit trees in the orchard and a rowboat waited for them. Stepping in first, Matteo then helped her climb into the little boat and introduced her to Signor Martini, a friend from the neighbouring town of Red Cliffs. Taking in the man's thinning, grey hair beneath his flat cap and his wrinkled, gnarled hands, Isabel wondered if the gentleman—who she guessed to be at least eighty years old—shouldn't be sitting up at the house relaxing. She changed her mind when he rowed the boat with the strength of a teenager and, once they'd tied up between two rows of lemon trees, began to pick fruit at such an impressive speed, it made her feel sadly lacking.

For the next few hours, standing back-to-back with Matteo in the unsteady base of the little rowboat, Isabel twisted the lemons from their branches and piled them into the big pocket on the front of her apron. She almost overbalanced a few times but managed to steady herself again. The gloves Matteo had given her were too big and hampered her movement, so she hooked them into the waist of her trousers. But it wasn't long before her poor hands were beginning to suffer with tiny nicks and cuts from doing battle with the branches and sharp leaves, not to mention the bitter cold.

Time moved swiftly as she worked, listening to the Italian conversations going on around her. She enjoyed it even more when they would suddenly break into song. How could they still be so cheerful when Mother Nature had been so cruel to them?

The work was hard, harder than it usually would have been since the orchard was now in the middle of a lake, but the pickers seemed to still be able to find joy in the occupation and being outdoors. It was a blessing that the rains had halted for the time being and Isabel was enjoying the warmth of the winter sun that somehow seemed to make the task a little less heartbreaking.

•

Farmers were resilient. You couldn't live in the region and not see that, Isabel thought. They dealt with everything Mother Nature could throw at them. Droughts, mice and locust plagues and, of course, flooding rains. It wasn't the first time the river had exerted its dominance over them and it wouldn't be the last.

At noon, a bell clanged in the distance and Matteo cheered. 'Lunchtime!'

'Already?' she said, surprised at how the time had flown.

Unfortunately, before Isabel had managed to take her seat, Signor Martini sat down and quickly began to row the boat towards the house in his rush to get back for lunch.

'Oh!' Her exclamation was more from her surprise at being caught in Matteo's strong arms than from her near fall into the murky waters. 'I'm sorry, Matteo, did I hurt you?'

'No.' He held her, cradled easily on his lap despite the extra weight of her apron full of lemons. Her eyes met his and his dimple winked. His smile faded slowly as his gaze moved to her lips.

'This is how we first met,' he said quietly. 'Do you remember?'

She nodded, speechless for a moment as she became lost in the blue of his eyes.

'I must be heavy.' It was a feeble response, but the only thing she could think of to say since her brain seemed to have stopped working the moment she'd fallen into his arms.

He shook his head. 'You are a mere leaf.'

'A leaf attached to twenty or so lemons.' She motioned to the pile of fruit in her apron pocket. 'And I'm all sweaty.'

'You smell like the fruit; tangy and sweet.'

He pressed his nose up to her neck, taking a deep inhale, and the world, and her heart, stopped. There was nothing but the warmth of his chest against her, his breath on her cheek, those beautiful eyes, the colour of faraway tropical oceans, that heated as they stayed firmly on hers. Oh, she hoped he would kiss her.

Maybe she could make the first move this time. If she just leaned in a little …

'*O sole mio*!'

She jumped. She'd forgotten they weren't alone. Signor Martini was singing again and winked at her as Matteo let her go when she scrambled from his lap onto the seat beside him. Horrified that she'd nearly kissed Matteo in front of their elderly companion, Isabel kept her eyes firmly on the lemon trees as they glided along the water.

'Is just like the gondolas of the great canals in Venice, no?' Signor Martini said with a rasping laugh around the cigarette perpetually between his lips. '*Molto* romantic.'

Matteo laughed and began to sing along with Signor Martini and finally Isabel relaxed again and enjoyed the song and the ride.

'Hungry?' he asked.

She nodded, unable to find her voice as his intense gaze washed over her once again.

Signor Martini sang all the way back to dry land and when Matteo helped her out of the boat, she emptied the lemons into the huge bucket as they passed. She removed her apron, and Matteo took it from her to hang over the fence as they joined the throng back at the house.

'Let's eat!' he said, taking her hand. 'Isabel, your hands are freezing.'

'Ow!'

'What?' he asked and lifted the hand he'd taken. His expression turned to one of concern as he studied the cuts beneath the little spots of blood she'd not been able to completely clean away.

'Where are your gloves? Didn't you wear them at all?'

'They were too big.'

'But your poor hands. A chef's hands are her tools. You cannot have damaged tools. Come, we'll fix them before we eat.'

He took her into the house and while he went looking for first aid supplies, she wandered slowly along the hallway. Photographs in black and white or sepia covered the walls. Family portraits, baby photos, faded images of men and women sitting outside what looked to be a cafe or restaurant. Italy, she guessed. Naples perhaps, since that's where Matteo had said his family, his parents, had come from. Incredible scents wafted through the house and her mouth watered as overwhelming desire drew her closer and closer to the fantastic aromas. She could hear women's voices coming from another part of the house. The kitchen, she assumed. She hadn't thought much about Matteo's offer to have his mother teach her to cook. Now suddenly it was all she could think about. She'd give away her soul to whoever could teach her to cook food that smelled like that. Before she could follow her nose into the kitchen, Matteo appeared again and dragged her out the front door onto the porch. Her disappointment was palpable.

He sat her down on one of the chairs and with a little bucket of hot, soapy water, he cleaned her hands before applying bandaids to the worst of the cuts.

When he was done, he lifted both of her hands, his eyes on hers, and kissed her knuckles. Swallowing heavily, she dared not move for fear he would let go and the moment would be broken.

A woman's voice floated out from somewhere in the house.

'Matteo! *Dove sei*?'

'Is that your mother?'

'*Sì*. I mean yes, come, let's go eat.'

When they walked around to the back of the house again, Isabel saw that a big bonfire burned in a pit, warming the workers who sat in little groups eating and talking. The tables that had been bare wood when Isabel and Matteo had arrived at the farm were now covered with red and white tablecloths and laden with huge, steaming pots, and plates of exquisite-looking freshly baked bread and cakes. The aroma—the same scents that had wafted out of the kitchen—made Isabel's mouth water again and her stomach grumbled embarrassingly loudly.

Matteo laughed. 'You are hungry. Well, you have earned your payment.'

He filled a plate with spaghetti, covered with a hot and chunky tomato sauce brimming with herbs, before handing it to her and repeating the process for himself.

'How come you get more than me?' she asked.

He raised his eyebrows. 'You think you can eat as much as me?'

'Matteo, I am starving. I could eat a horse and its rider.'

He laughed, delighted. 'Okay,' he said and added more of the pasta to her plate so that it matched his. 'Do your best.'

He carved huge wedges of crusty bread, giving her one. It was warm, straight out of the oven no doubt, and she put her nose down close to the bread on her plate to inhale the heady scent. Instead of butter though, Matteo tipped some olive oil over his bread and did the same to hers.

'This looks and smells amazing,' she said, taking a seat on a wooden bench as he poured two cups of homemade lemonade. She bit into the oil-drizzled bread and, closing her eyes, she moaned with pleasure as the warm bread melted in her mouth and the flavours exploded. 'Oh Lord, help me. That is heaven.'

When she opened her eyes again, he was staring at her.

'What?' she asked, unable to read the look on his face.

'Nothing. *Mangiare*. Eat.'

'Matteo!'

Reluctantly, he turned his head. 'Mama?'

He left Isabel, walking across to the woman standing at the table filled with food. Isabel listened as they fell into a conversation in Italian. His mama. Even if she hadn't called him over, the resemblance would be obvious to anyone. Gia Sorrenti was a very attractive woman. She had the blemish-free olive complexion of the Mediterranean cultures and the same midnight black hair and pale blue eyes as Matteo. Eyes that were now studying her with an unflinching stare as she listened to whatever Matteo was saying. She couldn't understand the words being spoken, but the look of suspicion in Mrs Sorrenti's eyes was plain enough.

Determined not to let it bother her, Isabel dipped her fork into the steaming pasta and took a bite. The combination of flavours hit her tongue and, moaning with gratitude, she commenced shovelling in the pasta as though she hadn't been fed in a year. She'd thought working in the pub on a Friday night was hard work. Harvesting fruit was so physically demanding. Though her hands hurt from the cuts and the cold, and her body ached, a warm sense of pride and accomplishment filled her as she glanced around at the huge wooden boxes with their mountains of bright yellow fruit.

Her bowl of pasta was empty in minutes and she went up for seconds. This time she was treated to a dish one of the women who was serving called gnocchi.

'It is potato,' the woman told her.

The sauce that covered the little balls was exquisite. Garlic, she guessed, and parsley. But the other herbs and flavours were a mystery—a delicious mystery—and as she took her seat again she began to seriously hope that Matteo's mother would teach her some of her wonderful recipes.

Nearby, Matteo continued to speak with his mother in Italian and Isabel enjoyed the melodic song of the language. She'd heard a cacophony of languages over the years as Mildura and the region was home to many immigrants, even before the war. Greek, German, even Russian could be heard at any store in town. But she'd always had a preference for the Italian language—even if she had no clue what any of it meant, and even if she knew they were talking about her.

Matteo left his mother, refilled his plate with food and returned to join Isabel on the bench.

'This food is excellent,' Isabel raved, accepting the second slice of crusty bread Matteo handed her. 'This is all lovely.'

'I know, the gnocchi, eh? I told you Mama does the best—'

'No,' Isabel interrupted him. 'It's better than excellent. There are no words to describe just how excellent this food is.'

He laughed at her exuberance and when he used the bread to scoop up the sauce—something her mother would have said was rude—she proceeded to do the same.

'What I meant was *this* is lovely.'

'What?'

She laughed and waved her hand at the scene before them. 'This. All of this. The food, the family. It's lovely how everyone comes together to work, to help out, and then share a meal together. Apart from Mum, her cousin Flo and her husband Albert, I've never had much to do with other family members. My mum has an aunt in Melbourne. I saw her last year when I was down there for the VFL grand final but she's getting on in years. I think I'd have enjoyed a big family.'

'Having a large family has good moments and bad,' he said, also gazing around the large gathering.

She nodded, slightly unnerved that Matteo's mother continued to stare across at her, the wary frown still evident on her face as she served the workers at the food table.

'Your mum is wondering why I'm here.'

'You're here to help with the harvest.' Matteo brushed off her concerns. 'Trust me, everyone is happy to have the extra hands.'

'She keeps looking at me like I'm stealing the baby from the bassinet.'

He laughed. 'The what? What does that mean?'

'Nothing. Never mind.' It wasn't the first time a mother had been displeased her son was courting her.

'She is just surprised. I don't think she expected you to last this long. Working the fields, picking, it is hard work.'

Isabel frowned at the insult. 'And you don't think running a hotel is hard work? It's not the same as picking crops, I'll grant you, but it isn't as easy as it looks.'

'No, that is not what I meant, and I am sure it is not what my parents think. I have no doubt that what you and your mother do is very demanding,' he agreed quickly.

'It is,' she insisted again. 'It's not just your mum, your father acted so strangely when we met. It couldn't have been my harvest abilities he was questioning, I hadn't even started work when we met.'

'I'm sure you imagined it.'

'He asked about my father. He said, "It's not your fault". What does that mean? What's not my fault?'

Matteo looked as baffled as she felt. 'Do you think they knew each other? Your papa and mine?'

Isabel shrugged. 'Has your papa ever spent time at the Riverside pub?'

'I doubt it. He's not the most sociable man. He prefers to keep to himself and I cannot see him spending time in your pub. Any pub.'

'It's not inconceivable that they'd have met somewhere. It's a small town, a small region. Especially on this side of the river. They could have met at the post office, the bakery. Nothing's impossible. What year did you say you all moved here?'

Matteo didn't answer and she followed his gaze across to where his parents were locked in what looked to be quite a heated discussion. She didn't miss the shared look of concern they shot her and Matteo.

'They don't like me.' Isabel put her plate aside. She'd suddenly lost her appetite. 'I should go.'

'No, please,' Matteo argued. 'I am sure it's nothing to do with you. Come, let me introduce you to my brother and his wife.'

Before Isabel could protest any further, he'd taken her hand and dragged her across the yard to where his brother sat with his wife under the shade of an olive tree. A child, about a year old she guessed, sat on a blanket at their feet.

'Antonio, Loretta,' Matteo started. 'This is Isabel.'

'So, this is the *bella* Isabel,' Antonio said with a cheeky grin that had Matteo swiping his hand across his brother's head, dislodging his hat.

As they shot insults and digs at each other, Antonio's wife shook her head and sent Isabel a smile so genuine, Isabel couldn't help but like her instantly. 'Come and sit with me, Isabel, and ignore them. I swear they get together and they act like twelve-year-old children again. Antonio! Behave. We have a guest.'

Isabel sat beside Loretta on the low seat in the midday shade, while Matteo dropped onto the rug to tickle and play with the little girl. The baby's giggles were infectious, and Isabel couldn't help but find Matteo even more attractive as he played with his niece.

'That's Lucia,' Loretta said. 'She is eleven months old tomorrow.'

'She's beautiful.' Isabel smiled down at the little dark-haired girl who found fun slapping at Matteo's cheeks while he blew raspberries at her.

'She's a happy little Vegemite.' Matteo sang the well-known jingle to his niece.

'Matteo says you cook at the pub your mother owns,' Loretta said.

Isabel was surprised Matteo had spoken so much about her to his family. 'Uh, yes. We serve lunch and dinner six days a week.'

'It is unusual for a hotel, no?' Loretta asked. 'And you do the cooking alone?'

'We had a head cook, Bruce, but his mother's house is—was—just down there.' Isabel pointed across towards the grouping of homes that were now abandoned, surrounded completely by the lake that had been formed when the levee burst. Bruce had been right. The water was about ready to overtop the sandbags and take the house. 'He decided it was time to leave and take his mother to Sydney. So now I am on my own in the kitchen, which is how I like it. Well, Mum helps when we get super busy, but she's not the most inventive cook and, honestly, she has so many other things she needs to do to keep the hotel running; the cleaning and making up the rooms for travellers. But I love creating dishes and trying new recipes,' Isabel went on. 'The science of it, the experimenting, it's such a challenge.'

'Perhaps we can share recipes one day,' Loretta suggested.

'If your cooking is anything like Matteo's mum's I would love that.'

'No one is as good a cook as Gia,' Loretta said. 'But did you try the *patati*? The flat bread topped with the potato and rosemary. I made that.'

'Yes! Oh! It's so simple but so delicious. Would you mind if I tried it at the pub?'

'No, please do.'

Loretta was easy to like. She exuded sincerity and warmth and, if Isabel was going to continue to see Matteo, she was hopeful she might find an ally in the young woman. Despite Matteo's denials, she was sure his parents were not enamoured with her.

'I would love to know how to cook that gnocchi. It was divine.' She patted her stomach at the memory of it. 'Matteo showed me how to make pizza.'

'Use that same dough recipe for the *patati*,' Loretta suggested.

'You gave her Mama's pizza sauce recipe?'

Antonio's horrified question had Isabel jumping in. 'Oh no, Matteo just fixed a sauce I was making already. Don't worry, I won't be serving it in the pub. Pizza isn't exactly in demand.'

Antonio simply grunted, giving his brother a kick in the leg.

'What?' Matteo slapped back.

'Mama will kill you if she finds out you're giving away family recipes.'

'Mama is going to teach Isabel how to cook,' Matteo insisted.

'She agreed to that?' Loretta asked, equally surprised as Antonio.

'Not yet,' Matteo said, standing when his father called for him and Antonio.

Isabel watched the brothers bump shoulders like young boys as they walked across to talk with their father.

'They are a handsome family, aren't they?' Isabel said, feeling a little thrill race through her when Matteo turned back and sent her a wink and a smile.

'Cursed with beauty,' Loretta said, rubbing the side of her head.

'Are you okay? You look pale all of a sudden.'

'Just a little nausea,' Loretta replied. Her smile when she said it had Isabel frowning. 'Baby number two is making me more tired than Lucia did.'

'You're pregnant?'

'*Sì*. But it is very early,' Loretta added, lowering her voice. 'I have not told the family yet.'

'Congratulations.'

'*Grazie*. Do you want children?'

'Someday.' Isabel nodded. 'I'd like some time for myself first. I want to study cooking, become a real chef. Maybe it can happen one day, but probably not. I'd love it if Mrs Sorrenti agrees to teach me to cook. Although that's not looking promising.' She gazed across at Matteo, who was helping his father and brother lift more containers into the rowboats. 'Has Matteo had many girlfriends?'

'A few,' Loretta responded. 'Like I said, the Sorrenti men are cursed with beauty. But I don't think I have ever seen him look at a woman the way he looks at you. And he most certainly has never brought anyone home to meet the family. And you are not Italian.'

Isabel's smile faded a little as she faced Loretta again. 'Is that a problem?'

'No,' Loretta said. 'Not for me. Not for Matteo. For Gia and Carlo? I can't say they would be happy if Matteo did not marry an Italian girl.'

Isabel must not have hidden her disappointment well because Loretta added, 'It is not a reflection on you personally, Isabel. Please do not think that. It's just that heritage and culture are very important to Italians. And how would your mother feel about you marrying Matteo?'

Isabel let out a little laugh. 'She'd be thrilled. She thinks he is lovely.'

'Your mama is more tolerant than many in this town then.'

'I suppose it's still hard for those who saw battle when Italy was an enemy and not an ally. People will forget all that hostility soon.'

'I hope you are right, but people have long memories when it comes to the war.'

The clang of the bell sounded the end of the lunch break and workers began to climb back into the little boats to head back into the orchards.

'It was lovely to meet you, Isabel,' Loretta said, standing and hitching little Lucia onto her hip. 'I do hope we will see you again soon.' She leaned in. 'And don't worry about Matteo's mama. She is more bark than bite.'

Isabel forced a smile and headed back towards the boats. Despite her warnings, she felt as though she'd made a real friend in Loretta. She'd given her plenty of food for thought and she'd just have to chew on the gristle for a while.

At the end of the day, as the sun poked its nose out of the clouds long enough to cast an orange glow on the flooded plains, the weary pickers assembled once again by the tables at the rear of the house where bottles of homemade beer and wine were handed out to celebrate a successful day.

Matteo approached Isabel with two small glasses and a bottle of bright yellow liquid.

'Here,' he said, pouring a small glass and handing it to her.

'More lemonade?' she asked.

Being thirsty, she tossed the drink back in one gulp. The burn in her throat led to a coughing fit as her eyes watered mightily.

'What is that?' she wheezed out as Matteo laughed uproariously.

'It is *limoncello.* A liqueur made of lemons, sugar and pure alcohol. It is a recipe from the Amalfi Coast.'

'Amalfi?'

'A stretch of coastline south of Naples. Very beautiful.'

'I thought you were born in Australia,' she said, mopping her watery eyes.

'I was,' he agreed. 'I have seen pictures and my nonno, he used to tell us stories about family holidays to the Amalfi Coast. Tiny towns that drop down the cliffs towards the Mediterranean Sea. Stunning blue water and pebble beaches.'

'Amalfi Coast sounds lovely.' She handed him her empty glass. 'That's tractor fuel.'

He laughed again. 'You sip it, don't swallow it like a beer drinker at "the swill".'

She had to chuckle along with him. His cheery nature was so contagious. And his smile never failed to have her heart doing a little flip in her chest.

The light began to change as the sun slipped lower.

'I should probably be getting home, Matteo.'

'Of course,' he said. 'I hope it was not too much work. I've enjoyed having you here.'

'Not too much work.' She smiled. 'I've enjoyed being here. But I do think I'll sleep well tonight.'

'I hope you'll dream of me.' His eyes stayed on hers for a long moment before he looked away. 'I'll get your things from the house.'

She said her goodbyes to Loretta and Antonio and thanked Mrs Sorrenti for her wonderful food, sighing at the woman's terse but polite 'Thank you for your help today'.

She wandered around to the front of the house to meet Matteo at the truck. Alone on the front porch in the old rocking chair sat Carlo, a bottle of wine in one hand and a glass in the other.

'Mr Sorrenti.'

'Miss Hayward,' he returned with a nod, draining the glass of wine before topping it up from the label-free bottle. 'Thank you for helping with the harvest today.'

'It was my pleasure,' she said. 'I hope we managed to save enough fruit. I'm sorry about your other gardens, the ones that have been flooded. I'm sure it's a big loss.'

'We will survive. We have survived worse.'

Isabel wondered what could be worse than losing your livelihood.

She smiled, determined to make him like her. She was a good person, a nice person. All she could do was be herself. 'You have a lovely home and a beautiful family.'

He nodded, a small smile touching his lips.

'Did you always want to be a farmer?'

'No. We used to live in Adelaide. I ran a delicatessen, a store.'

'Oh, of course.' Matteo had told her that.

He stared out towards the trees again, a faraway look on his face.

'And you decided to move up here and start the farm after the war?' she asked. Matteo hadn't told her much about their move up from Adelaide. Now that she thought of it, he hadn't told her much at all. Whenever she'd asked him anything about his background, his childhood, he would somehow manage to change the subject.

Mr Sorrenti didn't speak for a moment and Isabel wondered if mentioning the war had brought up some terrible memories. Perhaps he still had family in Italy. Had he lost relatives or friends in the war? Almost everyone had.

'It was not my decision, not my choice to leave Adelaide.'

Before she could ask any more Matteo arrived, carrying her purse and a small wooden crate of fruit and vegetables.

'Payment for services,' Matteo said, motioning with the box.

'Oh no, I can't take those,' Isabel argued. 'I was happy to help.'

'We have had to pick too much. We tried to save as much as we could before the water came. It will go to waste,' Mr Sorrenti said with a sad shrug. 'You may as well take it.'

She watched Matteo put the crate into the tray of his truck.

'*Ciao*, Papa, I'll be back soon.'

'Goodnight, Mr Sorrenti.'

'*Buona sera*, Isabel Hayward.'

In the truck as Matteo drove her home, Isabel stewed over what his father had said. Finally, her curiosity got the better of her.

'What did your father mean when he said it wasn't his choice to leave Adelaide?'

'He told you that?'

She nodded. Matteo looked genuinely shocked and didn't say anything else for a moment, but she could see he was turning something over in his mind.

'Did something happen in Adelaide? To his delicatessen?'

Matteo kept his eyes on the potholed road ahead. 'Did you know that during the war many foreigners who had made Australia their home—Germans, Italians, Japanese—were rounded up and sent to internment camps around the country?'

'No. I didn't know that.'

Matteo nodded as he turned the truck onto the Sturt Highway and headed for Gol Gol. Isabel waited for him to say more but he stayed quiet, a small frown marring his usually cheery features. She didn't want to push him but when he pulled into the car park at the hotel, instead of just saying goodbye and letting her out of the truck, he cut the engine.

Silence enveloped the cab of the truck and Isabel didn't know what to do. She was about to reach for the door handle when he spoke again.

'Italy had stayed out of the war until Hitler took Paris,' he began again. 'Many say Mussolini was waiting to see what happened, so he could align Italy with the winning side. When Italy declared war on France and Britain there were mixed sentiments. Some Italians were proud, others scared for family still in Italy. But none of us was prepared for what would happen here in Australia.'

'What happened?' she urged when he seemed to hesitate.

'Men from our community, from the Italian community, began disappearing, being taken away by the police. We would hear that a neighbour was taken.'

'Taken where?'

'At first, we could see they were taking men who were outspoken, openly on the side of Mussolini, vocal in their allegiance. They made themselves enemies of Britain which made them enemies of Australia. Over the months, as the war continued, the net was cast wider. It was the worst day of my life.'

The tension in the cab of the vehicle was so thick, Isabel could feel it pressing in on her.

'Fifteen years ago, but I still remember that day like it was yesterday.' He took a deep breath and continued. 'We were walking home from school—Antonio and me. I'd been whining about being bullied again. It happened a lot once Italy entered the war.

Kids who had any German, Italian—and later Japanese—features or names were treated like the enemy.'

'Children can be so cruel.'

Matteo made a sound of agreeance. 'It wasn't just the children. When we arrived home from school, just as we reached the shop, we could hear Mama's shouts and cries. I'd never heard my mama shout like that. Even when she was angry with us, she would never yell like that. We ran and ran, around to the back of the shop to where our little house was. Two men in the khaki uniforms and slouch hats of the Australian army had my father, one by each arm, and were dragging him out of the house with Mama following up, crying, trying desperately to hold on to Papa.'

He let out a shaky breath. 'Mama was yelling. "No! No! You cannot take him! He's done nothing wrong!". I was so young. I didn't understand what was happening. Mama just kept crying, "You can't take him away! You can't take him! Carlo!"'

Matteo let out a little laugh then. 'I stepped up to those soldiers and asked them what they were doing with my papa. Where were they taking him?

'"He's going to prison, little boy," one soldier said to me, "where all fascists belong."'

Isabel swallowed the lump in her throat.

'There was that word again. Fascist.' Matteo stared blankly out the windscreen into the darkening sky. 'The kids had been calling me that name for weeks. I didn't even know what it meant. The other soldier was kinder, but I hated him anyway. He was taking my father away. And for what? For what? I yelled at them that we were Australian. I even kicked one of them in the shins. He raised his hand like he would hit me, but Papa managed to free himself and pulled me behind him, protecting me even then, even as his life, his freedom, was being taken away. I still remember, he did not yell as they yelled, as Mama yelled. His voice was so quiet, and he said to them "I will go with you. But you will not touch my boys." Mama cried again, begged again. Antonio and I clung to Papa's trouser legs, trying hopelessly to keep him with us. I didn't understand. Why were they taking him to prison when he had done nothing wrong? They wouldn't even tell us where they were taking him or when we could see him.'

Isabel couldn't help the tears that fell on her cheeks now but she wiped at them, not wanting Matteo to see.

'We fought to hold on, but the soldiers were too strong, and Papa was dragged from us and shoved into the back of a truck with Mama screaming and fighting them all the way. There were so many faces I recognised in the back of that truck. Many Italian men from the area. Shopkeepers, barbers, Signor Centofanti, Signor Formicello and even Roberto, Signor Centofanti's eldest son. Where were they taking all these men? Mama swore at them and slapped one of the soldiers across the face. I will never forget how loud it was, the crack of her palm hitting his cheek. But Papa just told her to stop, to take care of us. Papa reached through the window of the truck and called to me and Antonio. We rushed forward and gripped his fingers.'

Isabel wondered if Matteo realised he was, even now, reaching out his hand as though trying to touch his father.

'He told us to be good boys, to take care of Mama. Then he was gone.'

Isabel wiped away more tears and Matteo shook his head as though waking from a dream—or a nightmare.

'He'd been allowed one small bag of belongings, clothes and personal items,' Matteo said. 'The soldiers searched through it, no doubt looking for contraband or weaponry. I kept asking why my papa, or any of those good upstanding citizens, had been treated like the enemy.'

'They thought your father was a spy,' Isabel said. She'd only been a child herself when Italy entered the war, but she'd learned plenty about Mussolini and fascism at school. 'Because he was Italian. Being Italian, they would think him a fascist.'

Matteo's head snapped around and he looked at her for the first time since starting his story. 'My papa was not a spy. He was not even a fascist. There were fascists within the Italian community, supporters of Il Duce. Papa never displayed any fascist propaganda at the delicatessen. They tried to get him involved, but he refused. He did not agree with this kind of politics.'

Isabel slunk back in her seat a little. She'd only been trying to understand why his father had been taken away. She hadn't meant to anger him.

'It was fear, Mama said. They feared foreigners who may have had sympathies towards the Nazis or Mussolini. After Papa was taken, the kids at school continued to tease us mercilessly. They called us "Mussolini's spies". The teachers hadn't been much better. The war, and Italy's alignment with Hitler, had made us undesirables. I started to skip school altogether. Instead, Antonio and I would go on adventures in the creek and foothills not far from home.'

'Your poor mother,' Isabel said. She'd heard stories from soldiers, stories of the war, of battles in Europe and Asia over the years, but she didn't think she'd ever heard anything about how people, civilians, had been treated right here at home. Of course, she'd only been a kid herself, younger even than Matteo, but it was interesting that she'd never heard talk of Italo-Australians being rounded up and taken away from their families. 'How did she manage? Raising two young sons on her own, with no idea where your papa was must have been so hard.'

'With Papa gone, we lost the store. People stopped coming in to shop once they heard Papa had been taken away, after he was accused of being sympathetic to the enemy. Without customers, we couldn't afford to pay the rent, to keep it going. It broke Mama's heart to write to Papa and tell him. She wrote him letters every day. Antonio and I would write a page each and we would get letters a few times a week. Papa didn't tell us much about the prison camp where he was held. He'd tell us mundane things like the time he got up and went to bed. His work in the gardens. He said they played football and poker, but as I got older, I began to think that he was lying to us. He was telling us things weren't so bad for him so that we would not worry, and that made me worry more. I began to wonder, I began to imagine what was really happening inside the camp.'

'How long was he gone?' Isabel questioned.

'Five years. He was in the camp for five years. Some internees were released earlier but for some reason, they kept him in there longer.'

Almost the entire length of the war, Isabel thought. She'd been without her father now for almost the same amount of time, but she'd been sixteen, not a child. Not a nine-year-old boy who would have desperately needed to have his father around.

'Five years is a long time,' she said. 'What did you do for money? How did you survive?'

'Mama went to work in the market gardens. Adelaide has a very Mediterranean climate, good for agriculture, which is why it drew many Italians in the first place. A lot of them settled near the foothills in the north-eastern town of Campbelltown. When the men who'd worked the fields went off to war, or internment camps, gardeners needed more workers. Many in the region refused to hire Italians. Women had to step up to lend a hand in all industries when the men went away to war. Some of the market gardens brought in groups of women from the Land Army to help during the harvests. Mama figured if those women could work in the fields, then why not her. Antonio and I did our bit after school—when we went to school that is—and when we in turn reached thirteen we left school to work in the fields full time.'

'Did you find out where your father had been all those years?'

'All I know is that he was locked up at an internment camp in some backwater place called Loveday.'

'He must have been so relieved to see you all, to be a free man again.'

'It took two more years after he was released before we could join him. The Civil Alien Service—that's what they called them. Prisoners who were released were forced to work in remote rural places. When they finally freed him, Papa managed to get a lease on the land we have now, and that's when Mama, Antonio and I moved up from Adelaide. So, you see,' Matteo said, 'it was not his choice to leave Adelaide. None of it was his choice.'

It was a lot to take in, Isabel thought. It still didn't explain why his papa had acted so strangely towards her.

'It's not your fault.' That's what Carlo had said to her. Of course it wasn't her fault. None of it was her fault. She'd been a child. *It makes no sense.* But one thing Matteo had said triggered something in the back of her mind.

'Did you say Loveday?' Isabel asked.

'Yes. Do you know it?' Matteo asked.

She shook her head.

'It's across in South Australia. Somewhere near Barmera, I think. At least that's where our letters were sent through the Australian Red Cross.'

They sat in a heavy silence for a moment. Only the sounds of the night permeated the cab of the truck. The pub sat dark and quiet. Sunday evening. No patrons. No music playing. The only vehicles in the car park were those belonging to overnight guests and Isabel's own ute.

'Matteo, I'm sorry that you, that your family, had to go through that,' she said, carefully reaching a hand over to place on his. 'I want to thank you for telling me. I admit, I don't know much about that time or the internment camps. It shames me that I don't.'

He looked at her for the first time. 'You were just a little girl too. Children shouldn't know about such sad and terrible things. I had no choice since it happened to me.'

'And I'm so sorry it did. I'm sorry for your father too.'

'It was a hard time for all of us,' Matteo said, his expression darkening. 'And no doubt harder for him. But he never speaks of it. Refuses to talk of those five years he was imprisoned. I try to be understanding but sometimes it infuriates me. He is a different man to what he was before the war, and I don't have the first idea what made him the way he is today. I just want to understand.'

'Maybe he wants to spare you from that,' she suggested. She'd heard stories from soldiers who'd been incarcerated in prisoner of war camps in Europe and Asia. She didn't think, couldn't believe it possible, that those kinds of atrocities would be going on here in Australian-run internment camps, but the war had made people do horrible things.

'It's the not knowing that is the worst part of it all,' he argued. 'My imagination runs wild with what might have happened to him during those years. If he would only tell us …'

She understood completely where his imagination ran to. Hadn't she spent the last five years wondering, imagining what had happened to make her own father do what he did? Hadn't she asked herself a hundred times why he had been so different, so distant, when he'd returned from the army? Why he hadn't talked to her, or her mother, about any of it?

'Would it be better or worse?' Isabel wondered out loud. 'To know what it was that changed them so completely.' She shook her head. 'I'm sorry. It's none of my business.'

He said nothing.

Isabel released a heavy sigh. 'I had a good time today. Matteo, try not to worry too much about what your father won't tell you. He survived those years and came back to you. Just be happy you still have him.'

His eyes widened. 'Isabel, I'm so sorry, I completely forgot—'

She shook her head; the wave of exhaustion, the weight of his story and her own memories threatened to knock her flat. 'It's okay. You have a lovely family who, despite what you have all been through, or perhaps because of it, have a close bond. Try to hold on to that.'

He lifted the hand she'd placed on his and kissed it. 'Thank you, and sweet dreams, *bella*.'

Nine

When Isabel stepped into the residence of the hotel her mother looked up from her relaxed position lying back on the comfortable green upholstered sofa. Noticing the photo album across her mum's lap, Isabel's heart sank. She often found her mum looking through old photos. Photos of her father mainly, their wedding pictures or the occasional snapshot of them with other young couples by the river during summer. It would make her mum sad, which then made her sad. And thanks to her conversation with Matteo in the truck, she'd just about had enough emotional upheaval for one day. Not to mention she was about to fall on her face from exhaustion.

Shaking off the melancholy, she looked for somewhere to put the crate of vegetables she carried. Discarded on the floor was that day's newspaper with its headline that screamed 'Flood Danger Faces Towns on Murray'. Squatting, she lowered the box onto the paper.

Her mum smiled, shifting the album aside. 'How was your day as a farmer? Thinking of moving to the growing end of the food industry?'

'Um, no,' Isabel said definitively as she removed her boots. 'Farming would be challenging at the best of times but harvesting from rowboats was an experience.'

'Boats?'

'Yeah, since the levee broke the Sorrentis' lemon orchard is partly submerged so we had to balance in the boats to get the fruit off the trees.'

'Inventive. Is their home under threat? Is there anything I can do to help?'

Isabel loved her mother's good heart. Audrey Hayward could never turn her back on those in need. The little menagerie of animals out the back of the pub proved that much.

'Their house is okay for now. Even with the break in the levee the water hasn't quite reached that high. Anyway, I think we got most of the lemons harvested. Sadly, the trees will die if the water hangs about for months like they say it will,' Isabel said, rolling her aching shoulders. Reaching up to pick the lemons for eight hours of the day had led to muscles she never knew she had screaming at her.

'They're saying they doubt the levees over in Mildura will hold,' her mum said. 'The river hasn't even reached its predicted peak yet.'

Isabel nodded. 'The Sorrentis seem like nice people. They have such a wonderful sense of community. Whole families came across from Red Cliffs and as far as Monak to help with the harvest and all for no more payment than a meal.'

'It's nice to know there are still good people in this world.'

'Sure is,' Isabel agreed. 'Then again, Mrs Sorrenti's cooking is more than worth the work. She made these little balls out of potato—gnocchi she called it—with a green herb sauce and cheese. It was a heavenly delight. So fluffy it almost dissolved in my mouth. And then there were the pastries!' Isabel rolled her eyes heavenward and licked her lips as if she could still taste them. 'I have no idea how to pronounce them but they were like fluffy tubes filled with a sweet custard—'

'Stop!' Her mum raised a hand. 'You're making my stomach growl.'

Isabel chuckled. 'Matteo asked his mother if she would teach me how to cook. She trained as a chef in Italy before they came over to Australia. Can you imagine? I hope she agrees to teach me. I would love to learn how she makes that sponge cake. I can't remember what it's called but they pour cream mixed with lemon liqueur over it. Oh, and the lemon liqueur! It's got a hell of a kick but it tastes wonderful.'

'What's in the box?' Her mum nodded towards the large, covered crate Isabel had brought in. 'Some of those cakes, I hope.'

'The Sorrentis sent home a lot of lemons, as well as some pumpkin, zucchini and a selection of other veggies from their market garden.'

'We have to pay them for it.'

Isabel shrugged. 'I doubt they'll take any money. They said they just want to harvest as much as they can in case the water rises any further. What they gave us was almost ready to turn and won't last the long trip to the city. I can make a huge pot of vegetable soup, use some of the carrots and onions in the stew for tomorrow's dinner and there'll still be plenty of veg left to go with the corned beef. I'm thinking lemon custard tarts to use up some of the lemons. Or maybe I can try and make that lemon meringue pie recipe in the Dione Lucas supplement from the *Women's Weekly*.' Excitement filled her at the idea.

'Well, at least you earned some of it with hard labour.' Her mum put her arm around Isabel and squeezed. 'I'm proud of you. Times of hardship bring out the best in people. I saw that sense of community you talked about during the war.'

The war. Her mother didn't talk about the war much. She'd lost her brother, Isabel's Uncle Rodney, in New Guinea. And then the war had taken Sam. Well, it wasn't technically the war that had taken her dad, but Isabel always suspected the war was to blame for what her father did.

Isabel remembered Matteo's dad's odd behaviour at the farm that afternoon.

'Mum, have you ever met the Sorrentis?'

'I don't think so. Why do you ask, love?'

'Matteo's father, he acted so strangely when Matteo introduced me. As though he recognised our name. To be honest I'm not sure what it was about really.'

'Perhaps Matteo has been talking about you.' Her mum grinned and raised her eyebrows suggestively. 'He seems quite taken with you.' She laughed when Isabel dropped her gaze to the floor as the heat rose in her cheeks. 'Everyone knows this pub, pet, whether they frequent it or not.'

'Yeah, but it wasn't so much the pub as my name that he seemed to recognise. Hayward. Maybe he knew Dad.'

'Sorrenti, you said?' Her mum narrowed her eyes thoughtfully. 'There's lots of Italians on this side of the river. I've probably spoken to plenty of folks in the post office or at the general store. I could have met the Sorrentis and not really been aware of it. Pretty sure they don't frequent our pub though.'

'Why is that, do you think?' Isabel had a feeling she knew exactly why. People had long memories and Italy would always be the enemy to some.

'They tend to keep to their community. What are Matteo's parents' names?'

'Carlo and Gia.'

'Doesn't ring any bells,' her mum said with a shrug.

Isabel still couldn't believe she'd never seen Matteo around the district given how many years they'd lived there.

Isabel eyed the photo album on the couch. 'What are you looking at?' As if she didn't know.

Her mum picked up the album again. 'Just a little trip down memory lane.' She flicked back to the front of the large book. The pages were black and separated by wax paper. Isabel hadn't looked at family photographs in years. It still hurt to see those happy family snaps back when her dad had still been her hero.

'Your dad bought a little Kodak folding camera second-hand from some guy when we were about sixteen years old.' She pointed to an image. 'Look, that's me and your dad with Trevor and Shirley at the school camp on Lake Cullulleraine in our final year. That's where Shirley and Trevor started going round together. Your dad only arrived in the region the year before.' She laughed. 'Believe it or not, I'd been going out with Trevor.'

'What? Ew!' Isabel was horrified. 'How did I not know you dated Trevor?'

Her mum waved it off. 'We only went out a few times, and only casually. Hard to see it when you look at Trevor now, but he was a looker back in the day. Oh, but when Sam Hayward arrived at Mildura High all the girls' hearts went a-fluttering.'

All the girls.

Isabel remembered what Ross had said about his mum being in love with some other bloke in school before she'd finally ended up with Trevor—and his money.

'Sam only had to look my way and I was his. We'd been together for about six months when that photo was taken.'

Isabel looked closely at the image of the four teenagers. Her mum and dad were wrapped around each other wearing matching grins. Trevor and Shirley were standing beside them, looking at her mum and dad with bland faces. Hardly the picture of a newly formed couple in love. Not much had changed then, Isabel thought. She wondered how she had never known her mum and Trevor had been a couple. It was impossible to believe she could have forgotten something like that.

Her mum turned the page of the album and side by side were wedding photos of her mum and dad on one page and Trevor and Shirley on the other. 'We were all married the same year,' she said, a wistful note in her voice. 'Trevor and Shirley had booked their wedding date already. Sam and I were struggling to find an available venue at all, but the Rowing Club had a cancellation and suddenly our wedding was two weeks before Trevor and Shirl's. I remember Shirley was so angry with me over that. Our friendship had become strained since high school. I never really knew why. Anyway, she demanded I change the date. She was marrying a Burrows which should have made her wedding the event of the year. In a region this size, you pretty much have all the same people attending every wedding. Of course, Shirl and Trevor's wedding was a huge event that would have cost a whole truckload of money. Sam's parents weren't wealthy and we certainly didn't have that kind of money to play with.' She sighed wistfully, running her fingers across her wedding photograph. 'But I wouldn't have had it any other way. Our wedding day was intimate and romantic, and I wouldn't have traded that day for the Burrows' gala event for all the world.'

Isabel compared the two wedding pictures. Shirley had been an attractive girl with chin-length, wavy blonde hair. Her satin gown with lace across the decolletage would have been the height of fashion no doubt. The long sweeping train fanned out ahead of where she stood arm in arm with Trevor, who looked about as happy as a kid forced to wear a suit to Sunday School. Everything about the photograph screamed 'money' but there was very little joy about the image they portrayed.

Her mum, on the other hand, had been a stunner. Despite the obviously less expensive dress, a white sheath with long sleeves and a simple neckline, she looked heartbreakingly beautiful and radiated happiness as she smiled up at Isabel's dad. A young—very young, it seemed to her now—and handsome, tawny-haired Sam Hayward was grinning like he'd just won the lottery.

Audrey flicked through the pages and found an image of Isabel as a baby in her dad's arms.

Her mother's sniff told Isabel that it was time to change the subject.

'One of the men at the Sorrentis' farm was saying the river has risen another half a foot. Do you think we have enough sandbags?' Isabel took the photo album from her mother and set it down on the side table. 'I hate feeling so powerless. I can't imagine what we would do if we lost this place.'

She looked around at the pale green walls of their small living room. Their residential rooms were part of the pub building and, if she was honest, they could do with a decent paint job. There were two bedrooms, a living room, a tiny kitchen—which was barely ever used because they mostly ate in the pub kitchen—and a miniscule bathroom that at least had an indoor dunny. It wasn't much, but it was the only home she'd ever known.

Her mother put her arm around her to soothe her. 'We'll be fine, love. The levee is built and should be high enough for when the water reaches its peak. Perry and Albert are taking turns on patrol and as long as that great dirt wall out there holds, we'll be fine. Don't worry yourself over it.'

Isabel dropped her head to her mum's shoulder and her eyes began to droop.

When she yawned hugely, her mum tapped her on the leg. 'Now, my girl, you're too big for me to carry you to bed these days, so off with you.'

Isabel pushed herself up off the couch and staggered, half asleep already, down the corridor to her bedroom. Matteo's revelation about his father's incarceration had been both fascinating and heartbreaking. But there was something about his story that kept nagging at her. There was something … something about the camps he'd mentioned, but her poor tired brain just couldn't seem to function enough to sort it out.

She yawned again. 'Tomorrow.'

Dropping face down on her bed, fully dressed, with the light still on, she was asleep in seconds.

Isabel woke with the same niggling feeling. Like a memory or a dream that you try to bring back that remains just out of reach. Throwing off the covers she must have pulled up some time through the night, she sat up.

'Ow.'

Every inch of her ached. She rolled her shoulders and stretched out her calves and ankles before she attempted to stand up. What's more—she sniffed and screwed up her nose—she should not have slept in the clothes she'd worn for eight hours of hard, sweaty labour. It would have been smarter to have had a hot bath the minute she'd got back from the Sorrentis' farm last night, but she'd been so tired. After stripping the bed, which now also smelled, she tossed the sheets into the laundry as she passed on her way to the bathroom. Despite wishing she could lounge and languish for hours to soothe her aching muscles in the hot, fragrant water, she quickly scrubbed herself clean, cringing at the colour of the bath-water as it drained away.

Clean and fresh and feeling slightly less like she'd been put through a meat grinder the day before, she dressed and wandered through the house to the pub kitchen. Passing by the living room, she bent to pick up the crate of vegetables she'd left by the door and spotted the photo albums her mum had left on the couch.

Meaning to just pack them away again, out of her mother's sight, instead she sat down, picked one up and began to flick through it. In the pages beyond the baby pictures of her that she'd seen the night before, there were photos from the many camping trips they'd taken when she'd been a kid. Prior to the war, she guessed, considering her age in the pictures. And if not for that, the smile on her father's face would have been a dead giveaway. He hadn't smiled that much after the war. She recognised Hattah Lakes, the ancient painted deserts and Great Wall sand dunes of Mungo, and the myriad river camping spots they'd visited. Trevor and Ross featured in many of those photos as well.

Towards the back of the album, there were some images of her father in uniform. The sight of him in his khaki green brought back a flood of memories, simple things she'd forgotten. She was struck with flashes of her rushing out of the pub to greet him when he'd come home from … wherever it was he was working for the army. She frowned. Did she ever know where he'd been stationed during the war? He'd never gone overseas, so where had he been all that time? She'd blocked out so many things about her father since that fateful day. Shaking away another unwanted memory that threatened to surface, she turned another page in the album. An image showed him and Trevor and several other soldiers standing in front of a lake. Lake Bonney perhaps? It looked like Lake Bonney down in South Australia but it was hard to tell from the picture. She admitted it could have been any lake, or any body of water for that matter.

She closed the album, then picked up the crate of veggies and carried them into the pub kitchen where her mum was just boiling the kettle for tea and slicing bread for toast.

'Good morning, sunshine. Cup of coffee?'

She thought of the coffee Matteo had brought her the day before and wasn't sure she could ever face their brand of instant swill again. 'I'll have tea, thanks.'

Isabel placed the crate on the floor near the Coolgardie safe and kissed her mother's cheek as she took the cup of tea from her. 'Thanks.'

The strength and warmth of the tea blew the last of the morning cobwebs away. 'Mmm, good.'

'What's on the menu today?' her mum asked.

'I'll whip up something from the box of veggies the Sorrentis gave us,' Isabel said as she looked out the window at the gloomy weather. 'It's another chilly, miserable-looking day so I'll definitely make the soup I mentioned last night.'

Last night. Isabel frowned as she remembered Matteo's story of his dad's internment. The photo of her dad and Trevor in their army uniforms, at what looked like Lake Bonney, popped into her head and something clicked into place.

'Mum, what was Dad doing when he was in the army?' she asked. 'He was gone all that time when I was a kid, during the war. I don't remember where.'

'He was down in South Australia,' her mum said absently, buttering toast. 'Near Barmera somewhere I think.'

Isabel paused, her cup halfway up to her mouth. 'Barmera?'

'Yes, he was working at one of those camps down there.'

Isabel's mouth was suddenly so dry she had to sip her tea again before she could speak. 'At the Loveday camp?'

'Yes, that's the one. He and Trevor were both stationed at the camps.'

Trevor too?

'Why the sudden interest in what your dad was doing during the war?'

'Matteo's dad, Carlo, he was ... there, at Loveday, um, imprisoned there.'

'Oh, I don't think they were prisoners as such,' her mum said as she handed Isabel a plate of toast and jam, before moving back to add more bread to the flip-side toaster. 'Lots of immigrants worked on the farms around the camps and in the poppy fields where they made medicine to send to the war.'

'Matteo said his dad was rounded up with other Italians, taken from their families by force and brought up to Loveday. They didn't see him for many years.'

'I'm sure we would have known if there'd been a prison camp just down the road.'

'Did Dad ever say what he was doing down there?'

'He just said he was overseeing workers in the gardens.' Her mum turned to face her, an expression of concern on her features. 'Were they really imprisoned?'

'Well, if they couldn't leave of their own accord, then yes, I guess imprisoned is the right word. How did we not know more about the camps? Or about what Dad was doing down there. Was Dad a guard or something at the Loveday camp?'

'Honestly, pet, he didn't really talk about it,' her mum said, quickly grabbing the toast before it burned. 'When he came home on his short furloughs he didn't want to talk about work or the army, he just wanted to be here with us. Maybe he wasn't allowed to talk about it. The army was secretive about many things during the war. You were so young, but you have to remember he'd be gone for weeks at a time. He'd come home for a few days and then he'd leave again.'

'I don't remember much about those earlier years, I mean, I was barely more than a toddler when war broke out,' Isabel said, trying to think back to what she could recall. 'Later, towards the end of the war, I remember him coming home. We always had a good time when he came back. But he was away so much. Then in those last years, before he came home for good, I was more interested in playing with my school friends on weekends than spending time at home.'

'Mmm,' her mum agreed. 'And by the time he came home permanently after the war, he was … well, you know he was different.'

That Isabel did remember. His sullen moods, his heavy drinking. He wasn't the same happy-go-lucky dad she remembered. 'If those camps were …' She struggled to say it. 'If they were prisoner of war camps, it might explain why he didn't like to speak about his time there. It also might explain how Mr Sorrenti recognised my name.'

'You don't really believe he knew your dad in the camp, do you? I mean, there must have been lots of soldiers working down there. It was so long ago. Why would Mr Sorrenti even remember Dad's name now?'

Isabel shuddered to think why, after nearly a decade had passed, Carlo Sorrenti would remember one guard in particular at the internment camp.

She chewed on her lip as realisation sank in. 'Mum, how do you think Matteo is going to react when he finds out my dad could have been one of his father's captors?'

Her mum moved across to her and ran a sympathetic hand down her arm. 'Only one way to find out, baby. You need to tell him. Relationships based on lies eventually break down. We both know that all too well.'

Isabel stood at the levee, peering over the top to where the water was now more than halfway up the levee bank. She had joined

Perry that morning, wandering along the length of the clay and dirt wall, looking for leaks or weak points. They'd checked and double checked the sandbags already in place and made a note of where they needed more.

It was nearing the end of July, and hundreds of families had been evacuated from the riverbanks of the Murray. Sultana vineyards and market gardens were inundated. Little hope was held for the remaining levees at Buronga to survive as another eighteen inches of water were still due to come down the river. Roads were closed due to flooding or damage, isolating properties in Boeill Creek and Merbein. Thousands of pounds worth of tomatoes had been destroyed with the loss of more glasshouses at Buronga. More families evacuated from Buronga and even in Gol Gol people had decided to leave early as the Sturt Highway threatened to be cut off by the rising Gol Gol Creek in the coming weeks.

Levees were patrolled day and night on both sides of the Murray, including the levee that had been built up in front of the Riverside Hotel. The levee now reached all the way from the bakery, not far from the Gol Gol Creek, around to the other side of the hotel.

It had been a few days since Isabel had last seen Matteo. He'd been busy salvaging what was left of their farm, clearing what could be saved of the tomato crops and then dismantling the glasshouses where they were able to save some of the glass sheeting for future use. When they weren't working the farm, they were shoring up the remaining levees over at Buronga—the last line of defence between their home and the constantly rising river. The Sorrentis were holding steady despite the loss of their lower gardens, orchards and vineyards. They still had the house, although it was sandbagged up to the bottom of the windows in readiness. If that final levee broke, all the sandbags in the world wouldn't save their home.

She'd missed him. She had. But selfishly, she'd also been grateful he'd been so busy and had been kept away. Isabel still didn't know how she was going to tell him that her dad might have been one of the guards at the camp where his beloved papa had been kept prisoner for five years. How would he react to that? Could she expect him to understand? Would he ever be able to look at her again with those patient, pale blue eyes she'd come to adore? Her heart felt heavy all the time, and she'd not slept well the last week. She knew she had to tell him. Her mum was right. Secrets were poison. Secrets broke families and relationships. But it wasn't exactly something you could just blurt out in passing at the post office. It wasn't her fault they hadn't been able to see each other this last week, she told herself a hundred times. And she was a coward. She had to tell him.

And as though fate had heard her, she turned and watched him walk towards her, down the hill from the hotel, his beautiful smile lighting up his face. It was time to pull the bandaid off and tell him.

'*Ciao*, Isabel! *Come sta*?'

She smiled and walked up to meet him.

He took her hands in his and kissed each of them, before moving in to kiss her lips lightly. 'How are you? It has been too long since I saw your pretty face.'

Her heart flew and ached at the same time.

'How's things at the farm?' she began, stalling.

'We are managing,' he said as they walked along the length of the levee.

They talked of the floods, of what they'd been doing over the last week.

'I have not been able to ask my mama again about teaching you to cook,' he said, apologetically. 'It seems the wrong time.'

'Oh, it's absolutely the wrong time,' Isabel agreed.

If only you knew how wrong a time it is.

'But I will ask her,' he said, and went on chatting happily.

Her heart was thumping in her chest. Her panic and her reluctance to tell him made her realise just how much she cared about him, but she couldn't hold it in any longer.

'Matteo, there is something I need to tell you,' she blurted, interrupting him mid-sentence.

He stopped walking and laughed. 'Okay.'

She pulled her hand from his and walked away while she tried to gather the right words.

'Let me guess. You're married,' Matteo joked.

She turned back to face him. 'No.'

'I know, you're having a secret affair with old Clarry.'

They looked across to where old Clarry was taking a nap in the cart as Sampson stood munching happily through their neighbour Dulcie's camellia bushes.

Isabel gave a nervous chuckle. 'No, nothing like that.' Taking a deep breath, she took his hand. 'You know how I feel about you, don't you?'

He seemed a little surprised at the turn of the conversation, but surprise turned to delight as he took her hand in his again and raised it to his lips. 'I think so. And I hope you know I feel the same about you, Isabel.'

'I think I do.' She swallowed over the lump in her throat. 'I do. But if we are going to have any sort of future together you need to know the truth.'

'The truth about what?' He must have seen something in her eyes because his easy-going joking was replaced with a concerned furrow between his beautiful dark eyebrows. 'Isabel, what is it? What's wrong?'

'You've told me about your father. That he was kept at the internment camp at Loveday.'

'Yes.'

'But I haven't told you much about my father.'

He ran a comforting hand across her hair. 'I did not want to push you. I know it was hard for you to lose him.'

'Yes, but …' She hesitated, her heart pounding. Could he hear it? Could he see it banging against her chest through her heavy winter coat? Was it possible for someone her age to have a heart attack? 'Matteo, my father didn't go to the war, but he was in the army.'

Matteo stayed quiet, respectfully waiting for her to tell her story. But when she struggled to get the words out, her mouth opening and closing wordlessly, he urged her on.

'He was in the army?'

'He was in the army,' she said again. 'We think … we're not completely sure what he did for the army but …' Her breath was coming fast and she thought she might just hyperventilate or pass out.

'Isabel, what is it?' He rubbed a hand along her bicep. 'What are you trying to tell me?'

'We—Mum and I—we think Dad might have been a guard when he was in the army.' She paused. 'A guard at an internment camp.'

Matteo shook his head, and she realised he didn't understand the bombshell she was about to drop.

'At Loveday.'

He was so still she wasn't sure he'd heard her. She wondered if he understood the implications of what she was saying until his smile fell slowly, his expression darkening.

'At Loveday?'

She nodded. 'We think so.'

'You think your father was a guard where my papa was imprisoned?'

She nodded again and could no longer meet his eyes, didn't want to see that look of accusation in them.

'Why didn't you tell me this when I told you my father's story? You could have said something then. Why didn't you?'

'I didn't remember it. Honestly,' she said quickly as Matteo pulled away abruptly and began to pace. 'I was young, just a kid like you, Matteo, when my dad went away. Eventually, I understood he was away with the army, but I didn't remember where he'd been stationed until you mentioned Loveday. Then, when I saw a photo of him in uniform at Lake Bonney with Trevor—'

Matteo turned back to face her then. 'Trevor Burrows?' he said, interrupting her rambling. 'Trevor Burrows was a guard at Loveday?'

'I guess so, but why does that matter?'

'It matters to me,' he interrupted with a ferocity that startled her. 'Your father and Trevor Burrows were friends?'

'Yes, they were friends for years.'

'And guards together at Loveday?'

'I mean, we're not completely sure but—'

He closed his eyes, shook his head. 'No wonder …'

She didn't understand his having a stronger reaction to finding out about Trevor being at Loveday than he had to her telling him about her father.

'My papa was kept at that internment camp for five years,' he said. A sort of quiet anger permeated his tone that had Isabel's heart kicking up again. 'For five years he was treated like a prisoner, a criminal. Locked up like an animal and no doubt treated like one by the guards who stood over him. No wonder he refused to talk about it. And now you tell me that your father and Trevor Burrows—one of the most vile and vicious human beings I've ever met—were in that camp with him? In charge of him? Controlling when he slept, when he woke, when he ate, *what* he ate.'

Fearful now, Isabel took a step back. She'd never seen Matteo so angry, and having that anger directed at her had tears pricking at her eyes. 'I don't know anything about what my dad and Trevor did in the camps. I didn't even know until a few days ago that they were even there—'

He raised his hand. 'A few days ago? You've known this for days and didn't come to tell me?'

'You've been busy.' Her voice was so small she barely recognised it herself.

She'd been a child during the war and only ten years old when her dad had finally come home for good. And then a few years later, he was gone again … for good. She didn't know anything about her father's time at the camp. All she did know was that she didn't want Matteo to look at her the way he was now, with such anger and disgust.

'Matteo, I—'

He put up a hand to stop her, stared at her as though seeing her for the very first time. 'I have to go.'

Tears tracked down her cheeks as she stood and watched him storm up the hill away from her towards the car park. She'd known he might not take it well, but this was infinitely worse than she'd expected. Her chest ached and walking back up to the pub in a sort of stunned daze, she heard the engine of his truck idling for a few more moments, as though he were thinking. She waited, hoped he would change his mind and come back to talk it out with her some more. Finally, she heard the gears shift and the engine lurched as he drove away.

Ten

'Marjoram. Marjoram. Where the bloomin' hell is the sodding marjoram?'

Well, she'd go without, wouldn't she. Just because Mrs Emily McPherson called for it in her shepherd's pie didn't mean she had to comply. She had a brain, didn't she? Hadn't she told Bruce for years that recipes were all about personalisation? Well, he was gone now, wasn't he, so she could bloody well personalise as much as she wanted.

'Shepherd's pie. None of those fussy customers can complain about something as simple as that, can they?'

Isabel went on mumbling to herself as she carved hunks of meat off the leftover lamb roast and jammed them into the cast iron mincer clamped to the benchtop. Taking hold of the handle she wound, battling against the chunks of meat.

'You've got too much lamb in that thing.'

Isabel looked up at her mother who was leaning against the doorway to the front bar. She hadn't heard her come in. She hadn't even noticed Perry Como wafting through the door as he sang about putting a picket fence around his rambling rose.

'How long have you been standing there?' Isabel asked, stretching out her aching wrist.

'Long enough to hear you mumbling to yourself about marjoram.'

'We're out,' Isabel mumbled again.

'Pretty sure we never had any to begin with,' her mum responded, wandering up to the bench where Isabel worked. She set about removing some of the meat from the top of the mincer. 'There. Try it now.'

Isabel turned the handle again and this time it rotated smoothly. She ground the lamb and added more to the mouth of the instrument.

'So, are you going to tell me whose head it is you're envisaging pulverising in that thing?'

'Huh? Oh, I don't know. Mine I suppose.'

'Why?'

'Because Bruce is gone and I finally get full run of the kitchen and I have absolutely no idea what to cook that won't make the customers turn up their uneducated, unadventurous noses. Hence, boring old shepherd's pie again.'

Okay, that was a lie—and unfair to her faithful customers. She wasn't ready to tell her mum that Matteo had reacted badly to the news that her father had been with the army at Loveday.

'Shepherd's pie is a classic for a reason.'

Isabel grunted. Having finished with the lamb, she picked up a knife and started quartering the onion to feed into the mincer.

'I mean, why can't people just be reasonable? Is that so much to ask?'

'Are we still talking about the menu or is something else stuck in your gullet?'

'Like what?' Isabel spun around, knife in hand, and her mum took a step back, hands raised in defence.

'Isabel, put down the knife.'

'No, I have work to do.' Isabel turned back to the workbench.

'And you'll do it. But first, you need a break,' she said, taking the knife herself and placing it safely in the sink. 'Honey, I worry that you're working yourself too hard. You need to find some balance.'

'But, Mum, I love cooking,' Isabel said. 'I want to be a cook.'

'You are a cook,' her mum said, pulling her in for a hug. 'You're a good cook.'

'No, I mean …' Isabel stopped herself before she said too much. No matter how frustrated she felt, or the current bad mood she was wallowing in, she couldn't let her mum know that she wanted to leave her to go to cooking school in Melbourne. How could she tell her she wanted to abandon her here to run the pub alone?

Leaning back, Audrey swept Isabel's hair from her forehead. 'Sweetheart, you're still young. You need to go out and have some fun occasionally. I don't want you ending up like an old spinster, cooking in this pub for the rest of your life. I want you to find love, get married, have babies.'

Isabel snorted with derision. 'Because marriage worked out so well for you, didn't it?'

The shocked hurt on her mum's face had Isabel wishing the river would flood in now and swallow her up.

'That's a terrible thing to say. I had a lot of good years with your dad.'

'But you never moved on. You talk to me about having a life away from this pub. What about you? When was the last time you went out with a man?'

'Don't be silly.' Turning away, she moved to the sink and started washing beer glasses that were piled on the bench.

'You're still young, still a beautiful woman,' Isabel said, calming her tone. 'Why shouldn't you meet someone else?'

'Because, Bella, I'm still married to your dad.'

Isabel stared at her, gobsmacked. 'Mum, Dad's gone. He's gone. He's not coming back. Why can't you just forget about him?'

'Stop it, Isabel, just stop it.' The hurt had returned to her mum's eyes when she turned back to face Isabel. She grabbed a towel to wipe her hands. 'I don't want to talk about this now. I have to get back out front.' Her smile was forced. 'If you're not going to take a break now, do so when you've finished making the pie. I'll serve dinner tonight. Hardly anyone is coming in for a meal anyway. Either go and see Matteo or go make yourself useful somewhere else until you get over this foul mood of yours.'

She disappeared back into the front bar and Isabel leaned against the bench, exhausted.

Did her mum still really think of herself as married? Her dad had been gone for so long. In the first few months, they'd both been left confused and devastated, but they hadn't had the luxury of falling to pieces. Her mum, always so strong, was not going to let it cause them to lose the family business. And so, while they mourned privately the loss of their husband and father, Audrey and Isabel Hayward continued to run the Riverside pub alone.

Audrey Hayward was still a young and attractive woman—Isabel was right about that. After that fateful day—when they realised Sam probably wasn't coming home again—it hadn't taken long for other men to come sniffing about. At the time, Isabel had been lost in her own grief, but thinking back over the years, she had never seen her mother with another man. Not once had she ever gone out to the movies or to a dance with any of the men who'd asked her. Audrey had just got on with the job of running the hotel and raising a strong-willed, angry teenage daughter.

Realising she'd been very self-involved for too many years, Isabel wasn't just grateful, she was proud that her mum had ignored all of those people who'd said the hotel would fail if left to two women to run. With stoic grace and determination, the Hayward girls had turned the Riverside Hotel into a thriving business. Isabel sniffed and bit her lip to stop it from wobbling. She was feeling neither stoic nor graceful at this particular moment. She knew she'd been behaving like a sulking, wallowing brat the last few days, waiting for Matteo to calm down, understand she hadn't lied to him purposefully, and come to see her. Unloading her bad mood on her mum had been convenient … and wrong.

She hadn't told her mum what had happened with Matteo. How could she explain that because of Dad, Matteo would probably never want to speak to her again? Her mum would be angry with Matteo, and Isabel didn't want that.

She hadn't meant to say those things to hurt her mum. Dad had put them both through so much and now, even when he wasn't here, he was still ruining her life.

She wasn't sure Matteo would ever be able to get past the fact that her dad had been one of the people who'd kept his papa captive. It wasn't her fault. Hell, when it came down to it, it wasn't even her father's fault. It had been his job. It had been war. The Hayward family had not been responsible for dragging Carlo Sorrenti away from his family and locking him up in the middle of nowhere for five years.

Was that how Mr Sorrenti had recognised her name? Because he'd met her dad in the internment camp? Had her father been a brutal guard?

It's not your fault.

Matteo's dad had said that to her that day at the orchard. He didn't blame her, so why did Matteo?

The tears that fell had nothing to do with the onions she ground in the mincer. She had so many questions about her dad—from both the war years and the years since. Isabel had been sixteen the last time they'd seen him. A teenage girl had no idea how to process what had happened. Isabel grabbed a tissue and wiped at the tears, before blowing her nose.

As for ever seeing Matteo again. Well, hell and high water may just come before that ever happened.

Matteo was grateful for the rain that battered the tin roof of the shed where he and his papa worked on the old pump engine. It meant he didn't have to make conversation. The broken irrigation pump would normally be used to bring water out of the Murray to the crops and gardens, but they were hoping they could set it up to pump water out of their block to try and save what they could of their orchards. The longer the tree trunks stood in water, the sooner they'd rot. They had about two weeks to try and pump out the water if the trees were to survive.

Matteo knew there was nothing they could do about the vineyards and gardens that were already well under water. At least they'd harvested the bulk of the lemons. Of course, getting them to market was a challenge in itself. Transport was becoming more difficult as roads closed.

The punt at Kingston had closed back in June. The main road to Adelaide was still open for now, but in the weeks ahead, the Sturt Highway would potentially be cut off between Renmark and Paringa and again at Monak on the way to Sydney. The Calder Highway to Melbourne was still in operation and would have no diversions in place as it veered away from the river. The train still ran, and was being used to deliver hessian bags and supplies before it loaded up again to transport fruit and vegetables to the cities. There was talk that the RAAF might be brought in to help fill sandbags and provide support on the ground. Unfortunately, with resources spread so thin across the length of the flooding river system, they'd yet to see any of that support in the small hamlet of Buronga.

Staring out the window at the river, Matteo played and replayed the conversation with Isabel in his mind. With each passing day his anger had subsided, and he began to wonder if he had over-reacted. Her revelation that her father had been a guard at Loveday had floored him. The fates could be cruel. To find a woman he thought he could be with, someone who challenged his mind as much as she ignited his passion, only to discover that her family was part of the worst time of his father's life? Yes, the fates, the gods, whatever you believed in, could be complete bastards. Had Sam Hayward been cruel to the inmates at Loveday? Knowing that he'd been friends with Trevor Burrows, a man who was known to have a mean streak as wide as the Murray, Matteo had to assume Sam was cut from the same cloth.

'*Per favore*, Matteo, please, the wrench.'

'Huh?' He snapped out of his thoughts, looking back at his father.

'The wrench, Matteo. I've asked you twice.'

'Sorry, Papa.' He couldn't even blame the rain anymore, since it had dissipated to a misty drizzle that matched his mood. Matteo reached into the box and held out a tool.

His papa shook his head at the screwdriver in Matteo's hand and leaned over to get the wrench himself. 'What is wrong with you today? You have a face like *Zia* Maria—grouchy, unpleasant woman, never wore a smile.'

Matteo grunted. His great-aunt had been an unhappy old woman, so different from her brother, Matteo's nonno. Both now rested in a cemetery in Adelaide, peacefully, he hoped, although Matteo was unsure Maria knew the meaning of the word.

'How is Isabel?'

Matteo shrugged a shoulder. 'Wouldn't know.'

With a grunt, Carlo finally wrenched the ancient nut off the bolt holding the casing of the pump together before eyeing his son. 'You have not seen her? Have not spoken to her?'

'No.'

'No? And why not? You looked very friendly when she was here for the harvest.'

'I've been busy.'

'Too busy to visit a woman you like? This does not sound like you. I thought you were enjoying getting to know her.'

'Turns out I didn't know her at all,' he grumbled, digging holes in the dirt with the toe of his boot like a petulant child. He'd debated for days about telling his father what had happened, about what he'd learned. Unable to bottle it up any longer, he let it spill out. 'Did you know her father worked at the internment camp?'

His papa froze momentarily. It was the only sign of surprise Matteo could discern. 'At Loveday?'

'Yes! Can you believe that?' Matteo could feel his anger rising up all over again.

His father continued to clean the pump casing. 'She told you that?'

'She did. Freely and unashamedly.'

He stopped working to face Matteo with a quizzical brow. 'Why should she be ashamed?'

'Papa, he was there. While you were imprisoned there.'

'What of it? Many people worked there. Many soldiers.'

'And that's how you know Trevor Burrows? Why you fear him?'

His papa stared out at the river as he rubbed grease from his hands. 'I do not fear Trevor Burrows, Matteo. I just choose to stay away from him. As should you.'

'Papa, please. Why won't you tell me?'

'Matteo, there is no point in looking backwards. We cannot change what has been, only what will be.'

Matteo hated it when his father spouted his philosophical sayings. 'Your letters from the camp, Papa, they didn't tell us much about your time there.'

'There was not much to tell,' he responded quietly.

'I have heard the stories, Papa, out of Cowra and Hay. Some internees, some of the other Italian men I have spoken to, say they were treated poorly by guards.'

'We were lucky to be here in Australia when the war broke out.'

'Lucky? Papa, you were imprisoned for five years for no reason. How is that lucky?'

'My boy, you still have a lot to learn about luck and fate. And what does this have to do with you and Isabel?'

'It just feels … wrong now. Ruined. How can I be with her knowing that her father kept you away from us all those years.'

'She did not work at the camps. It was not Isabel, or even her father, who put me there.'

'Yes, but she kept it from me.'

'Did she deceive you deliberately?'

Matteo dropped his head, digging at one of the shed's wooden posts with the screwdriver he still held. 'She said she didn't remember that he had worked there.'

'She was a child during the war, the same as you. Do you remember much about that time?'

'I remember you weren't there,' Matteo shot back. 'I remember the day they took you away. I remember Mama crying for you every night, I remember us struggling to make ends meet.'

Matteo regretted his words when his father's face crumbled with pain.

'I'm sorry, Papa,' he said, softening. 'I don't say these things to hurt you, but those years were hard for us too. I hated the Australians for what they did to our family.'

'Hate is a slippery slope. Do not let it consume you.'

Matteo couldn't help the knowing smile that touched his lips. 'Mama used to say that to us when we were children and the other kids would bully us.'

'Your mama is a smart and beautiful woman,' his papa said, his own smile peeking out. 'Do you like Isabel?'

'I did,' Matteo responded, frustration filling his tone. 'I do. I still do but I don't know how to get past this.'

He waited for words of wisdom from his father and when nothing came he asked the question that had been plaguing him since he'd last seen Isabel. 'Did you know him? Did you know Sam Hayward when he was a soldier at the internment camp?'

His father didn't look up, just kept on working on the pump, but finally he spoke. 'There were many camps out there. And many soldiers.'

That didn't answer my question.

'And Trevor Burrows was one of them.'

Again, his papa didn't answer. But Matteo pressed on. 'Isabel said Trevor and her father were friends. Does he remember you? Maybe I should go and ask Trevor—?'

'Stay away from Trevor Burrows.' The wrench clattered to the ground. Now he had his father's attention.

'Why?'

'Matteo, just … do it. For me. Please.'

Matteo had always assumed that his father didn't want to talk about his time in the internment camp because of how he was treated there. But now, it felt more like he was holding back for some other reason. Had he known Isabel's father in the camp? If he had, why wouldn't he just say so?

Isabel sat at the bar, tapping her fingers against the wood top. It had been a quiet couple of days. A few truckies had come and gone for overnight accommodation and a meal. Tourists were still passing through on their way to Adelaide, or just to get a look at the shocking beauty of the flooding river. But they generally stayed over in Mildura at one of the bigger hotels like the Grand. Most of the locals were working to shore up levees along the river or preparing to evacuate themselves and their belongings. The peak was still a month away. If business kept up like this, well, they might not lose the hotel to the river, but they could go broke from lack of customers.

The door opened and in came one customer Isabel knew they'd never lose.

'Trevor.' Isabel watched the man wander up to the bar.

'Pint, thanks, Isabel.'

She poured the pint, raising her eyebrows at the thick fold of pounds he pulled from his pocket as he counted out the payment. He was holding a lot of money.

'Win the lottery, Trevor?'

An expression, one Isabel thought looked remarkably like guilt, crossed his features. Features, Isabel noticed now, that looked much older than his years. Sagging, sallow skin drooped from his cheekbones. Red and purple broken capillaries marked his face like a roadmap. Too much booze over too many years. His hair—it used to be light brown, the same as Ross's—was mostly grey and greasy, like he hadn't washed it in a week. Bloodshot eyes, hard eyes, studied her as she put the pint in front of him. When had the laughter gone out of those eyes? She had to think back to the last time she'd seen Trevor Burrows smile. It was hard to believe he was only forty-two years old, still a young man really.

'Thought you'd still be moving furniture,' she said as he dropped himself on a stool at the bar and took a sip of his pint. 'I hear the levees are struggling at Buronga.' She hoped to find out a little more about what was happening near the Sorrentis' house considering how close the Burrows estate was to Matteo's family's farm.

She'd thought Matteo might have calmed down by now. At least enough to see reason, enough to realise that she hadn't deliberately tried to hide her father's connection to the internment camp. No, she had to accept that whatever they'd had was over before it began. But that didn't mean she'd stopped caring about him, or caring about what was happening on their stretch of river.

Trevor shrugged a shoulder. 'Done what we can at the house.' He looked around. 'Where's Audrey?'

'Mum drove out to the Sturt Highway to deliver some food to the police patrol there,' she said. 'The rising creek is due to cover the road any day now, so they've got a twenty-four-hour watch. Poor buggers are stuck sitting in their cold cars all night.'

She watched him for a moment, wondering if what she planned to ask next was a good idea. With her mum out of the hotel for a while, she was free to ask the questions that had been gnawing at her. Finally, her curiosity got the better of her. 'Trevor, you worked with Dad at the Loveday Internment Camp during the war, right?'

He didn't move from his stoop at the bar but his eyes, their little veins of red shooting out of the brown centre, met hers. 'What do you know about Loveday?'

'Nothing,' she said. 'Apart from what Mum told me.'

Suddenly he was all interest. 'Which was what exactly?'

She remembered what Ross said about how his father reacted whenever he was asked about the war and knew she had to tread carefully. 'She just told me that you and Dad were stationed there, at Loveday, during the war. Even Mum didn't know it was an internment camp, a prison.'

'It was secret army business,' Trevor grumbled, slouching over his beer again.

'Really? Well, anyway, I have a friend whose dad was at Loveday. I was wondering if you might remember him.'

'There were a lot of soldiers at Loveday over those years,' he said. 'What was his name and rank?'

'Oh, he wasn't a soldier,' she said, watching Trevor closely. 'He was an inmate.'

Trevor paused mid-sip.

'He was taken there from Adelaide,' she went on. 'Was held there for five years.'

'So? Lots of Japs, Nazis and fascists were kept at the camps. Spies. Place was full of 'em.'

Isabel ground her teeth together. She hated the vitriol that dripped from his tone. 'As I am just discovering.'

'Well, you'd be better off not discovering.'

'I just thought you might have known him, my friend's dad,' Isabel said. 'His name's Carlo. Carlo Sorrenti.'

This time the beer slopped out of his pint glass when his hand jolted.

'Dunno him,' Trevor said, wiping the beer from his hand onto his trousers.

'Oh. Are you sure?' There was something in Trevor's manner that told Isabel he was lying. 'He lives just down the road from here. Quite close to your place actually, in Buronga.'

'Never took much notice of any of the dagos in camp,' he mumbled. 'Prisoners, fascist bastards. Not likely to take notice of them now.'

'They weren't all fascists or spies,' she said, temper leaking into her tone. 'Some were just fathers and husbands stolen from their families, their livelihoods.'

'Look, Isabel, don't go dredging up the war,' Trevor said, his eyes darting left and right around the pub. 'It does no one any good bringing that stuff about Loveday to light.'

'I imagine there are a lot of people who'd be happy to keep that time in our history hidden. And they're doing a good job of it. I didn't even know there was an internment camp down in South Australia during the war. Certainly didn't know Dad worked there with you. But Matteo told me how his papa was dragged away from his home, taken from his family and locked up like a common criminal. All because he had Italian heritage.'

'Well, the government obviously thought he was a threat or they wouldn't have locked him up.' Trevor eyed her now, a sneer crossing his grizzled features. 'Ross said you've been dating some other bloke. Throwing over my boy for some foreigner. Town this size you can't hide anything, girly.'

'I'm not trying to hide anything. And he's not a foreigner.'

'If his old man was interned at Loveday he was an alien enemy. Part of the dago menace. You'd do well to stay away from them. What would your dad say if he knew you were dating the enemy?'

The enemy?

The comment knocked Isabel. 'What a horrible thing to say. Dad never had a problem with Italians, or Greeks, or anyone else for that matter.'

'Whatever. Look, the past is the past. It needs to stay there,' Trevor insisted, swallowing the last of his beer. 'If people didn't keep trying to bring up the past, the damn war, your dad might still be here.'

Isabel blinked. 'What does that mean?'

Trevor looked everywhere except at her. Yeah, he was definitely lying about something.

'What do you know, Trevor?'

'I don't know anything, just …' Trevor scrubbed a hand across his face. His bloodshot eyes held another look now, but Isabel couldn't quite discern it. 'I gotta go.'

Watching him leave, she had more questions than ever.

Perhaps she'd pushed too hard.

If people didn't keep trying to bring up the past, the war, your dad might still be here.

And just what the hell did that mean?

Eleven

It was just after lunch on Friday when the siren wailed. No one in the pub moved at first. It had been going on for days. Sirens wailing day and night in all directions and there was a sense of exhausted helplessness beginning to creep into the psyche of the region. But still, every patron in the bar and dining room fell silent, listening for the code to let them know where the levee had broken.

Isabel gasped when she discerned the siren's code. 'Buronga. The Sorrentis. Mum?'

'Bar's closed!' her mum called, and she rang the big brass bell with gusto. Groans and complaints could be heard from some of the patrons, but her mum's no-nonsense expression soon put an end to that. 'Anyone who's able, get over to Buronga now and see what you can do to help.'

The crowd of customers headed towards the doors and out to their vehicles but not before Audrey assessed their ability to drive.

'Barry, give me your keys, you're walking home,' she said, grabbing at the man's coat pocket before he could make a drunken run for it.

'But it's pissing rain!' Barry complained.

'You made of sugar, Barry? Walk home or come with us to Buronga to help out.'

His grumbling continued as he ran—or rather staggered—out into the pelting rain.

'Artie, we're calling your wife. Bella?'

'Got it!' she said and picked up the phone to be connected to Artie's wife in Mildura.

When everyone was out, Isabel and her mum donned coats and boots and headed out to the truck to make the short drive to Buronga.

'Mum, it's teeming,' Isabel said. Her heart was racing. The rain had barely let up all day but now it seemed to be getting heavier.

'Let's just see what we see,' her mum said. Her calm voice soothed Isabel's panic a little but what they saw when they arrived at the long road that led down to the Sorrentis' sent a wave of dread rushing over her.

'Oh, Mum.'

Before they'd even reached the Sorrentis' they could see the devastation as the water surrounded the Burrows' double-storey home. Shirley's prized roses that lined the path up to the front door were now a foot under water. Behind the house, the expensive levee had crumbled like a child's sandcastle at high tide; the old railway sleepers had been lifted by the strength of the inundation and tossed through the large glass windows of the home that had provided such a stunning view across the now drowning orange groves and the usually serene river below. Water was pouring in through smashed windows and had risen halfway up the ground floor. As they passed the driveway, she caught a quick glimpse of Ross and his mother, standing beside their usually spotless sedan that was now muddy up to the doorhandles. All the money in the world hadn't helped the Burrows beat back the river any better than the levees the lowly farmers beside them had built by hand.

Audrey carefully moved the ute further down the muddy incline and eventually had to park a few hundred feet away from the Sorrentis' house thanks to the number of other vehicles that lined the dirt road leading down towards the small collection of farmhouses. Even from there they could easily see the utter devastation that had befallen the farmers and families of the low-lying flats.

Tractors pulled trailers full of furniture and belongings of those lucky enough to have already been evacuating before the levee broke.

Walking quickly towards the Sorrentis' home, Isabel scanned the huge gathering of people for the person she most wanted to see. With so many hooded parkas and umbrellas it was a challenge to see faces. Pushing her way through the crowd, she saw Loretta first, standing under the verandah of a shed.

'Loretta!' she called and rushed to her.

'Oh, Isabel.' The woman was soaked to the skin and holding little Lucia close inside her raincoat as she did her best to shelter the screaming baby from the rain. 'It's so awful. The house is filling with water.'

'Where's Antonio?' she asked, throwing one of the blankets she'd brought from the car around Loretta's shoulders.

'He's inside with Mama trying to empty the house,' she said, her pretty face etched with worry.

'What about Mr Sorrenti and … Matteo?'

'The last I saw them they were running towards the levee.'

Isabel peered through the rain at the gaping hole in the dirt wall, but she couldn't pick either Matteo or Carlo from the large group of parka-clad men who moved about in a hive of activity, in a futile effort to plug the hole. Wishing she could go down there and find Matteo, instead Isabel turned towards the little fibro house that was already surrounded by knee-deep muddy water. Sandbags were askew, or hidden completely under water, as the torrent of the river had shoved them aside like they'd weighed nothing.

'Isabel! Wait!

She heard her mother's worried shouts as she began to run towards the house, but she didn't stop. She had to go, had to help. Slowly she waded in, gasping as the icy water hit her calves above her favourite pair of boots. The gumboots she'd forgotten to put on would have been more hindrance than help as the water came up to her knees even before she'd reached the verandah.

As she stepped up onto the wooden decking, she saw a line of people handing belongings out of the house, passing smaller items to each other until they reached utes and trucks. Larger pieces of furniture were being carted by several men to higher ground.

A small table appeared through the open front door and with it came Antonio.

'Isabel?' He looked surprised to see her. 'What are you doing here?'

'We closed the pub when we heard the sirens,' she said, brushing her soaked hair from her eyes as her mother joined her. 'What can we do to help?'

'Mama is inside. She won't leave,' Antonio said, his face etched with concern. 'She wants to take everything from the kitchen. It happened so fast. One minute we were eating lunch, the next we heard this almighty noise, like a freight train was coming for the house. The sirens sounded and then water started coming in under the floorboards, through the doors. Mama's credenza in the hallway washed all the way to the kitchen when the door flew open with the water. We had no time to do anything, but Papa and Matteo waded out to see what they could do. There is nothing to do. It is lost.'

She stroked Antonio's shoulder in comfort, then pushed past him and other folks who were helping to empty what they could from the house, and into the house with her mum now on her heels. They found Gia alone in the kitchen loading boxes. Muddy water swirled around her knees as she moved about the room.

'Mrs Sorrenti,' Isabel called, horrified at the state of the house and the woman who was wading in the cold water in only her dress. 'We have to go. The water is rising too fast.'

'I need to get all of my cookware,' she insisted, trying to open lower cupboards that wouldn't budge against the pressure of the water. 'And my linen and lace, please, they have been in the family for generations. I won't leave them.'

'Mrs Sorrenti, please,' Isabel begged. 'Your family needs you to be safe.'

That got her attention. She looked around at her kitchen, her eyes filling with tears. 'Where is my Carlo?'

'He and Matteo are down at the levee; they'll be back soon.' At least Isabel hoped they'd be back soon.

Isabel's mum grabbed a half-filled crate and began loading what she could carry into it. 'Isabel, take that tablecloth and pile into it whatever you can carry from the top cupboards. Mrs Sorrenti, the pots and pans won't break. We can come back for them later when the water calms.'

Snapping back into action, Gia took hold of what she could carry and with arms laden and the tablecloth full of linen slung over Isabel's shoulder, the three women made their way out of the house.

'Mama!'

'Matteo!' Isabel heard Gia call. 'Is your papa still at the levee?'

'Not anymore.' Carlo walked around from the back of the house.

When Isabel waded out the front door of the doomed house, she saw Matteo stop when he spotted her. The men were drenched head to toe and covered in mud.

'Isabel? What are you doing here?' Matteo asked.

She couldn't tell if it was shock or annoyance she saw on his face.

'I came …' She gestured to her mother. 'We came, to help.'

'It is too late to save the house,' Carlo said to Gia. 'There is too much water.'

Isabel's heart broke as Carlo took Gia's tear-streaked face in his hands and kissed her forehead.

'*Mi amore*, it is time to go.'

All they could do was watch.

Gardens disappeared beneath the water as the river continued to gush in and rise up the small incline, home after home succumbing to the rising waters.

The rain finally slowed mid-afternoon and as evening came, an even darker gloom descended as farmers surveyed the lake that had overtaken their homes, their crops, their glasshouses.

'What do we do now?' Gia asked, her face a picture of grief as they surveyed what was left of their home. Mud and water had flowed through the house, but the inundation had slowed now that the levee break had widened, and the water had reached its highest possible point. 'We have nowhere to live.'

'There is the migrant camp on the other side of the river, on Walnut Avenue,' Carlo said with a heavy sigh. 'We should go there.'

Isabel grimaced. They couldn't go to that place. There were already so many people there who'd been flooded out of their homes. Regardless of what had passed between them, she couldn't bear the thought of Matteo, or his family, being forced to squeeze into the shelter.

'Mum …' Isabel's eyes begged.

'Way ahead of you, sweetheart.' Her mum nodded, rubbing Isabel's shoulder. 'Mr Sorrenti, Mrs Sorrenti.'

Carlo and Gia turned away from the disaster that was their home, their livelihood.

'You can come to the hotel. One of the bungalows is free. We don't have as many travellers staying since the roadblocks have gone up over at Euston to stop the rubber-necking tourists. It's a little small. It has only one double bed. But we have some fold-out cots we can set up.'

Isabel looked hopefully at Matteo. He hadn't spoken to her, barely even looked at her, since he'd first seen her. 'I am happy to sleep on a cot,' he offered.

'Thank you, Mrs Hayward,' Carlo said sombrely. 'But we couldn't impose.'

'Impose?' Isabel piped up. 'You wouldn't be imposing. And I can share with Mum so Loretta and Antonio can have my bedroom. She shouldn't be sleeping rough with the new baby to come—' Isabel realised her mistake too late as four pairs of eyes, filled with surprise and confusion, turned to land on Loretta, who still snuggled Lucia under the blanket Isabel had given her.

'*Bambino*?' Gia turned to glare at her son. 'Antonio, you didn't tell us?'

Antonio was staring wide-eyed in shock at his wife, before his eyes dropped to her belly. 'I didn't know.'

'I'm sorry.' Isabel slapped a hand to her mouth, horrified. She'd just let slip with family news. News she should not have known. Especially before the father. 'I'm so sorry, I …'

But suddenly the sadness and despair that had weighed heavily on the family just a moment before turned to elation and cheers of congratulations as the Sorrenti family and their friends surrounded Loretta and Antonio.

Isabel felt her mum's arm go around her and together they watched the lovely family scene.

'I think you did a good thing, Bella. They needed the boost.'

'I didn't mean to,' Isabel said, making a face as she watched Matteo move in to hug his brother and sister-in-law.

'Mrs Hayward.' Carlo approached them. 'I am sorry. I was ungracious just now. We are honoured by your kind offer for lodging. We will stay for one night until we can find alternative arrangements.'

'Whatever you say, Mr Sorrenti.'

Isabel smiled. She knew her mum would simply coerce and outmanoeuvre the Sorrentis and they would stay as long as they needed to. Nervously, she glanced across at Matteo who stood back from the family, watching her with a look she couldn't read.

'Please, I am Carlo,' he said, and he took his wife's hand as she joined him. 'And this is Gia. We don't know how to thank you.'

'Pleased to meet you both. Isabel speaks very highly of you all. I'm Audrey.'

'*Grazie*, Audrey.' Gia nodded and in a quick change of temperament she began shouting orders at her family. '*Andiamo*. We go to the hotel. Boys, get those things into the truck. Do not forget my mother's lace.' She turned back to Matteo. 'And you, you need a shave.'

'*Mama!*' Matteo whined. 'I've been a little busy, eh?'

'That is no excuse.'

The men sprang into action and soon the trucks, including Isabel and her mum's, were filled to capacity with everything they'd been able to save from the house, as well as crates full of vegetables salvaged from storage sheds before the river took them over.

When they arrived in convoy at the hotel, Isabel directed the Sorrentis to their accommodation. Her mum dug out sheets, blankets and towels and helped Gia make the bungalow liveable, while Isabel swapped the sheets on her own bed for Antonio and Loretta. Matteo and Antonio had gone out to the shed to dig out Isabel's old baby cot and, after they removed the spider webs from the antique iron crib and gave it a quick wipe down, little Lucia was asleep the moment her body hit the mattress of folded blankets. Then Isabel and her mum left the Sorrentis to get settled. The family needed time alone to come to terms with their loss and to sort through the truckload of belongings they had managed to save.

Back in the kitchen, Isabel was thankful she'd prepared the menu for dinner service earlier that day before the levee had broken at Buronga—had it really just been that afternoon?—and was able to have everything cooked as the first of the dinner crowd arrived.

Two hours later, she was just filling her water glass at the bar when the sudden and very obvious lull in conversation had her glancing up.

Carlo and Gia stood at the doorway of the dining room with Antonio and Loretta, baby Lucia now wide awake on her hip. Casting her eyes about the room, Isabel couldn't miss the glares and sneers some of the patrons were sending the Sorrentis' way.

'Mr and Mrs Sorrenti!' she called out, walking out from behind the bar. 'Welcome. Table for four and one highchair?'

She tickled little Lucia's belly, making her laugh.

'Perhaps we should get something to take back to our rooms,' Carlo said quietly, his eyes casting about the busy pub the way Isabel's had.

'Nonsense,' she insisted.

Isabel led the family across the room to a table that was set for four, passing by Mrs Watson and her husband Stan. The look of disgust on the old woman's puckered-up face as she followed the Sorrentis' path across the dining room had Isabel scowling at her.

'You're not eating, Mrs Watson,' Isabel said, ensuring she put censure into the carefree tone of her voice. 'Is the food not to your liking this evening? See, how it works is, you open and *close* your mouth to chew.'

The woman's mouth snapped shut at the insult.

'It's not the food,' the old woman grizzled in her nasal voice as she stood and took her purse that was slung over the back of her chair. 'My boy fought the Italians in the war. Come on, Stan. We're leaving. I've lost my appetite.'

'Sit down, Gladys, I haven't finished my dinner.' Stan continued to read his paper as he chewed on a forkful of fish, but he looked up once Gladys's sizeable bottom hit the chair again. 'Cod is as good as it's ever been, Isabel.'

Isabel smiled. 'Thank you, Mr Watson, it's the special herbs I put in with the butter.'

'Herbs, you say?'

'Yes, herbs from the Sorrentis' farm actually,' Isabel added, waving a hand towards the family. She winked at Stan. 'How about I get you another pint once I've settled these lovely people at their table?'

Stan smiled broadly. 'Sounds like a great plan, love. Ta.'

Rodney Jamison made a show of slamming his pint glass against the bar and leaving with a parting shot of 'Bloody dagos'.

'Guess you'll be drinking back in Victoria from now on then, Rod. Enjoy the six o'clock swill,' Isabel's mum called after him. 'Anyone else got something to say?' She paused. 'No? Good. Dessert is on the house.'

'What's for dessert?' Bert Bagshaw asked from his seat at the bar.

'Lemon meringue pie,' Isabel called back.

'You haven't had a meal, Bert, you don't get dessert,' Audrey told him.

'Well, if I'd known dessert was on the house I would have had a meal.'

Isabel left her mum arguing good-naturedly with Bert and seated the Sorrentis as conversations started again and patrons went back to eating their dinner.

'I like this one, Matteo,' Gia said, one eyebrow raised. 'I like this one a lot. She has strength.'

Isabel shrugged a shoulder. 'Can't be a weakling when you run a pub.'

'Can't run a restaurant if you give away all the food either,' Gia said with disapproval.

'We're used to this sort of … welcome,' Antonio mumbled sarcastically. 'Happens all the time.'

'But it shouldn't,' Isabel insisted. 'And I won't tolerate it in my place. Neither will Mum. Now, what can I get you for dinner? We're serving cod with herbed butter and green beans from a local Buronga market garden I once knew.' She gave Carlo a sympathetic look and a shoulder rub. 'Or lamb chops baked in tomato sugo and mashed potato.'

'I'll have the lamb,' Antonio and Matteo said together.

The others ordered their meals and, trying her best to ignore Matteo's confused and suspicious glances, Isabel went back to the kitchen where she got to work frying more cod before pulling out the tray of lamb chops baking in the sugo in the oven.

Hearing the door to the bar swing open, she looked up, surprised to see Gia.

'Is something wrong, Mrs Sorrenti?'

'I thought you might need some help,' Gia said, her hands clasping and unclasping in front of her.

'Thank you but I have everything under control,' Isabel said with a nervous smile. 'Please go and relax with your family.'

'I am used to doing. I need to keep busy or I will lose what is left of my mind. Please.'

Realising Gia wasn't used to being waited on, Isabel looked around. 'You could check the cod for me while I mash some more potato.'

'Of course.' Gia took an apron off the peg and moved to the stove.

The door swung open again and her mother stepped in. 'A couple of truckies have arrived. We need one cod and two lamb chops.'

'I will handle the cod,' Gia offered, going to the Coolgardie safe to take out more fish.

'Thank you,' Isabel said as she finished plating up. 'Mum, can you take these out to the Sorrentis, please?'

Isabel stood for a moment after her mother had left and watched Gia Sorrenti move about the kitchen like the expert chef she was. Isabel knew she could learn so much from her. How could she possibly ask Gia to teach her now, with everything that had happened to them?

Wiping the sweat from her brow, Isabel leaned back against the bench. The dinner shift was finally over. What a mentally, physically and emotionally exhausting day it had been.

Despite Isabel's rejection of her offer, Mrs Sorrenti had insisted on doing the dishes. Desperate for some fresh air and a moment away from the kitchen, Isabel grabbed her coat and, slipping it over her filthy apron, stepped out the back door. The rain had stopped altogether, and she was almost sorry. She could have used the cool trickle of rain on her warm face.

Walking slowly out into the night, she let her mind wander. Since they'd left the Sorrentis' farm, she hadn't spoken more than a few words to Matteo, nor he to her. She had hoped that after a few days he would realise that she hadn't deliberately set out to hurt him. Why did children so often bear the brunt of the sins of their parents? And what had her father's sin been anyway? Had there even been a sin? So he was in the army, so he had been posted to an internment camp. She'd since learned that the camps had been staffed by veterans from the First World War as well as men who were unfit to go overseas to the fighting. All she remembered of that time was how happy she'd felt each time he'd come home on furlough. He was her dad and she'd worshipped him until … until she hadn't.

She wandered down towards the creek. The levee patrol—made up of Gol Gol townsfolk—were doing their rounds. She passed Mr Walker from the general store as he leaned against a tree under a kerosene lamp, huddled into his coat, smoking a cigarette and staring up at the wall of dirt and hessian bags.

'Evening, Mr Walker,' she said wearily as she passed.

'Isabel.' He nodded in greeting. 'Don't get too close to the creek now. It's been rising all day with all that rain.'

'I'll be okay,' she said, and she walked along the levee wall towards a collection of sandbags piled up, at the ready in case the levee should begin to fail. Making sure her waterproof coat was spread beneath her bottom, she sat on the pile of sandbags and stared out across the dark swirling waters only a few feet away.

It had risen, Isabel thought. A lot. Her favourite tree swing now floated uselessly on top of the water. How she'd loved to play here as a girl. Her dad had made her that swing.

She frowned as the memory pushed its way in.

She'd been on her swing, waiting patiently—or more likely impatiently—until he'd fixed whatever had broken around the hotel while he'd been away. Waited until he could push her on that swing. What had happened that day—the woman in the bright red dress with the shiny black car—had made no sense to her at the time.

But years later, it had meant everything.

Twelve

Matteo tapped his fingers against the table where he'd sat and had dinner with his family, his eyes glued to the kitchen door. He'd waited and waited but Isabel never came out again.

The fierceness with which she had defended his family when they'd walked into her pub shouldn't have surprised him. But given the things he'd said to her, the way he'd treated her the last time they'd seen each other, well, she had every right to ignore him, and to let the bigots have their say. He should have known by now that Isabel Hayward wasn't built that way. Despite his recent hostility towards her, on hearing the siren announcing the levee break, she'd closed the pub and driven herself and her mother down to Buronga to help them evacuate. Then, when they'd lost their house, she'd offered them hers.

Time, and the talk earlier in the week with his papa, had lessened his anger enough that he could see he'd been wrong—terribly wrong—to accuse her of lying. Wrong to accuse her of knowing all along that her father had worked at the Loveday camp, or even worse, that he'd had anything at all to do with Papa being imprisoned.

He still had questions. He'd *always* had questions about his papa's time in the camp, but it was his papa who needed to answer them, not Isabel. He wanted to talk to her. He needed to talk to her, but she hadn't come out of the kitchen. Instead, his mama had gone into the kitchen.

She'd simply stood and said, 'I go to help Isabel. Behave yourselves.'

At the end of the meal, Antonio and Loretta had taken Lucia off to bed, and when his papa stood to go out to the bungalow, Matteo began to follow.

'Don't you have someone to talk to?' his papa asked, looking pointedly towards the kitchen door. 'And send your mama out soon too; she needs rest after today.'

Matteo watched his papa leave the pub and stood where he was, surveying the bar. It was getting late and only a few barflies were in residence on stools, nursing their ale like it was a beloved family member.

Scanning the room, Matteo recognised Len Canarvon. It wasn't hard since the man, now in his late sixties, refused to wear anything but his khaki army uniform. Like him, it had seen better days. Len had served his country, not during the last war, but in the first one, and now spent his days leaning up against whatever bar he could find.

Matteo stepped up to the bar. The old man turned to sneer at him, mumbling something about dark-skinned thieves. He'd felt sympathy for the man a moment ago. Now? Not so much. Ignoring him, Matteo waited until Isabel's mum had finished serving a pint to the truckie at the end of the counter.

'You the one's got your eye on our pretty cook?'

Matteo groaned inwardly and turned his head towards the man at the other end of the bar. He appeared to be in his mid-fifties, and thankfully not too drunk by the looks of him, but Matteo was wary just the same.

'I might be. Is that a problem for you?'

'Can't say it is.' The man gave a one-shouldered shrug and puffed out smoke with a raspy cough. 'Can't speak for others 'round 'ere though.'

Matteo followed the man's glance back towards Len Canarvon.

'You Greek?'

'Actually, I'm Australian,' Matteo said, reciting his usual line.

'But your kin—your family—comes from one of them south European countries, right?'

'Italy.' Matteo prepared himself for the abuse that was bound to come.

Instead, the man surprised him. 'Better off being from Italy than from Adelaide, in my opinion. Bloody South Australians. Worse than Queenslanders.'

Matteo smiled, amused if not a little perplexed. 'Okay.' Good thing he hadn't told the man he'd been born in Adelaide.

He took a small step back, still prepared to defend himself if need be, when the man got up from his stool and brought his beer over to stand next to him at the bar.

'Name's Bagshaw. Used to be I could bag a girl for sure.'

The man laughed uproariously at his own joke, before falling into a coughing fit as Matteo reluctantly shook the hand he offered.

Bagshaw settled on the stool at the bar, taking a long swallow of his beer. 'Yep. Met me a nice girl in Italy during the war. Good-looking sheila, she was. Father ran a sort of butcher store in Florence. Did good sliced meat, good spice to them.'

Understanding the man meant him no harm, Matteo found himself mildly entertained by Bagshaw's story and, using the distraction, he relaxed, leaning an elbow on the bar.

'Spring of forty-five, I reckon it was, this sheila and I took off one day down to the coast,' the man went on, lighting another cigarette before offering one to Matteo. He shook his head. 'Wanted to see that leaning tower thingy everyone had heard so much about. There wasn't much fighting going on by then, so we figured it was safe. Got back later that night and her dad, the butcher, came after me with one of them big knives he used for cutting up meat.'

'What did you do?' Matteo felt obliged to ask.

'Ran for me bloody life, didn't I!' Bagshaw slapped his knee. 'He was set to butchering me. Nearly ended up on the tables of fine Eye-talian folks right there in Florence.'

The clang of the big brass bell made Matteo jump and he turned just as Isabel's mama stepped up to the bar in front of them.

'Where's the onions to go with this tripe?' she asked Bagshaw with a shake of her head.

'C'mon, Audrey. I'm telling Isabel's beau here about my time in his home country.'

It wasn't his home country, as Matteo had already stated, but he let it go. No point arguing with a man who was—what was the Aussie slang term?—three sheets to the wind.

Audrey rolled her eyes. 'Bert, you've been telling that load of codswallop to anyone who'll listen for nigh on five years.'

'It's God's honest truth.' Bert thumped his fist on the bar, then put his hand across his heart. 'Shame about the sheila. Never did see her again. She was a looker too. They were all lookers, them Eye-talian sheilas.'

Audrey snorted out a laugh. 'Leave the poor bloke alone, Bert, finish your beer, then out you go. You heard the bell. Last drinks.'

'Alright, alright, I'm just finishing this one and warning our mate here to behave himself with our girl or I'll come after *him* with a butcher's knife.'

'Well, she's not your girl, she's mine.' Audrey whipped Bert's unfinished beer out from under his arm and tipped it down the sink to his very verbal disgust. 'Bar's closed, Bert.'

'You're a cruel woman, Audrey.'

'Not as cruel as your wife, so get on your way or Margie will be down here with her rolling pin again. Now get. I've got cleaning to do.'

'It was nice talking with you,' Matteo said with a nod to his bar companion.

'You be good to that girl now, ya hear?' Bert gave him a warning shake of his finger. 'Makes damn good meat pies does that one.'

'Yes, sir.'

Bert mumbled his way out the door.

'Will he be alright?' Matteo asked as Bert, drunker than Matteo had realised, staggered into the doorframe with a sickening crack before finally making it outside.

Audrey started wiping off the bar. 'It's a short walk home for him. He'll be right as long as he doesn't fall into the river.' She stopped cleaning and looked at Matteo, a little frown of concern between her brows. 'Did he really threaten you with a butcher's knife?'

'No,' Matteo said with a chuckle but then he stopped and narrowed his eyes thoughtfully. 'At least, I didn't think that's where he was going with the story.'

She chuckled. 'Why don't you head on out to bed? Isabel put some extra blankets in the bungalow for you all. Gets cold out there.'

The mention of Isabel reminded him of his original mission. 'I'm under orders to find my mama and send her to bed.'

'She's just finishing up the dishes.' Audrey inclined her head towards the kitchen door. 'Why don't you pop in there and give Isabel a hand? Your mama has been a great help.'

She was being so nice to him it made him feel guilty. Had Isabel told her mother what a stupid, immature idiot he'd been?

When he stepped into the kitchen, his mama was just finishing drying the last pot.

'You know when to show your face.' She shot him a look of censure.

'Papa wants you to go to bed.'

She studied him with narrowed eyes. 'You should get some sleep too. You look dead.'

'Thanks, Mama.' He rolled his eyes. 'Is Isabel about?'

'She went outside to get some fresh air.'

Matteo looked towards the door that led out of the pub kitchen.

'She works hard, that girl.' High praise from his mama. She poured lemonade and handed him the glass and a cheese sandwich. 'Take this to her. She did not eat tonight.'

Matteo headed out the back door. It took a moment for his eyes to adjust to the darkness. Clouds disclosed only a hint of the moon, casting an eerie glow over the tall river gums down the hill in the distance, their broad trunks surrounded by dark water. The spreading river had reached the raised mound of dirt that formed a semi-circle around the pub. Two men patrolled the barrier and he nodded to them as he passed. The night shift, watching over the wall of dirt and sandbags, ready to raise the alarm should the levee start to leak. The scant light of kerosene lanterns, set at intervals along the levee, lit his way down the hill.

His papa's Fergie tractor was parked nearby. They'd used it to tow the trailer full of their belongings from their property. If there were no breaches on the levee tonight, the Fergie would rumble to life in the morning to help build up the new stretch of dirt wall up towards the back of the bakery. He'd overheard talk in the pub while they'd been eating dinner that the river was quickly backfilling the usually thin slice of estuary that was the Gol Gol

Creek. The bakery and other homes near the Sturt Highway were now very much under threat.

In the small spray of light from the kerosene lamps, he could see the water in the creek, deceptively calm in the darkness, a sneaky living organism, rising at a rate so slow you could barely discern it, as it gobbled up the grassy banks.

Walking along the edge of the creek, he spotted Isabel sitting on top of a pile of sandbags. The family of willows that would once have lined the edge of the estuary was now surrounded, their weeping green fingers dipping in and out of the water. He could hear frogs and bugs, thriving in the flooded inlet. In the near distance, a little wooden swing attached to a box tree floated on top of the dark water, its ropes straining as the river threatened to steal away its innocence.

'Mama said to bring you this.'

She jumped at his voice but didn't turn her head.

He stepped closer, handing her the glass and sandwich. She took a sip of soft drink but didn't unwrap the sandwich.

'May I sit?' he asked.

She just shrugged.

He took a seat beside her. The sandbags were cold and wet, but it didn't seem to worry her. She still wore her white kitchen apron under her coat, splatters of grease and food testament to the busy dinner rush she'd just endured. He took a peek at her face. She looked tired, and a little sad. It shamed him to know he was the cause of it.

'Isabel, I wanted to come and apologise for my behaviour. It was a shock to me, what you told me about your father. But it was wrong of me to react the way I did. To accuse you of lying to me.'

She nodded solemnly but didn't speak.

'I was angry. But more, I was frustrated. I know next to nothing about my father's time in the internment camp. He refuses to speak of it. Italians at the club, in our community, some of them talk about escaping or surviving the camps in Europe. It pains me to think that same mistreatment could have gone on here in the camps but my father, he says nothing. I can only assume the worst. Why else would he refuse to speak of it?'

She finally met his eyes. 'Did you ask him if he knew my father?'

'He didn't say. He *wouldn't* say,' Matteo said, feeling that same frustration rising again. 'He said there were a lot of camps, a lot of guards. I asked him about Trevor Burrows.'

'And?'

'He didn't confirm that he knew Trevor at Loveday, but I think he must have. I think there is something about Trevor that he won't tell me. He has this fear of the man,' Matteo said.

Isabel nodded. 'Mum said Trevor was definitely a guard at Loveday with my dad. I asked if Dad had ever spoken about your papa. She didn't think so. Matteo, I don't know if my father …' She hesitated, and he could see the pain that her own imagination was causing her. He realised that like him, she knew very little about her father's life during the war years. Was she wondering what horrible things her father might have done in the camps? And it was worse for her. She could never ask Sam Hayward about those years. He'd died before she'd had the chance.

'My father was not a saint,' she started again. 'I don't think I knew him, really knew him. At least, not enough to say what he was, or was not, capable of. I don't know if he could have mistreated anyone. If there were things he'd done at the camp …' She paused. 'When he came home, when the camps closed, he was distant. He drank a lot. I could see my mother was worried. They began fighting. I'm sure they thought I didn't know, but when you live in such close quarters in the hotel it's impossible to hide raised voices. Then one day he stopped drinking, started helping around the pub again. Things got better between him and Mum and we were happy for a while. Then he was gone.'

'You never told me how he died.'

She looked away into the darkness and Matteo almost wished he hadn't brought it up.

'He didn't die.'

Matteo looked confused. 'I'm sorry, I assumed … the way you speak of him, it sounded like he was dead.'

'He may as well be.'

It was rare to hear so much bitterness in her voice, Matteo realised. She was always so positive and light-hearted.

'I'm sorry. I know I made it sound like he had died but …' She sniffed, then wiped her wet cheeks on her sleeve. 'He left us. I came home from school the day of my sixteenth birthday and he wasn't home. It wasn't unusual. He sometimes went fishing or I thought maybe he was just in town getting more party supplies. I was throwing a party here at the pub with all my school friends, just down there.'

Matteo looked across to where she pointed. A stretch of land below the pub where gum trees stood. Land that was now several feet under river water.

'It was a hot day. We were swimming in the river, swinging off the rope. I kept looking for him, kept waiting for him to show up with some grand present, some grand gesture. He'd always been so good at birthdays. Hours passed; we couldn't wait for him any longer to light the candles and cut the cake. When the party was over, and everyone had gone home, I was pretty angry. Mum was angry. We waited up late, waited for him to come home. When he didn't, I was devastated. I stayed strong for Mum but I cried myself to sleep for days as we waited for him to come back. He'd left no note, no reason for his disappearance. Mum just assumed he'd gone on one of his benders again, but I didn't believe it.

Trevor came into the pub the next day—they'd usually go on a bender together, but he said he hadn't seen him. Dad may have stopped drinking, but … as the days passed and we still heard nothing from him, I began to wonder if he'd left us for another woman.'

'What would make you think that?'

'I know he had at least one affair while he was down in Loveday.'

'Did you ever go down there to the camp to visit your father?'

'No, we never went there.'

'Then how do you know he was having an affair there?'

'I've been sitting here, thinking, trying to remember those years during the war, when Dad would have been working at Loveday. I was so young when he went away to work for the army, at first I don't think I really noticed that much. Time works differently when you're little.'

Matteo nodded.

'But as I got older, towards the end of the war, I began to understand it all better,' she went on. 'He'd come home for short periods, and I would spend time with him and I got to know him again, I got to have my dad around to do fun things with. We were inseparable when he was back.' Her smile beamed out for a moment, and faded away just as quickly as she went on. 'And then he'd go away again. I always felt so sad, so upset that he would have to go. If I really let myself think about it, I must have been a horror to live with. I whined to my mum. God, when I think about it now I was awful to her whenever he went away. I just wanted him to stay with us. Why couldn't he stay with us?'

Matteo knew that feeling all too well. Her father may not have been interned. He may have been allowed to come home. But those war years had damaged her relationship with her papa as much as it had damaged his relationship with his.

'Mum would say that we were the lucky ones, and she was right. I lost count of how many families lost their fathers, their brothers, uncles. Every day, someone came into the pub with a story of loss. She'd say we were lucky that Dad was not in Europe or Asia somewhere, fighting on the front lines or in some horrible prisoner of war camp.' She gasped, eyes wide with horror and guilt as she looked at him. 'Sorry, Matteo, I didn't mean …'

Matteo shook his head. 'My papa said almost those exact words to me the other day. He said we were lucky to be in Australia when the war broke out. We were children, Isabel. We just wanted our papas with us. What's wrong with that?'

She glanced across at the swing, floating on the water, straining against the current.

'My dad made that swing for me when I was nine,' she said. A wistful grin, full of memories, brightened her features for a moment. 'I'd twist myself in circles, the ropes wrapping themselves around each other, then I'd lift my feet and spin and spin, watching the river go by until I was dizzy. Dad used to push me so high, if I let go, I would have flown right into the creek. It was terrifying and exhilarating. By then he was my best friend, my hero.' Her features darkened again. 'Until the day I saw *her*.'

She stood up and walked to the edge of the water where the levee hadn't been completed.

'I was here on my swing when I saw the car pull up. Big, shiny, black thing.' She turned to look back up to the pub car park, as though she was seeing it all again. 'Dad was chopping wood and he stopped when she called his name. She got out of the car and walked towards him. Red dress, dark hair, that's what I remember. She looked … expensive, at least to a nine-year-old's eye. Dad took her arm and all but dragged her back to the car. I don't think he remembered that I was there, waiting for him to push me on the swing. I'd never seen the woman before but she looked angrier than a cut snake as he hauled her back across to her car. A paddle steamer blew its horn out on the river and blocked out a lot of what was said, but then she kissed him. Full on the mouth. Even a child knows something is wrong when her dad kisses a woman like that who isn't her mum. I remember feeling sick in my stomach. Living in a pub you hear some colourful language, you can't help it, but what that woman said, the accusations she hurled at him before she drove away, I reckon they'd have made Bert Bagshaw blush.'

Isabel turned back to him. 'I can still remember the look of horror, the look of guilt on Dad's face, when he turned back and saw me sitting there on the swing, watching him. He'd definitely forgotten I was there. I don't think I fully understood then what was happening. It wasn't until a few days after my sixteenth birthday that I remembered that day. That's when I knew he'd left us. For her? I don't know. I'll probably never know.'

'I'm sorry.'

'It hurt, you know?' Tears streaked her face now and she was shivering in the cold. 'We weren't enough to keep him happy, to keep him here. I wasn't enough.'

He stood and walked to her, took her by the arms. 'No, Isabel. You can't blame yourself for your father's actions.'

'For years I beat myself up over him,' she said, dropping her head. 'I wasn't fun enough, I wasn't a good enough daughter. He would have wanted a son, right? Men want sons, not little girls. I was a disappointment.'

'No,' Matteo demanded. 'You stop that now. You must know his leaving had nothing, nothing to do with you.'

Isabel had never wanted to talk about her father and now he understood why. His papa may have been taken away from his family, but hers had left of his own accord.

'But why would he leave my mum? She loved him. We loved him.'

He pulled her in, held her against him. 'No one can truly know what happens between a husband and wife. You had no control over that. I don't know your mama well, but I can see she is a strong and independent woman. She cares about you.' He lifted her face to his, wiping her tears with his thumbs. 'And so do I. That is all you need to know now. You are cared for. You are loved.'

Surprise crossed her features. In fact, he'd surprised himself with his accidental admission. It was too soon, wasn't it? Too soon to know he was in love with her.

'Matteo, I am sorry that your father had to go through what he did. Being separated from his family, being locked up for no reason other than because of where he was born.'

'My father was quite baffled when I told him that I didn't think I should see you anymore.' He took her hand, linked his fingers with hers. 'That I blamed you, blamed your father, for something I knew nothing about. I only hope my misplaced anger hasn't ruined what you and I have between us. I've missed you this past week.'

She smiled. 'I've missed you too.'

He lifted her hand and kissed her knuckles, before leaning in and pressing his lips to hers, lightly at first. As he felt her reciprocate, he moved his hand to her cheek and deepened the kiss. He wanted to be tender with her. She'd been so fragile when he'd found her sitting here alone. But his blood was rushing, and when he felt her press herself to him he could feel the thumping of her heart against his chest, matching the beat of his. He'd wondered if it was too soon to know it was love, but her kiss, her reaction, made him question how it couldn't be.

He took his lips on a journey across her cheek to her ear and throat. Her scent was sweet and sweaty, a wonderful smell that tugged at him, made him wish they could slip away somewhere and be together so he could show her just how much she was loved. His mouth found hers again and his control was a thin, taut line waiting to snap when her hands swept up his back, pulling him closer still.

They stood embracing, kissing, surrounded by the night, the sounds of the river lapping. When he felt her shiver again, Matteo pulled back despite her trying to hold on.

'You're cold,' he said, rubbing her shoulders.

She shook her head, reached for him again.

He smiled and took both her hands in his, kissing each of them. 'We must go inside or they'll find our frozen bodies here in the morning.'

Wrapping his arm around her, he walked her back up to the kitchen door of the pub. He turned, looked into her bright green eyes. Eyes that even in the pale light emanating from the hotel windows mirrored his own desires.

He pressed his forehead to hers, kissed her lips one last time. 'I wish I didn't have to say goodnight to you.' Using every inch of willpower he had, he stepped back, ready to head to the bungalow he'd be sharing with his parents. 'Tomorrow, we will go to the property and see if I can tow my caravan out of the mud.'

'Oh!' Isabel's hand went to her mouth.

'What? What is it?'

'I forgot to get the old folding bed out of storage. With everything going on and then dinner …' She looked thoughtful for a moment then, grinning, she took his hand and pulled him around to the door to the residence and inside into the warmth of the hotel and through to the living room.

Isabel's mother was just wandering through to her bedroom. 'I've just helped Loretta warm some milk for the baby. She's such a darling little girl. Oh, Matteo!' Her confused glance flicked to Isabel. 'Matteo, aren't you sleeping out in the bungalow?'

'I forgot to get the camp bed out,' Isabel explained. 'Matteo can sleep here on the couch.'

'It will just be for tonight, Mrs Hayward,' Matteo insisted.

Isabel moved into her mum's bedroom and came out a moment later with blankets and a pillow.

'I'll be in in a minute, Mum,' Isabel said as she helped him spread the blankets out on the couch. 'Go to bed. You look done in.'

'Thanks a lot, kiddo.' But she hesitated at the door, her wary eyes moving from him to Isabel and back again.

He should probably go out to the bungalow. He could sleep on the floor for one night. But Isabel had other plans.

'Mum. I've got this. Go to bed. I'll be one minute.'

'Okay.' She pushed the door behind her, leaving it slightly ajar.

Isabel chuckled quietly. 'My mum is worried you'll take advantage of me.'

'I'm afraid I no longer have the energy to do so,' he said, dropping exhausted onto the couch. It wasn't quite long enough for him, but he was so tired, he doubted it would matter. 'It has been a challenging day, for both of us.'

'I'm sorry about your home, your belongings.' She ran a hand across his hair, her touch sending sparks through his body. Maybe he wasn't too tired after all?

He kicked off his boots. 'We'll survive. We have survived worse.'

'Yes, you have.' She leaned over and kissed his cheek, but before she could move away, he took hold of her arm to keep her there, turned his head to lay his lips against hers. His fingers reached up to run lightly across her cheek.

'Bella,' came her mother's voice from the next room.

She stood upright and rolled her eyes. Matteo chuckled.

'Get some sleep,' she said. 'Things always seem less bleak in the morning light.'

'Goodnight, *bella*,' he said, repeating her mother's nickname, and he kissed her palm before letting her go. She stepped into her mother's room, then turned to give him one last longing look he knew would keep him awake all night, before she closed the door behind her.

She wished she could have stayed with him. Beneath the smouldering eyes, she'd seen his pain. She'd opened the door again, just a tiny sliver, to peek out once more. He'd looked so forlorn, so lost, so exhausted, sitting there on their ugly green couch. It hurt her heart to see the sparkle had gone out of his smile now that he was alone with his thoughts, his pain at losing his home.

Isabel changed into her pyjamas, then proceeded to climb into the big bed next to her mum who immediately rolled over and cuddled her in.

'Mum!' Isabel groaned, wriggling.

'You always hated being cuddled in bed,' her mum said with a quiet chuckle. 'Even as a toddler. You wanted to climb into bed with us but you would spread out your little arms and legs like a starfish so your dad and I would be squished to one side of the bed and you'd have the whole other side to yourself.'

Isabel couldn't muster a laugh at the faded memories of being curled up in bed with her parents—the story she'd just told Matteo was too fresh in her mind. Her wonderful moment with Matteo out by the river had temporarily pushed it away but the hurt her father had inflicted was a raw cut again. She'd pulled off the scab and all the betrayal and deceit had flooded out.

'I'm so proud of you, baby.'

Isabel lay very still. 'Of me? Why?'

'You've grown into such a good woman, with a beautiful caring heart. You offered that family support when they needed it most.'

'*We* offered it,' Isabel corrected her. 'It wasn't a hard decision. They needed somewhere to stay and we have plenty of room. Although, it means no income from truckies looking for a room as they pass through since we're full to overflowing now.'

'They'll just have to sleep in their trucks. They're used to it. And they'll understand. As long as they get a meal and a pint they'll be happy.'

The thickness in her voice told Isabel that her mum was on her way to dreamland. She, however, wondered how she would ever get to sleep.

The tension of the day, the loss of the Sorrentis' home and her revelation to Matteo that her father hadn't died as she'd led him to believe, coupled with the knowledge that Matteo slept in the next room, had her staring wide awake at the ceiling. Considering that morning she'd thought he would never want to see her again, she was stunned by how the day had ended.

Not to mention the kiss they'd shared that was still tingling on her lips. If her mother hadn't been watching her like a hawk, she may just have curled up on that couch with him. Squeezing her eyes closed, she played and replayed the moment he'd kissed her, revelling in the sensations, the excitement of it all. No one had ever incited such deep and … lustful feelings in her before. She began to imagine how it would feel to be with him. To let him touch her in intimate ways. She'd fumbled around in the back of cars with a few boys in high school. Inexperienced boys. But since she'd left school, since her dad had disappeared, she'd concentrated on making a life for herself and her mother and increasing the draw of the pub, as one by one her friends got married and left the region or started popping out babies.

Men and marriage hadn't really been a priority for her. Her dates with Ross, or any other man for that matter, hadn't progressed past the occasional innocent kiss. Matteo had woken something in her. Feelings she didn't really understand, desperate feelings that made her want to do something reckless.

Rolling onto her side, she sighed. With Matteo's beautiful blue eyes the last thing on her mind, she drifted off to sleep.

Thirteen

It felt like she'd only been asleep for five minutes when the whir of sirens in the distance pushed her out of a deep slumber. Another levee had broken its banks.

Isabel sat up, her body aching from all the heavy lifting the day before helping the Sorrentis save their furniture. She rubbed gritty eyes and squinted at her mother, who was already out of bed and pulling on clothes. The clock out in the living room chimed seven.

'Where?' Isabel asked, her voice still husky from sleep.

'Mildura side of the river.'

Sirens repeated the signal and Isabel strained to hear the distant drone as she counted the specific code.

'Brickworks?'

'Not sure. That's the Cureton Avenue signal, so it could be.'

Moving quickly, Isabel dived out of bed, pulled on the clothes she'd worn the night before and followed her mother out into the living room. She was disappointed to find Matteo already gone. He'd no doubt already be down at their property, seeing if there was any way to salvage any other furniture or farm equipment.

When she headed outside to the verandah of the pub, there he was, looking out over the top of the levee to the other side of the river.

'Brickworks?' Isabel asked again as she stepped up next to him.

Matteo shook his head. 'We cannot see from here. I was going to drive across the bridge and see if they needed any help. Want to come?'

'Yep.'

As they rushed across to Isabel's truck, Carlo wandered up from the bungalow with Gia.

'Matteo, where are you going? We need to go back to the house to see what we can retrieve from the sheds.'

'I'll be back soon, Papa.'

'If they don't need any help over there we'll come right back,' Isabel called as she climbed into the passenger side of the truck.

Gravel spat out from the rear tyres as Matteo turned the truck onto the highway and headed for the border. As they began the slow drive across the bridge Isabel gasped.

'Good Lord, would you look at that!' she said, craning her neck to peer down between the steel girders of the bridge at the spread of the river. 'It must be miles wide now.'

'Never mind the river, look at *that*!' Matteo said, pointing out towards the brickworks.

'Wow, it's like a geyser.' Isabel marvelled at the column of steam rising in the cold morning air. 'The river water must have flooded into the kilns of the brickworks. That's going to be a mess. Hope no one's been injured in the explosion of steam.'

Matteo pulled the truck up on the corner of Cureton Avenue. In the distance, they could see that the levee had a gap at least two hundred yards wide. A torrent of water had gushed, and continued to gush, through the hole, flooding the low-lying land to the east of the town of Mildura. They could see at least ten homes had been inundated.

Matteo continued to move the truck along Cureton Avenue but soon ran into the police roadblock.

Isabel wound down her window. 'Constable Masterson!' she called out to the policeman, who appeared to be directing traffic out of the flood zone and stopping rubberneckers from heading in. He looked like he hadn't slept in months.

'Hey, Isabel, what are you doing on this side of the river so early?'

'We saw the steam geyser,' she said. 'Must have hit sixty feet.'

'I'd say a hundred,' he corrected, waving a truck overloaded with furniture out of the flood zone.

'Anything we can do to help?' Matteo asked.

'It's too dangerous to go in,' Jim said. 'We've evacuated most of the residents now.'

'Anyone injured?' Isabel questioned, gnawing at her lip.

'Nope, all accounted for,' Jim said as he directed a ute forward out of the doomed area. 'Alright, Gordon? Got everyone out?'

'Yep, reckon we're the last of us,' Gordon replied, leaning an elbow out his open window. The man was soaked to the skin, as was his wife who sat teary-eyed and staring straight ahead out the windscreen. 'I heard the roar of the water when the levee broke at about half six. Hell of a racket. Then water just started coming in under the doors and up through the floorboards. Levee must have been leaking before that, but no one noticed till it was too late. The dirt just crumbled under the pressure. Wave of water had to be five foot high. Barely got my suspenders up before the house lifted off the foundations. We had to make a dash for it with what we could carry. Fifty years we'd lived in that house.' His voice broke and he wiped at his nose.

Knowing Gordon wouldn't want them to notice the loss of his usually stoic demeanour, they all looked away until he got hold of himself again.

'Got your mail out of the letterbox though, I see,' Jim said, obviously trying to lighten the moment.

Gordon waved the envelope and hissed. 'Yep, just got my rates notice. Water bill's due. Ain't that a kick in the head. Bloody water company's got a sick sense of humour.'

'Take it easy, Gordon, Amy.' Jim nodded to the couple and sent them on their way before turning back to Matteo and Isabel. 'I heard the final levee in Buronga went last night.'

'Yes, we lost the farm, the house,' Matteo said with a sad nod.

Isabel put her hand over his on the seat.

'I'm sorry to hear that. And you came over here to see if you could help?' Jim shook his head with admiration. 'Go home. Nothing you can do here. Take care of yourselves, eh? Evacuation orders are in place for lower parts of Gol Gol and the last houses at Buronga. What's left of it.'

'Got it,' Isabel said. 'Thanks, Jim.'

They drove back across the bridge and, after a quick stop for breakfast at the pub, headed over to join Carlo and Antonio at the house in Buronga to see if they could rescue anything they hadn't managed to take the night before.

Wandering through knee-high water and ankle-deep mud that had settled, Matteo swore loudly when a snake dropped out from the roof space.

Isabel grinned. 'Just a green carpet snake thankfully. Watch out for king browns and tiger snakes though.'

Matteo shivered, letting fly with a string of words Isabel was sure were Italian curses, as the snake swam its way out the door. 'I hate snakes.'

They saw two more snakes and a rather soggy kangaroo that bounded up from the remains of the orchard. The roo shook itself like a dog and sped away up the hill.

Matteo's caravan was bogged, but the water had only reached the first step and luckily none had made it into the van. They hitched it up to the Sorrentis' ute and after an hour of trying different methods to free it from its muddy prison, they managed to pull it out and up onto higher ground. By lunchtime they'd loaded the van with pictures they'd taken from the walls of the house, some furniture Carlo was sure he could reupholster, and a collection of tools and machinery from the shed that was now waist deep in river water and muck.

Matteo stood with his brother and his father, staring silently at what had once been their home, their farm, before they turned their backs and headed for their vehicles.

'Can you start again?' Isabel asked.

Carlo nodded. 'We can and we will.'

'When the waters subside we'll see what root stock is still viable in the vines, check the orchards for rot,' Antonio added.

Back at the hotel, they unhitched the caravan in the car park behind the kitchen.

'At least you only had to sleep on our uncomfortable couch for one night,' Isabel said, trying to lighten Matteo's mood a little. He'd watched his father closely, she'd noted, as they'd worked their way through the little flooded house, as he'd collected items from their damaged property. It was as though he expected his father to break down at any moment. And who could blame him. She'd only once let herself imagine what would happen if the river took their pub, their home. It was too frightening to dwell on for too long.

'It was not so bad, sleeping on the couch,' Matteo said, lifting a hand to her cheek. 'I enjoyed knowing you were so close in the next room.'

His eyes looked tired, and there was heartbreak behind his smile as the reality of losing his home sank in. He leaned forward, pressing his lips lightly to hers. She closed her eyes and let the warmth of his mouth, his breath, wash over her. She felt the loss when he moved back.

'I'd better get into the kitchen,' she said.

'I need to go help Papa and Mama sort through what is left of our lives,' he said, the sadness returning. 'Perhaps I can give you a tour of the caravan later.' A little frisson of excitement skittered across her skin at the thought of being alone with him. She nodded, not trusting her voice, and they went their separate ways.

Days passed in a blur. For months they'd fought against the cruelty of Mother Nature. Everyone was exhausted. August had arrived and with the heavy rains both in Mildura and further upstream, the river was rising and flowing even faster as they headed towards the predicted peak. The last of the Buronga homes were evacuated, leaving a ghost town surrounded by inundated vineyards and orchards. The decimated levees were abandoned. The mighty Murray, a victorious foe, staked its claim on its acquired land. New rivers were formed, pouring in and around the back of Gol Gol as the previously tiny trickle of a creek rose and followed the path of least resistance towards the already overflowing Lake Gol Gol. The little hamlet of Gol Gol watched with increasing nervousness as the river crept higher up the levee bank that stretched from one side of the hotel, along the frontage encompassing Dulcie's house, the bakery and the Fultons' home before it curved in front of the Gol Gol Creek to the now impassable Sturt Highway.

It wasn't uncommon to see barges full of livestock on the river, being shifted from flooded properties to higher ground. Sadly, it was becoming just as common to see dead livestock floating down the river. The little zoo at the hotel expanded by half as people brought in near drowned or starved wildlife; echidnas and wallabies rescued from fast-flowing water or pockets of land where they'd been trapped without food.

At the hotel, they were drastically short of both manpower and heavy machinery to continue to build up the levee and the call went out to anyone who could help.

'Here's my Italian mate.'

'Bert Bagshaw.' Matteo greeted the man with a grin.

'You two know each other?' Isabel asked, surprised.

'Matty and I go way back, right, Matty?' Bert slapped Matteo heartily on the shoulder.

Matteo smiled. 'I met Bert in the pub the night we moved in here and he told me about the time he spent in Italy during the war.'

'Love those Italian sheilas.' Bert winked.

Isabel raised her eyebrows. 'You here to work, Bert?'

'Thought I'd see what I can do to help save my favourite pub,' he said, hooking his thumbs into his suspenders beneath his coat. 'Be a blasted disaster if she should go under. Where would I drink then, eh? Have to cross the border into Victoria to do me drinking.' He snorted. 'Imagine pubs still shutting at six in the evening. Un-Australian if you ask me.'

Isabel stifled a chuckle. 'Well, Bert, we will be happy to put you to work. There's a new pile of earth that's been dumped up on the highway near the school. We need to shift as much of that down here as we can move. We're just waiting on Carlo to return with the Fergie tractor.'

'You need a bigger bit of machinery than one little Fergie to cart enough dirt to fill those sandbags.' Bert puffed on his cigarette, surveying the group of helpers standing about helplessly as the water now lapped at the top of the levee.

Isabel felt weary and worn down. Bert was right. How were they ever going to shift enough dirt with one lone Fergie tractor to stop the levee from overflowing?

'I might have an idea,' Bert said, a devious look in his eye. 'Old mate over in Wentworth told me there's a bulldozer at the Main Roads depot there.'

'Well, Wentworth is practically an island now, so it's probably trapped,' Isabel said.

'Nah,' Bert puffed and coughed. 'The depot is outside the town centre. The dozer's been sitting idle all weekend.'

'Are you joking?' Isabel was gobsmacked.

'Why is it sitting idle?' Matteo asked.

'Apparently, there's no one to drive it since those blokes don't work weekends.'

Frustration had Isabel wanting to scream.

Matteo was uncharacteristically quiet as he scratched at the growth of beard on his chin. The small smile and gleam in his eye had Isabel studying him, and worrying a little at how much it resembled the look Bert wore.

'What are you thinking?'

'Antonio!' Matteo called his brother over. 'Do you still play cards with Sevvy in Wentworth?'

'*Si*, he owes me a pound.'

'Even better. He's a locksmith, *si*?'

'*Si*. What's going on?'

'We need to go visit Sevvy. I have a job for him. He can pay you that pound back in trade.'

'What are you up to?' Isabel had a horrible feeling it was lots of no good.

'Nothing you need to know about,' he said, dropping a light kiss on her nose. 'Antonio, let's go see a man about a bulldozer.'

Isabel's mouth dropped open. 'Matteo. Matteo, no!'

But Matteo was already heading up to his truck. 'Coming, Bert?'

'An adventure!' Bert exclaimed heartily and tossing his cigarette aside he followed the two brothers, his umbrella hoisted into the air like a bayonet as he called, 'Once more into the breach, dear friends!'

Isabel scrambled up the hill behind them. 'Matteo, you can't!'

But they were already piled into the truck and waving as they headed out onto the highway in a spit of mud.

'Everything okay, Isabel?'

She turned to see Constable Masterson standing at the back door of the pub with two cups of coffee in one hand.

'Um, uh-huh, yep. All good.' Her voice sounded so high and squeaky she was sure he wouldn't believe her. 'Is Mum inside?'

'Yes, she asked me to take these out to Perry and Albert at the levee before I have to leave. Thanks for the mutton sandwiches for the patrols out on the highway too.' He clicked his fingers in front of her face and chuckled as she continued to stare after the truck disappearing down the highway. 'You sure you're okay?'

She snapped back, grinning a little too broadly. 'Yep, yep, fine.' She'd always been a terrible liar.

He looked at her like she'd gone crazy, before continuing on his way, disappearing around the side of the pub.

'God, we're all gonna be arrested.'

Isabel spent the next few hours as a nervous wreck. She tried to convince herself there was no way Matteo, Antonio and Bert—blasted Bert and his ideas—were about to commit auto theft. She just hoped they were unable to get the dozer out of the depot and would return without incident. But when the wind picked up again and the water began to dribble over the lip of the levee, she prayed they would be successful. They could ask for forgiveness later, but if they were going to save the pub, they needed that dozer.

She was about to get in her own truck and go after the men, when Gia walked into the kitchen. It was quiet for the moment, between meals for volunteers and hotel guests, and Isabel was preparing the veal for dinner.

'You are a good cook,' Gia said, washing her hands and then moving in to help Isabel flatten the veal with a rolling pin. 'I have been watching you these last days. You have a good feel for food combinations and a nice eye for presentation.'

'Thank you, Mrs Sorrenti,' Isabel said. The compliment thrilled her to her core. Matteo's mum had been a great help to her in the kitchen over the last few days, but she still frightened the hell out of her.

'Matteo says you want to be a chef.'

'I do.' Her dream was slowly moving further away from her, the higher the river rose.

'There is a school for this in the city?'

Isabel nodded. 'It's a six-month course. Starts in September. But I can't leave, obviously.'

Gia made a sound Isabel couldn't discern.

'Matteo asked if I would teach you some things.'

'Oh, I … you don't have to—'

'My son, he likes you, very much.' Gia interrupted Isabel's babbling.

Isabel could feel the blush creeping up her neck. 'I like him, too. He is a good man.'

'He is,' Gia agreed, the smile of a proud mother touching her lips. 'Most of the time. I have decided. I will teach you some of my home recipes, but you must promise never to share them with anyone.'

'I promise, but I can't ask you to spend time teaching me when you have just lost your home, your livelihood.'

'Which is why I have time.' Gia glanced out the kitchen window towards the river, and her lips quivered for a moment before she firmed them up, her expression turning to one of determination.

'We will begin again. It is not the first time we have dealt with loss, and not the first time we have had to begin again.'

Isabel remembered the Sorrentis' lost delicatessen in Adelaide. She thought of the woman who had been without her husband for years when he'd been taken from her so cruelly, and everything she had done to raise her sons and earn money to keep them all alive. 'Mrs Sorrenti, you are the strongest woman I have ever known.'

Gia stopped hammering the veal and stared at Isabel, blinking in surprise. 'I ... *grazie*. Thank you. You have been very kind to us, to my family. Now, we will start with this veal. I will teach you the saltimbocca. Do you have prosciutto?'

'Prosciutto?' Isabel asked. She'd heard of it but wasn't a hundred percent sure what it was. Not much of the cool foods at the Sorrentis' had survived the inundation of their house. They'd had to throw out a lot of cured meats according to Matteo.

'Ham,' Gia said.

'There's cold baked ham in the Coolgardie safe.'

'Hmm, it is not the same but it will have to do,' Gia said, and she went to the Coolgardie to get the ham. 'If you are going to cook Italian food, we must teach you to speak some Italian. But for now, go and get some sage from your little herb garden on the verandah. We begin.'

For the next hour, Isabel was kept occupied in the kitchen with Gia, learning how to make saltimbocca. At one point Loretta wandered into the kitchen as well and once the veal was ready to be cooked for the evening meal, the women worked together to make the Italian pastry *sfogliatelli* from scratch. Gia was so fast, with agile hands that rolled the dough. After leaving it for thirty minutes in the Coolgardie safe to cool, Gia split the dough into four pieces and rolled it through a contraption that looked like a smaller version of the machine Isabel used to wring out the washing.

'It is a pasta maker,' Gia explained, rolling the dough through the wringer, folding it over and feeding it through the machine again. 'I brought this over from Naples with me when we came. It has been in my family for many years.'

'I'm glad you were able to save it from your home,' Isabel said when Gia paused momentarily, sadness crossing her features.

'*Finché c'e vita, c'e speranza.*'

Isabel just stared, no idea what the woman had said.

'While there is life, there is hope,' Gia translated. 'We have been through a lot. But you must always face what comes at you head on. Challenge gives life its flavour, and flavour is everything to Italians. Next, we make the gnocchi!'

When Matteo stepped into the kitchen a few hours later, he stopped dead at the sight before him. His mama and Isabel sat at the kitchen island, flour on their faces as well as all over the bench where they hand rolled little balls of gnocchi and laughed deliriously. A bottle of grappa sat between them.

'Oh, Matteo!' Isabel called between giggles. 'Your mama is teaching me to make her gnocchi.'

'Looks like Mama is getting you drunk.' Matteo leaned against the doorway, amused.

'She has a gift, this one,' Gia said, pouring another glass for Isabel.

Matteo stepped forward and took the drink himself, downing it in one go.

'Hey! That was mine, *stronzo*!'

Matteo's eyes went wide. 'Mama, what have you been teaching her besides gnocchi?'

'She wanted to learn Italian so I have been teaching her things she can say to people like that Rod Jamison who called us dagos.'

'You're teaching her all the swear words in Italian?'

'Not all of them.' Gia brushed him off. 'What? You think only men get to use curse words?'

Matteo shook his head in disbelief.

'Where have you been?' Gia asked.

'Oh, no! The secret mission,' Isabel said, slurring her words as she slipped off the stool.

Matteo put a hand out to catch her before she went right over.

'Okay, you are cut off,' Matteo told her. 'Mama, no more grappa for Isabel.'

A deep distant hum broke through, increasing in volume, and the building began to shake a little.

'The levee!' Gia exclaimed, standing unsteadily. 'It is breaking!'

Matteo went to the kitchen door. He'd driven the truck back from Wentworth and now the bulldozer they'd liberated had finally arrived.

'Antonio and Bert are here with a bulldozer!' Isabel's mum called as she shot through the kitchen from the bar and out the door, nearly knocking Matteo over in the process.

'A bulldozer?' Gia asked, excitedly wiping her hands on a tea towel as she joined Matteo at the door.

'I'm not sure you'll be so happy when you find out what they've done,' Isabel murmured, drinking the large glass of water Matteo handed her.

'What did you say?' Gia asked.

'Nothing.'

Matteo helped Isabel untie her apron and together they followed Gia out to where the huge dozer, complete with bucket full of dirt, was slowly moving down the hill to deposit its precious load.

Jim Masterson stepped up beside them. 'Where did that come from?'

'They st—' Isabel started to explain but Matteo took her arm and pulled her behind him.

'Bert knew a guy,' Matteo interrupted her.

'Great to have some help,' Jim said, and he wandered across to where Antonio had taken the driver's seat when Bert jumped down.

'*In vino veritas*, hey?' Matteo laughed as he turned back to Isabel. 'You'd be no good as a spy. One drink and the truth comes tumbling out.'

'What did you do?' she hissed at Matteo quietly as they stood together at the kitchen door. 'You're gonna get thrown in gaol when Jim works out where you got that from!'

Matteo just smiled and shrugged. 'How will he know where it came from?'

'The depot will report it stolen.'

'We'll return it before Monday,' he said easily. 'They won't even know it was gone.'

'It serves them right,' Isabel exclaimed. 'Bastards! Locking away precious machinery that could help save land and homes. All because they won't pay men to work on the weekend.'

Matteo chuckled. 'Come on, let's get some coffee into you.'

The delivery of dirt revitalised the workers and with renewed energy they went back to work, filling sandbags, while Carlo in his Fergie drove buckets of red clay up to the lip of the levee.

Fourteen

Emotions were raw as day after day reports came from all over the region.

More crops were lost, low-lying homes were taken off their foundations by the raging floodwater or inundated where they stood. The lucky ones had time to get out and take some belongings with them. Others, those who had nowhere to go, stayed to fight until all hope was lost, and they drove away from their homes for the last time—their vehicles filled with whatever they could carry—with the river sometimes literally chasing them down the street.

At Gol Gol, Mrs Barnes was evacuated from her home for the second time in her life, having been forced out during the flood of thirty-one too. The McEntees' house was sadly too low to be protected by the levee bank and the family had to evacuate, with no choice but to stand by and watch as the creek rose and inundated their home.

Audrey and Isabel worked tirelessly in the pub, cooking meals and handing out drinks to volunteers, as the Sorrentis and others from the town fought to save their home and livelihood.

As the sun rose on what looked to be a beautiful clear day in August, mists swirled and rose like smoke off the water as the sun swished its warm hands across the serene-looking river.

'It's awful to say but it looks quite stunning, doesn't it?' Isabel said, standing on the steps of the pub with a tray of coffee and tea for the exhausted workers who'd shown up yet again to help them save the pub. 'Appears deceptively calm with the sunshine sparkling on the surface like that.'

'Some days it barely looks as though it's moving,' Matteo agreed, wrapping his hands around the mug for warmth.

'Hard to reconcile that beauty with the devastation it's causing.' Just that morning she'd read in the newspaper that South Australia was copping as much, if not more, flooding, thanks to the Darling River also being in flood. The Renmark Paringa Road was impassable and this week the town of Mannum had been hit hard, its main street so flooded that people were rowing their boats up to the first-floor balcony of the hotel for a beer.

The rumble of a tractor broke into the peace of the morning as Carlo drove his Fergie down along the side of the pub.

'Papa!' Matteo waved, heading over to speak with his father.

Isabel handed the tray of coffees to her mum and taking a cup, she followed Matteo and handed the cup to Carlo when they reached him.

'*Grazie*.' He swallowed the coffee in one gulp and gave the cup back to her.

Matteo jumped up onto the side of the tractor with his father. 'The Mildura boy scouts are down by the bungalows filling sandbags. Let's pick them up in the rear loader, give them a ride back up to the pub for breakfast.'

'They'll get a kick out of that,' she called, and she waved, stepping back up to the verandah.

'How long can we keep this up?' Dulcie asked as they stood on the steps of the pub. She'd arrived with fresh bread, and the smell made Isabel's stomach rumble as she took the paper bags filled with loaves still warm from the oven.

Some of the workers changed shift as the rain abated for a short spell. Men disappeared in cars, going home to rest before they'd return again later that day to take the night shift once again. Others went in for breakfast, enticed by the smell of the bread, coffee and frying bacon.

'We'll keep it up as long as we need to,' Isabel said in answer to Dulcie's question. 'Until the rain stops and the worst of the waters head downstream to South Australia and leave us be.'

Isabel stepped back into the hotel and wandered through to the kitchen where her mum was watching over breakfast.

'Bacon is done and staying warm in the oven,' her mum said.

Isabel moved about the kitchen, checking on the food. 'We'll have fried eggs ready for bacon and egg sangers in a jiffy. Mum, can you slice the bread and toast it? Those boy scouts will be hungry little men.' She turned to look at her mother when she didn't respond. There were tears in her eyes. 'Mum? What's wrong?'

'Oh, sorry, love.' Her mum took a hanky from her sleeve and wiped her nose. 'It's all just getting to me. I heard Dulcie before. She's right. We can't keep this up forever.'

Isabel left the stove and her eggs to throw her arms around her mum.

'Come on, Mum, you're tougher than this. We'll survive.' Isabel took the hanky and wiped her mum's tears herself.

'I've lived here my entire life. I don't know how to do anything else. If we were to lose it all, like the Sorrentis have lost everything—'

'That's not going to happen,' Isabel interrupted.

'But everyone is so tired.' She welled up again, and it broke Isabel's heart. Her mother was usually so strong. 'And every day the river takes more land, more farms, more homes.'

'I know, Mum. It's hard to see friends lose everything.' She thought of the Sorrentis. They'd lost so much they could be forgiven for sitting back and sulking while they counted their losses. But no. Here they were working so hard to make sure the same thing didn't happen to her and her mum. 'Even if these levees break, we'll probably only lose the bungalows. This pub has stood on this land, in one form or another, since the last century. It survived the flood of thirty-one and it'll survive this and any more the Old Man Murray wants to throw at us.'

Audrey nodded and wiped her tears just as Matteo stepped through the rear kitchen door.

'Sorry, I am interrupting.' He was about to back out again but Isabel shook her head.

'No,' she said, moving back to check the eggs frying on the grill.

'Okay, well you need to come outside for a minute.'

'I can't. I have eggs on the stove.'

'Take a break for a minute.' Matteo took matters into his own hands and removed the pan from the stove, taking Isabel's hand and then grabbing her mum's too, leading them outside.

'But you've just sent the boy scouts back in for breakfast. It'll be ruined if I don't …'

Her complaints trailed off as she saw what Matteo had called them out into the drizzling rain for.

Two small buses had pulled into the car park and stepping out were the coaches of the Red Cliffs Tigers and the Mildura Demons Aussie Rules football teams.

The men stepped up to Isabel's mum. Once captains of their own high school teams, Barry McKechnie and Graham Stokes had both had a crush on Audrey Hayward for as long as Isabel could remember. They occasionally frequented the Riverside after games and over the years, one or the other would get up the guts to ask her mum out. She never said yes, of course, and Isabel remembered the night, not so long ago, when her mum had said she still believed she was married.

'G'day, Audrey. Thought you might need a hand over here, so we've brought you some helpers,' Barry said.

'No games today?' Isabel asked.

'All matches forfeited today,' Graham said, joining the conversation. 'All the coaches agreed. We've played on throughout the flood crisis, but today it was decided there were more important things we ought to be doing. So, the lads are here, ready and willing to help.'

Isabel studied the group of men between the ages of seventeen and thirty, alighting from the buses. At seven in the morning, none of them looked particularly ready and willing.

'The Imperials are working over at the Mildura power station and the Magpies are on home turf at Merbein to help raise the levees there,' Barry explained. 'But we saw this as the next place in need, so here we are.'

Isabel laughed as her mum threw herself at the two men and kissed them full on the lips. Both men's faces turned red as beetroots. Yep, there were definitely still torches burning. Shame her mum couldn't see it. It was past time she found a good man—her dad was never coming back. Isabel's smile soured. Even if he did come back, there was no way Isabel would ever forgive him for leaving her mum, for leaving her.

'Alright, well, thanks, men,' Audrey said, and Isabel was glad to see the fight back in her mother's eyes.

'Coffee is on in the dining room and grub will be up in about ten minutes. We'll fill their bellies before they start filling sandbags,' Isabel called, hoping they'd have enough bacon and eggs to go around.

The footy players, who'd looked mostly bleary-eyed and annoyed, were soon smiling at the idea of a free feed and eagerly headed indoors. As she watched them go she took a mental inventory of the pantry and figured if she fried up some onions and potato slices, she could make it all stretch far enough to feed them all.

'Hi, Isabel.'

'Ross!' Though he was a dedicated member of the Demons team, she really hadn't expected to see him given the Burrows' property was in the inundated disaster zone of Buronga. 'I thought you'd be with your parents.'

He shrugged and she thought he looked sadder than she'd ever seen him.

'You lost your home, Ross,' she said, laying a sympathetic hand on his arm. 'Go be with your mum.'

'She and dad are fighting,' he grumbled. 'I can't stand it. We were still moving stuff out when the water started pouring into the house. Mum's fretting 'cos when we evacuated we had to leave so fast we left Pepper and Salt behind and now she can't find them.'

Pepper and Salt were the Burrows' annoying little English terriers.

'We've been searching the area but there's no sign.' He looked around at the levee, the rising creek. 'You haven't seen them, have you?'

'If I'd seen them I'd have called you,' Isabel said. 'I'm sure they'll turn up.'

'For the last week we've been wading through mud at the house, trying to salvage anything we could. Mum and Dad are at each other's throats, but that's not what they're fighting about. Mum gave Dad some money a few days ago to hire a truck.'

Alarm bells went off in Isabel's head. She remembered the thick wad of pounds Trevor had brought to the pub a week earlier.

'But no truck ever showed up. They've been yelling at each other ever since. Anyway, I needed to get away from the fighting for a while, so I thought I'd come and see if you needed a hand.'

'Thank you,' she said, giving him a hug. 'It means a lot that you're here.'

It had been almost a month since she'd seen him last, she realised. She hadn't deliberately kept her distance from him since they'd argued, she'd just been so occupied with the floods, the pub and Matteo.

He nodded. 'I'm not the selfish bastard you seem to think I am, Isabel.'

'I never said you were a selfish bastard,' she argued.

'But you'd rather go out with some dirty farmer, some foreigner, instead of me.'

'Ross, please don't start that again.' Isabel didn't have the energy to fight with him, so instead she turned and led him inside and out of the miserable misty drizzle. 'Head on into the front bar and get some coffee. I've got to get back to the kitchen and finish cooking your brekkie.'

'Isabel—'

'No!' She'd said it so loudly, the other football players who'd been making their way into the pub smirked. 'If you're really here to work, then thank you. We can use all the hands we can get.'

She pushed back through the door into the kitchen and closed it firmly behind her so he couldn't follow. It saddened her just how much of his father she was beginning to see in Ross.

The boy scouts were fed and sent home for some well-earned sleep. Isabel cooked while her mum refilled coffee and tea provisions, in between toasting bread and delivering trays of food out to the hungry football players who ate like they'd not been fed in weeks. Once full, the lads headed out to be put to work.

'Hollow legs, those boys,' her mum commented, leaning against the sink. 'Bella, I'll finish those dishes. Walk these ham and cheese toasted sandwiches up to the police at the roadblock on the highway, will you?'

'Okay, Mum.' Isabel moved to take the tray of toasted sandwiches but as she grabbed hold of it, her mum held tight, her eyes narrowing as she studied Isabel's face.

'You need some rest.'

Isabel smiled tiredly. 'So do you, Mum.'

'You both need rest,' Gia announced as she and Loretta entered the kitchen. 'Isabel, do as your mother tells you. Take those sandwiches across to the police up on the highway and then go to your bed for a few hours.'

'Oh, but—'

'Listen to Gia, my girl.'

'And you.' Gia turned to Audrey with that 'I'll take no nonsense' look Isabel recognised. 'When did you last sleep?'

'Um ...'

'*Si*, I thought so.' Gia shook her head. 'You go to your bed too.'

'Gia, I can't—'

'Go. I can handle the kitchen and food for the workers for a few hours,' Gia insisted, pulling on an apron. 'You're both dead on your feet. No good to anyone. Go!'

'Yes, Mrs Sorrenti.' Isabel swallowed. The woman could be a little scary.

After Isabel delivered the food to the police officers at the barricade on the Sturt Highway, where the creek was now well over the road, the Hayward women did as they were told and went to get some sleep.

When Isabel woke, she discovered she hadn't quite made it to bed. She was stretched out on the couch where she'd dropped when she and her mum had come back into their quarters.

Leaning up on an elbow, she was surprised to see a body on the floor beside her. Once her eyes had adjusted, she realised it was Matteo. She smiled wearily. He'd been working so hard to save her home. With so much to do they'd barely spent any time alone together over the last week, despite him living on the property.

Carefully she dropped down to the floor beside him and lying down at his back, she curled her arm around his waist, nuzzled into his shoulder and promptly fell back to sleep.

'I knew it!'

Isabel opened one eye slowly and looked up to see an upside-down Ross glaring down at her. Shifting slightly, she realised she was curled into Matteo's chest, his arm around her, holding her to him. He must have rolled over as they'd slept.

'Ross,' she said, her voice husky as she started to push herself up.

'Shh,' Matteo said without opening his eyes. 'Sleeping here.'

He pulled Isabel back down into his arms, kissed her forehead and sighed as though he would go back to sleep again.

'Isabel?'

Isabel pushed up again. 'Ross, I'm tired. We're all tired. We're catching some sleep whenever and wherever we can. You should go home and do the same. Thank you for being here to help, but you really need to be with your family right now.'

'I gave you the space you needed to realise we would be good together, and you end up sleeping with this … this—' His face wrinkled up as though he'd caught a whiff of a bad smell as he studied Matteo.

Isabel jolted when Matteo jumped quickly to his feet.

'This what?' he urged Ross as they faced off.

'Stop! Now, Ross!' Isabel demanded, standing and getting in between the two men. 'Before you say something we'll all regret.'

'You can't be serious about him, Isabel?' Ross asked.

Facing Ross and holding Matteo behind her, Isabel tried to keep her tone calm. 'Despite what you think, Ross, what I do or don't do, and who I do or don't do it with, is really none of your business. Now, let me walk you out.'

She took Ross's arm and led him through the hotel residence. Matteo moved ahead and opened the door. Before they'd even stepped outside, Ross gave Matteo a quick shove in the back, sending him staggering down the stairs. He managed to keep his footing, but only just.

'Stop it!' Isabel yelled, as Matteo turned and lunged straight for Ross. 'This is stupid. We have bigger problems to deal with here.'

'What is this about?'

Isabel was relieved to see Carlo wander up. 'Mr Sorrenti, thank God. Maybe you can help me talk some sense into these two idiots.'

'No, let them be.'

Isabel turned at the voice. Trevor Burrows walked across from his car. He looked even more dishevelled than usual. 'Let them fight it out.'

'For what reason?' Carlo demanded of Trevor.

Already struggling to keep two bull-headed men apart, Isabel wondered if she was going to have to do the same with Carlo and Trevor. The looks they exchanged were almost as incendiary as Ross and Matteo's. They were glaring at each other as though they were lifelong enemies. The last thing she wanted was for the fight to escalate into an all-out brawl.

Trevor stepped closer to Carlo. 'I don't need a reason, dago, I don't answer to you.'

'Aren't you tired of this, Burrows?' Carlo asked, wearily.

'Of what?' Trevor said with a grunt.

'Do you even know why you hate me?' Carlo asked. 'The war is over. It has been for many years. Even if it wasn't, I have more reason to hate you than you do me.'

'Wait. What does that mean?' Matteo asked.

The face-off between Carlo and Trevor had effectively stopped the battle between their sons as both Matteo and Ross were watching their fathers with interest and confusion. Tension crackled in the air as the men stared at one another.

Isabel turned as she heard a vehicle pull in and was overwhelmed with relief when she spotted the police car. Constable Jim Masterson and the younger Constable Winters stepped out of the vehicle. It didn't take long for them to size up the situation before them.

'Something wrong, gentlemen?' Jim's eyes tracked from Carlo and Trevor to Matteo and Ross.

'Nope. Nothing,' Matteo said.

'Nothing at all,' Ross agreed, his eyes narrowing as he looked with disgust between Isabel and Matteo.

'Okay,' Jim said, watching the men warily. 'Then how about you all go to your separate corners and we'll call this done—whatever it is.'

'Thanks, Constable Masterson. How did you get here so fast?' Isabel asked. 'Did Mum call you?'

'No. We were already on our way here.' Jim wore an expression she couldn't quite read, except it reminded her of the day he'd announced little Christopher Phillips had gone into the river.

'Why?' Isabel asked, a sense of dread rising within her. 'What's happened?'

'A body was found out by Lake Ranfurly,' Constable Winters began. 'Spiro Vassilakis called us.'

'A body?' Isabel winced. 'Not another child I hope.'

'Do you know who it is?' Matteo asked, moving across to stand by Isabel.

Jim gazed around at the large group that had gathered and then up at Audrey, who had stepped out onto the verandah. 'Perhaps we should talk inside, Isabel.'

Isabel's frown deepened as she followed the two policemen and her mother into the house.

Matteo watched Isabel and her mother disappear into the hotel with the policemen.

'What's that about, do you think?' he asked. 'Whose body do you think they found?'

When he turned back to his papa, he was confused by the way he and Trevor Burrows were eyeing one another. Trevor looked uncharacteristically nervous.

'Matteo, go inside,' his papa told him, his eyes still on Trevor. 'Go to Isabel. I think she is going to need you.'

'Why?' Ross asked. He looked just as confused as Matteo felt by their fathers' strange behaviour. 'Why would Isabel need him?'

'Ross, come on. Let's go.' Trevor stepped in and took his son's arm.

'What? No,' Ross argued, pulling his arm from his father's grip. 'If he's staying,' he nodded at Matteo, 'then so am I.'

'Ross, get in the damn car. We have to go,' Trevor said through gritted teeth.

'Then go, Dad. What are you even doing here? I'm sure there's a beer somewhere with your name on it,' Ross shot back over his shoulder as he followed Matteo into the pub.

'You shouldn't talk to your father that way.' Matteo couldn't help the dig.

'Shut up.'

Matteo took the few steps up to the covered verandah followed closely by Ross. When they arrived in the living room, Isabel and her mum sat together on the couch holding hands. Their faces were deathly pale.

Jim was holding up a bronze disc on a broken chain. 'We found this near the body.'

'I don't know what that is,' Isabel said, eyeing the disc. 'Mum?'

Her mum took the plastic bag with the disc inside and studied it, a small frown marring her tired features. 'It wasn't his, but … it looks familiar—'

'What are you doing with my dad's medallion?'

Everyone looked at Ross.

'You recognise this?' Jim took the medallion from Audrey and moved across the room to show it to Ross.

He gave it one quick look and nodded. 'Yeah, Dad said he won it in a poker game. I liked to play with it when I was a kid. I thought it was cool. But he said he lost it a few years back.'

'Five years back?' Jim questioned.

'Don't know.' Ross shrugged. 'About that, I guess. Why?'

'Is Trevor still outside?'

'No, he just left. Said he had to go. What's going on?'

'Bones in a shallow grave were unearthed when the crew down there were shifting dirt,' Constable Winters said. 'We believe it could be the body of Sam Hayward.'

Stunned, Matteo looked to Isabel. He didn't understand. Sam had run off with another woman on her sixteenth birthday. Hadn't he?

'Are you sure it's my dad?' Isabel asked, her bottom lip quivering. 'How could you tell? It could be anyone, right?'

Matteo wanted to go to her, wanted to comfort her, but seeing the two Hayward women, curled together on the couch, he didn't want to intrude on family.

'Some forensic guys are coming out from Melbourne to take a look, but we also found a wallet amongst the remains. Leather holds up well,' Jim said, nodding to Winters who opened the wallet and carefully lifted something from inside, handing it to Isabel's mum. The small rectangle was tattered and torn. Matteo couldn't see what it was, but as Audrey looked at it, she closed her eyes. A single tear fell from beneath her lashes.

'What is it, Mum?'

'It's a photograph,' Audrey said, as Isabel leaned over to see.

'That's me. That's me and Dad.' Her voice was small and full of grief. 'He didn't leave us?'

'No, baby.' Audrey took Isabel in her arms. 'He didn't leave us. He didn't leave you.'

Matteo could only watch with an aching heart as Isabel broke into sobs in her mother's arms.

After a few moments, Isabel pulled herself together. 'I was so awful about him. I said such hateful things when he disappeared. I thought he'd run out on Mum, that he'd left us. I was so angry for so long. I told people he was dead.'

'You did what?' Audrey asked, horrified.

'I'm so sorry, Mum. But the idea of him leaving us made me so sick, so furious.' She looked back at Jim. 'And he really was dead? All this time? I don't understand. What happened to him? Why was he out at Lake Ranfurly?'

'We don't know. We may never know that. But we need to speak with Trevor.' Jim stood and dropped the medallion and the wallet back into a plastic evidence bag.

It wasn't an accusation, but the insinuation hung in the air like acrid smoke.

'You think Trevor had something to do with Sam's death?' Audrey asked. 'Because his medallion was on the … with Sam?'

'What? No!' Ross met every suspicious set of eyes in the room. 'They were best mates. What reason could my dad possibly have to kill Sam? How do you even know he was killed by anyone? He could have died lots of ways.'

'An autopsy will show how Sam died,' Jim said, raising his hands in a 'calm down' motion. 'Let's not go jumping to any conclusions or accusing anyone of anything. I simply want to ask Trevor some questions. He may have been the last person to see Sam alive.'

'Constable Masterson.'

Matteo hadn't even realised his father was there until he'd spoken.

'May I speak with you alone for a moment?'

'What can I do for you, Mr Sorrenti?' Jim asked.

'I believe I have some information that may help in this matter.'

'Is that so?' Jim waved his hand in a 'come ahead' fashion, urging Carlo further into the room.

'I think Trevor Burrows may have killed Sam Hayward. And I think I know why.'

Fifteen

Matteo stared at his papa. He'd had his suspicions that Papa had known Trevor Burrows better than he'd let on but never in his wildest imagination had he expected the accusation his papa was throwing out now.

'What would you know about any of this?' Ross demanded. 'You didn't even know Sam.'

'Yes, he did.' Isabel spoke up.

Carlo crossed glances with her and after a moment he nodded in agreement. 'There was a time when I saw Sam Hayward and Trevor Burrows every day.'

'And that would be when?' Jim asked.

'During the war.'

'At Loveday.' It was Audrey who'd spoken and Matteo saw that she was also looking knowingly at his papa. 'Isabel told me. You were there. At the camp where Trevor and Sam were stationed. You knew them.'

'You were an internee, Mr Sorrenti?' Jim questioned. Matteo saw the hint of sympathy on the policeman's face.

'I was held at Loveday Internment Camp for five years. In the last few months of the war, I was at the river with another Italian internee named Massimo Conti. Sam and Trevor were guarding us as we worked on one of the irrigation pumps that had broken down. While we were imprisoned, we were allowed to leave the camp to chop wood, to work the gardens, to work in the fields where the poppies were grown for medicine. We were paid if we worked. Sam and Trevor bathed in the river while we worked, and they drank from a small hipflask. Whiskey, I think, from the smell of it. When we finished our work, I too swam in the river to cool off. It was an unusually warm April day. Massimo did not swim. He did not know how. Sam and Trevor teased him about it. Massimo walked up the bank a way to where he dropped a line in to fish. When I had finished my swim, I sat on the sandy beach of the river to dry off.'

He took a breath then and Matteo could see that dredging up the memory was hard for him. He'd never heard his father speak for so long on anything to do with his time at the camp at Loveday.

'When it was time for us to head back to the camp, Trevor and Sam mounted their horses,' his papa went on. 'They were very drunk. Massimo had just caught a fish and was reeling it in. Trevor was yelling at him to hurry up, to let the fish go, but Massimo kept trying to get the fish onto the bank. Trevor moved his horse towards Massimo, laughing and herding him closer to the river edge, tormenting him. Sam was calling Trevor back, asking him to stop. The edge of the bank gave way and Massimo fell into the river. They just laughed at him as he flailed in the water, yelling for help. I rushed down to the beach again and swam along to try to save Massimo. He went under—once, twice—and he never resurfaced. I do not know if he drowned, caught a snag underneath or was just taken by the current. I dove for him, but I could not find him. He was lost. Trevor yelled at me to come back to shore and they herded me back to camp. I begged them to send help for Massimo in case he had resurfaced further down the river, but Trevor said he would make my life a living hell at the camp, that he would kill me if I ever told anyone what had happened.'

The room was silent for a few heavy moments after his papa had completed his story.

'What happened when they couldn't find Massimo?' Jim queried. 'The camps used to hold a roll call, didn't they?'

'Three times a day they counted us,' Carlo confirmed. 'But when we returned to camp, Trevor reported immediately that Massimo had run off into the bush. He said they had given chase but lost him in the river. The officers sent the Aboriginal tracker out to look for Massimo. The tracker had found many men who had tried to escape before, but in this he had no luck.'

'Did the army ever ask you what had happened?' Jim had been taking notes and looked up from the notepad he'd been scribbling in.

'When the commandant of the camp asked me, I agreed that Massimo had escaped. I needed to survive for my family. At the time, I did not know that within weeks the war would be over, the camps closed forever.'

'You're not actually listening to this rubbish, are you?' Ross snapped at Jim before turning on Matteo's papa. 'Anything you say is hardly believable, is it? You were a prisoner. They kept you locked up. Of course you'd want to get back at them. You hate them.'

'He has a point, Mr Sorrenti,' Jim said, rubbing the back of his neck.

Matteo saw Audrey's expression change. She looked as though she was trying to figure something out. 'This all happened that last April? Before the war ended?'

'Yes.' For the first time since he'd started telling his story, Carlo looked at Matteo.

In his father's eyes he saw all the shame and guilt he'd been hiding. He understood now why his papa had been so reluctant to speak of his time in the camp.

'Sam came home for a few days around that time. He was different; sullen, sad. He began to drink more, became almost as bad as Trevor for a while. I tried to ask him what was wrong, but he got angry, refused to tell me.' Audrey sighed. 'Mr Sorrenti, were you mistreated by my husband during your time in the camp?'

'No, Mrs Hayward. I was not,' he said. 'Some soldiers did enjoy the power they held over us. Bullies can be found anywhere in life. Your husband was a good man, a fair guard. He never hurt anyone. In fact, Sam and I were friendly at the camp. We talked sometimes and he shared his tobacco with me. But after the incident with Massimo, Sam never spoke to me again. He was scared or ashamed. I do not know which.'

'I'm sorry you had to go through all that, Mr Sorrenti,' Jim said. 'But it doesn't explain what happened to Sam Hayward or why you think Trevor Burrows had something to do with it.'

'After the camps closed, many of us were still forced to work as part of the Civil Alien Corps. We had to do two years' servitude outside of the camps. I was sent to Wentworth and worked as a picker on a citrus orchard. When my two years was completed, I decided to stay on in the region, leased the land at Buronga and sent for my family. Before they arrived, I ran into Sam one day in town. He was very shocked to see me. We talked for a while and the incident came up. He asked why I never told anyone, after the war, what really happened.'

'Why didn't you?' Isabel asked. Matteo couldn't miss the censure in her tone.

His papa lowered his head. 'I am not proud of my silence. You must understand that after five years of internment, and two years of indentured service, I just wanted to find a normal life, to have my family with me again, to let the past go and start fresh. It seemed pointless, not to mention painful, to bring it all up again. I would not have known even where to begin. I saw Sam more often as the years went on. We would go fishing together sometimes out at Psyche Bend. Sam said he had been thinking about coming clean to the army. Telling them that Massimo had not run away but died. He'd found out after the war ended that Massimo had a daughter. He said he felt guilty that the poor man's family would never know what happened to him.' The pain on his papa's weathered features hurt Matteo's heart. 'His daughter would never know why he didn't come home.'

'I know what that's like.'

Carlo looked at Isabel, his eyes full of sympathy. 'I know you do.'

'When he came home for good, after the war, after the camps were closed, Sam was a mess,' Audrey said. Matteo had always thought of Mrs Hayward as one of the happiest people he'd ever met. Now she looked tired and older somehow than her years. 'He drank and gambled. But then something changed. He just suddenly stopped drinking, started working around the pub again. I never understood why he'd worked so hard to pull himself together, and then left us.'

'The guilt was like a shackle around his neck. Perhaps when he made the decision to tell the truth, his guilt left him and he could face his family with pride once again,' Carlo said with a weak smile. 'He said he felt lighter just knowing he would do the right thing.' He turned to the constable again. 'This is why I cannot stay quiet any longer. Only a week after he'd said he was going to tell the military, and to try to find Massimo's family, I heard that Sam had disappeared. I had always wondered if he had told Trevor what he planned to do. Now I am sure of it.'

'Bullshit!' Ross spat.

Matteo had been so enthralled by finally hearing some of the story his papa had held so tightly to him, he'd almost forgotten Ross was even there.

'He's making this all up to get back at my father.'

'Are you calling my papa a liar?' Matteo demanded.

'Okay, you two, just take it easy,' Jim said, manoeuvring himself between them.

'I'm not gonna stand here and listen to this "prisoner" call my father a murderer.'

Ross took off out the door. *Good riddance*, Matteo thought.

'Trevor killed his best mate to keep him quiet.' Constable Winters shook his head. 'What a bastard.'

Jim cleared his throat. 'Constable, why don't you put a call out to all other police vehicles to look out for Trevor Burrows.'

'Audrey, Isabel.' Carlo called their attention back to him. 'I am very sorry. I kept my silence for too many years. If I had told the authorities about Massimo sooner, Trevor and your father may have faced some charges, but at least Sam would still be alive.'

'My father made his own choices,' Isabel said. 'They were bad choices, but they were his and he should have owned them.'

'Trevor Burrows always had a strong hold over Sam,' Carlo said. 'Even in the camp we could see it. Sam was kind and fun. Unless Trevor was around. That man has a mean streak that goes very deep. I never understood why Sam went along with Trevor like he did.'

'They'd been mates since school,' Audrey said. 'A mateship only made stronger by the fact that they'd been the only two in their age group in the region who hadn't gone to the fighting when they'd joined up. It was a hard time for us, when all the men were going off to war and Sam stayed behind. His disability wasn't something you could see easily. He got a white feather in the mail. I assume Trevor did too, although he'd never admit it.'

'White feather?' Isabel asked.

'It was what people did to men who refused to go to fight in the war. They were calling him a coward,' Audrey explained. 'Sam wasn't a coward, the army just refused to send him overseas because of his dodgy leg. He'd had polio as a kid and as a result he couldn't run very fast. Trevor, on the other hand, was originally kept back as an essential worker. His mother saw to that. His father put the transport side of their business in his hands, but he was hopeless at managing it. He was about to be sent overseas to the fighting, but Sam was already serving at Loveday and somehow managed to get Trevor assigned there with him. I really didn't know what Sam's job was at Loveday. He never spoke about it and I never asked questions. Perhaps I should have.'

The room fell silent as the heaviness of the revelations sank in.

'Okay.' Jim put his hat back on his head. 'We'll go find Trevor and have a little chat. Then we'll need you to come down to the station and give an official statement, Mr Sorrenti.'

'Of course,' Carlo agreed.

'Audrey, Isabel,' Jim addressed them. 'It'll be a while before we can release Sam for burial. Probably for the best considering the cemetery is an island at the moment anyway.' He shook his head. 'My apologies for that. I'm very sorry for your loss.'

'Thank you, Jim,' Audrey said, and she walked him out of the pub.

'Matteo, we should leave Isabel and her mother,' his papa said.

Matteo moved to sit beside Isabel, took her hands. They were so cold. 'Are you going to be okay?'

She nodded slowly, her eyes wide and staring, and he could see the shock of the morning beginning to settle in.

'I'll be here if you need me.' He kissed her cheek before he stood and followed his papa out of the room, out of the hotel and into the drizzling rain once again.

Matteo walked quietly beside his papa. He'd learned more in that one afternoon than his father had ever revealed to them, but still a thousand more questions flooded Matteo's mind. He promised to hold his tongue for once, tried to tell himself it was enough for now.

'I know you are ashamed of me.'

He stopped walking and waited until his papa turned, lifting his gaze from the ground to meet his son's eyes.

'Ashamed?'

'A man died, and I stayed quiet to protect myself, to protect my family.'

'Papa, I could never be ashamed of you. You did what you had to to survive. No one would ever blame you for that.'

'I know my silence has been hard on you, Matteo. Harder even than on your mama, or Antonio. You were always one who needed to know how everything worked, even as a young boy.' Matteo studied his father's face. He looked as though he had aged in the last hours. 'Go and find your brother and Loretta and come to the bungalow,' his papa said, staring out towards the river. 'There have been too many secrets held. I think it is time I told you all about my time at the internment camp.'

He watched his papa walk down the hill to the bungalow where his mama was sitting on the steps, scrubbing mud from items they'd salvaged from the house, then he turned and rushed back into the hotel to find his brother.

Alone in the living room Isabel stayed on the couch, her entire body numb. After the noise and revelations of the last hour, the room seemed deafeningly quiet. But her mind swirled with everything she'd just learned. Her father hadn't left her on her birthday as she'd believed.

'You okay, baby?'

She took a deep breath and groaned as her mum dropped onto the couch beside her. 'Oh, I'm just sitting here going over all the horrible things I've said or thought about Dad over the last five years.'

Her mum pulled her close to her side, squeezing her tightly. 'Don't do that to yourself.'

Isabel sat back and studied her mum. It broke her heart to see her look so tired, and suddenly so defeated.

'You never said much about Dad after he left,' Isabel said. 'What did you think had happened?'

Audrey shrugged. 'In the first years, after he disappeared on your birthday, I hoped he'd just gone on some trip to find himself. I believed he would be back some day.'

'I recall that day in so much detail, but not for all the good reasons a girl should remember her sixteenth birthday,' Isabel said, feeling bone weary. 'I had half the school over for the party. It was so much fun. But I couldn't really enjoy it because I spent all afternoon watching the pub, the car park, wondering when Dad was going to finally show up. Then, after everyone had gone home, I sat up in the front bar and kept waiting.'

'I remember. You didn't cry.'

'I did,' Isabel told her. 'You just didn't see it.'

'Oh, baby.'

'I didn't want you to know how hurt I was. You were so angry with him. I preferred that to seeing you sad. Then Trevor showed up,' Isabel said, her expression darkening. 'God, I remember, I leaped on him the minute he stepped in the door, demanding to know where Dad was. He looked guilty. I remember clearly now how guilty he looked. I had just assumed Dad had been out drinking with Trevor. But he said he didn't know where Dad was, assumed he was here at my party.'

'And I walked in just as you were yelling at Trevor,' her mum continued the memory. 'Not your finest moment. I think it was the first time I'd ever heard you swear.'

'I really lost my temper.' Isabel cringed as she recalled her vicious accusations. 'I called Trevor a drunken, lying bastard. Then I said Dad was a lying, drunken bastard and I …' Isabel stopped abruptly. She couldn't repeat the words she'd said that day. Not now. Not after everything they'd just learned.

'You said you wished he was dead,' her mum finished for her. 'That's what I heard when I walked in. I knew why I was so angry, but I didn't understand your fury. I expected you to be upset, yes, and sad that he'd missed your party. But I thought he'd be back the next day with a present and you and he would be the best of friends again. You were so close. He loved you so much, Bella.'

'I was so angry because I thought he'd left us, left you, for another woman.'

'Another woman?'

Isabel pressed her lips together. She hadn't meant to blurt it out like that, but it was too late to take it back and there'd been too many lies already.

'I saw Dad talking to some woman. She kissed him.'

Her mum looked shocked. 'What? When was this? Around your sixteenth?'

'No, I was about nine. It took a few years for me to understand what I'd seen but I know now, he'd been having an affair.'

'You saw them?'

The pain on her mother's face cut straight to her heart. 'I'm sorry, Mum. I'm sorry, I shouldn't have told you. I should have let it alone. We've had enough revelations for one day.'

Her mum slumped, rubbed at her temple, and Isabel wished the couch would swallow her up. How much more pain could she, could her dad, cause them?

'Honey, you didn't tell me anything I didn't already know.'

Isabel's mouth dropped open. 'You knew?'

'Of course I knew. I knew all about that woman. Your dad told me. He'd been unfaithful. Just once, he said. He'd met her down in Barmera. The soldiers would go to dances in town. It gave them something to do when they weren't working at the camp. He said they had a fling one night. He told her he was married but she hounded and harassed him for months.'

'And you believed him? That it was only the one time?'

'I loved your father. He chose to tell me the truth about his mistake. It was hard but I forgave him. Yes, I believed he only had the one slip.' Her eyes took on a faraway sad look. 'I told him if he ever did it again, he'd better run, get gone good and quick or I'd kick him out on his arse so fast his head would spin. And then when he disappeared after your sixteenth birthday—' A sob burst out. 'I wondered … I wondered if he'd … I should have known he didn't leave. Even if he stopped loving me, even if he'd left me, he would never have left you. He loved you, baby, he adored you. Don't ever think he didn't.'

'He loved you too, Mum. Now we know he didn't leave us for anyone else. Someone took him from us.' Isabel felt the tears welling, her throat closing. 'He'll never come home. I wished him dead and now he is.'

'Oh, honey, please don't blame yourself.' She felt her mum's arms come around her again and they cried together.

Maybe Trevor was responsible for her dad's death, Isabel thought as the tears fell freely. But even if they discovered who killed her father, he was gone. And she would never get him back.

In the tiny bungalow his parents had been sharing for the past few weeks, Matteo held his breath. His mama took baby Lucia and insisted Loretta lie on the bed and rest. Matteo wondered if Mama was using the little girl as a shield, as something tangible to hold onto as Papa stood at the window gathering his thoughts, staring out at the levee that was built up almost to the doorstep of the bungalow. Antonio perched on the edge of the bed while Matteo stood in the corner, waiting anxiously for his father to begin.

'The time has come for me to tell you everything.'

Matteo exhaled the breath he'd been holding. He crossed glances with Antonio, then his mama. He had so many questions, and it seemed he might finally get some answers.

'You were so young when the war began,' his papa said, still staring out the window. 'I didn't think you remembered much about that time. And when we were reunited, I hoped we could just move on with life. I felt it was for the best to put it all behind us.' He turned his head to look at Matteo. 'Clearly, I was wrong.'

'But I still don't understand—why?' Matteo couldn't stop the question before it jumped out. 'Why were *you* interned? Why were *you* treated like an enemy alien? You were naturalised as a British citizen.'

'It did not matter. When Italy joined itself with Hitler's Nazis, our delicatessen lost a lot of business. Our Australian customers began to stay away. We began to hear rumours that anyone who was not of Anglo descent was being *indagare*.' He frowned as he sought the word in English. '... investigated. Then that day—the day you boys came home from school and saw those army men taking me—they told me the government deemed me to be an enemy alien and that I was to be interned.'

'Imprisoned,' Gia corrected. 'They kept you in a concentration camp.'

'No, Gia, no,' Carlo said with conviction. 'You cannot, you must not, compare what I went through at Loveday to what the people faced in Europe, or how soldiers were treated in the camps in Asia. I was lucky.'

'Lucky?'

'*Allora*, you are right, I did not feel lucky at the time,' he acquiesced. 'I had been largely cut off from the world in the camps. In the first years we weren't allowed a radio and the newspapers were carefully censored. As internees we were ignorant of many things outside of the razor wire. We did not know of the horrors of the Hitler concentration camps in Germany with their gas chambers, or the prisoner of war camps in Malaya and Thailand. Those soldiers returned home in terrible condition, if they returned at all. Lucky is perhaps not the right word, but things could have been much worse for me, for us, if we had stayed in Italy.'

Gia said no more and so Carlo went on.

'The soldiers who came that day, they searched the shop and they found some fascist literature in the storeroom. They accused me of spying for the dictator Mussolini.'

'Were you?' Matteo asked.

'Matteo!' His mama shot him a furious look.

Matteo balked. 'What? It's a fair question.'

His papa merely shook his head and went on. 'The literature was not mine. I had never seen it before. I was not a *fascista*. I had no political affiliations. We left Italy because life there was an endless struggle and we wanted better for our children. On the train from Adelaide to Barmera, I spoke with Rico Centofanti, who owned the fruit store. We both wondered how and why we had been targeted, and by process of elimination, I can only guess the fascist papers were put there by Mr McAllister.'

'The old guy who owned the milk bar down the street from our shop?' Antonio asked.

Carlo nodded. 'It seems we were putting him out of business.'

Matteo's blood boiled. 'He had you sent to internment because he was jealous?'

'They were strange times. But it would not have mattered anyway. The government did not see the difference between fascists and anti-fascists or communists, or those without political affiliation at all. We were Italian, Italy was disloyal to Britain, and so we were the enemy. It does not matter now why I was interned. I want you to know about my time in the camp. I know that my silence troubles you. You imagine how it was for me. I fear your imagination has run wild especially, Matteo, and while it was not easy for me, I know you think the worst.'

Matteo finally sat down in the old rocking chair they'd saved from their house. He knew it would not be easy for his papa to talk about those years and he was determined to stay quiet from now on.

'When we arrived in Barmera on the train, there were not enough army trucks to take us to the camp and so we had to walk for miles to Loveday. It was hot and dusty. The camp was surrounded by a long, double razor wire perimeter with very tall guard posts at intervals. It was a distressing sight indeed. For weeks we slept in tents on the ground with only a thin straw mattress. At first, the camp was mostly housing men who already lived in Australia when war broke out; doctors, professors, farmers, shopkeepers. Soon after, other Italians came from the cane fields of Queensland and from Western Australia. There were thousands of us spread across the many camps, separated by nationality—Germans, Italians, Japanese. Then later, boatloads of prisoners of war and internees from camps in England arrived. Some internees could continue their chosen trade inside. The camp needed gardeners, carpenters, barbers, cooks and medical staff. I could not be a shopkeeper, so I worked in the gardens and volunteered for labour outside the camp.'

'You were allowed to leave the camp?' Antonio blinked in surprise.

'Under guard of course,' he added. 'I tended the crops, cut timber to build the new dormitory buildings and worked in the poppy fields that made morphine for the soldiers. I would do anything that needed doing offsite just to be free of the depressing atmosphere behind the wire fences. Plus working earned me a shilling a day. We were not allowed money in the camps for fear that we would try to escape, and so the army kept it for us in deposit accounts. Instead, we were given tokens that we could use to pay for items like tobacco. But there was much unrest within the camps as well. Anti-fascist Italians were forced to live in the same camp as the fascists. It displeased the fascist activists that many of us chose to work. They said that we were supporting the Australian war effort. I tried to stay out of the politics but men who were sympathetic to Mussolini called me a traitor. A man was nearly strangled, I was punched in the face, slapped about a few times. I was seen as a traitor to Italy and treated like a criminal in my chosen home of Australia.'

'Did men die in the camp?' Matteo asked, thinking of the drowned man, Massimo.

'There were deaths. A man named Francesco Fantin was murdered by the fascists for standing up to them, for his principles. Some men took their own lives out of loneliness and depression. It was very hard for most of us at times. Your letters, and working outside of the camp, were the only things that kept me going in there.'

Matteo asked the question he needed desperately to know the answer to. 'Were you ever physically abused by the soldiers?'

'The soldiers were, for the most part, civil and we generally held a good rapport with the officers. But we were still prisoners.'

Antonio asked, 'How did you pass the time for five years? Did you always have to work?'

'Internees did not have to work at all if they did not want to. Many of us did simply because it was something to pass the hours and a way to earn some money. But there were also games. We could play poker and football. There was *bocce*. Some internees would sculpt out of the wood we collected, others would paint or draw. We even held plays and musicals and sometimes the soldiers would join in. It was very boring out there, for everyone.'

'All the soldiers were friendly then?' Loretta spoke up for the first time.

'There were some guards who were not very nice people,' Carlo said, but then he met Matteo's eyes. 'Bullies will always be bullies. Trevor Burrows was one of the worst.'

'*Che*?' Gia asked, wide-eyed. 'Trevor Burrows was a guard at the camp?'

'And you knew this?' Antonio looked accusingly at Matteo.

'I found out recently.'

Carlo nodded. 'Trevor arrived at the camp a year after I had been interned. It didn't take long to see that he felt the work he was asked to do with the army was beneath him. He took pleasure in treating us like criminals.'

'Why didn't the commanding officers of the camp do something about him?' Antonio asked.

'Bullies are always very good at hiding their attacks,' Carlo said. 'And we had no power. A younger man tried to tell one of the officers about Burrows' mistreatment. The next day he returned from work covered in excrement. He'd been on sanitation duty, digging new latrines, and Burrows had tripped him, pushed him into the bog. It was best to stay out of Trevor Burrows' way.' He crossed glances with Matteo. 'Then, one day, I was at the river with another Italian inmate ...'

Matteo listened again as his papa told the story he'd heard just that afternoon in Isabel's living room. The reason he believed Trevor Burrows had killed her father.

'Oh, *Dio*.' Gia put her lips to Lucia's soft hair as the little girl slept in her arms. 'Those poor women. What they have been through.'

'It is why I have urged you boys to avoid him to this day. I am sorry, Matteo. I should not have kept my silence for so long. You all deserved to know the truth of that time. I just wanted it all to be behind me. I did not know just how much my past would affect your future. And now, I fear Isabel will blame me, and perhaps you, because I did not speak up sooner about my suspicions.'

It was Matteo's turn to look wistfully out the window towards the hotel. Was he right? Would Isabel feel that his papa was in part to blame for her father's death? How was she dealing with the revelation that her father may have been murdered by his best friend?

'Trevor Burrows and Isabel's father let a man drown in the camp and then lied about it,' Antonio clarified. 'And you were friends with Sam Hayward in the internment camp?'

'Not exactly friends, no, but we would talk on occasion. I did not know that Trevor Burrows or Sam Hayward lived in this region when I moved here. The first time I ran into Sam in town he was as shocked to see me as I was him. The guilt he carried was etched on his face. We talked for a while and then continued to meet up again once a month or so. Just before he went missing, he told me he wanted to tell the truth about what had happened to Massimo Conti. While he was still at the camp, he discovered that Conti had a daughter. He tried to find her after the camps were closed, but she had moved when her mother had died and he did not know where to begin to look for her. I said I would see what I could find out. I was still in touch with some of the other internees. I wrote letters, asked if anyone had known the Contis, might know where his daughter would be now. Then one day,

Sam did not show up to one of our planned meetings. I heard a few days later that he had left. The gossip in this town is worse than the Italian grapevine. It was said that he had abandoned his family with no word. He hadn't even taken anything with him. I did not like the sound of this, but the talk was that he'd gone on a drinking binge and that he would be back. I remember wondering if he'd ever told Trevor Burrows what he intended to do, that he was trying to find Massimo's family. Then I heard that he had perhaps left his wife and daughter for another woman.'

'Did you wonder then if Trevor could have killed Isabel's dad?' Matteo asked.

His papa shook his head. 'It seemed impossible. They were friends. Time passed and I let it all go. I had my family, our farm to build up. It wasn't until you brought Isabel to the house for the harvest, when she told me her last name, and that she and her mother ran the Riverside Hotel, that I even thought of Sam again.'

His papa moved to him now, put his hands on his shoulders. 'I hope that my actions have not ruined what you and Isabel are beginning to find together. I have not been honest with you all and I fear I have caused you undue grief.'

Matteo looked back up towards the hotel again. 'I want to go to her, to see if she is okay.'

'Give her time,' his papa said. 'She will come to you when she is ready.'

'She is not what you imagined for me, is she?'

He glanced back at his parents just in time to see them exchange a look that said he was right.

'She is not Italian, she is not Catholic,' Matteo went on. 'I know that if Isabel and I somehow find a future together, we will face anger and resentment from many people—both her friends and ours. I have to say that I don't care. I hope that, at least, I can count on my own family to support me, to support us.'

'You have grown into a good man, Matteo. And from what I have seen, especially in these last days, Isabel is a very good woman. I know you will find your way. You do not need your papa to tell you how to live your life.' His papa grinned in a way Matteo hadn't seen in years. Like a huge burden had been released from his shoulders. 'You have your mama for that, eh?'

'And don't forget it.' Gia gave them all her most frightening narrow-eyed glare before handing Lucia back to Loretta and moving to put her arms around Carlo. She kissed his lips, and touched a hand to his cheek in a way that made Matteo wish even more that he could go to Isabel and console her.

'Now, I want to go over to the kitchen at the hotel. Those women are in mourning. We must do what we can to help them.'

'I'll come with you, Gia,' Loretta said.

'You need rest, Loretta,' Antonio told her.

'I am pregnant, Antonio. I am not made of glass,' she told him, settling the little girl on his lap. 'You can take care of Lucia for a few hours.'

'But I need to help Papa sort through our things,' he argued, looking scared as Lucia began to cry.

'Matteo will help me,' Carlo put in. 'Spend some time with your daughter, Antonio. I missed too many days with you boys, too many years. And there is a woman over there in the hotel who lost her father too soon. You must cherish every moment you have with your children.'

Matteo felt lighter for seeing his father's smile. He could almost see the papa he'd known as a child. Before the war, before Loveday.

Matteo couldn't remember a time when he'd felt more physically and emotionally drained. And that was saying something considering the last three months. Floods aside, the loss of his house, and his papa's admission that afternoon was enough to break even the strongest back. But what Isabel was dealing with was infinitely worse.

Matteo had left Isabel alone while she came to terms with the loss of her father for a second time. He had learned so much about his own papa and had let the stories he'd told him swirl through his mind and sink in. Hearing what his papa had faced was hard, but it was so much better than not knowing.

Worn out by all the emotion, Matteo was ready to hit his bunk in the caravan. He stripped off down to his singlet and long underwear, dropped onto his bed and was about to turn out the light when a knock at his door had him sighing.

What now?

He hadn't heard the siren so the levee hadn't broken. He moved to open the door and blinked, surprised, as he was forced to step back when Isabel pushed her way into the caravan and shut the door behind her.

'Isabel? What—?'

'Sorry. There are so many eyes out there. I had to get out of sight fast.'

'Out of … why? What are you—?'

He staggered back again when she grabbed his shirt and yanked him down so she could lay her lips against his in a sort of fevered rush.

Shock at the sudden assault had him pulling back just to regain his breath. 'Isabel, what is going on?'

'I just want to be close to you tonight. I don't want to talk. I don't want to think. Is that okay?'

'It's okay, but—'

'Life is so short, so precious, so up to the gods or Mother Nature, whoever. I don't want to waste any more time. Be with me, Matteo.'

She kissed him again and every nerve ending in his body went on high alert, sizzling sparks of electricity shooting across his flesh as her mouth stayed locked to his. Her tongue danced along his lips until he opened and let her in. He almost lost his grip on his control but remembering the revelations of the day he forced himself to step back and break the connection.

'Isabel. *Mi amore*. You've had a shock. Are you sure you're thinking straight?'

'I told you, I don't want to think at all.'

'Sweetheart, slow down.'

She blinked, staring up at him with wide, green eyes filled with hurt. 'Don't you want me?'

He pressed his forehead to hers as he fought to catch his breath. '*Dio, bella*. I want you every time I see you. I want you even in my dreams.'

He kissed her lightly, but still held her at a safe distance, summoning a strength he never knew he owned.

'You've just found out—'

She put her hand across his mouth. 'No. Don't say it. I'm tired of thinking about it. I'm tired of talking. I'm … I'm tired.'

He kissed the palm across his mouth before gently removing it and kissing the top of her hand. 'Isabel, I know what it's like to learn that things were not as you always thought. For many years I thought my father's silence was about the horrors he endured at the hands of his captors. I held terrible prejudices against this country, against the people. Now I find out all of my biases were misinformed. Internment aside, my father's pain was built from his own guilt. Guilt for not speaking up about an injustice that happened all those years ago.'

'Guilt for not speaking up about something *my* father was involved with. And that is what is so painful to me. Not just that he cheated on Mum with some other woman, but that my father could be responsible for the death of another man.'

'I am sorry your father was a part of that,' he said. 'War time does strange things to people. He was away from you both, he had a drinking problem. From what I heard, it sounded like it was all Trevor.'

'But Dad was there, and he never spoke up.'

'Trevor threatened my papa,' Matteo said. 'Maybe he threatened your dad too.'

'But Trevor was his friend,' Isabel cried. 'I thought they were friends. I still can't believe Trevor could be responsible for killing my dad. It seems so …'

'Vicious? Callous?' Matteo suggested. 'From everything I know about Trevor Burrows those two words fit him perfectly. I do not have such a hard time believing he could hurt your father. But we should wait until the police have investigated, until they find Trevor. Maybe you could talk to my papa. I think it will help both of you. He can tell you stories about your father. It might help you to know him better.'

'I'm not sure I want to hear them.' Isabel's face was a picture of weariness and confusion. 'I came here because I wanted to forget for a while. I wanted you to hold me. I just wanted to feel … something else, anything else. I can't take this pain, this emptiness of losing my father all over again.'

He stepped to her and rubbed his thumb across her cheek to remove the tear that had fallen. 'I am sorry you have to go through this. And I want to be with you, Isabel. I do. I want to make love with you and sleep the night with you and wake up with you in my arms like we did this morning. But I want it to be because you want all that too. Not because you are trying to replace bad memories with good ones. And they will be good memories when we finally make love.'

She smiled through sad eyes. 'Can I at least stay with you tonight?'

He opened his mouth to object, but she got in first.

'Not to make love. Just …' She hesitated. 'Just … I want you to hold me. We don't have to make love. At least, not tonight.'

The offer was there. Not tonight, but sometime. And he wondered how he'd be able to control himself with her lying all warm and sleepy beside him. Not on the floor of her living room, as they had been just that morning, but in the privacy of his caravan. He didn't have the heart, or the strength, to turn her away.

'I can offer you that comfort tonight.'

She tugged on his hand and he moved to sit beside her on the bed. She leaned into him, laying her head against his chest as he put his arms around her. Her hair smelled like the rain she'd walked through to get to him. They stayed like that for a long time and when he heard her sigh, and felt her body relax, he knew she needed sleep.

Leaning back, he pushed her jacket off her shoulders.

'Let's get into bed,' he said softly. He lifted her legs one at a time, untying the laces of her sturdy boots and dropping them to the floor with a thud. They crawled under the covers and within minutes of being cocooned in his arms beneath warm woollen blankets, she was breathing heavily in sleep.

'I love you, Isabel,' he whispered, kissing her forehead and following her into sleep.

In that soft place between sleep and waking, Isabel floated for a moment before remembering where she was. In Matteo's caravan, in Matteo's bed. Her eyes flew open and locked immediately onto the pale blue of Matteo's.

'Good morning, sleepy head,' he said, his voice low and quiet.

Sultry. That was the word she would have used to describe it. It reverberated through her and it was then she realised just how close she had snuggled in to him in sleep.

'Good morning.' She knew she should move back but she didn't want to. He was warm, hot even, and taking a chance, she lay her palm against his chest. The heat radiated through the thin cotton singlet he wore.

'Did you sleep well?' he asked, brushing a loose strand of hair from her forehead.

'I did. What time is it?'

'About five. You should probably go back into the hotel before people begin to wake,' he suggested, trying to move away and sit up.

She grabbed at his singlet and pulled him back down, taking his mouth with hers before he could object.

'Isabel—'

She looked into his eyes again. 'Did you say you love me last night?'

He hesitated momentarily. '*Sì*. I did. I didn't think you'd heard me.'

'I did. Say it again.'

He smiled. 'I love you, my *bella* Isabel. So very much.'

She grinned and kissed him again. 'Your mama taught me something else in Italian yesterday too. *Ti amo*.'

His grin beamed out at her use of Italian.

'I love you too, Matteo, *mi amore*. So very much. Be mine,' she pleaded, kissing his cheeks, his neck. 'Here, and now. Be mine, Matteo.'

He murmured to her in Italian, words she didn't understand, but didn't need to. It romanced her. He romanced her as his arms held her against him, as he kissed her dreamily, as his hands swept down her body, inciting and igniting little sparks across her sensitive skin.

He removed the last of her clothing, slowly, never taking his mouth from hers. There was nothing but the smell of him, the feel of him. His hard body pressed against hers as now, fully naked, they joined together. They moulded to one another in a way she never had with another man. Because this was love, she realised. She loved him and so their lovemaking was perfect.

He was tender, but still managed to have her fighting the urge to call out as he sent waves of lust and excitement rolling through her body. And when they had sated the tension in both of them, he curled around her, protective and loving.

Birdsong heralded the coming morning although it was still very dark outside the windows of the caravan.

'I don't want to leave you.' She spoke into the silence that had fallen.

'It is only for a while.'

She sighed, relaxed and sad all at once. 'I'd better get back into the hotel. Will I see you for breakfast?'

'Of course.' He kissed her nose, then her lips. One long, lasting kiss to send her on her way.

'Get some more sleep,' she told him.

Isabel rolled out from beneath his arm and the warmth of his bed. Dressing quickly, she slipped as discreetly as she could out of the caravan into the freezing, mist-covered dawn. Hoping that the remaining darkness would hide her from the morning levee patrols, she made a dash for the door to the residence wing of the hotel. Once inside, she leaned back against the door, closed her eyes and let the dreamy smile spread across her face.

Sixteen

There hadn't been any point to Isabel going back to bed once she'd left Matteo's caravan. Breakfast had to be made for the volunteers. Mrs Sorrenti and Loretta would no doubt also be in the kitchen soon, ready to help with the cooking.

She thought of Matteo and wondered when he would wake and visit her in the kitchen too. Her belly clenched deliciously as she remembered the exquisite night she'd spent in his arms. And he loved her. He loved *her.* That beautiful, wonderful, sensual man was in love with her. How had the last few days gone from her feeling so devastated at the loss of the Sorrentis' home, so heartbroken at learning her dad had been dead all this time, to feeling so much love that she was bursting with it? Lack of sleep or not, she danced around the kitchen with a newfound energy.

Still thinking of Matteo, Isabel rushed to open the kitchen door when she heard a knock.

She couldn't stop her expression of disappointment. 'Ross?'

And suddenly she was tired again, her good mood smothered simply at the sight of him.

'Yeah. Can we talk?'

'If this is about us again, there is nothing more to say. You and I are never going to happen.'

'It's not,' he said. When she eyed him, unsure, he crossed his heart. 'I promise.'

Reluctantly, she grabbed her coat from the peg and stepped out into the fresh morning air. The wind was gusting, and in the east, the sun was fighting a losing battle, trying to push through dark grey clouds that hung heavy, ready to drop yet more rain onto the saturated land.

'What are you doing here so early?' She wrapped her coat around her to stave off the chill, not only from the near freezing wind that was blowing a gale, but from the memory of what she'd learned the day before about his father's possible involvement in her dad's death.

'My dad's gone.'

'Gone? Gone where?'

'I don't know. After he left here yesterday, he didn't come back to the house. The cops have been round asking us all sorts of questions. Mum's a wreck. Grandad's got his lawyers involved, trying to manage everyone and everything, as usual.' Ross spoke to the ground, wouldn't meet her eyes. 'I think they actually believe he killed your dad.'

Isabel didn't say anything. If the police were accusing Trevor, they must have had evidence to back it up.

'He didn't kill your dad, Isabel, you have to know that.'

'Ross, I don't want to talk about this now.' She turned her back on him, aiming on heading inside.

'Dad is a lot of things,' Ross continued. She stopped with her hand on the doorknob. 'A drunk, and, yeah, he has a temper. I know that better than anyone. But your dad was his best mate. He would never have killed his best mate.'

Facing him again, she rubbed her tired eyes. 'He might have if he thought my dad was going to come clean about the death of that man in the internment camp.'

'That was a decade ago,' Ross argued. 'Who does it help bringing that to the police now?'

'Oh, I don't know, his family maybe,' Isabel threw back, irritated. 'Speaking as someone whose own father disappeared without a trace, I'm sure Massimo Conti's daughter would like to know what happened to him. It will break her heart to hear that someone let him drown, but not knowing what happened to your own father is torturous, Ross. She needs to know.'

'You just said it, he drowned. Our dads didn't kill him.'

'Maybe not, but they stood by and let it happen. They could have helped him and they didn't. The guilt must have eaten Dad up all those years. It's no doubt why he ended up drinking so much. It's all making sense to me now. Carlo said Dad was going to tell Trevor what he'd decided to do. If Carlo's right, and my dad wanted to tell the police what had happened, then maybe Trevor decided to make sure he didn't.'

'But Dad's not a murderer. Come on, Isabel, you know him. If something happened between Sam and my dad it had to be an accident. That Italian bloke just wants revenge for being locked up during the war.'

Isabel sighed. She still hadn't sorted through all the revelations of the day before. 'The medallion proves that Trevor was with my dad out at Lake Ranfurly. Why would he have it otherwise? Even if it was an accident, why wouldn't Trevor call the police or come and tell Mum what happened?'

Tears began to build, and Isabel felt her throat closing on sobs as everything she said started to make sense. Her father had been murdered by one of his best friends, buried in a shallow grave out in the treeless dirtlands that surrounded Lake Ranfurly. Every time she thought about it, she wanted to be physically sick.

'Ross, if your dad is so innocent, why is he hiding from the police? Why did he run when they arrived? Why won't he talk to them about the last time he saw my dad? If it was an accident, he shouldn't have anything to hide.' She wanted to scream, wanted to throw things, wanted to punch Ross right in his arrogant, ignorant face. 'Go home, Ross. Mum and I have a lot to deal with. The police investigation is ongoing, the floodwaters are rising and if the levee breaks, we'll lose our livelihood and our home and somewhere in there we have to find time to bury my dad. Go home, Ross,' she repeated. 'I can't face you right now.'

She turned her back and was about to close the kitchen door on him when he spoke again, this time with disgust in his voice.

'I saw you, you know.'

She sighed and looked back at him. 'You saw me what, Ross?'

'I saw you coming out of that dago's caravan this morning.'

Caught between shock and anger at the rapid change in his demeanour from conciliatory to vicious, Isabel just stared at him.

'You're sleeping with him? With *him*?'

'I don't have to explain myself to anyone,' she shot back. 'Especially not to you. You can't hate a man simply because of his heritage or the colour of his skin, Ross. If you do that, you'll be no better than your father. Do you want to end up like him?'

Ross couldn't have looked more shocked than if she'd slapped him across the face.

She rubbed a hand across her eyes. 'I'm tired and I have to get breakfast started. Go home, Ross.'

But before she could turn to go back into the kitchen, Ross grabbed her arm, tugging so hard she nearly lost her footing.

Isabel struggled against his iron grip. 'Ross, you're hurting me.'

'Let her go.' Matteo's deep voice was dangerously quiet as he joined them at the kitchen steps.

Ross pointed a finger at Matteo. 'Stay out of this, dago.'

'Do what she says and go home, Burrows,' Matteo said with a calmness that surprised Isabel. 'Don't make things worse for your family.'

'You go home. Go back to where you came from. Just because you managed to talk Isabel into slumming it and sleeping with you in that shitty caravan of yours—'

Ross didn't see the punch coming and neither had Isabel. She gasped as Matteo shook the hand that he'd ploughed into Ross's face.

Ross wiped at the blood that trickled from his nose. 'This is all your fault, you bastard.'

He moved so quickly and Matteo's head snapped back with the return punch before the two of them hit the ground with a sickening thud when Ross leaped on him. The two men rolled on the wet ground, trading punches.

'Stop it! Stop it, both of you!' Isabel tried to get in between them and Matteo jumped up to move her out of the way just as Ross scrambled to his feet. Matteo turned and landed a gut punch to Ross that had him whooshing out a heavy breath.

'Isabel, stay back!' Matteo shouted as the two men circled each other as the rain began to fall in heavy sheets. They slid on the wet, muddy ground, throwing punches that missed more than they connected. Still, when the occasional blow struck, Isabel winced.

The yelling and fighting soon drew people out of their beds and bungalows despite the rain.

'Isabel, what on earth is going on?'

She turned to her mum as she stepped out of the pub in her dressing gown. 'Mum! We have to do something. They're gonna kill each other.'

'Men!' Her mum rolled her eyes. Scanning the watching crowd, she zeroed in on Garry, one of the regulars that passed through and stayed at the hotel. 'Hey, Gazza! Grab a few of your cronies and break that up, will you?'

'Right, Mrs H.'

Garry, with the help of several of the large truckies, moved in, dodging legs and fists as they, too, slipped around in the mud and rain trying to separate the battling men.

'Oi, blokes! Most ladies aren't worth all this,' Garry said to Matteo as he dodged a right hook meant for Ross. Ross managed to duck it, and throwing off the restraining hands, ran at Matteo again and the two men tumbled to the ground, rolling over the wet grass as the truckies tried their best to break things up without copping a fist or foot to their nether regions.

Isabel saw Gia and Carlo emerge from the bungalow. Carlo grabbed at Antonio's collar before he could run in to help Matteo. Carlo walked out into the rain and Isabel could see he was gauging his moment to step in, but the truckies had it in hand.

Beneath the yells and cheers, Isabel heard the rising whir in the distance. She pushed in to stand between the men again as the two fought against the now vicelike hold the truckies had on them.

'Stop!' she yelled, looking furiously back and forth between Matteo and Ross. 'Shut up or I'll kick both your stupid arses.'

'Isabel!' her mum said. 'Take it easy.'

'No!' Isabel yelled again. 'Stop! All of you! Just listen!'

In the small lapse, between the heavy breathing of the fighters, the pelting rain and gusting wind in the trees overhead, the whirring got louder as it went up an octave. Then another sounded. All along the river, sirens began to wail.

'It's all this rain and wind. The levees can't take the pressure,' Carlo said.

Then the bell they'd all come to recognise—the big brass bell known for calling last drinks that now served as an early warning system—clanged from the river side of the hotel.

'Oh, Lord. That's our levee,' Isabel's mum said, her eyes wide.

The truckies let Matteo and Ross go as everyone rushed around to the river.

Perry was still ringing the bell as they reached him. 'I wondered where everyone had gone. There!' He pointed to where the dirt wall was crumbling.

The fight forgotten, anyone who wasn't already dressed donned boots and coats and headed down to where the water had begun to overtop the levee. The waves on the river, whipped up by the wind, crashed against the wall of dirt and sandbags. Small trickles began to widen between the bags and dirt in several places.

'There's another break here!' someone called from the levee wall by the creek.

Moving quickly, Isabel followed Carlo and rushed with Matteo and Ross towards the breach. Men were already taking spare sandbags and piling them over the holes in the levee where water was seeping through.

'We have to get on top,' Carlo called out. 'The waves are eating the levee away, the dirt there is sinking.'

'Let's get a line formed,' Matteo called, pulling himself up the side of the wall. 'Send those sandbags up one at a time.'

Isabel watched nervously as Matteo and Ross stood on top of the levee. She didn't like that the two men were in such close proximity given recent events. Matteo sported a bloody lip, and the blood from Ross's split eyebrow was running down his cheek, mixing with the rain and mud. With no choice but to leave them, she jumped into a line of men and women, Albert and Flo, her friends, the local baker, and together they handed the sandbags along and up to the two men who did their best to build up the wall where the earth was being eaten by the river.

Every now and again she'd look up at where Matteo and Ross balanced precariously on the edge of the levee wall, adding sandbags to the top to try and stave the flow of water. They were soaked through as they worked together to fill the holes. It seemed they'd put aside their differences, for now.

Thank God.

A dump truck had arrived late the night before, full of sand. Its driver had been bunked down, asleep in the cab, but now he backed the truck down towards the levee. Matteo and Ross scrambled back out of the way as Antonio guided the driver up. The tray lifted slowly to dump the earth on top of the weakest part of the levee wall.

Antonio joined Jack from the bakery at the edge of the tray as they scooped out dirt with their shovels. The winds were howling now, causing waves to push against the levee as the river tried to reach over the wall.

'Look out!'

The call came too late.

Both Antonio and Jack jolted as the tray of the truck was struck by powerlines that were waving in the strong winds. Antonio fell against the lifted truck tray, unconscious, but Jack shook in a horrific dance as two hundred and forty volts of electricity shot through the men.

'Antonio!' Matteo dropped his shovel to run to his brother's aid, but Ross grabbed him quickly.

'No, don't touch them!'

'Let me go!' Matteo shoved at Ross with force, but Ross held on.

'You'll get zapped yourself, if you try, you idiot!'

The driver, realising what had happened, lowered the tray, effectively breaking the connection with the dangling wires.

People dashed to the aid of Antonio and Jack.

They lifted Antonio carefully down from the truck. Jack simply shook his head, insisted he was fine and picked up a shovel to continue working.

'You need to see a doctor,' Carlo insisted.

'Balderdash!' Jack argued. 'I'm fit as a fiddle.'

Isabel shook her head at the stubborn old fool and looked back to the top of the levee.

'Where's Matteo? Where's Ross?'

She and Carlo looked around, expecting to see that the two men had come down off the levee to check on Antonio, but they were nowhere to be seen.

Isabel crossed terrified glances with Carlo before they both scrambled up to the top of the levee.

'Help!'

Looking down the swollen creek where it joined the widened river, they could only just see Ross, further down the levee wall, flat on his stomach and leaning out into the turbulent water. He had hold of Matteo by the collar of his shirt.

'Hurry! I can't hold him much longer!' Ross called out as Isabel and Carlo rushed towards him.

'No! He can't swim!' Isabel called, panicked.

Matteo was struggling against the force of the river, the waves constantly rushing over his head. Carlo leaned down to help Ross pull Matteo from the river back onto the relative safety of the levee wall. He flopped onto the top of the levee like a landed fish.

'Are you alright?' Isabel asked, dropping to her knees next to Matteo. She pushed his hair from his face, kissed his cheeks. 'Oh my God, you're freezing.' She turned and started slapping at Ross. 'You bastard! What did you do?'

'Ow! Isabel, stop! I didn't do anything!'

'You thought you'd finish him off by pushing him into the river?' Isabel yelled against the wind, slapping him again once more for good measure.

Matteo coughed up dirty Murray water for a moment before catching his breath enough to speak. 'Isabel, don't. I was trying to get to Antonio. Ross stopped me.'

'He would have been electrocuted too if he'd touched them or that truck,' Ross explained, his arms crossed defensively in front of his body until Isabel stopped smacking him.

'I was fighting him and we slipped,' Matteo went on between chattering teeth. 'We both fell into the river. It was my fault. Ross caught me and dragged me to the edge of the levee. He saved me, Isabel. He saved me.'

Isabel was speechless but Carlo laid a hand on Ross's shoulder. 'Thank you, Ross. You are a good man.'

'Unlike my father, you mean.' Shrugging Carlo's hand away, Ross stood, gracing Isabel and Matteo with one last resigned look, before sliding down the muddy levee bank and disappearing into the busy crowds still working below.

Isabel felt bad for accusing Ross, but she was more concerned about Matteo for the moment.

'Are you sure you're okay?' Isabel asked as they all slid down the side of the levee.

'I'm fine,' Matteo said, coughing again. He turned to his father. 'How is Antonio?'

'He was unconscious,' Carlo said. 'The police have taken him to the hospital. Loretta and your mama have taken the truck and gone with them.'

Matteo nodded, shivering uncontrollably now.

'You need to get some dry clothes and something warm into you,' Isabel said as her mother joined them.

'I need to keep helping fix the levee,' Matteo argued.

'We've got it for now,' Perry said. The man was barely recognisable under the layers of mud. 'Both breaks are plugged but the river is still rising and the wind and those waves aren't helping. If we don't get this section by the creek built up, it'll overtop and the bakery and the hotel will be history.'

Audrey turned to the exhausted crowd of helpers. 'Anyone who's not patrolling get into the pub to dry off by the fire.

Isabel, let's get back in and get on some brekkie and hot drinks for everyone. Then we come back out into the rain and do it all over again.'

'I'll just go get changed in the caravan and see you inside the pub, Isabel,' Matteo said, looking across to the hotel where Ross sat on the steps of the verandah, his head in his hands. 'Don't be too hard on him,' he told Isabel. 'I owe him my life.'

Exhausted, soaked to the skin and still reeling from the thought she could have lost Matteo to the river, Isabel threw her arms around him and squeezed tight. 'I was so scared.'

'I'm okay, *bella*,' he said quietly in her ear. 'I'll be back soon.' He kissed her cheek and walked across to his caravan, leaving Isabel with her mum.

It was hard to stay angry with Ross when he looked so forlorn. In her own pain and confusion, she really hadn't given much thought to what Ross was going through as well. Finding out his father was possibly a killer had to be weighing on him.

'Come on, Ross,' Audrey said. 'We owe you a feed.'

'Thanks, Mrs H,' Ross said, standing to follow her up into the pub.

Out of the corner of her eye, Isabel saw Shirley Burrows walking towards them, wrapping her winter coat around her.

'Ross.' She elbowed him.

'Mum? What are you doing here?' He looked around. 'Where's Dad?'

'That's a good question, isn't it?' she responded as she stepped under the shelter of the verandah.

'You drove yourself?'

'I do know how to drive, my son,' Shirley told him with a pointed look. 'I just choose not to. You are going to drive me home, but first I need a word with Audrey.'

Isabel exchanged a wary glance with her mother. What could the woman possibly want? Isabel wasn't feeling overly generous towards the Burrows family just at that moment and if Shirley Burrows was about to blame them for Trevor's disappearance … well, Isabel was having none of it.

'Isabel, you can find some of your dad's old clothes for Ross to wear home.'

Ross shook his head. 'I'm good. I'll change later.'

'And I'm staying put,' Isabel said, her eyes narrowed on Shirley.

'Isabel—'

'She can stay,' Shirley said. 'Ross, wait in the car. I will be there in a minute.'

'I'm ready to go now, Mum. Come on, I'll take you home,' Ross said.

Isabel studied Ross's face and wondered if he too was expecting her to launch into accusations.

'Home is under water,' Shirley said, turning back to Audrey and Isabel. She paused momentarily, as though carefully thinking over what she would say. 'You and I used to be close, Audrey.'

'We did,' she agreed.

'I can't change my behaviour from years ago. I am sorry we lost that friendship and went our separate ways,' Shirley said.

'I'm sorry for that too, Shirley.'

'There's not much I can do about that now, but I want to … I can … apologise for the … grief that my family has caused yours.'

Isabel looked at her mum. Surprise was quickly replaced by sympathy on her mum's face. 'Shirley, your family didn't cause it. You didn't cause it. Even if the police find that Trevor killed Sam, you have nothing to apologise for.'

'All the same.'

The awkwardness could have been cut with one of Isabel's chef's knives.

'I'm sorry to hear you lost your home,' Audrey said, and Isabel was astounded at her mother's endless supply of compassion. 'Do you have somewhere to live?'

Shirley nodded. 'My father-in-law, Roy, has plenty of room for us. Speaking of which, he is waiting at the police station. Ross, we need to go.' She looked out towards the river and the hive of activity that continued between the pub and the river. 'I hope you are able to save your home.'

Shirley turned away from the hotel. She popped up a large black umbrella and walked to the car.

'I'd better go,' Ross said, staring after his mum. He looked terribly sad.

Isabel walked him to the edge of the verandah. 'Sorry I smacked you.'

He just shrugged.

'I can't thank you enough for what you did,' Isabel said. 'Helping with the levee, saving Matteo.'

'I thought about letting him go.'

Isabel stared at him, horrified. 'Ross—'

'But that would make me as bad as my dad. I'm sorry, Isabel. I don't know if my dad killed yours. I don't know if I can believe he is capable of that. Don't want to believe it, probably. I'm sorry for whatever part he played in it.'

Isabel nodded. She wasn't as ready to forgive as her mum had been.

Ross rubbed his hand across his still wet, muddy hair. 'I hear what people say. That I'm just like him. That I'm going to grow up to be a drunken bully too. I don't want to be like that.'

'Then don't, Ross. You have a choice. You can choose to be a good person.' She wondered if perhaps it would be a blessing in disguise if Trevor Burrows never came home. Ross might just grow to be a decent man if he was out from beneath his father's bad influence.

He walked out into the rain, climbed into his mother's car and shut the door. Winding the window down a touch, he called out, 'I'll pick my car up later. See ya round, Isabel.'

The engine purred to life, the radio blaring as Joan Weber cried for her lover to let her go. Ross sat for a moment as the lyrics rang out the open car window. He sent her a sad smile, shook his head and drove away.

The levee was holding.

Men continued to patrol the wall of dirt that surrounded the hotel and the bakery, watching every inch with eagle eyes.

By sundown, the hotel dining room was finally emptying out as people who'd been there working to shore up the levee most of the day began to head home for a well-earned sleep. Isabel stood inside the window watching the lanterns light up over the levee with worry and a weariness she'd never known. She must have cooked a hundred bacon sandwiches that morning, then about twice that many sausages and boiled potatoes for lunch. The soup on the stove would serve for those who remained and the workers on the night shift.

'Isabel.'

'Hmm?' she asked, turning away from the window to see who'd called her.

Gia stood in the middle of the front bar, hands on hips as she studied her. 'You need to eat something.'

'No, I'm fine,' Isabel argued, rubbing her face to try and wake up a bit as she wandered back into the kitchen with Gia on her heels. 'How's Antonio?'

Gia and Loretta had brought Antonio home from the hospital that evening. He'd regained consciousness in the police car on the way to the hospital and then spent the next few hours complaining that he was fine until the doctors let him leave.

'Antonio is whining like a little boy, so he is fine. Loretta has him confined to bed for the night. You should also go and lie down for a few hours before the dinner rush. I can do the preparation.'

'You've been so kind, Mrs Sorrenti, but a chef is always in charge of her kitchen,' Isabel said, repeating words Gia had said to her during one of her teaching sessions.

'*Mula*.'

Isabel frowned. 'What does that mean?'

'It means mule. Stubborn as a donkey, you are. You're as bad as Matteo. You deserve each other.'

'You don't mind the idea of me and Matteo, do you?' Isabel asked, then quickly shut her mouth. God, she must be tired. She shouldn't have dared ask.

'Why do you think I should mind?' Gia asked, her eyes narrowed.

'I wondered if I might not be what you pictured for Matteo. Not the type of girl you would want for him.'

'Because you run a pub or because you are not Italian?'

Her heart sank. Both were no doubt reasonable excuses for Mrs Sorrenti to wish for someone else for her son—culture and religion being top of the list. An Italian Catholic boy and a non-practising Australian Protestant girl would do more than raise eyebrows in the region. But there was another reason for her fear that far outweighed what the local gossips might say. 'I was thinking you would not want me in Matteo's life because of my father and his involvement in the death of a man, and because of the guilt and anguish he caused your husband.'

Gia sank down onto a stool at the kitchen bench. 'I had a lot of anger for this country during the war. For taking my Carlo from me, from my boys. For leaving them without a father for so many years.'

'I can understand that.'

Gia nodded. 'But anger and hate only cause suffering for the person who holds onto them.'

It was very wise, Isabel thought. And so true. She'd suffered for years being angry at her father for leaving them. Only to find out, he'd never left them at all. At least, not of his own accord.

'I see how my Matteo looks at you,' Gia said, her eyes softening. 'I see how you look at him. If it is love, what I think or believe has no place to come between you. As it happens, I like you. You are a kind and generous woman. You have showed us that, taking my family into your home without question. Even after Matteo had been a fool.'

Isabel smiled. 'He wasn't a fool, not really. He was hurting. He loves you and Carlo so much.' She paused. 'And I love him.'

Gia stood and moved to Isabel, placing her hands on either side of her face. 'Then I bless your love and hope you will find happiness. Matteo will survive for a few months while you go to Melbourne to the cooking school.'

'Cooking school?'

Isabel spun around to face the door to the bar. She hadn't heard her mum come in.

'You're going to cooking school?' her mum asked again. 'In Melbourne? When did this happen?'

'Oh, I haven't … I didn't.' Isabel fumbled her words.

'You haven't told your mama you want to go to school in Melbourne?' Gia asked, judgement written all over her features. 'You do not lie to your mama.'

'I didn't lie.' Isabel nervously faced her mother. 'I just didn't tell you. And anyway, it doesn't matter. I can't go. The course starts in September and goes for six months. I can't go away for six months now. Not with the floods still on our doorstep and the investigation into Dad's death …' She faltered at her mother's wince.

'The investigation will happen without you here.'

'But I can't leave you to face all that alone,' Isabel insisted. 'It's okay, Mum, I want to stay and be with you. I need to.'

'I need you to be happy.'

'I am happy.'

'I've been so blind.' Tears welled in her mum's eyes. 'I thought you were hiding here. Just working in the kitchen because you didn't want to leave me alone. I didn't realise just how desperately you wanted to be a cook, a chef. You've been saving all your wages to pay for the school, haven't you? That's why you don't go out that much. Why didn't you tell me?'

'I tried to tell you, I did, sort of.' Isabel sniffed. 'Anyway, it doesn't matter. I can't leave you alone here. Who'd do the cooking?'

Audrey dusted her daughter's fringe from her eyes. 'I've always said you should have a life outside this hotel. I won't let you put your dreams on hold because of me. We'll figure something out.'

Isabel and her mother began to argue until Gia interrupted. 'If I can make a suggestion.' She'd stood so quietly in the corner of the kitchen Isabel had forgotten she was there. She was horrified at her behaviour in front of Matteo's mum.

Gia stepped forward. 'I would be happy to take care of the kitchen while Isabel goes to school.'

Isabel felt hope bloom, but her mother's answer deflated her again. 'Oh, Gia, we can't ask you to do that.'

'Please. My offer is not entirely selfless,' Gia explained. 'It is going to take time for us to find a new home, somewhere we can live until the water subsides and we can get the farm going again. If we could stay living here at the hotel until then, we can pay you for our accommodation by working. Antonio, Matteo and Carlo can help with handyman work. The mess this flood will leave behind will be very big. We can help with the clean-up and … I could take over the kitchen from Isabel. Until she returns, of course.'

Isabel was so moved by Mrs Sorrenti's offer she wiped at her tears and took a deep breath. 'Thank you, but the investigation, Dad's funeral … I can't leave Mum.'

'You can and you will,' her mum said, the determination back in her voice now. 'Gia, we accept your kind offer.'

The two women shook hands as Isabel looked on in shock.

Her mum turned back to her and took her by the shoulders. 'Isabel, I want you to go and do your studies; become the chef you want to be. Then, when you've got your diploma, you can come back here and run the kitchen at the pub if you want to. And if you don't want to, if you find a fantastic job at a restaurant in the city, that's okay too.'

'I'll be back,' Isabel said, grinning like a crazy person. 'There is nowhere else I want to be.'

'Does a certain young man have something to do with that?' her mum asked. 'I hope he's as happy with you going away for a few months as I am.'

Isabel's smile faded. Their love had only just started to bloom. How would he feel about her leaving him for half a year?

Isabel found Matteo down by the levee at the creek. She shook her head at the sight of him. He'd changed out of his clothes, sodden from his unexpected swim in the river earlier that day, but was once again soaked from the continuous rain.

Walking up behind him, she was suddenly overwhelmed by the emotion, the memory of the fear of what could have happened if Ross hadn't been there to save him. With no regard for who might see them, she threw her arms around him from behind and just held on.

He turned his head to look at her, surprised. 'Isabel? *Bella?*'

'You're safe.'

'*Si*, I am safe.' He turned to face her, and she just pulled him in again and squeezed him tight. 'But I am wet.'

'You're always wet.' She laughed. '*We're* always wet. Every damn one of us. I don't think we will ever be fully dry again. I don't care. Just hold me.'

A few whistles and catcalls rang out from those patrolling the levees.

He pushed her back, took her face in his hands and kissed her, quickly and chastely. 'Are you alright? You look worried. It has been a terrible few days, an exhausting few months.' He lowered his voice. 'Will you stay with me tonight? I want to sleep beside you again.'

'Just sleep?'

He pressed his forehead to hers. 'If that's all, it will be enough.'

She nodded. 'But first, I have something I need to tell you.'

His smile faded. She couldn't fault him for that. The last time she'd had something to tell him, he'd discovered her father was his papa's guard in the prison camp. She was nervous. How would he react to her going away?

'Your mother has kindly offered to look after the kitchen at the pub over the next few months,' she started.

'She has? I thought you were happy about being in charge of the kitchen now?'

'I am,' she agreed, swallowing hard. 'Matteo, remember how I told you I want to go to Melbourne, to the Emily McPherson College of Domestic Economy?'

'Yes.'

'What I didn't tell you is that I was already accepted,' she said. 'I was accepted to start in the September term. I'll be leaving here in a few weeks. Are you okay with that?'

He stared at her quietly for a moment, not giving away any clues. 'Am I okay with that?'

'Yes.'

His eyes narrowed. 'And what if I was to say that I am not okay with you going away to chase your dreams of becoming a chef in Melbourne?'

She frowned, her heart sinking. 'Is that what you're doing?'

He shook his head. 'If it was, I would be beyond disappointed if you listened to me.'

She nearly exploded with the relief she felt.

'Isabel, I am not Ross. I want you to achieve everything you desire. Did you think I would try to hold you back? That I could ever stop you from pursuing something that you have worked so hard to obtain?' He grinned broadly. 'You are going to be a chef. And I am so proud of you.'

'But we will be apart for months.'

He kissed one hand, then the other, then her nose. 'And I will miss you terribly. But I will visit you in Melbourne, and you will come home for Christmas, yes?'

'Yes.'

'We will make it work, Isabel. Because I love you, so we must.'

'I love you too, Matteo.'

He put his arm around her and walked her away from the light of the kerosene lamps and into the shadows. 'You do not know this about me, but I am a wonderful letter writer.'

She chuckled. 'Really? Will you write me romantic letters?'

'I will. September is not far away. I think you should come with me now and I will give you a little preview of just how romantic I can be,' he said, leading her towards his caravan.

She chuckled. 'I think that's a splendid idea.'

Epilogue

Christmas Day 1956

The midday sun shone brightly, and damn hot, as Isabel lifted the lamb roast from the oven and set it on the bench to rest. She wiped the sweat from her forehead and gulped down water like her life depended on it. It had to be pushing the century mark outside and that meant inside the kitchen with the wood stove burning was even hotter. After filling her glass with water once again, she moved to where the kitchen door was wedged open so the faint breeze could blow in. She stared down towards the river.

Four months since the peak of the flooding and the river had finally subsided back to its normal path. The mess of debris that had been left behind had been hideous and sometimes surprising. Among the tangle of tree limbs, reeds and other natural waste, they'd found two bicycles, a canoe, three mattresses, thirteen different types of pots and pans, several rotten animal carcasses and—strangest of all—a Coolgardie safe still with food inside. The stench of the mud left behind when the waters receded was overwhelming. On the lower-lying flood plains, cut off from its source as the river receded, the water hung around, stagnant and swarming with mosquitos now that summer had arrived.

The Mildura Show had gone ahead in October as the show-grounds had not been affected by the floods. It was hoped the frivolity of the yearly event would give those who remained in the region something to enjoy after so many months of exhaustion and bad news. And the news was bad. The final tally reported that thousands of people had lost their homes and been displaced. The loss to business and agriculture in the region was unfathomable. Thousands of pounds worth of livestock and crops had been destroyed. Roads were impassable and the estimate was two hundred and fifty thousand pounds worth of damage. Food shortages followed and the Red Cross Society in the southern parts of the state of Victoria was called upon to send butter, eggs and tinned milk to the Sunraysia district.

Other than little Christopher Phillips, there had been one other known loss of life in the region. A nineteen-year-old man had driven his car into a hidden sinkhole on the Sturt Highway and, after having climbed out onto the roof of the vehicle, had been swept into the swirling waters. Several other vehicle occupants had had to be rescued from cars, but luckily no other deaths had been reported.

The wall of dirt that had saved the hotel from ruin now lay in ruins itself. Once the water had crept back down the hill, the sandbags had been emptied and carted away, to be stored for the next event or reused on properties. The long, muddy levee between the hotel and the river had been levelled flat. But the barrier remained along the creek and the other side of the hotel. It was crumbling in sections, and Isabel noticed that grass and weeds had already begun to sprout atop the mound. The infinite cycle of nature. She shivered despite the heat, looking at the spot where Matteo had fallen into the creek. How close had she come to losing him? Thank God Ross hadn't been like his father, and let a man drown.

Trevor Burrows. Her anger rose again at the thought of him. He'd run, had never returned to the district, and was now officially a wanted man. Wanted for the murder of Sam Hayward. Once the coroner had made his finding—Sam had been hit over the head with something, his skull fractured—she and her mum had buried their father and husband in the Nichols Point Cemetery once the water had receded enough. Hundreds had turned out for the funeral. Ross and Shirley Burrows were conspicuous in their absence.

Ross had sent her a letter though. He'd taken his mother to Melbourne to live with his sister to escape the scandal. Isabel had heard recently that he'd taken a job in a bank. She often wondered if she would run into him in Melbourne while she was staying there for school, but she never had.

Isabel turned back to watch Gia removing the panettone from where it had hung upside down by a knitting needle overnight. Gia had started to make the traditional Italian cake two days before and Isabel had paid close attention. It was not your average Christmas pudding and Gia had balked when Isabel suggested they insert sixpence into the mix.

Her first three months at the Emily McPherson College in Melbourne had been exciting and enlightening. She'd been lucky that her great-aunt Silvia had been happy to let her stay with her for the duration of her semester at the college as it was a short walk from Silvia's house in Fitzroy. Isabel had learned so much already and was looking forward to her return to Melbourne after the Christmas break so she could continue her studies.

Watching Gia now, so at home in the hotel kitchen, Isabel felt so grateful. Before she'd gone away to school in September, the two women had worked side by side, with Gia tutoring Isabel, teaching her Italian recipes, and Isabel showing her the fine art of 'pub fare'. The kitchen was a well-oiled machine and Gia had been dubious but gracious when Isabel suggested she show her how to cook some of the Australian cuisine the patrons enjoyed so much. The Sorrentis had continued to live at the hotel, with Matteo and Antonio doing odd jobs about the place.

Her relationship with Matteo had only grown stronger. She had fallen so deeply in love with him and when they weren't working, they spent every second together. It had been hard to be away from him in Melbourne, but he wrote the most beautiful romantic letters and when she'd arrived home just before Christmas, he had picked her up from the bus station and that night … she blushed just thinking about that night.

An hour later, Isabel and Gia moved the food into the dining room. They laid it out onto the long table they'd set up by pushing all the tables in the dining room together.

Perry stood behind the bar and poured drinks for everyone just as Albert and Flo came in to take their seats. Loretta, now heavily pregnant with only three months to go, sat with little Lucia playing with presents beneath the squat Christmas tree in the corner of the dining room.

Carlo arrived with Antonio just as they were ready to sit down to Christmas lunch. The Sorrentis had been offered a small plot of land with the Johnston family in Trentham Cliffs so they could begin to earn money while they waited for their own land to become workable again. The Johnstons had purchased the land under the government's Soldier Settlement Scheme back in 1949 and, situated high up on the cliffs, the block and its sultana grapes and vegetable crops had survived the flood.

'Where's Matteo?' Isabel asked when she hadn't seen him follow his brother and father in.

Antonio grinned. 'Oh, he's on his way.'

'Alright, well, dinner is ready, so everyone take your seats,' Isabel announced.

The rumble of an engine had everyone looking at each other as the noise came closer and closer.

Antonio, still grinning like a crazed man, moved to the rarely used main double doors of the pub and pushed them open. Matteo, seated on a Fergie tractor that over the last months had had no trouble navigating the skinny tops of levees, drove through the doors with ease and straight up to the big wooden bar.

Isabel stood staring, open-mouthed. 'Are you mad? Get that thing out of here!'

'Do not berate the ever-faithful Fergie tractor,' Matteo said, patting the front of the tractor, as though he were stroking a beloved pet. 'We would never have survived this flood without her.'

'You've lost your mind,' she told him.

'Come sit, take a ride with me, *bella*.'

'No. Dinner is ready and you've got dirt all over the floor,' she told him, walking from behind the bar and looking at the mess he'd brought in with him. 'Your mama is going to kill you.'

But when Isabel looked to Gia for support, she was curled into Carlo's arms, watching with a knowing smile on her face.

Isabel looked back at Matteo, who still held out a hand to her. With a confused frown she took it and let him help her up onto the tractor.

'There's no room,' she said, pointing at the little bucket seat he sat on.

He slapped his thigh and reluctantly she sat, feeling the heat rising up her neck into her cheeks as everyone who was gathered watched on with curiosity and amusement.

'You *are* mad,' she said, shaking her head even as her heart was melting.

'*Si*. I am mad about you,' he said, his deep voice reverberating quietly in her ear. 'Isabel. *Mi amore*. Will you marry me?'

Her mouth dropped open as he held out a gold ring with a small but beautiful diamond.

'It was my nonna's, my grandmother's,' he translated. 'Mama gave it to me to give to you … if you will agree to be my wife.'

'Matteo …' She was lost for words. Looking around the dining room for her mum, she found her. Her fingers were steepled at her lips, her cheeks wet with tears, but she was smiling too. She nodded her consent and it was all Isabel needed.

'Think you can wait three months until I finish my time at cooking school to get married?'

'I've waited a lifetime for you,' he said, quietly, dusting her always wayward fringe from her forehead. 'I think I can wait a little longer.'

'Then yes! Yes, Matteo, I will marry you!'

The crowd cheered as they kissed.

'*Buon natale!*' Antonio called, popping a bottle of the Sorrentis' home-made sparkling wine.

Isabel laughed as her mother rang the big brass bell behind the bar. The sound was no longer associated with panic and despair, but with joy and hope.

'Drinks all round!'

Acknowledgements

In 1956, towns along the Murray River, from Echuca all the way down to Goolwa in South Australia, saw one of the largest flood events in Australia's history. This fictional story of the flood includes some real stories gleaned from newspaper articles from 1956 and also from friends and family who were in the region at the time. Names have been changed and, as with all fiction, some of the stories may have been exaggerated for dramatic effect, but many didn't need to be. Coffins were indeed rowed across floodwaters to the island that was the Nichols Point Cemetery. Hundreds of glasshouses with thousands of pounds worth of tomatoes were smashed and destroyed in Buronga alone and the river breached eight-foot high levee walls all around Mildura, flooding the brickworks and sending a one-hundred-foot geyser into the sky when water hit the kilns. I have tried to keep to the timeline of the flooding, including the constant breaking of so many levees around the Mildura region that caused such widespread devastation. It really was a twenty-four hour a day battle to save farms and towns and sadly it was often in vain.

The Riverside Hotel depicted in this story is a fictional one, loosely based on the Gol Gol Hotel across the border from Mildura in New South Wales. A giant thanks is owed to Gary Wilkinson and his sister Regina Maas, of the original Wilkinson family who owned the pub from 1917 until the 1970s. They grew up at the Gol Gol Hotel and shared wonderful stories and descriptions of the pub as it was—including the little zoo of animals and birds—and they provided me with a hand-drawn map of the levee that was built around the hotel to protect it from the river and the rising Gol Gol Creek. The Gol Gol Hotel is still there today and just recently faced the 2022–2023 flood crisis which gave me an incredible live-action point of view of how high the river came up back in 1956. Luckily these recent floods didn't reach as high as 1956, but many properties and towns along the Murray, especially in South Australia, have been inundated and levee walls surrounded the Riverland once again.

Thanks also to the Barmera Visitors Centre, and in particular Rosemary Gower, for the invaluable information about the Loveday Internment Camp. This camp in the South Australian Riverland reportedly became the largest internment camp in the southern hemisphere during the Second World War between 1941 and 1946, housing thousands of Italian, German and Japanese internees, many of whom were naturalised British citizens and had been living in Australia for decades. There is not much left of the camp today, except for a recreation hall at the group headquarters, a small prison block, and a few concrete slabs that once housed a hospital, bakery and pay office. You can see a display with photographs and artefacts from the camps at the Barmera Visitors Centre.

During my research I read the diaries kept by several Italian and Japanese internees during their stay at Loveday. I wanted to know what daily life was like inside the camps. Boredom seemed to be the predominant feeling. But despite being taken from their families and being locked away—in many cases simply for their nationality—most internees reported being treated well by their Australian military captors. In hindsight, several internees commented that they felt lucky in comparison to what people were facing in Europe, both in and out of camps. I'm sure not everyone held there felt the same, but it was a theme I wanted to express in this particular story. I could have written more about life in the Loveday Internment Camp but, as an author of fiction, there are some stories I feel aren't mine to tell.

I don't enjoy writing racist language, it never sits well with me. But to stay true to history, sometimes authors need to write the language that was often used by some people at the time, if it forms part of the story. It does not reflect all thought or sentiment of the era but would have been what many immigrants faced—and sadly still face—in Australia.

Thanks to my mum, Lorraine, who grew up in the Gol Gol–Trentham Cliffs region during the 1956 floods, for her insights into rural town life in the 1950s in Mildura and its surrounds.

Thanks as always to the super team at HQ HarperCollins Australia for helping me be the best writer I can be and supporting me and my storytelling. *Grazie mille*—a thousand thanks to you, the readers, for your voracious love of stories based on our unique, multicultural Australian history.

talk about it

Let's talk about books.

Join the conversation:

@harlequinaustralia

@hqanz

@harlequinaus

harpercollins.com.au/hq

If you love reading and want to know about our authors and titles, then let's talk about it.